Something Resembling Love

Enjoy!
Elizabeth

Something Resembling Love

A Novel

Elizabeth Standish

2025

Copyright © 2024 Thistle and Phoenix Press, Ltd.

All rights reserved.

Published in the United States by Thistle and Phoenix Press, Ltd.

Something Resembling Love is a work of fiction. Names, characters, places, and incidents are the products of the author's imagination or are used fictitiously. Any resemblance to actual events, locales, or persons, living or dead, is entirely coincidental.

PUBLISHER'S CATALOGING-IN-PUBLICATION DATA

Names: Standish, Elizabeth, author.
Title: Something Resembling Love / Elizabeth Standish.
Description: Parker, CO: Thistle and Phoenix Press, Ltd., 2024.
Identifiers: ISBN: 978-1-961842-02-1 (paperback) | 978-1-961842-03-8 (ebook)
Subjects: LCSH Scientists--Fiction. | Man-woman relationships--Fiction. | Italy--Fiction. | Love--Fiction. | BISAC FICTION / Women
Classification: LCC PS3619.T36 S83 2024 | DDC 813.6--dc23

First Edition

No part of this book may be reproduced in any form or by any mechanical means, including information storage and retrieval systems, without permission in writing from the publisher, except by a reviewer who may quote passages in review.

This book was written entirely by a human. No form of artificial intelligence was used in the creation of this book. *The author expressly prohibits any entity from using this publication to train any AI technologies or models, or to generate text or imagery, including, without limitation, technologies capable of generating works in the same style or genre as this publication. The author reserves all rights to license uses of this work for generative AI training and development of machine learning language models.*

All images, logo, quotes, and trademarks included in this book are subject to use according to trademark and copyright laws of the United States of America.

Cover designed by Elizabeth Mackey

Interior Layout by Katherine P. McGraw

Copyright owned by Thistle and Phoenix Press, Ltd.

For The Chestnut Gang, who didn't judge me when I was not as capable as they (or Jane!) were in the Tuscan hills.

Author's Note

The condition Jane suffers from, hereditary hemorrhagic telangiectasia, or HHT, is a real medical condition, with potentially fatal consequences. The statistics in this book about the risks of carrying a pregnancy to term with HHT are estimates, but they are very real, even if symptoms can be as mild as bloody noses or as severe as strokes. More information can be found at the Cure HHT website.

Jane

I rounded the last curve of the track, its rust color blurring at the bottom of my vision, ready to start my final sprint. The girl ahead of me had been beating me in most races this season. I was so close. I knew I could catch her this time.

With an extra gulp of air, I pounded out three more long strides—I could almost tap her on the shoulder. I lengthened my stride a hair further, and then—

When I opened my eyes, faces were crowded all around me. My coach, Mary, was next to my left shoulder. She was speaking, but I couldn't hear her. I rolled my head to the other side. My left leg ached. My side hurt, a familiar dull pain I got every time I pushed hard. Then I started to feel the burn in my hands. I lifted one to look at it. Scuff marks had been gouged into the heel. A similar sensation pulsed on the outside of my shoulder.

God damn it. My leg ached, feeling like it might explode. And my head was throbbing.

I tried to sit up, but several hands held me down on the hard surface. Voices came into focus.

"Jane, stay down. We need to get you to an ambulance," someone said.

I looked at Mary again. "I'm fine," I said. Or at least those were the words my mouth formed. I shifted again and the hands pressed more firmly. "Get off!" I roared.

People jumped back. I must actually be talking. Slowly, I rolled up to a sitting position. My head pounded, and tiny sparkling spots appeared in my vision. I brought my hand to the front of my temple.

"Ambulance is here," someone called, sounding far away.

And then the people who had still been crouched around me moved back.

"Miss, lie down. We're going to put you on this board."

I was too tired to argue with them. As the EMTs lifted the board and set me on a stretcher, I turned to look for Mary. I could see my teammates huddled together and other competitors watching. Fear. Pity. I closed my eyes.

At the bump of being loaded into the back of the ambulance, I reopened them. One of the EMTs sat next to me. I reached my hand out toward him.

"What do you need?" he asked.

My fingers flexed, grasping. He took the hint and held my hand. The badge on his lanyard, near my face, said Joshua. He was cute.

"Your coach said your name is Jane Davenport."

I gave a small nod.

"You're seventeen?"

I nodded again, eyelids feeling heavy.

"We're trying to get a hold of your parents to meet us at St. Luke's."

I was too worn out to tell him not to bother.

The next time I opened my eyes, I was bumping back out of the ambulance. A person in light blue scrubs came and reached across me for a clipboard. "Sweetheart? Jane? Where are your parents?"

Tears rolled out of my eyes, and I shook my head. "I don't have any."

The nurse looked up over the top of me. "She must have hit her head."

"No." God, why did everything feel so fuzzy? My leg throbbed, but the rest of me wasn't in pain.

"Take her to CT. I'm going to try to call the school."

"I don't have any parents."

Something Resembling Love

The nurse looked back down at me. "Of course you do, honey," she said with a pat on my arm. "We'll find them and call them."

I gritted my teeth in frustration. Why didn't anyone believe me? My parents were dead. I wasn't hallucinating that they were gone, my sadness, or the overwhelming feeling of being alone I had these days. If they hadn't been in that car accident six months ago, I would have had Thanksgiving with them. They'd have been at the meet, cheering me on. One of them would've walked with me to the ambulance.

"I'll call the school," a new voice said.

Dumbasses, it's Saturday. My eyes closed, resigned. Someone would figure it out eventually.

I felt something bite at me and realized it was an IV.

The next time I woke up, I was in an all-white room. Everything was much clearer now. The pain in my leg was gone, but the road rash still burned. I rubbed at the plastic bracelet on my wrist.

"Ah, you're awake."

At the end of my bed, stood a new person, name stitched on his white coat.

"Yep," I said with more enthusiasm than I felt.

"We've been trying to reach your school or your track coach so we can locate your parents. Now that you're awake again, maybe you can tell us how to reach them." The doctor had salt and pepper hair, carried a little extra weight around his middle, and was short.

"You won't be able to get a hold of them."

"Why? Are they military or something?" He probably thought he was very clever.

"No." I crossed my arms over the medium-blue hospital gown. "They're dead."

"Eh?"

"My. Parents. Are. Dead," I said, looking him square in the eye. "I'm emancipated."

"Ahhh ..." He said on a nervous chuckle. "Okay, well, I guess I'll just talk to you?"

"I'm the only one there is."

Why did people have to be such assholes about this? I'd had the same conversation with the school principal, and my lawyer had even talked to him beforehand. I had court documents that said I had a right to make legally binding decisions for myself.

"Right." The doctor shifted back to medical mode and pulled up a monitor with grayscale images, pointing and circling, using big words. "Basically," he finished, "there's something going on with your blood vessels."

"Is that why I fell?"

"We think so. It looks like a small clot broke off and traveled into your carotid artery. Possibly cut off enough blood supply that you fainted, but not enough to cause a stroke or kill you. Yet."

"Yet. That's cheerful," I said and glared at him.

"Just trying to give you the information."

"And what other information do you have?"

"Well," he began, using the pen to scratch his head, "not much. One of our vascular specialists has only seen vessels like this a few times. So, we're not sure."

I rolled my eyes. "How do we fix it if you don't know what it is?"

He looked away from me and back at the images on the screen. "Unfortunately, we don't."

"We, as in you and me, or we as in the hospital?" I hoped I didn't have to rely on this idiot for anything.

"We, as in the hospital. I can refer you to a vascular specialist. He's at Rush. In Chicago."

My eyes widened. "You're telling me there's no one in the entire state who can help me?"

The doctor shook his head. "Unfortunately, no. We've looked already. No one has seen anything this complicated before."

"Motherfucker," I muttered under my breath. I'd developed a sweary habit as a coping mechanism. Me and Samuel L. Jackson, dropping f-bombs whenever we felt like it. That was probably why I'd lost a bunch of friends. Could be worse, though, right? I could be shooting heroin into my eyeballs.

"We've arranged for you to meet with him, Dr. Joseph Chay, by video conference. He's at Rush."

"And when will I meet with this so-called expert?" I was really being a bitch. But I was not impressed. And I wanted to go home.

And I really wanted my parents. I bit the inside of my lip so I wouldn't cry.

"Tomorrow morning."

Something Resembling Love

I spent the rest of the day flipping through the hospital's limited movie selection. My cell phone was delivered, but Coach Mary didn't come visit. She wasn't family, the nurse said, and I nearly screamed.

The next day, just before ten, someone brought in a laptop and set it on the rolling tray. She poked at keys until the videoconferencing screen was set up, and stepped out of the room.

The screen filled with a face that looked much younger than I was expecting for someone who was an expert across multiple states.

"Jane?"

I nodded.

"Dr. Joe Chay. Nice to meet you. Sort of," he said with a deprecatory smile.

"Do you know what happened to me? They said I had a blood clot in my carotid?"

On screen, Dr. Chay nodded, dark hair trimmed into a banker's cut. At least he looked confident.

"That's not what happened. I'm fairly certain, looking at your imaging, that you have a condition called hereditary hemorrhagic telangiectasia. The short explanation is that your blood vessels form abnormally. Sometimes they're tiny, and don't create issues. You might see the telangiectasias on your skin—small red dots or a tiny red spider web?"

I nodded. I'd seen some of the webbing on my legs and assumed it was the spider veins my mom had had. *Maybe she had had this too?*

"The other, larger, thing that can happen with HHT, is that you develop arteriovenous malformations. You're a junior in high school, right?"

When I nodded, he continued, "So you know your veins and arteries connect by ever-smaller vessels, down to capillaries."

"Right," I nodded, thinking of my earliest science classes.

"With arteriovenous malformations, or AVMs, the vessels attach directly, without capillaries. They can occur anywhere, although it's common to have them near organs or your brain. Because of the improper connection, the AVMs shunt de-oxygenated blood that's headed for the heart to get re-oxygenated, back into the body."

"Um." I frowned. "Can you explain that more?"

"I know it sounds weird," Dr. Chay said with a reassuring smile and started again, this time sharing his screen to show me drawings.

"The hospital says your oxygen was below 90 percent when they brought you in, but it stabilized. You were at a track meet when you collapsed?"

"Yeah. One of the last ones of the season. I was trying to beat fucking Meli—sorry."

Dr. Chay gave me a genuine smile, broad and almost excited. "I'm glad you have that kind of passion. My guess is that when you were running, trying to outrun fucking Melissa Whomever—"

A surprised laugh escaped me, and I felt almost ... happy? It was hard to tell. Happiness wasn't something I'd experienced much lately.

"Your body just used up all of its oxygen. Your scan looks like there could be some blood in your calf muscle as well. Perhaps one of the smaller connections ruptured. That's not terribly concerning to me, since it looks small and wasn't in your brain. That being said, you're going to need a lot more testing to confirm my diagnosis and for us to get the lay of the land. You'll need PET scans, maybe an MRI, and I want you to keep track of your oxygen several times throughout the day."

I nodded, grateful to have a plan and be in the care of someone who seemed to know what he was doing.

"The other doctor said you're emancipated? At seventeen?"

"I was emancipated after my parents were killed in a car accident last fall." I felt my eyes fill with tears again and swiped at them angrily.

"I'm really sorry to hear that, Jane." Dr. Chay's voice was full of sincere sympathy. "Do you have health insurance?"

I nodded, sniffing back my emotions.

"Okay, that's good. Is there any other family that can support you?"

"Um," I sniffed, tipping my head back to contain the tears, "no. My parents were both only children. I think everyone is afraid of me now. After."

"What about a teacher?"

"M-maybe my track coach, Mary. I could at least talk to her."

Something Resembling Love

"Why don't you do that? Then, the three of us can get on the phone together. Just so someone else knows what's going on. In case this happens again."

He was looking at me with such kindness that I almost felt like he was in this sterile-feeling white room with me, sitting on the bed to talk.

"Are you going to make me give up running?"

Dr. Chay looked serious for a moment. "I don't think so. But until we can get a better handle on what's going on, I'd prefer if you didn't compete the rest of the season. Can you do that?"

"I can. I don't want to, though." Just one more thing taken away from me.

"I ran track in high school, too. I get it. But if you don't, something worse might happen."

"Fine," I said, sounding like the teenager I was.

"Great. I'll tell the doctor you've been working with at St. Luke's which tests I need, and then we can use those to create a plan. I'm going to give you my cell phone number. Call me when you get home, and we'll arrange a time for the three of us to talk." He said the digits slowly while I typed them into my own phone. "Jane, I know this is a big, scary-sounding diagnosis, but I'll be here to help you."

"You're not here, though," I scoffed.

Dr. Chay paused for a moment. "You have every right to be angry. You got dealt a shitty hand. Nothing will ever replace your parents or make that hole go away. But you're not alone."

16 years later...

Peter

If anyone had been watching, they would have noticed the tall, dark-haired guy. They would have pegged him for a senior, maybe on the lacrosse team. As he sauntered, tanned and shirtless, from one small group of people to another, stopping to sub in for a round of sand volleyball, anyone watching would have assumed he was just another athlete there on scholarship. But on nearly all counts, they would have been wrong. He wasn't a ladies' man; this wasn't his following, exactly. He certainly was not a senior or on the lacrosse team.

He was my best friend, and this was his annual kick-off-to-summer-grill-out-and-beach-volleyball party.

Chris easily mingled with the group of twenty-ish people spread out along the grass and beach at the edge of Lake Michigan, some of whom I knew too. I, on the other hand, was stuck by the picnic bench, holding the mustard I'd been about to splat on my now-cold burger, staring out in the distance at the woman who had caught my eye. I didn't see Chris headed my way.

Her hair was like the bark of an old evergreen tree, untouched by the sunlight. *Jesus.* I shook my head at myself. *Do people even think like that?* Though she seemed tall, her short haircut made her look like an actual pixie. A pixie with bright red retro eighties sunglasses and cutoff shorts that showcased long muscular legs. Even from yards away, I could see the rise of her chest above the scoop of her nearly see-through tank top.

"Whassamata?" Chris slapped me on the shoulder, jostling the burger dangerously close to the edge of its bun.

"What? Oh, nothing, the sun blinded me for a minute." I blinked down at the plate in my hand.

"Sure, sure. So. Which one?" Chris scanned his friends.

"Which one what?"

"Which girl?" he prompted, picking up the burger patty and beginning to eat it himself.

"None, nothing, I told you," I insisted.

I glanced sideways at my lab buddy. Had we been in California, he could easily have been mistaken for a beach bum, with his longer hair waving back from his face, Pakistani skin, and muscular body. I dropped my head, noticing as I did that the tops of my feet were already beginning to burn despite the SPF 50 I'd slathered on earlier. Same with my forearms.

Unlike Chris, I looked like I belonged in a research lab.

"At least tell me what she's wearing, then maybe I can be blinded by the sun, too."

I didn't want to give him the satisfaction of being right, but as Chris finished the burger, still scanning the beach, I mumbled, "Red sunglasses."

Chris considered the view. "Huh. Cute. She might be the friend Alicia said she was going to bring. Think I'll go check it out." He turned back to me. "You coming?"

"I think I'll stay here." Hiding under this massive tree from all things hot. Like the sun. And that girl who is too hot to talk to.

Chris shook his head at me. "Did you look at the statistics I emailed you last week?"

"Yeah."

"And?"

"I'm not depressed, Chris. Or anxious. I get plenty of sleep."

"Twenty-one percent of people who got poor sleep failed one or more years of school." He was studying me, probably taking stock of how well hydrated I appeared or how many grey hairs I'd developed since he started keeping track of my sleep. "We're not in college anymore."

"You're still pulling all-nighters like you're in grad school."

I glared at him.

"Fine. Guess I'll have to go meet the new girl on my own."

I was certain I would look like a fool next to his easy banter and dark good looks, so I stayed put, watching Chris saunter down the short slope to the edge of the sand and wedge his way between the two girls. "Hellooooo, ladies," he said, as he draped an arm over each of their shoulders.

"Chris, this is my good friend Jane," the second woman, our friend Alicia, said. "Jane, this is Chris. He's …"

"The reason this party exists."

I imagined Alicia rolling her eyes as her laughter carried to me. Alicia had been in and out of the microbiology building for a couple of years after being hired during a leadership restructuring, and made responsible for setting research stage gates. Chris had befriended her, as he did everyone, and invited her to a few Cubs games. Now Alicia was a regular fixture. "He is. But don't let him convince you he's actually cool. Oh! Lauren!" She waved at someone else off to my left.

From my spot under the tree, I saw Chris' girlfriend pause, a small hitch in her step, as she walked toward them. Chris waved her over, his arm still resting on the shoulder of my girl.

My girl. Jesus, Peter, get a grip; you haven't even talked to her.

Then Lauren was jogging, calling, "Jane?"

At the same time, Jane tried to answer, "What are y—?"

Lauren closed the gap and threw her arms around the neck of the girl I'd been staring at. They jumped up and down, squealing like little girls.

"Oh my God, this is so random! How? It's been forever!"

"Babe, this is my college bestie, Jane," Lauren said, grabbing Chris' hand.

"Yeah, I know. I went out and found her for you, for a present. I knew how much you missed her," Chris said as he unwound his arm from the girl's neck.

"You?—Oh, you did not! You didn't even know about her." Lauren smacked Chris on the shoulder, and he feigned rubbing it for a moment. Below his mirrored sunglasses, his face split into a grin.

Chris turned to Alicia. With a dramatic flourish, he said, "Alicia, this is Jane."

"I'm the one that brought her," she said dryly.

Lauren gave a little jump in the sand, her straight blonde hair surging up with her.

I scowled at my burned feet and ruined appetite. I supposed I could go over there and say hey to Alicia. She was the person I felt the least awkward next to. In meetings, she was forthright and even pushy, unfazed by whether her opinions would be dismissed, the bright purple streak in her white-blonde hair reminiscent of my sister, Catherine's. Outside a conference room, she was quick to strike up a conversation. Like me, she carried extra pounds.

I hadn't seen Alicia since we'd been at the Cubs home opener, but maybe she could introduce me to Jane. Without all the joking and teasing that Chris would inevitably do.

"It's like you have a whole history without me," Chris said with a fake pout so exaggerated I could see it from where I stood.

That was exactly the kind of thing I couldn't do—joke with people.

"Indeed, we do!" Lauren threw her arm over Jane's shoulders and beamed at Chris. Jane immediately wrapped her arm around Lauren's back, and grinned as well.

Nope. Not happening. I pitched the bun that Chris had left on my plate in the trash.

"Come on, Chris," Alicia said. "Let's go play volleyball, while these lovebirds catch up on their long-lost days apart." She hooked her arm through his and led him toward the net.

I squinted against the blazing blue sky and then turned to walk up the hill before Alicia could see me and want to bring me into the conversation. I headed toward the Northwestern campus. It was only two in the afternoon. I could grab a bite and hit the lab for about eight hours. I'd done a methylation on a sequence of DNA earlier, and it was awaiting analysis. On a Saturday afternoon the lab would be empty, and I could concentrate.

The goal had been to finish my postdoctoral work this spring, and finally get a faculty position somewhere. Anywhere. That ship had sailed several months ago when the DNA strands in the project kept disintegrating during methylation. I'd readjusted my expectations and thought maybe I could get it done by the end of the year.

I glanced back at Jane, now deep in conversation with Lauren, when I reached the sidewalk.

Nope. Still too hot to talk to.

Three days later, I was still thinking about her. Not as often as I had been the afternoon I left the BBQ, but enough to be distracting and make me mad at myself. I was a serious professional, a researcher, a postdoctoral fellow. One who had neither the time nor the inclination to be mooning over women generally, and those who I had never met, specifically.

Someone suddenly grabbed the back of my lab chair and tipped me backward. I snapped out of my reverie and found myself looking up into Chris' grinning face.

"Solving the great mysteries of cancer?" he joked, as he set my chair back down.

"No, I was thinking about—"

"Dude, what's the matter? You look like you've been sitting at your computer since I last saw you at the park three days ago!"

"Hmm. Well, not quite." I had gone to my apartment to sleep for about six hours one night. And I had used the shower in the research building a couple of times. But he didn't need to know that I'd hardly been away from the desk other than that. I edged around my desk a little further to hide the trash can that held the evidence of my vending machine foraging.

Chris and I were trying to solve the problem of cancer replication. The study of epigenetics was quickly taking a more prominent place in medicine. How could our DNA change over three generations instead of thousands of years, as Darwin's slow process of evolution posited? Could being bullied as a child and having hormones and chemicals related to anxiety rushing through your body daily for years make a person more susceptible to contracting diseases? Could those same hormones and changes cause a person's grandkids to be more susceptible? And the big one Chris had alluded to: Could we cure cancer by changing the structure of an individual's DNA so that their body wouldn't host it?

I stood up to pace as Chris went from computer to computer checking on datasets, codes we were running, and then the coolers that held the DNA samples we were manipulating manually.

"I already checked those, Chris."

We'd met in graduate school, gone through together, and started the same doctoral program. Chris had presented his dissertation sooner, though, and was always exploring offshoots.

And he's already been the lead author on a paper, the little voice in my head taunted. I ignored her—the voice was always a her—and focused on Chris again, who was now staring at me.

"Your apartment is like a block away; you should use it."

It seemed he knew what I'd been up to, anyway. "If I had a cute girlfriend and a killer house to go home to, I probably would."

In addition to his PhD, Chris was heavily invested in real estate and owned a company that focused on fix-and-flips. He'd worked on Wall Street for a few years after college, earning a boatload of money, before going back for the master's where we'd met. He was just plain smart, and efficient, and on top of everything. I couldn't understand how he did it all and slept. Maybe he didn't sleep, but if so, he probably also had some magic shake every morning because he always looked fully rested.

"Nah. You just need to get laid so you can let off some steam! You'll feel better and be able to sleep again."

Aaaand back to thinking about the girl with the red sunglasses ...

JANE

I admired the Gaudi-esque arched doorways of the restaurant Lauren had suggested. Carved vines framed the patio entrance. It didn't surprise me at all that Lauren would pick a place like this. Even when we'd been young and ridiculous twentysomethings at the University of Oklahoma, she'd always had a flair for design.

"Like it?" she asked as she sat down across from me on the patio. Between her real estate season and my work, it had taken months to find a Friday evening together.

"I love it! My salon is just down the street. I have no idea how I've missed this." The tree-lined streets and diverse-but-still-small-town main street feel were some of the things I liked best about living in Evanston.

"Chris brought me here for one of our first dates; I've been hooked ever since."

Lauren ordered the vodka tonic I remembered her favoring, and I asked for the Prosecco. When the server reached for the menu, she withheld it from him for a moment. "We have a lot of catching up to do."

"Sure thing, ladies."

"And on that note, go! What have you been up to in the last, gosh, eight years since we last saw each other?" she prompted.

"Haha," I said. "You're not getting out of it that easily. I see something sparkly that wasn't there the last time I saw you."

Lauren blushed, but burst into a huge grin. "I'll tell you all about it. But will you at least give me a few details about your life first, so I don't monopolize the entire conversation?"

I laughed for real, shaking my head at the way the independent and decisive friend I had known was glowing, a huge, happy smile on her face. "I'm afraid there's nothing terribly exciting. The short answers are, I'm in a different job since we last connected, directing research, or at least part of it, instead of just following orders—monkey see, monkey do. But I'm still with the USDA. My boss is fabulous. He listens, instead of ordering us around."

"Are you still playing with dirt?"

I laughed again. "Yes, I'm still 'playing with dirt.' 'Soil science' when I want to sound less like a five-year-old making mud pies."

"Recess for adults?"

"Something like that! Our lab group has gotten into mud fights when we've been out collecting soil samples in the field. You come back covered in dirt, mud smeared in your hair, grateful your car is ten years old, impossibly tired, a little sunburned. Even as you're logging samples, wishing you could be at home in a hot shower, you can't help but feeling like you have the most entertaining job in the world, and you wouldn't trade it for anything. And then you end up going out for a beer with your lab buddies before you have a chance for that shower. It's a little less awesome in winter weather, but once the ground freezes, we're stuck in the lab, anyway."

"You make it sound like a diversion, not real work. Maybe I should go back for a degree in soil science, too."

"Most of the work is in the lab; you'd be bored out of your mind. Trust me, stay with real estate, Lor!"

"Are there any cute guys you work with? I'll bet most of them are in shape." Lauren wiggled her eyebrows across the table at me.

"There are a few, although most of them are married. I've gone out with a couple guys I've worked with, both at this lab and the old one. But nothing special." I sighed, then covered by taking a sip of my bubbly wine. No sense dwelling on what was missing. "Anyway! Tell me about Chris and that rock!"

"He came looking for a house a couple of years ago. Alicia had referred him. I helped him find a house here in town—he had said he wanted a place to start a family, and Evanston made sense with his work here. I couldn't

Something Resembling Love

figure out why he wanted such a big house when it was just him, but he claimed to entertain a lot. And he does, I learned." She shrugged, as if that were a normal answer for a single guy in his thirties. "Then he asked me to sell his condo on Lakeshore. So I did—he had a place in Marina Towers! It sold in about two and a half weeks." A wistful smile flitted across Lauren's face. "He asked me out, but I turned him down. It didn't seem ethical."

"But weren't you a little curious? He's a good-looking guy, to put it mildly."

"Well of course I was interested! But dating your clients is getting into sketchy territory. Could be a conflict of interest."

"But he wasn't your client anymore." I shook my head.

Lauren nodded, taking a drink of her cocktail. "Well, then he was again. He asked me to list a property for his fix-and-flip business. When he kept asking me out, I finally gave in. I'm sure glad I did! And that huge house he bought? It's the perfect size for us, Sebastian, home offices, and spare rooms for guests."

"Good lord, is it really that big?"

"Just over seven thousand square feet, ground level done in stunning cherry hardwood floors. Acres of granite countertops in the kitchen, including a twelve by eight-foot island, and two large den spaces perfect for the entrepreneur. The upstairs features an owner's suite with a Jacuzzi tub, and three separate guest bedrooms, all en suite. The luxury home is situated on nearly a half-acre of beautifully landscaped, emerald-green grass carpeting."

"You sound like a real estate ad," I half laughed.

"That's pretty much verbatim from the listing."

"How does Sebastian feel about this?"

"He likes it much better than the small apartment we shared. There was never any room for him to express himself, he says." Lauren rolled her eyes at her absent thirteen-year-old son.

At the gathering along the lake, Lauren had told me she'd left Dean and moved north, aiming for Chicago, but landing near her sister, Vanessa, for a while before getting transferred.

She said a friend in corporate had encouraged her to get her real estate license. I had no doubt she'd hustled, building her reputation as she'd skyrocketed as an agent in the ensuing two years.

"And now?"

"Well, now I guess I'm getting married again!" Lauren wiggled the fingers as she extended her hand toward me again.

"Here's a toast to more of a new life for you." We drank in tandem. "Now." I leaned forward. "Does he have a brother?"

"He does. But he's gay ... and lives in California. But I will make it my mission to get you hooked up!"

"I know that look in your eye. I don't know if I should be excited or terrified," I laughed.

Despite our warning, the server gave up on our lingering conversation and we were left to flag him down. After a battle for the bill, we hugged goodbye and promised to get together again soon. "And Alicia, too!" Lauren called back as we started our separate ways down the sidewalk.

As I walked home, the sun was just low enough to cast a golden light on everything. Evanston was my favorite part of Chicagoland. In summer, huge old trees full of dark green leaves provided much-needed shade along the sidewalks. In the fall—all the colors! And then, in the winter, even if it could be bitterly cold with the wind off Lake Michigan, it could be one of the last areas to get snow. As much as I hated being cold, I always loved seeing the landscape covered in silvery white dust.

I soaked up the late summer warmth, enjoying the light breeze off the lake, and even the humidity, as I strolled underneath the stately deciduous trees. The chance reconnection with Lauren had put a sweet spin on my late summer and fall. I'd been expecting to muscle my way through more lonely days stuck indoors in the lab. In truth, I loved my job as much as I had made out to Lauren, but sometimes I wished I had a family to go home to, rather than sending my lab mates home to theirs and shouldering the extra work myself. Since I rarely had an excuse to not stay later, if there was a need, more often than not, I would.

But with Lauren around, and Chris, who, according to Alicia, was always planning some social event, maybe I would have a reason to skip out early now and then. On the other hand, Lauren had Chris and Sebastian. Presumably, she'd be with them when she wasn't working; and I knew she worked a lot. And now she'd be planning a wedding. So maybe I wouldn't have that many excuses after all. Still, one night a month with a legitimate social plan would be better than what the last year or so had looked like.

I paused in my front yard. My place was a sweet brick duplex, built in the late forties, that I'd bought after grad school. It was bigger than I

Something Resembling Love

strictly needed, but I'd been able to afford it using money from the sale of my parents' home. The thought of them made me sigh wistfully and smile at the same time. My retired neighbors were good-natured, and watered my garden and fed my cat, a very large, very fluffy orange tiger cat named Otis, when I traveled. It was such a warm and comfortable home, and it was perfect to share with someone. How badly I wanted someone to share it with. Not that I begrudged Lauren her happiness, but I wanted some for myself, too.

I date, I reminded myself. Or perhaps more accurately, went on many first-couple-of-months dates. Sometimes it was easier to stay late at the lab. A girl who played with dirt all day put off most guys. Or, at least, the ones who were otherwise drawn to my online profile.

"What are we going to do though, Otis?" I asked him as I bent to scratch his head where he lay sunning himself in the yard.

Otis didn't have any ideas, and only followed me inside, asking for his dinner. While I fed him, I pondered. Friends had always said I was too smart, even though they admitted I didn't come across as a know-it-all or stuck on being right. The guys at work didn't mind the smart microscope-loving girl, but then again, neither of those first few dates had gone anywhere, either. Maybe I was destined to be an old maid. The non-family aunt to my friends' kids.

I scratched Otis as he ate and let out a sigh. That wasn't the real issue, though. I knew what it was, and I didn't want to think about it. We were all entitled to one thing that made us different. Weren't we?

※※※

"Jane, I thought we were all leaving for the bar?"

I picked my head up from the microscope and blinked to bring my boss's tall, lean frame into focus. "We are."

Director Kip Thompson glanced at his watch, his professionally cut brown hair staying in place as he looked down. I did the same.

"Sorry, Thompson, you know how my boss is. I was trying to finish this one thing ..."

He shook his head on a half laugh, a broad gesture that revealed more about his personality than anything else. "Our resident workaholic."

"I'll be there soon, but I want to finish a few notes on this slide."

"What is it this time? Bull shit?" He chuckled at himself.

"Heifers, actually," I said, resetting my eye and blinking to force my brain to see only through that one.

"You're not seriously going to tell me there's a difference between bulls and cows."

"Heifers, specifically. And there might be." I jotted a last detail on the page next to the microscope before switching off the light and removing the slide. "I'll let you know if non-lactating female bovine has a different nitrogen output than bulls, or, as you so eloquently said, cows."

"Next, you'll want to add deer to your study."

"Hm. That's a good idea." Thompson was teasing, but I wasn't above stealing the idea and making it mine. "All set," I said as I dried my hands at the wash station.

"Grab your coat."

I did as he said and was glad he'd reminded me when we stepped out into the brisk fall air.

Kip followed me into the suburban sports bar our lab team went to once each month. A half-dozen people crowded around the table, and I saw two more at the bar, probably ordering pitchers for the group.

"How's your shit coming, Jane?" someone called from the end of the table.

"Better than yours, Rodriguez."

"I doubt that. My shit don't stink." Rodriguez laughed at his own joke.

"But is it nicely formed? I guess we'll find out in the dirt building contest."

"Okay, children," Kip said in his Director Thompson voice. "Enough taunting. We're all friends."

Behind our boss's back, I stuck my tongue out at Rodriguez. But I was grinning, too. This rowdy, obnoxious group of people was the closest thing I had to family. Even though Kip was fifteen years my senior, he often felt like more of a big brother than the boss.

PETER

"Look, are you coming to the damn party or not?" Chris leaned back in his chair and tossed a ball against the wall. Catching it and lobbing it again.

"Sure, man, sounds fun," I said from where I squinted at my screen.

He sat forward quickly, feigning a heart attack. "You mean it? You're really going to? Spend a weekend away from the lab!??"

I gave him a dry look. "Ha. Ha. And no, not the entire weekend. Just the part where there's a turkey, lots of food I didn't have to find for myself, football, beer, and someone prettier than you to look at."

"Fine," he said, standing. "Suit yourself. Just don't show up after kickoff, or I'm not coming to let you in."

"Lauren will—she's nicer than you!" I called after him.

Chris yelled out something crass as he left the office we shared, papers in hand, making me smile. I suspected that he'd run over to grab the printed reports, take five minutes reviewing them, then mostly spend the next couple of days hanging out with Lauren, cozied in against the grey cloudy skies that were forecasted, and doing whatever you did to get ready for a party when you had a fiancé. Or anyone.

I'd been going to Chris' for Thanksgiving since grad school, usually using it as a reason not to go home. For years it had been a few bachelors and whatever girlfriend we might have had, until slowly, over the seasons, our friends had paired off and moved away. When Chris met Lauren, he'd gone from expansive catered meals at his swanky condo to expansive catered meals at his new mini-mansion. And from a friendly meal to an event.

I wasn't at all surprised to see a mix of friends at the house again this year. A couple of school friends were still around, as well as several people who came to Cubs games with us, friends of Chris' from his finance years, Lauren's sister Vanessa—the brunette version of Lauren—and Alicia.

I grabbed a beer from the fridge and settled on the couch to half watch the game, knowing I'd only be in the way if I offered to help.

A flash of red at the edge of the entry hall and living room caught my attention, and I looked over. And that was how I met her the second time. Or, if I was honest, how I finally met her.

"Hey, sorry I'm late," she said breathlessly, holding out a bottle of wine to Chris, toeing off her shoes, and wriggling one arm out of her puffy, knee-length, bright red coat all at the same time.

"Well, it's not kickoff yet, so I guess you're okay," he said as he took the bottle.

From my spot on the couch, I could just see her. Same short haircut, same athletic legs in leggings, long sweater. She reached over to hug Chris, then Lauren, who came out of the kitchen to grab the coat before it hit the floor.

"Jane," Alicia stood up and leaned over the back of the couch to give her a hug.

What is it with girls hugging everyone?

"Everyone, listen up, this is my friend Jane." Heads turned at the command. "Jane, this is everyone," Lauren announced, gesturing Vanna White style.

People waved and called out their names. I opened my mouth to do the same, but Chris cut me off. "Oh, and this guy in the corner is Peter. He doesn't get out much."

She leaned over the couch again to shake my hand.

"H-hi," I said, swallowing over the dry spot in my throat.

"Hey, nice to meet you," she said with a warm smile.

Something Resembling Love

The game was not memorable. Two teams I didn't care about. But her? Jane? She was still as alluring and elusive as I remembered her from the summer beach.

Jane didn't sit down to the game, so even if I'd been brave enough, I wouldn't have had a chance to talk to her. I'd seen the size of the turkey in the oven, and the massive pile of potatoes to be peeled and cooked. Whatever Lauren was making for dinner, she sure wasn't going to be doing it all on her own.

Over the next several hours, Jane and Lauren, along with Vanessa, Alicia, and Lauren's son, Sebastian, were in and out of the kitchen. Occasionally, they would sit down in front of the TV, together or individually. Jane seemed to at least follow along with the few plays she did see. A couple of times, I thought I caught her looking at me. But that was probably wishful thinking on my part.

"Happy Thanksgiving!" Lauren said, by way of calling us to the table. Her hair, which had been in a messy bun, was now in a sleek braid, and her apron off.

"How long did it take you to drag this thing out of the woods, Lauren?" one of her real estate colleagues joked as we sat down.

"I delegated that task," she said, gesturing for us all to take our seats. "We'd like to welcome you all to our first Thanksgiving together, in this house, as a family. Some of our closest friends are here, and we couldn't be more pleased."

"I bought this house expecting to be entertaining, but not like this," Chris picked up Lauren's opening. "Then I met Lauren, and Sebastian," he added, ruffling the kid's hair, "and I knew they had to be here too, or it wouldn't be complete." He and Lauren exchanged a look and a smile behind Sebastian.

A half smile formed on my own face. I was happy for my friend, who'd always wanted a family but had been through a string of unfulfilling relationships. Now he had an insta-family.

"As most of you know, both of our families are scattered. Which is why I've always done Friendsgiving. It's nice to have you all here!"

I was sitting next to Jane, who'd teared up at the toasts. The tears only highlighted her eyes, which up close were a tawny gold color, like a dog or a lion. Her eyelashes were so dark and thick, I couldn't even tell if she was wearing mascara.

At first, I didn't know if she was talking to me because she was sitting near me, and was merely being polite, or if she was legitimately interested in my work. She obviously understood something about the work Chris and I were doing in the lab, though.

"The idea," I explained in answer to her question, "is to add a carbon and hydrogen molecule to DNA, which allows us to control how the gene it's attached to expresses."

"Do you know where to add the methyl groups specifically?"

I blinked at her for a moment, trying to get my bearing in the conversation. "Ah … do you know about cancer replication?"

She lifted one shoulder in a small shrug. "I took some biochem."

"Ah, okay?" I reached for my glass and took several swallows. She was pretty, *and* she could talk science? I was screwed. "Most gene-linked cancer is related to hypomethylation, not hyper."

She nodded, like what I said made perfect sense, and I had to pause again.

She wasn't at all what I'd expected. Beautiful, yes, but I'd expected her to hold herself away from people. Or at least people like me. But she … didn't.

"I work in a lab, too. Science, it's what's for dinner!" She gave an awkward smile. "Sorry, that's what we say at the lab—I'm a soil scientist. We work on improving soil quality and enhancing yields without adding chemicals. Thus, we get more dinner. Potatoes?" she beamed as she handed me the bowl.

I swallowed. "Thanks."

I imagined other women disliked her for her curves—the ones guys always talked about wanting their women to have. On every trip out of the room, I had noticed her butt. What Chris always said, something to hold on to. And breasts. Even under a sweater my eyes were drawn to them. I usually didn't consider myself a guy much concerned with physicality. How could I, when I was carrying fifteen extra pounds myself? She might have been a runner with the muscles outlined by her leggings. And she was clearly smart. The whole package was intimidating.

When dinner was over and everyone headed their separate ways home, she hugged me. A big, warm, welcoming kind of hug. Feeling her press up against me, I suddenly understood everyone's enthusiasm when she'd come in. She felt good, both her body and the genuine warmth she projected in her embrace.

"It was really nice to meet you," she said.

Nice to meet me? Me?

"Yeah, you too," I returned lamely, turning to leave. But she'd been smiling when she'd said it; maybe she meant it.

I took my warm fuzzies with me as I went back to my little apartment. I hadn't ever really compared my place to Chris'. He had way more money than me. But having met Jane? Now it seemed severely lacking.

JANE

"Oh good, you're here," Lauren said when she opened her front door for me, dragging me inside.

"I am." I admired the way the entry opened into the living area's cathedral ceilings. "Is Alicia here?"

"Did you think I was going to miss out?" she answered from behind me, pushing the door open.

"I made soup. I know it's mid-afternoon, but do you guys want any?"

"You're such a mom," Alicia said as we followed Lauren into her spotless kitchen and its acres of granite.

"I know." She grinned over her shoulder as she got out bowls for us.

It had only been a week since I was here last. After helping clean up Thanksgiving dinner, Lauren had asked what I was doing for Christmas.

"Drinking eggnog and having a fire."

"You should come here. For Christmas dinner."

I'd debated, but ultimately gone. It had been the first time in years I hadn't had to accept Kip's invitation to join his family. Christmas had been much smaller than Thanksgiving, with just her, Chris, Sebastian, and Vanessa's family. It had been nice, if a little awkward so obviously being the odd woman out, but I'd kept myself occupied playing Grand Theft Auto with Sebastian for part of the afternoon.

Something Resembling Love

"Earth to Jane," Alicia said, waving her hand in front of my face.

"Sorry," I gave a sheepish smile and sat back.

"You were daydreaming," Lauren said, setting her chin on her hand, her elbow on the table to scrutinize me.

I had been. It was easy to do on a relaxed afternoon with friends.

"What do you guys know about Peter?" There had been something there at Thanksgiving, a flutter of excitement. Someone to talk science with. On my few intra-lab dates, conversation had always become about work; most other guys weren't interested.

"He's super sweet. Kinda shy, so I don't know him super well. But I like him." Lauren got up from the table, and we followed her to the kitchen.

When I didn't say anything, Lauren turned around from the sink. "Why, do you have the hots for him?" She gave me a pointed look.

"Maaaybe."

"I know him. He's a nice guy. Kinda quiet. Pretty absorbed in what he's doing at the lab," Alicia added.

I wanted to know more. How he'd gotten into his line of research, and what it was like to think about possibly making such a big contribution. Plus, he was cute in that nerdy way that I found endearing.

"He was involved in several of the projects I managed. He rarely had much to add, but what he did say was well-thought-out and usually got other people talking." She picked up a piece of peanut brittle from a plate on the counter and nibbled. "He hangs out with us at the bar occasionally, goes to baseball games. He's social, even if he doesn't go out much."

"Are you guys talking about Peter?" Chris asked as he came in from the garage.

"Yeah." Alicia wandered to the end of the counter and leaned against the dishwasher, making her hips seem even more like a fertility goddess than usual. Of all my friends, Alicia was the one who best understood what it was like to not look like a nineties stick figure model.

"Jane has the hots for him," Lauren announced.

"You do?!" Chris' voice went up in surprise.

"I didn't say that. Exactly. But he seems like a nice guy. I asked Lauren what she knew about him." If I was being honest, it was a bit more than that. As I had walked into the living room a month ago, I'd felt my whole body sit up and take notice. Not in a sexual way. More like a little flag saying, "Yoo-hoo, pay attention! This is im-por-tant."

"And I said I didn't really know; that he was your friend." Lauren picked up the ladle and held it out to Chris. "Here, put the soup away and tell us everything you know." She pushed a stack of glass storage containers towards him as well.

"Ah … Okay."

All three of us watched him expectantly as he got into position at the counter.

"Peter spends more time in the lab than anyone I know. He's super smart. Um, I kind of have to drag him out to socialize."

The room was quiet for a moment as Chris carefully measured the soup out.

"And?" Lauren prompted.

"And he's not super close to his family. He's not dating anyone. He—"

"Does he want to date?" Lauren asked with a small line forming in her forehead.

"Of course he does. Every guy wants to get lai—sorry Jane."

"Chris!" Lauren scolded.

I suppressed a smile. "Not offended. Dating is as much about the physical stuff."

"Don't let him off like that!"

"What?" I shrugged. "It's true. Besides, I like sex, too."

"Do you want us to set you guys up?" Alicia asked.

I glanced at where she leaned against the counter, her hands resting on the edge. Chris was concentrating on stacking the small containers in the freezer. I assumed Lauren sent Sebastian to school with them. "What do you like about him?" I asked Chris. "As a friend."

"We were classmates before we became friends. He was quiet in discussions, but I think Alicia would agree, that when he does speak up, he's got something meaningful to add. I went to him a few times with questions about some of the more advanced concepts I didn't remember after five years away from a lab. He seemed surprised that I was coming to him for help, but he was generous with his time and his explanations. I took him out for beers occasionally—to say thanks, but also because I genuinely liked him. It took him awhile to figure out that I saw him as an equal, not the smart kid to do my homework for me. He's genuinely a nice person, and one of my closest friends."

"We should all have dinner or something," Lauren said. "Where we're not watching a football game. Alicia's date was nice, maybe we could have, like, a double date with six of us."

"That sounds like something that would be easier for him," I observed. "Rather than getting set up on a half-blind date."

"We could toss you guys together tonight?" Lauren suggested.

"New Year's Eve! Are you crazy?" Chris asked.

"What?"

"A setup on New Year's Eve. That won't backfire at all!"

Lauren shrugged. "He's coming, anyway."

Chris turned. "Alicia, help me out here. Peter will freak."

She shrugged too. "Maybe don't tell him it's a setup."

"Getting him to come at all was a big deal. He's even more skittish than you were."

"I wasn't skittish; I was independent!" Lauren said with a toss of her hair.

One corner of Chris' mouth lifted in suppressed amusement, and I suspected he teased her about this a lot.

Lauren made a fake mad face, and said, "Peter's already coming! What harm can it do to reintroduce them? Maybe force them to sit next to each other? Ooh!" Her eyes widened with inspiration. "Have him escort Jane."

"I think it's going to take more than having them in the same room," Chris said with a skeptical look. "They spent half a day together last month, and he didn't ask her out."

Lauren rolled her eyes at him. "That's because he doesn't know she's interested."

"You're going to have to hit him over the head with it," Alicia added.

"Which is why tonight would be perfect!"

"You guys." I breathed out a laugh, shaking my head at their back and forth. "I can probably manage some of it on my own. It's not like we don't know who the other person is."

"Worth a try," Chris agreed with a quick shrug. Then he glanced at the clock.

"Are you ladies going to spend *all* afternoon getting ready?"

"Of course," Lauren scoffed at the same time Alicia said, "It's five p.m."

"I don't know what you could spend all that time doing."

"Making ourselves beautiful. For you men to gaze at all night." Lauren batted her eyelashes.

"You couldn't possibly be more beautiful if you tried." Chris walked over to her to plant a kiss on her lips, and then grinned back at us with a wave as he strolled out of the room.

Alicia pretended to gag.

"Come downstairs, and let's have a glass of champagne. We can talk about New Year's resolutions. Or hopes for New Year's Eve," Lauren said with a wiggle to her eyebrows, looking at me.

In the lower level—there was no way to call this a basement—a big screen TV hung on one wall and a pool table stood nearby. There were also two more bedrooms, and the biggest guest bathroom I'd ever seen.

"Right, so first stop, that new Asian-fusion place, Zengo," Lauren said, sounding like a cruise director. "Then that party one of Chris' friends from his finance days, Stewart, is hosting. He said this guy throws bigger parties than he does."

"If that's true, I'm surprised Peter said yes to Chris' invite," Alicia said.

"He didn't so much ask, as inform," Lauren said as we sat on the couch. She handed me a bottle of bright red nail polish and unscrewed the top on a sparkly purple for her own toes.

"I'll bet Peter loved that," Alicia said sarcastically.

I let their chatter wash over me. Peter might always need to be dragged out to socialize, but I rarely went out for the new year myself. A few years ago, the whole lab had had a party, but even there, I'd felt alone. But this year felt different, an inevitability quietly simmering in the background. Intrigue about the possibilities. Curiosity about what Peter was like, who he was, and what he wanted out of life.

"I'm excited!" Lauren said as we migrated to the bathroom. She'd been saying the same thing since Christmas dinner, and I had to admit, I had gotten caught up in her enthusiasm. We spread out makeup along the counter. Seriously, this room belonged in a spa.

"I am, too, but also nervous now. Nothing like pressure when so obviously setting up two people on New Year's Eve."

"Enh, you'll be fine. With a couple of drinks everyone will lighten up," Alicia said, as she curled a piece of her hair that had an artful bright blue streak.

"Do you think Chris is up there texting Peter, suggesting there might be someone who is interested in him? Do guys even do that, the way we do?" I wondered, eyes wide as I smoked my eyeliner.

"I doubt it. Chris says Peter's not great with social plans, so he either commits last minute or bails if he's had too much time to think about it."

"Great. So, I'm getting set up with a guy who's not sure he wants to be social." Although I had done the same thing, hemming and hawing until I'd taken Lauren up on her offer to come for Christmas dinner.

"You're the one who said you had the hots for him," Alicia reminded me.

"That is *not* what I said! I said I thought he was interesting! I specifically said nothing about his appearance. Even if he is kinda cute in an overly smart guy kind of way," I finished with a mumble.

Lauren arched an eyebrow at me, as if she didn't believe me.

"You know how Superman is super-hot, but when he's Clark Kent, he's kinda nerdy and gets passed over?"

Alicia snorted. "Peter looks nothing like Clark Kent. He doesn't even wear glasses."

"Maybe not in physique, but he's, you know, a cute nerd."

"You *do* think he's hot!" Lauren pounced.

"Maaaybe …" I smirked, meeting her eyes in the mirror. "Do you think I look like I'm trying too hard with this dress?"

"Only if by 'trying too hard' you mean trying to scare the poor guy to death."

Lauren turned to Alicia, aghast.

"What? She's wearing, like, half a dress. The guy is terrified of his own shadow. He stays in the lab for a reason. Once he relaxes, he's a super fun person to be around but, I don't think he's dated much. Certainly not anyone who looks like that," Alicia said, waving her hand at my bare back. "So yeah, she might scare the bejesus out of him. But it will be fun to watch!"

"So maybe not these, then?" I held up a pair of four-inch red stilettos, and we burst into laughter.

An hour later, we were collecting the last of our things, and Chris was helping us into coats and then into the town car that would be our ride for the evening.

PETER

I stood in front of my bathroom mirror, furiously untying and retying the bowtie. I'd never had occasion to wear a tuxedo before, so I'd had to rent one, because Chris had informed me, we were all going out to a big party for New Year's. The suit felt ridiculous, but I was going to put on a good show. Especially since Chris had, not at all subtly, told me that Jane—*red sunglasses girl*—was coming, along with him and Lauren and Alicia and whomever she was dating.

Spotlight on the dorky guy who can't get laid by himself, I muttered to myself.

The bowtie looked better after about the fiftieth attempt, and I decided to leave well enough alone. Dinner was in thirty minutes, and it would take me every bit of that time to reach the restaurant. Some French-Polynesian fusion place Chris had picked. I'd refused to ride with Chris and everyone else; if Jane was going with them, I didn't want to be trapped next to her, getting sweaty with nerves.

I checked my wallet again for the credit card I was sure I'd need and shook my head as it flopped open on its worn spine. It certainly didn't match the pressed lines of the tux.

Blue icicle lights adorned the front awning and windows of the restaurant, and the entrance was laminated in gold for the evening. Men and women wearing party clothes rushed up and down the sidewalk.

"Here goes nothing," I muttered to myself. As I closed the cab door behind me, I heard my name. Turning, I saw Chris handing Lauren out of the car, followed closely by Alicia.

"Get the other door, buddy."

I silently obeyed, dreading what might happen next. In the dark interior, Jane was facing toward the other side of the car.

"Oh!" she exclaimed when I opened the door behind her.

"Let me help you," I offered my hand.

For three seconds, it felt like a scene from a movie. The moment the overlooked nerdy guy helps the beautiful woman out of the car, and she notices him for the first time.

Then a horn blared behind me.

Still, Jane took my hand, and I didn't let go, savoring the small moment as I led her through the front door and followed the hostess to a dark corner. Everything was lit by candles, and Christmas lights in whites and golds sparkled along the walls.

When I helped Jane out of her coat, I was relieved to have followed Chris' advice on the tux. A navy suit, no matter how nice, would have looked out of place next to the rest of them; especially Jane's white satin dress, which seemed to be missing a fair amount of back.

"How's the methylation sequencing coming?" Jane asked as soon as we had ordered drinks. "Chris told me you were running and re-running a bunch of previous attempts."

"I—um, good. Well, not good, since we were trying to pinpoint why it wasn't working the way we thought it would."

"Like maybe there was a different enzyme you should use instead?"

"Right!" I was euphoric that she got it. "When a genome is hypermethylated, it adds a methyl group to the nucleotide. Sometimes hypermethylation turns on genes that were not previously expressing. But we were trying to turn off the cancer genes, and instead our process was making it grow faster—are you sure you want to hear about this?"

Jane nodded enthusiastically as I looked for boredom in her eyes. "I don't understand it all, of course—no cancer cells in dirt. But the work that you guys are doing is fascinating."

"What about your lab?"

She laughed. "My boss is always giving me a hard time about the various manure samples I look at. But it's good to see if different animals have different microbial byproducts we could harness."

The mention of manure made me want to cringe, but then again, I knew the compost sold at the garden center was just that.

"Does it really make that much difference?"

"No one has studied it, at least not in-depth. Cheers!" She raised her coupe glass of champagne to my pilsner glass.

Once appetizers were served, she transitioned easily to talking with Alicia's date, following along with Lauren's ideas for the wedding, and trading insults with Chris. I felt the conversation buoy me. Jane knew enough about the science to ask good questions, and it was nice that someone—a girl!—was interested in the science part of things, not just the potential fame. That alone made the night worth it, and I relaxed, the meal seeming to fly by instead of dragging with the awkwardness I often felt, being the only single person.

But dinner felt like a warmup, compared to standing at the entrance of The Signature Room. I'd seen photos of it but never been inside. Giant square chandeliers hung from the ceiling, looking like a combination of Art Deco and the 1970s. The walls above the high tops, leading to a second level, were painted with bright vintage scenes of Chicago. It felt a little like stepping into a time warp.

In one corner, a DJ mixed music, while the bar in the center attracted movers and shakers who were looking to make a deal even on New Year's. I found a spot near the windows that overlooked Navy Pier with the Ferris wheel lit up for the night.

Although the guests were savvy and successful, some of whom I recognized from trade publications, tonight they were lavish, extravagant, and ornamented. There was a flair that pushed the party from an upscale celebration into a frenetic, Gatsby-like atmosphere. I tried to blend in with the wall.

"I want you to meet my friend and lab partner, Peter," Chris said as he walked toward me. "Peter, meet Fritz Klüssendorf, he works for Roche Pharmaceuticals, in Zürich. I was just telling him about our research."

"*Hallo*, Peter, very nice to meet you." The corners of his eyes crinkled with a genuine smile at the introduction. I shook his extended hand. He had slightly greying hair and wore his tux like he was in one every weekend.

"Fritz is wondering if we have any research we'd like to share with him. Roche hopes to develop a drug targeting prostate cancer."

"I don't think we have much to provide," I answered.

"I would like very much to speak with you about what you have found. I am in town for a few more days; perhaps we could meet?"

I read the business card he handed me. Principal Associate in oncology discovery. I glanced at Fritz again. He couldn't have been older than his late forties, and yet he had a job like this. Well, I was only a little behind. In a decade I supposed I could have his job.

"Sure," I agreed.

We watched him walk into the crowd. "We don't have anything to give him, Chris. The research isn't anywhere near ready for publication, let alone use for drug therapies!"

"Maybe not, but Roche could provide more funding than we can get at a research lab attached to a university! It could be an incredible opportunity. Just think about it. All you have to do is meet with him for an hour."

"Why aren't you going? You're the charming one."

He slung his arm around my neck. "I learned it from you. Now let's go find our ladies and celebrate this opportunity."

"I don't *have* a 'lady'!" But I followed him anyway.

Chris reached to slide his arm around Lauren. As he leaned forward to kiss her cheek, Fritz walked up to Jane and handed her a glass of champagne.

"This dress you are wearing is stunning. I do not see this often outside of Europe. Is it always you look like this, or only for special events?"

She laid her hand on his upper arm, laughing, "Ha! Limited to special events, I'm afraid. I'm usually covered in dirt or fertilizer. Soil science. We make dirt better."

His chin tipped upward with his hearty laugh at her witty comment.

I took a step back and retreated further from the circle. Only a fool would have thought she was interested in me. No, her dinner conversation had been politeness, nothing more.

Not long after, Chris found me along the same wall. "Come on, man, we're dancing!"

"You know I don't really dance." I looked over his shoulder at the revelers on the dance floor.

"Who cares? It's New Year's, there's free booze and hot women!"

"You have a hot woman. Dave, or whoever Alicia's date is, has a hot woman. I," I pointed at myself, "do not." Like I should need to remind him of the facts.

"What are you talking about? This whole thing was a reason to go out and be social, for you to get to know Jane."

"The Jane who was flirting with Fritz?"

"For cryin' out loud." Chris threw his hands in the air. "You are the most ridiculous excuse for a man ever."

"Yep." Hard to disagree with facts.

"She was being nice, but not giving him any come on."

"She had her hand on his arm."

"He's married! And European. You've had your cheeks kissed before."

He was right.

"You're the only one who got his card tonight. Besides, if Jane was interested in Fritz, don't you think she'd be hanging out with him right now, instead of making sure you were included in our group dance party?"

"She was?" I brightened, then deflated again. "But I'm a terrible dancer. I have no moves."

"It's New Year's Eve." Chris jerked his hand wildly through the air in annoyance. "No one gives a shit!"

I watched Chris intently for a moment. "All right, I'm coming."

"Yay, here he is!" Jane clapped her hands overhead as we approached. "I was beginning to think you had fallen in the special toilet."

"The special toilet?"

"Yeah, you know, the one antisocial people use, and then get flushed to the first floor. They only use it when there are big parties up here. But Chris told me you wouldn't use that one," she winked.

I grinned in spite of myself. "Nope, just getting a refill on my beer." I lifted it slightly to prove I wasn't making something up.

Before too long, the DJ quieted the music. "The new year is only a few minutes away, so be ready by making sure you have a glass of champagne and the one you want to spend the next year with close by. You never know what might happen with a New Year's kiss!"

People took the flutes from servers and started counting down the last minute. Couples moved closer together, Alicia and her date swinging their hands. I took a step backward, wondering if I could get out of the crowd. And then I saw Jane's hand. She was holding it out to me.

I glanced at her face and saw only a genuine smile. *What the hell*, I thought, taking a breath as I grasped her hand.

She stepped closer, and I felt her arm come around my waist. It took all my willpower to not look at the spot at my waist where her hand rested.

"Six, five ..." Jane raised her glass to me.

I raised mine as well and joined the count. "Three, two, one, HAPPY NEW YEAR!"

Happy couples surrounded us, kissing as the strains of "Auld Lang Syne" began. I hesitated, wanting to thank Jane, hoping that maybe I could kiss her. Just a little one. On the cheek. It was New Year's, after all.

I leaned in, closing my eyes. But what I felt wasn't the smooth plane of her cheek. It was ... my eyes flew open. My lips were pressed to hers, and ... I inhaled sharply, not moving until Jane pulled away. She was smiling, and her arm didn't move from my waist.

As the fireworks exploded out over the lake in front of the windows, I wrapped my arm around her shoulders.

After the last of the blues and whites filled the sky, the DJ blasted music again, and the dancing began in earnest.

JANE

It was nearly three in the morning when Peter helped me into my coat, and we piled into the Livery SUV Chris had gotten to fit all of us on the way back to his house. Hours of dinner, drinking, dancing, and general partying had made us all silly and raucous with laughter.

"Careful on the ice here," Peter said, as he held out a hand to help me out of the SUV.

"Noon brunch, if you're interested," Lauren slurred just a little over her shoulder.

"If you're awake by noon, I'll be surprised," Chris told her as he supported her up the front steps.

Peter smiled, looking at them, and then turned to me.

"Well, that was fun!"

He gave me a shy smile. "It was more fun than I expected."

"I'm glad you came. It was nice to talk to you when there weren't twenty other people and a football game in the background. We could do something like that again."

"I hope you mean the dinner part, not the party."

I smiled and laughed. "The party was fun, but yeah, it was a little over the top."

Peter stared at me, still smiling. I waited, hoping he would say something more. "Right, well, it's cold out here—"

He yanked his hands out of his pockets. "Er, look, why don't I give you my number, and, um, if you want to go out some time, you could call me?"

"No."

"Oh, I thought …"

"Dr. Livingston, I presume …" I began, trying to find a balance between serious and teasing, "you know how to ask for a girl's number."

"Oh. Er." He flushed in the cold. "Well, I could call you sometime?"

"I'd love that!" I said and flashed him a smile as I recited my number for him to save in his phone.

"Great, that's great." His arm moved forward, as if he wanted to shake my hand, and I noticed the slight eye roll at himself. But he didn't pull his hand back, and I suspected he couldn't, not without feeling ridiculous. I took it, then moved closer to brush a kiss over his cheek. "Good night, Peter. Nice bowtie," I whispered in his ear. Then I turned and walked to the house. I waved from the door.

"Good night, Jane," he called from inside the SUV.

I turned to call over my shoulder, "Good night, Peter."

On the first workday of the new year, I was sitting at my lab bench, humming while I prepared Gram stain slides of three new samples of manure.

"Happy New Year, Jane," Rodriguez said, as he used the sink across from me.

"Hm? Oh, same to you. Did you have a good one?"

"We did." He yawned. "The kids convinced Sarah and me to stay up until midnight."

I pictured their five- and seven-year-olds bouncing on the couch. "Sounds like fun." It sounded exhausting.

"Sounds like you had a *festive* evening, too."

I stopped concentrating on the slides. I couldn't talk and do them at the same time. "Went to a party at The Signature Room." I couldn't quite keep the giddy smile off my face.

"Swanky!" Rodriguez shook his fingers like something was hot.

"Complete with the Chicago fireworks, nearly bursting through the windows."

"And did something else get lit that night?" He leaned forward across the countertop, resting on his elbows.

"Uh."

"Come on, Jane, you were *humming*."

Yes, I had been. "Fine," I huffed. "Yes, I had a good night, and yes, there was a guy there, and no, I don't know when I'm going to see him next."

"But you'll tell me when you do? Actually, don't bother. I'll know just by looking at you." His entire face lit up with a teasing grin, and I saw the mischief in his dark brown eyes.

I rolled my eyes. "Whatever. Let me get back to work."

When I'd graduated from high school, I'd left everything behind. If I went back now, likely no one would remember me. Which was all right with me. I didn't need to be remembered, and I'd only been looking forward when I left.

I'd met Kip during my sophomore year of college at a career fair, before he was *Director* Thompson, but he'd refused to hire me until I had worked in an industry lab. "Keeping experience balanced," he'd said. It had been good advice, and two years after I graduated, he'd connected me with a different department within the USDA. Two years after that, he'd finally given me the job he'd been dangling in front of me.

I looked around. High-powered microscopes, most covered by protective plastic, dotted the lab. Two of the other women were labeling something in the far corner.

I glanced at Rodriguez again and shook my head before looking through the microscope lens.

It didn't take long for my mind to wander, the colors of the Gram stain blurring in front of me as I thought about Peter.

His enthusiasm for his work, the way he'd asked about my own—and not been grossed out when I'd mentioned manure. The way he'd helped me out of the SUV and warned me about the ice.

When Chris had retrieved Peter from wherever he had gone to hide, he'd half-shoved Peter into the center of our group. And then walked up behind him and started grinding on him. Watching Peter get flustered and then do three quick twerks to get Chris to back off had been worth it.

Then he'd noticed me and flushed a bright red. That was why, when the countdown had begun, I'd put my hand out to him. I hated being the only single person out somewhere. Even when I knew that "only" wasn't true.

If he'd been wearing glasses, he could definitely have pulled off a sandy-brown-haired Clark Kent look. While I doubted Peter was going to turn into Superman—he wasn't trim in Chris' surfer dude way—part of Clark Kent's charm had been his ordinariness. A kind word, a smile on someone's bad day.

"Must have been some guy for you to still be humming …" Rodriguez said.

I flushed, smiling at the top of the lab bench in front of me.

Peter

January began bitterly cold, as it usually did. After another pep talk from Chris, I reached out to Fritz, and we met over coffee.

"I'm afraid I don't know how much more information I can provide than Chris has," I confessed.

"Explain again to me what processes you have used and where you think it is unraveling." He looked completely relaxed in his brown suit. As I walked him through the work again, a part of me nagged that I shouldn't be sharing our techniques—what if he was able to take them back to his lab and correct them, publish a paper, develop a drug? This experiment was supposed to be my ticket—to finding a way to cure prostate cancer, to writing a well-received peer-reviewed article, to finishing my postdoc, and to getting out from under the thumb of our boss, who clearly favored Chris, and kept telling me I needed to set up the research differently

"I see." Fritz sat back, considering. "I do not have any ideas to fix your problems with the replication processes, but we have in-house resources to work on this further, if you are interested."

Chris would jump at the chance. The fear of our work being stolen made me hesitate. But Chris' instincts were usually right on this kind of thing. "Chris and I would both appreciate opportunities to hear more ideas," I hedged.

I needed to think, so on a dark Thursday evening a week later, I booked a rental car and drove into Wisconsin, to a small lake where I could throw up a windshield and ice fish for the weekend. Fritz had said he'd be in touch. But I was still struggling over the data. What it was and wasn't saying.

I wished I could turn off the circular rumination my brain was doing in favor of something more ... fun. With the sun warming my back, I screwed up my courage and called Jane.

Despite her invitation, all but saying that if I called, she'd go out with me, I had hesitated now for a couple of weeks. She had seemed sincere, but her invitation could have been given out of pity or fueled by drinks and the energy of the evening.

The adrenaline tasted sour when I got her voicemail, and I shoved the phone back in my pocket, scowling at the ice.

When my phone rang, I jumped, fumbling through heavy gloves to answer. "He-hello?"

"Peter?"

"Yes?"

"Oh good, you didn't sound like yourself there for a minute. It's Jane."

"Jane. It's nice to hear from you, thanks for returning my call."

I sounded like I was on a business call. *Lame.*

"I'm glad you did." She sounded enthusiastic, and I thought I heard a smile.

"Sorry. You just startled me. I'm ice fishing and didn't think my call went through," I lied.

"That sounds ... cold," she laughed.

"It's not so bad in the sun."

"It's—like four. Isn't it getting dark?"

"Well. Yeah. I guess I was having a good day." I relaxed as we started to talk. After a bit, I got to the tricky part. "Do you think you might want to have dinner sometime?"

My breath came out in a whoosh when she said, "I would."

"Great! There's a corner restaurant a couple of blocks off Chicago Ave. They have a great sampler happy hour menu."

"Sounds interesting. Is Chris keeping you chained to the desk, or do you have a night free this week?" This time there was definitely a smile.

I didn't bother to look at a calendar. My evenings were always the same. "How about Wednesday?"

"Wednesday's good for me," she agreed.

By Wednesday, the cold, damp weather had turned to heavy snow, and I watched people sliding on roads, accidents piling up, on my walk to the restaurant.

Jane entered in a whirl of frigid air and a swirl of snow, and I waved her over to the table.

"I love winter as much as the next person, but brrrr!" She rubbed her hands together. "Then again, you said you ice fish, you probably love this!" She was wearing heels, despite the several inches of snow.

"I like the frozen lakes part," I laughed. "But heels? In this weather?" I looked at them skeptically.

"I know, right?" she agreed, pulling off her hat. "I was presenting findings to the Under Secretary of Research, Education, and Economics today. Gotta look like a professional for those, you know." As she shrugged out of her coat, I saw she was serious. The dark-colored suit hugged her tightly.

"Your hair is longer. Then when I first met you, I mean."

The question in her eyes reminded me we hadn't actually met on the lakefront beach. "Maybe it was a picture I saw at Alicia's," I hedged.

"It was short! I can only stand the pixie for so long before I get fed up with not having any options."

"This is cute. Sleek." It reminded me of the hairstyles in old photos from the 1920s, and I wanted to reach out and feel if it was as silky as it looked.

"Thanks! Any menu suggestions?" she asked as she picked up the sheet in front of her.

I ordered the charcuterie and cheese platter, but rather than try the wine flights, Jane ordered a chardonnay. "What do you do?" Such a lame question. "Alicia said something about the USDA?"

Jane said a quick "Thank you," as her glass was filled. "It's more complicated than that. I'm at the National Institute of Food and Agriculture, but that's part of the USDA, so it's easier just to say that. I've been there almost ten years. My second employer out of college." Jane took a sip. "How did you end up trying to cure cancer?"

"By accident, mostly. Chris and I were doing similar work, so we partnered together. It took off on its own, and now here we are."

"So you've been at Northwestern for about a decade?"

This was why I hated dating; it was like playing twenty questions with the things I least wanted to talk about. "Feels longer! Two years of master's, six for the PhD. Now I'm two and a half years into my postdoc." I sat back and crossed my arms. "It can take time."

"It's pretty amazing work you're doing." Jane showed no surprise at how many years I'd been at this. "Do your parents live close?"

"About six hours. In Kentucky," I said with a flinch. Kentucky could be associated with being dumb, and I didn't want Jane to think I was. "After my sister, Catherine, and I graduated, in Cincinnati, they moved closer to family. Yours? You seem like you could be close."

Jane looked at the table. "I lost my parents in high school."

"I'm so sorry, Jane." I reached to put my hand on her arm, but pulled it back. Yet another reason I hated dating. It was so easy to put your foot in your mouth. "You don't have to talk about it." I rushed to cover the awkwardness. "Let's talk about something else entirely. What made you choose Evanston?"

By the time we'd finished, we were the last people in the restaurant. Jane had stayed far longer than the polite ninety minutes I'd assumed she would.

"Maybe I should just take my heels off and run out in bare feet," she joked, as we looked out the restaurant window. "Less treacherous."

"Let me help." Offering her my arm was as much a way to touch her as anything else.

"Let me just start my car," she said when we got there, leaning through the driver's door. She stretched further and then backed up, reemerging with her windshield brush.

"Here, give me that." I held out my hand.

She looked at me strangely before handing it over.

"No one's ever cleared your windshield before?"

"I have a garage at home, and yeah, no, I guess none of the guys at work think I need help."

"You have a house?" I asked, surprised.

"I do."

"There you go." I handed the window brush back. "You should be all set for a safe drive, now."

"Thank you." Her voice was warm and sincere as she took the brush. "That was very nice of you." She paused, waiting.

"It was nice to see you," I offered lamely, then hesitated. Should I kiss her, or hug her? I really wanted to kiss her.

Still undecided, I leaned forward and watched her eyelashes sweep down, anticipating an embrace. I wrapped my arms around her waist, felt her hands on my back. Pressing a kiss to her cheek, I stepped back.

"Good night, Jane, drive safely."

Confusion barely touched her face. "'Night, Peter."

I all but bounced on my toes as I stood, watching her pull out of her parking spot. Ebullient. Unbalanced. A disturbance, which I liked a lot, had just occurred. Did I have time for this? Maybe it wouldn't matter. Perhaps we wouldn't even go out very many times. Or maybe it would be spectacular.

I watched her drive away to make certain she didn't get stuck, then walked to my apartment.

JANE

Outside my window, everything was white. Condensation crystallized on the pane, white fluff on the trees, white clouds covering the sky. It had been a few days since I had gone out with Peter, and I was still rolling it around in my head.

I lay in bed, watching tiny rainbows from the frost on my window sparkle on the ceiling, absently scratching Otis between the ears, wondering. We'd had a perfectly nice time. Nonstop conversation, laughter, interest.

And then bam! Brush-off kiss-on-the-cheek.

I had had many different endings to my dates. Everything from sneaking out a side door because it was A, awkward, or B, creepy, to full-on sex in the backseat of someone's car.

But never, never on a good date, had I not been kissed.

I picked up my phone and dialed Alicia. "Peter and I went out," I said without preamble.

"Good morning to you too. Let me just—coffee first." In the background, cabinets slammed, and I heard the beverage hit the mug. Obviously, I was on speaker. "Okay. Peter." I could all but see her rubbing her face to wake up. "You went out—"

"Yeah, Wednesday. And it was great! We spent like three hours together; he cleaned off my car for me. And then BAM! He kissed me on the cheek!

Something Resembling Love

What the hell?" I gestured wildly in the air above my bed. Otis got up and left. "Did I get friend zoned?"

"I doubt that; I know he was really looking forward to seeing you."

"And you didn't tell me you'd talked about me?"

"We didn't talk about you. He just mentioned you guys had traded numbers and he was excited to see you again."

"You're a terrible friend!" I laughed through the phone.

"Just give it some time, it *has* only been three days."

"Fine," I agreed on an irritated exhale. "Breakfast?"

"Can't. The guy is over. Later though."

I dropped the phone on the down comforter and snuggled in. I hated being cold.

When Peter did call, a week after our date, I was pleased. My choice this time, a pizza parlor. Pizza was always a litmus test, I thought. Would you be able to share, or were your tastes too different, and you'd need separate pizzas? We planned for a weekend date, and I waited. Was I anxious because of him in particular, or because he seemed to fit my criteria?

Peter suggested he come pick me up, which seemed silly since he didn't have a car with which to pick me up, and it was close enough to walk from my house. But I had to admit, it was a sweet gesture.

I watched Peter study the menu. "I'm not a big fan of vegetarian pizzas."

"My favorite is the duck and fig," I offered.

"That sounds great!"

I smiled at his ready agreement and the good start.

"How long have you known Lauren?" he asked.

"About thirteen years, if you count the years we weren't in touch," I said as the pizza arrived. "We were besties in college, but she was a year ahead of me and had Sebastian. Then I moved here to start my career …"

Peter nodded. "I've only known Lauren a couple years, since Chris bought that monstrous house. But he's always been the king of socializing."

"I was warned," I laughed, swirling my wine glass. "It's nice to have that one friend who's always planning something."

"You seem like you're pretty comfortable in a crowd." As he said it, Peter was spinning the cork from the wine bottle.

"Mostly yes. I didn't have a ton of friends when I was young. While my little girlfriends were playing with Barbies, I was using my microscope looking at dirt."

"Microscope that young?"

"I know, it sounds silly. Maybe that's why I didn't have lots of long-lasting friendships."

"I think it sounds cool. But dirt?!"

"To this kid," I pointed at myself with my slice of pizza, "it was a great mystery. It was dark in this field, sandy in that one, and I saw pictures of the rocks in the Grand Canyon in a *National Geographic*—they were red. I wondered how come, if it was all dirt, it looked so much different?"

Peter set his piece down and sat back with an amused smile. "You really do have a thing for dirt."

"I do! I've been making mud pies since I was a little kid. I'm sure I ate some of it, but oh well—healthy immune system! My mom had the greenest thumb, and we had a huge garden. Strawberries, asparagus, tomatoes, broccoli, even corn. She taught me about nitrogen and phosphorus, shared her gardening errors with me. She was a great cook, too. I only got the baking gene."

"Is that what you do in your lab—share information on what you find in fertilizers?"

"Yeah, kinda. Mostly it's about what's already in the soil. What bacteria or nutrients or fungus. We all have different areas we specialize in though, just like every other area of academic science." I twisted my lips, considering my lab and what I thought Peter's was like. "I guess the difference is we aren't in it for the money. Fertilizer chemicals are patented, but not cow shit. The point is to undo the need for chemicals. Whereas for you, it's all about money."

"It's not, though!"

"I don't mean for you personally." I leaned forward onto the table. "But in order to slow down or stop cancer, there has to be a treatment. And treatments are high value."

"Don't you have to compete for grant money?"

My hair swung into my eyes as I shook my head. "No, we're entirely funded by the USDA."

"Wow." Peter paused with his slice of pizza halfway to his mouth, looking shocked, and I thought maybe a little envious. "That's—" He stopped mid-word, his eyes straying to my shoulder, where my sweater had slipped off, revealing an intricate bra strap.

"Sorry, I, uh …" His eyes dropped to the table. "Got distracted."

I blushed, even though I had worn this sweater on purpose.

Peter's eyes rose again and lingered on the lace for a moment before he held out his hand to help me from behind the table. "Right. Shall we?"

"I have to ask," I said as we walked back to my place, "What was that last week, when you kissed me on the cheek?"

"I was being polite."

"That was the most chaste kiss ever."

"I thought it would be rude to jump you in the parking lot." Without seeing his face, I could still tell he thought his answer was obvious.

"You wanted to jump me?" I felt the surprise on my face in the dark.

"Yes. Well, er, I mean no, not jump exactly. Maybe … wanted to kiss you. For real. But I didn't want to come on too strong, too pushy," he said in a rush. "I think people should have their space," he stuttered through the end of his explanation.

"I see," I said slowly as we approached my house. "And would I be coming on too strong if I asked if you wanted to come in for a drink?"

"That's different, because you know I'm interested in you."

"Do I, though?" I tipped my head with skepticism. "I mean, you did give me what most women would assume was a brush-off." I gave him an amused smile as I unlocked the arched wooden front door.

"You have a cat," Peter said as Otis regarded us from the couch.

"Don't mind Otis. He likes to cuddle, but he's pretty good at taking no for an answer if you're not a cat person," I said, heading for the kitchen. "All I have is red right now."

"I don't dislike cats, I'm just allergic."

"Oh crap," I said as I held out a glass. "I'm sorry. Do you need to leave?"

"No, no. I'll take a Benadryl when I get home, I'll be fine. Could I have some water, too?"

"Of course. With or without ice?" I turned away from the cabinet, hand on the knob.

"With."

I froze, looking at Peter looking at me. He took a step closer, and I couldn't have let go of the knob if required. He set his hands on my hips, then his lips on mine, waiting.

After a moment, my useless free hand grabbed onto a belt loop. The kiss was firm, but not demanding. A small sound lodged in my throat, and he stepped back abruptly, my fingers still caught in his belt loop. I didn't let go, and Peter glanced at my hand.

"Maybe I don't need any water right now," he said hoarsely.

I nodded and made a beeline for the couch. I barely waited for him to sit down before I reached for him. All I wanted to do was make out with him for the next three days.

Many minutes later, I sat back, letting my hands rest on Peter's thighs. His hair was mussed, and my sweater was askew again. A wry smile spread across my face.

"What's that look for?"

"Nothing, I just—well, given that kiss last week, I expected it would take us a lot longer to get here." I gestured to where we sat on the couch.

He reached forward and set his own hand on the outside of my knee. "Do you want to slow down?"

"No!"

"Okay then." He slid his hand under my sweater and pressed his lips to mine.

When his tongue swept across my bottom lip, I hummed in appreciation, and he kissed me even more deeply. I lost track, letting myself feel the longing I'd been stuffing down. I wasn't in lab clothes; I wasn't being eyed on the street. It was just me, being both groped and valued at the same time.

Rodriguez was going to have a field day with this when I saw him next week.

PETER

I'd been telling the truth; I hadn't wanted to jump Jane. Or I had, but not in the way she probably meant. I almost hadn't called her again. She was way out of my league. What would she say? "Hi, Peter, I had a nice time, but you're not exactly my type. You're too geeky." I'd argued with myself that she knew what a lab looked like, and so was unlikely to say any of that. Maybe she'd reject me for other reasons—like the fact that I didn't look like Chris, or because I'd been working on my postdoc for over two years and was likely to be doing so for … who knew how long.

Finally, I'd convinced myself that I'd never know if I didn't try. And I did want to try.

I stared, gaze unfocused, at the place where the wall and ceiling met, thinking about last night. I had thought it somewhat forward when she'd asked me in for a drink. On the other hand, maybe that was just me; maybe I was too cautious. Regardless, I was glad I had gone along. Because wow! That was some second date. I smiled to myself.

Admittedly, I hadn't dated a lot in the last couple of years. I'd been buried in the lab, working on my dissertation. The few dates I had had been awkward, like we were trying to figure out why we'd thought we could match. Jane and I didn't have any of that clumsiness, we just fit.

The back of my chair rattled, startling me.

"Are you solving all the world's problems, or just fantasizing?" Chris asked.

"Neither. I'm thinking about coding." I typed some to make the lie convincing.

"You don't get that look on your face when you're working."

"What look?" I turned to him, hoping my face was blank.

"That one—the one that's smiling." He grinned at me.

"I'm not smiling. This is my regular lab face." I looked back at the monitor.

"Have you seen Jane since New Year's Eve?" he asked, flipping through the papers on his desk.

"I'm working here!"

"So that's a no."

I remained silent, focused on the screen in front of me.

"Or maybe it's not a no … Pretty sure you're thinking about Jane. How was that date?"

How the hell did he know about our date, and how good it may or may not have been? I stopped typing and glared at him. "Why bother asking if you already know?"

"I wanted to hear the sordid tale from you. Don't worry—if Jane shared any of the gory details with Lauren, she didn't tell me."

Naturally. The joys of dating inside a friend circle. "Jane and I had a very nice time." I sounded prim even to my own ears.

Chris snorted. "I certainly hope you had a nice time. Does 'nice time,'" he air quoted, "include getting laid?"

"I would never tell on a lady."

"That actually *is* a no," he observed, straightening from his keyboard.

"I'm a gentleman. I wouldn't force myself on her like you would." *Still prim.*

"Is that really what you think of me?" Chris asked, genuinely wounded.

"No," I sighed. "But you would have taken things further. We're not all Greek gods who can get people to open up based on charm." My good mood faltered. Chris definitely would have had sex.

"You're far more charming than you give yourself credit for. Lauren also told me that Jane's dated a lot—"

"Of course she has. I mean, look at her!"

Something Resembling Love

"—that Jane's dated a lot," Chris continued, "and she has no issue sending guys packing quickly if they don't measure up. Stop selling yourself short, buddy."

"Fine. Yes, we've been out. Twice. No, I don't know if I'm going to marry her, but probably not as I doubt this will last long. Can we *not* talk about my shortcomings as a potential suitor?"

He set his hand on his heart. "I won't pop the bubbly until you've gotten laid."

"Gee, thanks." I rolled my eyes at both of us.

Chris' teasing had me thinking about how long it had been since I'd last had sex. Or even a second date. And that it wouldn't be long until Jane figured out how much of an uninteresting geek I really was.

I shook my head to clear it and refocused on the results I'd been working on. Within moments, I had stopped typing again and was lost in the memory of making out with Jane.

JANE

Work crushed me over the next couple of weeks. I'd told Peter that my work was entirely funded by the USDA, and watched his eyes widen at the thought of not having to compete for grants. But that didn't mean there weren't stage gates and milestones for continued funding.

I wanted to run a six-month composting experiment using manure from different species, and, as I'd been working on last fall, the different sexes and sexual maturities of bovine. In my mind, I saw piles of compost left behind, and the resulting plants I would grow. There would be a clear winner and a clear loser, and several acceptable alternatives.

In order to get to that stage, though, I had to convince Thompson and his boss, Undersecretary Aziz, that my current data showed enough of a difference between the groups to continue.

"Don't you have a date tonight?" Rodriguez asked as he put on his coat.

"It's for dinner, so—hey! How did you know about that?"

He shrugged. "I can't be blamed for you leaving your calendar open."

I narrowed my eyes at him. "It was on my desk."

"Sometimes people need things from your desk."

"It's a good thing I like you so much."

Something Resembling Love

"You better get out of here if you want your date to like you so much." The mischievous look in his eyes told me exactly what kind of liking he was talking about.

"I have plenty of time, it's only …" I said, glancing at the clock on the wall. "Oh, crap!"

"No pun intended," he said with a grin. "Have a good time," he called as he walked down the hall.

I hurriedly stored my samples and ran out the door.

"Hey there, good looking," I said when Peter opened the door to his apartment. I had made it on time, but just barely.

Peter flushed, but didn't look away. "I—um. Let me grab my coat, and then we can walk?"

"Sure."

The details of our days flowed back and forth as we walked the half mile to the restaurant. His, he admitted, were often the same. Test tubes, pipettes, coding, algorithms, more coding. They sounded like my days, minus the coding. A reagent here, a smear of cow dung (or deer droppings or worm castings) on a slide there.

We arrived to find Lauren and Chris, and Alicia and her date, at a table in the back corner. I smiled, seeing my friends had gotten a table away from the cold air of the front door. Reconnecting with Lauren, and being pulled into this sphere, I had a pleasant sense of familiarity.

As we stood at the end of the meal, Peter helped me into my coat, and I reached for his hand. On the sidewalk, we turned toward Peter's apartment, waving as our friends made their own way home.

"This is my humble abode. I'm sorry about the mountain of mail," Peter said as we passed through what was best labeled as a sitting room, with an alcove that held a table. The apartment occupied the top floor in a greystone, with a wide window, which I assumed looked out over a post-age-stamp sized yard. The detritus of life covered every surface.

I surveyed the room, checking out the books on his bookshelf, noting the half-empty coffee cup on the edge of one shelf.

"All through dinner, I kept thinking about coming back here," he said as he walked across the room from the coat closet. "About having you to myself."

That was all the encouragement I needed. "Good!" I breathed, reaching to pull him toward me.

In a matter of moments, I was on my back beneath him, in a good old-fashioned make-out session. Peter's hand slid under my dress, bunching the fabric up, and caught my breast in his hand. With eager fingers, he tugged the lace of my bra down and grabbed the V neckline of the dress from inside, baring my skin. His head dipped and trailed a line of kisses along the exposed edge. This boy, for all his nerdiness, had had some practice kissing somewhere. My body lifted involuntarily, pressing against his mouth.

"God, you are so sexy," he whispered hotly in my ear.

Hands on his waist, I pulled him closer against my hips. Peter raised his head to my lips, and I kissed him with urgency.

I yanked his shirt out of his pants, racing to put my hands on his back. I felt his body stiffen, then relax. His lips left mine and skipped along my neck, back to where he'd started, at the edge of my bra. I gasped at the wet slide, pressing my hands into the soft flesh of his back, holding him tight against me. I could feel the hardness of his excitement.

He left the skin he'd been tracing, planting kisses along my chest, back up my neck, coming to rest on my lips. "I think you should go home," he whispered.

"I—"

"You're so beautiful, and I want you so much, but I—" He looked at my lips.

"So beautiful you don't want to sleep with me?"

"No, Jane! It's not that! I do want to sleep with you, but I … I want to enjoy this."

The look he gave me made one side of my mouth lift in an ironic smile. His face was sad; bummed, really, like nearly getting in to see the newest movie and being the next person in line after the last seat was filled. His eyes searched my face, and I felt like he was looking for clues that I was okay.

"I do, too."

There had been plenty of times I'd rushed into sex. And now that we were here, I wanted to rush with Peter. But he was right, we should enjoy this. As much as I found his nerdiness sexy, there was excitement in getting to know each other, in going slow.

"So, I'll go home."

Something Resembling Love

The next morning, I picked my phone up off my nightstand and read a late text from Peter.

> Maybe we could have dinner tomorrow night— or, I guess that's tonight 😊

I smiled into the sunshine streaming in my window as I replied.

> I'd like that a lot.

"Tell me something few people know about you," I requested, as we sat on Peter's ratty couch, eating Chinese that evening.

"I got into epigenetics by accident."

"As so many of the best careers happen!"

He gave a self-deprecating smile. "I was working on my master's and was asked to help write some code for a translational medicine computer program, because I'd had more biology than anyone else in the program. It was so successful that they kept asking me to work on other projects. Somehow, I ended up taking extra biology classes, and getting a master's in biomedical engineering, instead of computer programming. And now I'm here, working with DNA every day," he said, looking baffled.

"Why don't you seem happier about it? That's a very cool transition. And I doubt you would have made it if you weren't interested in the biology side of things."

"I'm not really a scientist. I'm an engineer."

"You could be both?" I suggested.

"My boss doesn't think so."

I tilted my head and frowned.

"The head of our department, he's crazy about medicine. I want to engineer a solution that will prevent the mutations from happening. He only wants to stop it once it gets started. He keeps telling me to look at the problem differently."

"Have you? Tried his way?"

"No, that's not the point of the research Chris and I are doing!" He stabbed his fork into the takeout carton.

Clearly, I was exasperating him, too.

"I was just thinking that if you found a way to stop the process once it started, you could reverse engineer to prevent it from happening at all."

Peter kept quiet for a moment, eating bean sprouts and being irritated with me.

"Your turn." He gestured with the fork. "Something few people know."

There were a couple of options here, but I chose the easy one. "My parents were killed in a car accident my junior year of high school. The weekend before Thanksgiving. I don't talk about them much, so most people just assume that I'm not close with them. But I was, we were, very close. Sometimes too much," I gave a wry smile. "I still really miss them—especially my mom. She was like my best friend."

"I'm sorry, Jane. That must make every Thanksgiving hard." Peter reached his hand to my knee, and I covered it with my own.

"It does. This year was the first year I really celebrated."

"Don't you have any siblings?"

"No, I'm an only child."

"Family friends?"

I shook my head. "When I left for college, I basically disappeared. I stayed in state so I could pay for college and not take any loans. I was so focused on my studies I didn't make much time for friendships."

"Weren't you still a minor?"

"I was seventeen when they died, and I petitioned for emancipation. I used the money they left behind to pay the mortgage and take care of myself until I graduated. When I left for college, I sold the house. I couldn't bear to be there without them. Maybe if I'd been their age when they died, but not in my teens and twenties …" I took a breath and forced a smile. "How about you, what's your family like?"

"Dad's an engineer, mom's a science teacher," he outlined. "My younger sister is an actress."

"So you come by it naturally!"

"Ha! I'd never thought of that." He watched me closely before raising his hand. Tentatively he pushed my hair behind one ear. "You're so beautiful."

I looked down, trying not to squirm.

"Can I not tell you that?"

"No—it's just—"

"You are a beautiful woman; surely you know that?"

"I do." My eyes stayed down as my hand came to his wrist, where his hand rested on my cheek. "Sometimes it feels like that's all I am." I paused. "We both want to be seen for our successes, and that would be easier if I looked … different."

"I know that you're more than your looks. But I—" Peter dropped his hand and looked down at his own lap. "I'm surprised every time you agree to go out with me."

I grabbed his hand. "You shouldn't be! I think you're attractive and smart, and I really want to keep getting to know you."

He looked at where I held his hand, and then back up at me. "I won't ask you to stay," he said, and then hesitated. "But if you'd like to, you're welcome."

"Do you have boxers and a T-shirt I could borrow?"

He studied my face. "I do. I'll put them in the bathroom for you, then I'll take the trash out."

When Peter left, I wandered his small space. The desk was piled with pages of scribbled notes. A few open journals were pushed to the side of the coffee table. Another coffee cup sat on the bookshelf. A rack of drying laundry was visible through the bedroom door.

I was sitting on the couch, still in my clothes, reading an article in a cancer journal when he came back. "Do you need anything else?"

"No. I was just waiting to change until you came back because I didn't want to get cold."

"Are you cold?" He looked at me like he didn't understand. "I can turn on the radiator."

Twenty-two degrees outside … and he didn't even have the radiator open. The tile in the bathroom confirmed the weather.

When I came out, wearing his T-shirt that bagged on me and a pair of well-worn flannel boxers, he was setting his alarm clock. "What time do you need to get up?"

"Six?"

"God, that's early!"

He flipped the covers back for me, and I climbed in, shivering.

"Are you cold?" he asked again.

"A little."

"Let me warm you up," he offered, sliding his arm around me. "Since you're so close, and in my bed, I can't be entirely blamed if I do something like this."

I leaned into a kiss that wasn't hesitant, but painfully, enjoyable slow. He trailed kisses down my neck and tugged at the shirt to reach the top of my breast. I arched underneath him, and in response, he ran his hand along the outside of my thigh.

When he removed his hand, I caught it and brought it to my lips, kissing the palm of his hand, then swirling my tongue in the same spot.

His breath hitched. "What are you doing to me?"

"Do you want me to quit?" I asked, all innocence.

"No! Don't stop." His hand was shaking.

"If you're sure," I licked from his wrist across his palm again.

PETER

I stared, unseeing, at the screen in front of me. Once again. Jane had come back. And slept in my bed.

I'd wanted to strip my shirt off of her. And I wanted to go slow and enjoy.

Jane seemed breakable in a way that I couldn't have imagined. But just because she was pretty didn't mean she hadn't been through a lot, as I was finding out.

And then, to know about her history, at the same time as she pressed herself to me, kissing me back … the feeling of her thigh pressing gently against my crotch, the pressure making me want her even more.

Hours later, and I was still turned on just thinking about it. Sure, I'd had sex before, but I'd always thought of it as the guy's job, my job, to make sure my partner got what she needed. But with Jane … a ghost of a feeling across my wrist made me shiver.

"Daydreaming?" Chris said from behind me.

"Uh, yeah." I blinked to bring the screen in focus. "That the changes we made work, and we can move on to the next stage."

He narrowed his eyes, studying my face. I squirmed under the scrutiny.

"Uh-huh." He turned away. "You're in luck. The intel you got from Switzerland worked."

"I saw. On to updating coding."

"How's Jane?" Chris asked, watching code scroll on a computer screen.

"Fine."

"I heard you guys have been talking a lot."

"No one said there was anything wrong with your hearing." I turned away from Chris and the main screen.

"I'm going to miss you while you're gone," Jane said as she snuggled under my arm where we leaned against the headboard.

"You are?" I heard the surprise in my voice. "It's only ten days."

"You're the one who's going to be out having fun, meeting people, advancing your career, drinking excellent beer, sightseeing. Meanwhile, I'll be sweeping mouse droppings out from under the cabinets."

I sighed, thinking about the upcoming conference in Germany, where I would have a poster on our attempts. "I hate the pressure to network," I sighed. "I always feel like I'm begging for a job."

"Don't we all."

"I'll bet you're great at it." I paused, picturing the last big conference I'd been to and the feeling of being lost amongst all the ideas. "I'm not ready; I don't know what I'll say to people who ask about the research."

"You'll tell them the truth—that curing cancer, or treating it, is complicated, and you are learning a multitude of things about how DNA responds to external pressures."

"When you put it like that …" I chuckled. "Are you sure you're okay taking me to the airport in the morning?"

"I'm sure. But it's such an early flight, we should probably go to sleep now." She shifted out from under my arm and turned off the only lamp in the room. "'Night, Peter."

As my eyes adjusted to the dark, I kept looking at her, lying in my bed. I had hoped that we might make out some more. But she was right; I would never be able to wake up if we did.

Something Resembling Love

I lay down behind her, pulling her close to me. Well, her breast was right there, I couldn't exactly be blamed if it was where my hand was most comfortable. Or if it was just the right shape to be squeezed.

I felt Jane's laugh as much as I heard it. "Go to sleep, Peter."

It was surprisingly easy to do so, even with her next to me.

Before dawn, in my dream, I felt her on top of me, our bodies pressed together. I shifted, wanting to get away from the sensation. Some half-awake part of my brain insisted it wouldn't be nice to wake her with a hard-on poking her in the back.

Dream Jane kissed me lightly, and I turned my head. This was going to be embarrassing. Under the covers, I started to stiffen. I could feel her legs on either side of my hips, and then she pressed more of her body against me.

It was physically painful. I jerked awake. My hand flexed just before I opened my eyes, and it felt like flesh under my palm.

And then there was Jane, straddling my hips. I felt myself harden the rest of the way.

"Good morning," she said, her eyes on my face. Her voice was husky.

"G-good morning." I glanced down, taking in my hand disappearing under her shirt and the pressure of her against my—oh God, it wasn't a dream. "Wh-what are you doing?"

"Finding a better way to wake up than a jarring alarm clock."

I swallowed hard.

"Touch me," Jane whispered.

I watched her for another minute, my thumb sweeping back and forth over her nipple. It was almost incredible that she wanted me. But here she was, in my bed, waking me up like ... this.

I flipped her to her back.

"Like this?" My voice was husky, too. I pushed the fabric of her panties to the side and gently slipped two fingers inside of her.

Jane moaned, her whole body tensing.

"Is this what you want?"

Jane cupped my balls through the boxers I was wearing. I closed my eyes and groaned.

We touched each other slowly. My fingers moved inside of her, drawing out the fine agony of wanting.

There were so many competing interests in my body. The part that didn't want to rush through the new intimacy warring with the part that wanted to take my hand away and dive headfirst into her. And then the part of me that just wanted to look at her, limp in my hands, eyes closed as she bit her lip. Even as I watched her, Jane's hips raised, lifting to meet my hand, her hand clenching in the sheet, and she cried out.

She lay there, panting, while I smoothed a hand along her thigh.

After a moment, she let out a long breath and opened her eyes to look into mine. "This is *your* wake-up call."

I smiled down at her. "And a nice one. What—"

Jane's hands were on my waist, pulling my boxers over my hips, which lifted of their own accord. She tossed the clothing away, settling me on the bed, on my back the way we had started. Her hand came to rest around me, tightening in increments as she slid her curved palm up and down.

The feeling of losing control was overwhelming. "Jane . . ." I choked out.

She shoved my shirt up my chest and spread her palm along the skin.

"Jane!" I cried, louder, grabbing at her forearm as my body strained upwards toward her grasp.

My face contorted as I felt the release of the last months of tension. I lay there panting, eyes still closed, trying to determine if it was all a dream. But when I opened my eyes again, Jane was still there, lying on her side next to me, palm resting on my stomach.

"You're right, that is a much nicer way to wake up than a stupid alarm clock," I said, as I trailed my fingers along the back of her ribcage. I frowned. "What's this?" Under my fingers was a small indentation of hard skin.

"A scar."

When I didn't say anything, Jane continued, "From surgery several years ago. I have a vascular condition."

From the way she'd taken a steadying breath, I could tell she didn't really want to talk about it, so instead, I pulled her close for a thorough kiss. "I'd go out of town anytime if it meant that kind of wake-up. Hmm. Well, except then, I'd have to be away from you more often. You *are* beautiful. Darling Jane." I sighed with weariness, remembering why I was getting up so early. "And now, I have to leave this bed and finish packing. Don't move, I want to look at you every time I come in here."

She grinned at me. "How about I go make coffee instead?"

PETER

Meeting up with Fritz had made the conference in Germany, already a month ago, feel less like hurling myself down a gauntlet and hoping for the best. He seemed, surprisingly, pleased to see me, was complimentary of my work, and introduced me to several people. He had also offered to host me in Zürich, any time I wanted, and take me on a tour of Roche's lab.

I found one free night to go to the opera. The ticket was for standing room, but I didn't mind. What I did mind was that Jane wasn't there to enjoy it with me. At the end of my fifth day, I flopped into bed after midnight. Every moment of every day felt like a desperate bid to get someone to talk to me. And the conference reception tonight, walking around with beers and tiny cups of wine? So much worse.

After a few minutes, I levered myself up. As I rummaged through my disorganized suitcase, I felt paper. A small, folded square flipped out as I retrieved my boxers.

I sat on the bed as I unfolded it. There was nothing written on the page. Just a lip print in a deep burgundy that I'd seen Jane wear a few times. I'd traveled while dating other girls, and no one had said they'd missed me. I smiled, touched by the gesture.

Still holding the piece of paper, I dropped backward on the bed. With my eyes closed, I could almost feel where her lips had touched my body. I lay there, rubbing my thumb over the small paper. My body remembered the way she had touched it, too.

My whole body flinched as I closed my hand around myself.

Knowing I was coming home to Jane had made everything feel better. As if my entire life weren't hanging solely on my career. Even if it was.

But then I had returned to my third-floor cave and was disgusted by the mess. I'd left my suitcase by the door and decided the sheets, still rumpled from the morning Jane had woken me up, were the easiest place to start.

After I'd taken them to the building's basement laundry, I stared around the living area. It was no wonder I liked being at Jane's so much more. I took the journals off the coffee table and stacked them on the bookshelf. I retrieved a few notebooks from the scarred table by the window, and moved them to the shelf, too. *What the hell were these coffee cups doing here? Ugh, I was a such slob.*

The table was supposed to be a table and desk, but mostly it was a catchall for notebooks, magazines, and my computer bag. Usually I just sat on the couch, hunched over the laptop on the coffee table. I cleaned the table off, thinking I could keep it picked up, use it as a table and desk as intended, then turned as the small mountain of mail caught my attention.

Jane teased me when she'd come over the day after I returned. "You cleaned!"

"Some. Your place is so much nicer. It always smells like you just polished the furniture and looks like you vacuumed the carpets."

"That's because I usually have just vacuumed," she'd said, setting a carryout bag on the counter where I'd only just cleared space. "If I know you're going to be there, I try to vacuum the floors and couch since you're so allergic to Otis."

"Oh! That's really ... thoughtful." I had paused, stumbled really, like usual, watching her unpack the Italian takeout. "I got you something while I was gone."

"You did?"

I retrieved the small black box from my bag. "Just a little something." I set it down gently.

Curious and a little wary, Jane tugged the lid off, and unfolded the tissue paper. Inside sat two small, hand-carved, wooden Edelweiss flowers.

"They're illegal to pick. I thought you might like these instead."

"They're gorgeous!" She twirled one between her fingers, and I saw her eyes soften. "Thank you, that was incredibly sweet."

She'd leaned to kiss me. Which had inevitably led to less sweet places.

She would be here in a few hours, but she'd refused to tell me where we were going. I hoped she hadn't planned some big birthday party. I *hated* my May birthday. But then again ... Maybe I wouldn't hate it so much with her.

When she drove us further out into the suburbs, I started to wonder what was going on.

"Where are we going?" I asked, when she parked in front of an arcade and bowling alley.

"Bowling."

"I can't bowl." I crossed my arms.

"Neither can I. I'll probably get a gutter ball on every roll. We can always just play arcade games. C'mon." She waved her arm as she got out of the car. "Let's go find our table."

I huffed as I followed her. Lauren and Chris were picking up shoes at the shoe rental. "This was Chris' idea, wasn't it? And you went along with it."

"We planned it together."

"*Great.*"

"What's wrong, babe?" She turned to face me, setting her hand on my arm.

"I *told* you I didn't want to do anything. And then you planned something anyway!" A tiny part of my brain registered that I was behaving like a jackass.

"Okay. Just pretend it's not your birthday tomorrow. Or better yet, remember that your birthday isn't until tomorrow, and we can have terrible nachos, maybe play a couple of video games, and hang out with our friends."

I felt something squeeze in my chest, and not in a pleasant way. A panicked clutching.

Something Resembling Love

"That's going to be hard to do with the giant balloons Chris brought." I stared at the grass-green mylar "three" and "four" that bobbed in the air.

Jane looked over her shoulder and laughed. "Um. We can pop them if you want."

"Nah. Besides, it's just us four, Alicia, and I think that guy is Zach," I said, squinting to see across the alley. "I'm pretty sure Chris can't help himself from always inviting at least one more person."

"See, if you don't know that guy, this can't be your birthday."

Jane was right, she got a gutter ball on almost every try. It didn't matter though. My mood lightened as we drank crap beer and threw balls down the alleyway until Chris set a pie on the table with a flourish. "Cherry?" I asked, wary, irritated, and curious all at once. As Alicia lit the candles, I thought of birthdays past, of the pie I'd seen on a menu but hadn't ordered, when Jane and I had gone out a couple of months ago.

"If you hate it, I'll take the pie, and you can lick this off Jane instead," Chris said, holding up a bottle of chocolate sauce.

"How about you just give me that?" I reached across the table.

"I know I said this wasn't for your birthday ..." Jane started.

"She lied. Jane's a crap girlfriend. She dragged us all, all the way out here, and said we had to sing to you," Chris said, and then Jane, Alicia, and Lauren started singing *Happy Birthday*, joined quickly by Chris and Zach.

I held my breath as I took the first bite. As I chewed, I felt my face relax into a smile. "None of you get any," I said, pulling the pie plate close.

"No way, man, I had to bring that thing here and not eat any. I better get some!" Chris whined like a schoolboy.

We polished the pie off quickly and, bowling finished, said good night, everyone wishing me a happy birthday again.

Chris turned back around from the exit, and said, "Here you go, Pete—since you're the birthday boy and all," as he handed me the chocolate sauce.

"Jane," I said, catching her attention before she turned on the car. "I'm sorry I was a jerk earlier. I was cranky about my birthday, and I just didn't want to do anything ..."

"Did you think I was going to let you not celebrate?"

"Maybe?"

Jane gave me a half smile.

"I'm sorry," I repeated. "Do you think we could go home and try this?" I held up the bottle of chocolate sauce.

"Nope." Jane set her hands on the steering wheel. "This wasn't a birthday celebration, you just said so."

I could see she was trying not to smile.

"Tomorrow then," I agreed and sat back to buckle myself in.

"Okay, but before I let you put any of that cold sticky stuff on me," Jane said in the morning, holding on to my wrist, "I want to know why you didn't want to do anything for your birthday."

My shoulders dropped where I sat on the edge of the bed, and I set the bottle on the floor.

"It's nothing." My reason was stupid for a thirty-something guy. I looked out the window. But Jane was watching me, clearly waiting for an answer. *What the hell.* "I always wanted to see the special museum exhibits for my birthday, but because my birthday is mid-May, and inevitably at the end of the school year, I could never get my parents to take me, because of my mom's schedule. And I got cake from the grocery store. Catherine always had better birthdays, because hers is in the middle of summer break."

Jane frowned, not following my logic. Which wasn't logical. I sighed. "Right now, I'm just really frustrated with my boss. Each new hypermethylation we try causes the DNA to disintegrate. Like, the DNA doesn't fall apart, but now it won't express at all. Every time I talk to him it's a totally different conversation, a new suggestion, a new metric. I keep thinking he wants to shut down my research."

I thought about the relationship between Chris and our boss. Chris was always poking around with new ideas, which seemed counterintuitive to me, but I'd seen the two of them looking at data together and the excitement in our boss' face. It was like Chris didn't even have to try and he had everything. Whereas, until I, last night, I'd never really had a great birthday.

"Do you ever think about leaving the program and working for a company? Didn't you tell me that Fritz is interested in what you have been working on?"

"Not really," I said, staring across the room at the wall, the way I sometimes zoned out on algorithm results. "They're a pharmaceutical company, not a research institution." The implication was obvious, wasn't it?

"Surely, with the methylation process, you can't fudge the results. It either works or it doesn't." Jane frowned.

"How it was funded still taints the results," I insisted. Jane should know this from her own work.

"Hmmm ... I don't know. If you can cure cancer, I'm not sure it matters who funded it."

I shrugged irritably. "Anyway. That's why I don't like my birthday. School. Mom. Now work reminding me I'm falling behind. It doesn't really feel like I have anything to celebrate."

"Should I have taken you to see the mummies at the Field Museum instead?" Her voice was teasing.

"No. Well, maybe." I felt my lips curve a bit.

"We could go this weekend. Or whatever you want to do."

"Last night was fun." I shifted to her fully and looked at her beautiful face. "It was good to blow off some steam. I've never been dating someone on my birthday. It was exceedingly nice to have someone think of doing something for me."

Jane trailed her fingers along my hand. "I'd do whatever you needed to make you happy."

My heart constricted in an unfamiliar way. Warm this time, and not unpleasant.

"Like I said, I've never had a girlfriend for my birthday. That's what I'd like now: to have you."

Jane rolled backward and grabbed a gift bow from the nightstand. She stuck it to her chest. "Now you can! Come here so you can have the rest of your birthday present."

I lay down, facing her. "There's more? Maybe I do like my birthday after ah—"

My thoughts scattered at the warmth of her tongue sliding down my sternum, her fingers pressing into my side. I reached up to put a hand on her shoulder and realized with shock that it was trembling. Before my next thought, she was pulling off my boxers.

"Wait," I blurted. "Up, stand up." I followed her off the bed, wanting to put my arms around her, kissing her as I pushed at the pair of my boxers she was wearing—*mine*, I thought with a smile.

Goosebumps sprang up along her arms and abdomen.

"Are you cold?"

"A little. Er, yeah," Jane admitted with a shiver. I pulled her closer to my body heat, and she shivered again.

The screen printing on her shirt (Dirt isn't dirty!) scratched against my chest when she shuddered, and all my nerve endings took notice. I realized I was trembling all over, too. I was conscious of her hands on my bare back as I watched her; she was watching me too.

For a long moment after we were both naked, I waited, breath coming in short bursts, my body frantic.

I bent to kiss her, and Jane jumped, carrying us over onto the bed. The instant we landed she was reaching to guide me.

"Wait," I said, stilling her hand.

"We've done too much waiting. I want to make up for all the waiting we did. I don't want to take my time." She slid closer.

She had a point.

Was this birthday sex? If so, I liked it. And the time we had waited made the feel of her, warm and wet around me, even better.

She rocked. Once, twice. I felt myself jerk inside of her and I squeezed my eyes shut, trying to hold on against the sensations. "I'm—I can't—I—Jane, I'm not going—"

"Good. Don't. I don't want you to hold back anymore," she breathed in my ear.

She rocked against me. Between her warm breath on my neck and the feel of her around me, my vision blurred. "Oh, *God*," I groaned. She hummed in appreciation, still rocking. When her breath caught, I lost all control.

It was minutes before I put enough brain cells together to form a sentence. "I—Did you?"

"Um. No."

"I'm such a jerk."

"You were enjoying yourself."

I was silent, contemplating her words as she lay down next to me, her head on my shoulder. I had always been able to hold off until the girl came first. This had never happened. I vowed to myself I would make it up to her next time.

"My parents called yesterday," I said after a few minutes. *Parents, while naked. What am I saying?*

"They did?" She picked her head up.

I looked at her. "Yeah. And they want to come visit."

"Peter, that's great!" She settled her head on my chest again.

"They're going to want to meet you. Probably dinner at least once. They're thrilled I'm dating someone so smart." My lips twisted. "They're thrilled I'm dating anyone."

"It's nice you got to talk to them for your birthday, that they want to visit you." I felt her exhale a long breath. *Had I stuck my foot in it again? Mentioning my parents had probably been an insensitive, asshole move.*

JANE

I sat at the utilitarian metal desk in my office, hands flat on the cool surface, fingers spread in front of me, my computer screen staring back at me.

Two weeks ago, I'd been in for the nuclear PET scan I'd gotten every year since we'd discovered the HHT.

I'd been radioactive for a day and had stayed home, away from my coworkers. I didn't need to go all Marie Curie on them.

Today, I was finalizing plans for the lab. As the weather warmed and crops were being planted or even sprouting, soil experiments were ramping up. The questions we asked were always a variation on a theme: How could we change the dirt and still have seeds grow, or could they grow better? What changes would allow for less water usage, what nutrients would make up for an overly dry summer or an absence of sun? We would take investigational trips to the farming lands south of the city and up into Wisconsin, and there would be a trip to the dry southwest this fall as well.

Inside the concrete block that was my office, so very circa 1984, a notification pinged from my hospital app at almost the same time Joe's office called, wanting me to come in. I'd stopped calling him Dr. Chay before I'd been his patient for a full year.

Alicia would be the better person to talk to, and I hoped she'd be at her desk. Peter didn't know I'd had the scan.

Something Resembling Love

"When are you going to tell him?" Alicia asked when I finished telling her that the PET scan had shown that my blood vessels were back to their quirky, twirly tricks.

"He's already asked. About the scar on my ribs. I just told him I had a vascular condition."

Every time I had the conversation, I hated it. I'd heard so many variations of *You're so beautiful, you're so sexy, how can you be this pretty and so smart?* Since I'd hit college. Take your pick, *how could you not want to be a mother and pass those genes along to your daughter? You're too sweet to not be a mom; you'd be perfect at it.*

When it got obnoxious, I would explain my health in excruciating detail. I got one of two reactions. *Why are you such a bitch; I was only giving you a compliment.* Or more well-meaning, but just as wearing: *You're too pretty to be so tough.*

"I guess ... maybe this weekend? I don't want to talk about it on a work night. Peter will—well, actually, I have no idea what he'll do. Research the hell out of it? Take me at my word? Want to come with me to see Joe? Run away?"

Alicia stayed silent while I stared at where the wall and ceiling met. "I think I'm most hesitant because I don't know how he'll react."

"Maybe you should just rip the Band-Aid off." The suggestion was pure Alicia. Practical and a little in your face.

"Usually, I don't care what people think. This is ..."

"Different," she finished for me. "My best advice is to bring beer. Then you'll each have something to hold on to, and by the second beer, it'll seem less scary."

I breathed a half laugh. "Sage advice."

"I'm here all week. All my best tips and relationship advice for a limited time," Alicia said in an overblown comedic announcer voice.

I was still laughing when she said goodbye. As soon as the call disconnected, I texted Peter and confirmed he was coming over on Friday.

Two nights later, I'd gone through as many ways of presenting what I had to say as I could think of. From shouting it out to beating around the bush with analogies.

"You know you don't have to knock; you can just come in," I said when I opened the door.

"What if you weren't dressed?"

"What if I wasn't?" I raised an eyebrow and gave him a coy smile.

"Oh." His eyebrows went up with excitement. "Good point! Hey, babe." He kissed me hello.

"Hi," I said, reaching for a hug, absorbing the feeling of being close with him. He didn't let go either. It felt good to be held, and suddenly I was no longer concerned about how he would react.

"There's beer," I said, sticking my head in the fridge and then standing up again, having taken one last calming breath in the cold air.

"Thanks," he said, taking one from me.

"There's something I need to tell you." I took his hand and led him to sit on the couch. "Do you remember that scar you asked me about?"

Peter nodded.

"And how I said, rather vaguely, that I have a vascular condition?"

"Yeah." He was wary now.

"I went to the doctor the other day. Well, I go every year, for a PET scan to look at my blood vessels."

His forehead wrinkled with a frown. I looked at him for a moment, gauging how he was doing. So far, he hadn't run away. "It's called hereditary hemorrhagic telangiectasia. Or HHT for short. The range of symptoms is pretty wide; everything from tiny red spots on the face and nosebleeds to anemia and seizures."

Peter's eyes widen, and he opened his mouth to say something, but nothing came out. This is why I preferred the acronym—people tended to freak out when you said *hemorrhagic*.

"Thankfully, I don't have most of those things, but HHT makes my body grow clusters of blood vessels in erratic places. Sometimes it's not a big deal, a small bundle in an out-of-the-way place. But the way my blood vessels grow can have other serious consequences like strokes or organ damage, depending on where they are, and how big."

Peter's eyes grew even larger.

"I get a scan to see what it looks like, and then we do surgery to block them off when they get too big. Sometimes they are little and it's nothing. Other times …"

"This sounds like this might be an ... 'other' time?"

I nodded, still holding his hand. "I haven't seen my doctor yet, or the imaging. But based on how quickly he wanted to see me, I'm sure he's going to want to do surgery."

Peter stilled.

If he was going to pull away from our relationship, or even the situation, because it was too much, better to know now. So I plunged on, and told him about the year I was exhausted because I'd had an arteriovenous malformation growing off a branch of my pulmonary artery, affecting blood flow close to my heart, and how, as a result, my oxygen saturation plummeted. I'd felt like a new person when I'd gotten that one taken care of.

"Is that what the scar on your ribcage is from?"

I nodded. "Usually, they just thread a catheter through my arteries. But that time, it was laparoscopic so they could remove the bundle, not just fill it up."

"You seem so healthy, though." Peter's gaze intensified, and I tried not to squirm.

"Pretty much I am. I just need to have random things cut apart in my body." I made a face, ignoring that "pretty much" might be a stretch.

"What do your doctors say about exercise?"

"Exercise is fine; it's good, in fact, since it keeps everything working well, in case I do have to have something taken care of."

"That is serious." Peter's face changed again, a frown of concentration. "Can you have kids?"

"Kids are ... less certain," I hedged. "They'd be concerned that even if there isn't a bundle we could see, that there might be smaller ones we can't, that might burst with increased blood pressure. I've decided I'm not having children because of that. Plus, that additional strain on my body can cause birth defects."

"Why didn't you tell me before?"

Because sometimes it's a big issue. I shrugged. "Because I didn't want to talk about the fact that I can't have kids right away. I'm usually really up front about it, and it just always ends up being an elephant in the room."

"But you can have kids? You're just choosing not to."

What did that *mean*? "Sure, it's *possible*. But I never know how these things will show up. Or when. I don't want to put my life at risk, and I won't subject a child to a fate they have no control over just so I can reproduce. It's five times more likely a child I bear would have Down Syndrome. It's also genetic, so I could pass this on. And I don't really know what the future holds. It's so unpredictable."

When Peter didn't say anything immediately, my heart sank. "Do you want to break up with me now?" I asked tentatively.

"No! Why would you think that? No. I was just thinking … if the risk of a child developing Down Syndrome is 1 percent in the general population, that means the risk for a child of yours is only five. Those are still pretty low odds."

"I suppose. But I've never really wanted to have kids, anyway; I've never had that biological impulse. So, it wasn't really a big deal for me." I paused, watching his face. "Do you want to have kids?"

"I haven't really thought about it much. You wouldn't even want to adopt?"

"No. I—I just don't really like kids all that much. And this makes it that much harder. What if something happened to me? I should just leave them motherless? I know what that feels like, and I would never forgive myself. I'm not even sure I could pass a screening. Unfit mother," I joked.

His face split in a grin. And then he said, "I bet you'd make a great mom!"

"Thanks, Peter." I took it as a compliment. Even if I didn't want kids, that didn't mean that I didn't want to be thought of as kind, loving, and supportive.

"Did you, that is, did your parents know, did they help you?"

"No," I said on a shuddering breath. "They were already gone." I closed my eyes against the fresh pain. Of losing them, missing them, not having had them when I'd needed someone most. The general dull ache of being family-less.

Peter shifted, and we repositioned ourselves to sit, legs stretched out, facing each other. "Will you tell me about them?"

For a moment I hesitated, but even in the pain there were wonderful memories. "My dad was an engineer for IBM. My mom taught classic drawing at Loyola. They were so amazing. As individuals, but also together."

Something Resembling Love

I closed my eyes for a moment, seeing them each so clearly. The way they had admired each other's work and respected the other person, the obvious affection and love.

"My mom has a couple landscapes hanging at the Art Institute," I finished around the squeeze of my voice.

"It's hard for you to talk about them?"

I nodded past the lump in my throat I always felt when I thought of them. "We were so close, and even though I was almost out of high school when they died, it still felt like all my support was gone. I miss being able to talk to them."

"I can't talk to my parents at all." Peter shook his head slowly. "My dad is always trying to give me advice about how to do my work, how to reverse engineer the methylation. He works for the Kentucky state government now, as a data administrator—basically running their coding. And my mom," he sighed. "She's just, she smothers me. It's like she thinks I'm one of her high school social studies students who needs to be told what to do. Telling me to go to bed, telling me to eat better, calling to check on me."

"You don't think that's just because she loves you and wants to make sure you're healthy and happy?"

"Yeah, but I've moved out!"

I gave him a wistful smile. "I don't think parents stop worrying or caring as soon as kids are adults."

What else was I going to say? I would have loved to still have a mom calling to check on me.

"When do you see the doctor? Do you—do you want me to come with you?"

I heard the hesitation, but it wasn't as bad as I had feared, not nearly like what other people, women included, had said to me over the years.

"I think I should go alone. But I really appreciate you offering."

<hr />

"Jane, it's nice to see you," Joe said when he walked into the exam room the next week. "I'm glad we were able to get you in so soon." He met me with open arms.

I felt myself relax into the hug. "I know you like me and all," I said as we stepped apart, "but you didn't just miss me, did you?"

"No." His voice was a low, almost sandpapery sound. "It's somewhat what we were anticipating. There has been more growth of the abnormal veins in your left leg, and they are extending up through your pelvis."

I thought about when I'd first been diagnosed, fifteen years earlier, and Joe taking time over weeks and months to teach me everything I needed to know about my new condition.

"It grew much faster than we were anticipating."

Shitballs. How was I going to explain that I didn't just have a medium-sized thing Joe wanted to get ahead of, but something much larger tangled in my body?

Sometimes, small growths could be managed with an injection; other times, larger ones needed surgical intervention. No matter the size, the aberrant blood vessels could not only reroute blood bound somewhere specific, and the pressure in the malformations could be quite high, leading to rupture. Malformations could appear anywhere in the body, too, wreaking havoc and even causing strokes.

"What's your plan?" I asked Joe.

"I think we start with the mass that's in your thigh and see what we can work on there. We map out what else is growing once we get in there, and then we make a plan for more surgeries, as needed. These will probably be more painful because of how extensive they will be." Joe's face was stoic, but underneath, I knew he was as concerned about my emotional state as he was about my body. "We'll do a big one as soon as we can get you scheduled and see how we go from there."

"How soon do we have to do this?"

"Why?" Joe asked, voice and face filled with suspicion.

"My boyfriend's parents are coming to visit. Over Fourth of July. And I'd like to not be broken when they visit."

He chuckled at my description. "I think we can wait a few weeks. But no longer. I want you in here the day after they leave."

"Yes, doctor."

"And while we're at it, let's talk about this 'boyfriend' thing." Joe peered at me, knowing me too well.

"Ah—yeah?" I glanced at my lap.

"Jane, there's no problem with that. But I want you to remember the potential risks and complications if you do get pregnant."

"Don't worry, Joe," I said as I sighed out the last of my emotions, shaking my head. "We're using protection. I'm not getting pregnant, and even if I did, I wouldn't carry it to term."

"It's your choice, of course. Some women with this disease successfully carry pregnancies to term. Although …"

"I'm more complicated than most. I know."

"Yes. I want you to be especially careful until we get this thing taken care of. No flag football, no rock climbing," he kidded.

I shot him an unamused look. "I'm always especially careful."

"I know you are," he said around a supportive smile. He gathered his iPad and logged out of the computer, then swiveled on the chair toward me. "How did he take it? The new boyfriend."

I thought about the statistical analysis of my risk of having a child with Down Syndrome. "Well, he's a PhD postdoc in cancer research, so …"

"Ah. Say no more. As long as he's supportive, that's all I want for you."

I felt better after talking with Joe, as I always did, but somehow still out of sorts when Alicia called to check on me in the evening. I sat, curled up on my couch, Otis perched on the back next to me.

"It's not like I've never done this before!" I flung my hand out, as if she could see my exasperation.

"But now you're in a relationship." Alicia's voice was calm and rational. When I didn't say anything, she continued. "Well, you're not hysterical or irate, so I'm guessing he didn't break up with you."

"No," I choked out a laugh. "I rarely get this far in a relationship. It either comes up earlier on—"

"Because you're proactive and realistic, and this time you wanted to enjoy things."

I could see Alicia so clearly, sitting on her curved lime-green modern couch, drinking some foreign beer I'd never heard of, in her condo with floor-to-ceiling windows that looked out over Lake Michigan.

"Yeah," I agreed. What else was I going to say—she was right.

"Peter's going to be okay. Even if he didn't have a grade-A response, he was probably just surprised. He works in science; he'll understand what's going on. If he's spending all this time and energy to develop a cure for cancer for people he doesn't even know, don't you think he'll have the same care with his girlfriend, whom he adores?"

"Yeah, but this one is big! I could be in the hospital for a couple days after. I could be helpless for weeks afterward."

Alicia cut me off, out of the spiral. "What did you do for your last big surgery? How did you get through?"

I snorted. "Thompson put me up for several days while I rested. I took a lot of pain pills, I walked slowly. I swore a lot."

"And do you think any of us are going to let you suffer on your own? Lauren would be happy to have you with her. You and Otis can stay here if you don't want to deal with stairs. But probably Peter is going to want to stay with you until you feel reasonably good."

"I'm sure you're right."

"I know I'm right. Now, do you want me to come over, or are you good?"

"Otis will probably have to listen to me rant some more." I patted him where he had settled on the chunky knit cream throw.

Alicia choked with a laugh. "Call if you need to. Or tell Otis to call if *he* needs backup."

JANE

The way Peter prepared for his parents' visit told me all I needed to know about how anxious he was. We spent an entire day sorting through the mountain of mail that took up most of his kitchen island, and he scrubbed every surface until I was afraid he'd wear through the Formica.

The night before they arrived, we sat down on the couch.

"It feels better in here," Peter said, surveying the open living area. "Now I can sit at the island to eat breakfast."

I snorted a laugh. "All that breakfast you take time to have."

He chuckled too, and took a drink from his beer. I saw his eyes slide toward the bedroom.

"What?"

"I need you to take your toothbrush and slippers home with you."

I turned to look at him, blinking my surprise and confusion. "I don't want my parents to know you spend the night here." He didn't look at me when he said it.

"Are you serious? Peter, I'm absolutely sure they know we are sleeping together. And anyway, it's just a toothbrush. Maybe I'm obsessive about dental hygiene."

"I know it seems ridiculous. But my parents are very old-fashioned." And then a shrug, like it was normal for a thirty-something to have his parents stay in his one-bedroom apartment and completely rearrange his life to accommodate them.

My next thought was to wonder if I was the one being ridiculous and if I'd measure up to what they envisioned for their son.

"They'll get in the way the whole time they're here," he said, rolling his eyes. "I won't get any work done. I wish they weren't coming."

"Why not? Do you not want them to meet me?" My face fell at the idea.

"No, it's not that at all! They'll love you."

The next day, I went with Peter to pick them up at the airport. Was I ready to be loved by someone's parents, even in a friendly way? My family was my friends; I didn't have any aunts or uncles. I didn't even know the parents of my closest friends. What would it be like to be around parents again, like this?

"It's really helpful that you're driving. Normally I take the L and ride back with them in a cab." He stretched across the console to kiss me, leaning in. "That's the last kiss for the next few days."

It seemed odd to me that Peter's parents would be weirded out by their mid-thirties son kissing his girlfriend. But what did I know about the relationship between parents and their adult kids?

"Peter!" a woman with greying brown hair called across baggage claim, coming toward us with open arms.

"Hi, Mom," Peter said with a small sigh as he hugged her. When she let go, he and the man I assumed was Peter's dad hugged awkwardly, patting each other's backs.

"And you must be Jane!" When she said my name, I heard a faint Southern accent.

"Hello, Margaret. It's really nice to meet you."

She only came up to my eyes, but what Margaret lacked in stature, she made up for in warmth. Brown eyes and a welcoming smile. She hugged me closely and then handed me over to William. Clearly, Peter had gotten his coloring from his mom, but he'd gotten the calm lake-blue eyes from William.

"Jane," he said, holding me away from himself to look at me, as if we'd been separated for a long time, "it's a real treat to meet the girl Peter will barely tell us anything about."

Behind him, I watched Peter roll his eyes, and I smothered a smile. "I feel the same way, William."

As William and I stepped away from each other, Margaret shifted back to me, beaming. "What a sweetheart you are. And so thoughtful of you to pick us up. I know you don't really need a car in Chicago, but it sure is nice," she said as we rolled luggage toward the parking garage.

We dropped Peter's parents' luggage at his place and then headed for an early dinner nearby. After we were seated at the restaurant and had gotten drinks, Margaret leaned forward. "Peter said you work for the USDA. That's very prestigious!"

"It's not as glamorous as it sounds. I'm a scientist for a division. I'm in the lab, albeit a different kind than Peter's, almost as much as him."

"Dirt, right?" William asked.

"Soil science—it's what makes dinner! Sorry," I said with a sheepish grin. "We have terrible jokes."

"How did you and Peter meet?" Margaret asked.

"Mom," Peter sighed, "I told you guys this. We met through mutual friends."

"Well, I know, but I want to hear Jane's version." The look she gave me was motherly and loving.

I shrugged. "There's not much more to say. We have mutual friends, we were both at a few social gatherings together, and he decided he didn't mind me dragging him out occasionally."

William turned to Peter. "Still working at your lab so much?"

I saw the way Peter's shoulders came up around his ears, resisting the conversation, even as he answered the question and fielded a request from his dad to visit the lab. From the outside, I could see the genuine interest William had, and I wished Peter could see it for what it was. "Peter said you do data administration."

"I do. Even though Peter thinks I'm an old fuddy-duddy who doesn't understand what he's doing now." He winked at me, and I smiled, suppressing a shiver.

"You all right?" Peter rested his hand on my knee under the table.

"Just a little chilled in the air conditioning, is all. I should have remembered to grab my sweatshirt."

"I hate when they crank the air up so much in the summer. It's nice to come in from a hot day, but if you sit around in it too long, it makes you start to wish for a sweater!" Margaret agreed.

"I always keep my house warmer than Peter would like. He's a good sport."

"You have a house, here in Evanston?" William asked.

"A duplex, but yeah, I bought it about eight years ago." I smiled, thinking of opening the door with my own key the first time, of the curved wooden banister leading upstairs and the stained-glass inlay in the top foot of the window over the kitchen sink.

"You live there by yourself?"

"Unless you count my cat. I gave up roommates a while ago," I said with a deprecating smile as I glanced at Peter. "It's a great location for me to get to work, it has some wonderful trees, and the small backyard lets me garden."

"You must have a lot of birds, if you have trees and a garden." William's face took on the same eager look I'd seen on Peter's.

"William is an amateur bird watcher. Always has his binoculars ready at the kitchen window." Margaret patted William's arm.

"Oh, that sounds like fun! There are a lot of birds, but I'll admit I don't know what most of them are. I have cardinals, and those are my favorite. I can tell you about the trees, though!"

Peter and I trailed behind his parents as we left the restaurant, and he leaned to speak in an undertone. "I'm sorry you can't stay tonight. I'd rather spend the evening with you."

"Not like we could both fit on the couch anyway. Tell me again why you insisted they stay with you instead of at a hotel like they had planned?"

Peter looked over to where his parents were standing, waiting for us, and I could see the internal war between having always had his parents stay with him on other visits, and wishing they weren't now. "Hotels aren't cheap."

"It's only three days; we'll manage. But I would like to kiss you goodbye."

"Me too," he said, but hugged me instead.

Something Resembling Love

I left Peter and his parents in front of the restaurant. Margaret was enthusiastic, but maybe it was because her son was dating someone—anyone. Or possibly she was trying to make up for her short stature. Being petite and trying to teach high schoolers social studies couldn't be easy. She seemed more like a kindergarten teacher.

William was harder to read. But Peter had clearly gotten his inquisitive nature from his dad. Peter might not have liked his dad's questions over lunch, but he probably didn't recognize he did the same thing.

As nice as it had been to meet them, and as relieved as I was that they were friendly and seemed to like me, I took the rest of the day, and the next, for some time to myself. I'd been spending a lot of evenings with Peter, and while he could stay up and work after I went to sleep, I was behind on laundry, weeding, and grocery shopping.

The next morning, I sat in one of the Adirondack chairs on the tiny brick patio in my back garden, drinking coffee and reading. "This is nice," I said to Otis, as he wound his way under my chair and bumped his head under my hand for scratches. "I know, we haven't had any time for you and I to sit out here and read, have we? We should make sure we do that."

Otis purred in hearty agreement as I scratched under his chin.

I joined Peter and his parents at the Botanic Gardens a few hours after my quiet morning. Peter hugged me hard when I got out of my car.

"Did you miss me?" I teased when he didn't let go.

"More than you know."

"Ready to go look at flowers?" William asked.

"And some birds, right dear?" Margaret winked as she took his hand.

They were cute together, I thought, holding Peter's hand while the four of us wandered through the gardens.

William chuckled when I bent to observe a bed of hostas and the mulch that surrounded them.

"Sorry. Habit," I said with a self-deprecating smile. "I like dirt. When I was a kid, I liked digging up worms and mixing sand with clay. We always had a full garden, and watching my mom use straw for mulch, and rotate where we planted things each year just kind of sunk in. Now I can't help myself."

"Your parents must be proud you took something you did as a family and made it into a career," he said as he stepped next to me and peered at the ground himself.

My hand flexed over the top of the short post it rested on. "I imagine they are, but I have to imagine. They died during my junior year of high school."

"Oh Jane, that's awful! I'm so sorry for your loss." Margaret's drawl grew more noticeable, and she covered my hand with hers.

"Thanks." I gave a crooked smile, half in thanks and the other half as sad as I always was. "Anyway. We're getting better at understanding how the cycle of farming impacts the ground, and vice versa, but also about forests, and how prairies function. It's a lot like what Peter does. You know some things about the process, but you don't know everything. So, there's a lot of trial and error."

"He doesn't share much about his work," William commented with a glance at his son.

"I do, too," Peter scoffed. "Computer modeling for business is different than modeling for science. And computers can't tell you everything. Like Jane said, it takes trial and error."

"Well of course it does, Peter." Margaret let go of my hand and reached for his arm. "But I think what your dad meant was that you don't tell us about the details of your research. What you are working on is exciting and important. We're both interested. We want to know more."

"Errors are good points of data, too," William said, looking expectant.

"Sure they are," Peter begrudged.

"Gives you a place to start from for your next set of experiments. Isn't that right, Jane?"

I did not want to be in the middle of William and Peter, even if I agreed with William. "I think that can be true sometimes. Other times it just takes you back to square one."

Peter squeezed my hand.

The conversation shifted back to the flowers, or the starkness of the Japanese garden, and the birds that were attracted to the various landscapes.

At the restaurant after zigzagging through traffic down 94, William pulled out a chair for both me and Margaret.

Something Resembling Love

"Now, Jane, you can tell me this is none of my business if you want, but Peter said you're going to have surgery soon?" Margaret's face was etched with concern.

"I am. How much did he tell you?"

"That was all!"

"Oh," I laughed. "Well. I have a vascular condition," I said, explaining in simple terms HHT and the repercussions, and what my surgery would likely look like.

"You'll let us know if there's anything we can do?"

"Mom, you live six hours away."

"I know. But it can be nice to have someone else take care of you. Although, I suppose you have all your friends, plus Peter."

"That's very sweet of you to offer, but I'm sure I'll be fine." I smiled at Peter, who looked completely exasperated.

At the end of the meal, we stood and walked outside, where it was still sunny and hot. I immediately felt my muscles relax.

"Jane," William said, hugging me. "You're a lovely and resilient young woman. Margaret's right, it was great to meet the person Peter is with."

"Thank you, William, that's nice of you to say."

"Peter, will we see you for the holidays?" he asked.

"We'll have to see."

"It would be great to have you home." There was no missing the hopefulness in Margaret's expression.

"Maybe. We'll see," he repeated, and turned to give William an awkward hug.

"Let us know. And Jane is welcome, too. Jane," she said, looking around Peter's shoulder, "you're welcome, too."

Peter hugged Margaret, cutting off my reply.

A cab pulled up next to the curb almost as soon as William raised his arm. I shook my head and laughed. "That never happens for me."

"It's one of his special talents, isn't it, dear," Margaret said, smiling up at him.

"Handy!"

As William opened the door for Margaret, Peter hugged me tightly, as if I was the one flying home. "I know you're going to the lab, but I'll come over this evening?"

"I can't wait to see you," I said in his ear. Then I waved goodbye and got in my own car to drive to the suburbs.

The lab was empty at the end of the holiday weekend. I sent a few emails to confirm I'd be out of the office for at least a week, including a long one to Kip letting him know the status of my projects and how I thought the week or more away would affect their timeline. I watered the grasses I was growing in the various soils I had created ahead of a large-scale experiment.

After a couple of hours, I felt my work was organized ahead of my impending surgery, and I drove home.

"Getting them ready this morning took forever," Peter said when I let him in that evening. "They were up early, and they wanted coffee, and then they wanted to sit around talking. Before we even met you, for more coffee and more talking and lunch!"

I kissed him hello, chuckling against his mouth as he finished venting. "Peter, they love you and were thrilled to spend time with you."

"They did have a good time," he said as we sat on the couch. "They said so about fifty times just this morning. The entire cab ride, Mom couldn't stop talking about how nice you are."

"I like your parents. They're such warm and friendly people. They remind me a little of my parents."

"My dad—wanting to go to the lab with me. Ugh."

"Why didn't you take him?"

"What was he going to see? A bunch of glass-fronted fridges with petri dishes and a room full of computers. Not very exciting."

"Peter, you should have taken him! He just wants to spend time with you and understand what you are doing."

"He wants to tell me how to do it," he huffed.

"That's not true; he wants to contribute what he knows. You have similar paths even if you ended up applying your engineering backgrounds in different ways."

Something Resembling Love

He picked up the beer bottle I had set in front of him. "I just want to live my life, do my work, and be done with this postdoc! I don't want to have to make my dad feel better in the process."

"It's something you share."

"And then, they were so, like, they were trying to ingratiate themselves with you!" Peter waved his hand up and down in front of where I was sitting.

My head tipped as I raised my eyebrows in skepticism. "They were trying to make a good impression with their son's girlfriend."

"It just seemed over the top." He slumped into the couch cushions and crossed his arms.

I hadn't minded. It had been nice to have parents around, asking about my work, concerned about my well-being.

PETER

I watched Jane take extra care all the next week. She did laundry and shifted furniture, cleaned her entire house, and vacuumed twice.

I chuckled as I watched her straighten the tablecloth on her dining room table. "You look like you're preparing for the Pope to visit."

"I know." She rolled her eyes. "I've gotten more … particular, when I know there's a chance I'm going to be in pain for a while. Coming home to clutter just makes it worse. It's the same when I travel."

She gave a quick shrug at herself, like, *What can you do?* But if her house was cluttered before, I didn't want to know what she had really thought of my place before we'd cleaned it for my parents.

I gazed over her shoulder and out the window in her small dining room, unseeing. Thinking about what Jane had told me about her condition, and her appointment with the doctor she called by his first name. I thought that was weird. I had a doctoral degree, although a different kind, and I wanted people to call me "doctor" in a professional setting.

"You're really quiet." Jane reached her hand across the table to mine. "Is this too much?"

Maybe. "No. I'm just thinking about everything you said. Have you been dealing with this all your life?"

"Yes and no. It's always been there, but it didn't really start to have an effect until late high school. I found out when I collapsed at a track meet."

"Wow. Scary." I tried to imagine losing my parents before I graduated from high school. And then finding out I had a life-threatening and rare disease. How was she as calm and well-adjusted as she was?

"It was, but Joe has been with me since the beginning. He's at least as much my friend as he is my doctor. Surgery is kind of a big deal, but in some ways, it's also not."

I thought about that. *How could surgery not be a big deal?*

"The no kids thing has been more of an issue in the past," she said as she stood.

"Mm."

"Are you sure you want to go with me?" She bent to pick up a small clump of Otis' fur. "Lauren and Alicia both said they could take me to the hospital tomorrow."

I followed her into the kitchen and covered the takeout I'd brought from Trattoria Demi, our favorite Italian place, while she washed her hands.

"You think I can't handle it."

"No. But maybe I'm a little worried you'll freak. Working in a lab is one thing. Hospitals are different."

I wasn't sure what to say. Did she not trust me? Did she not want me there?

"There won't be anyone there to answer questions."

"There wouldn't be for Lauren or Alicia, either." Even to my own ears, I sounded defensive.

"I just want you to know, it's okay if you don't want to, if you'd rather be with me here, after." It was hard to miss the concern for me in her voice.

"And leave you alone going into a big surgery like that? Not a chance." I took the scrub brush from her hand. "Go upstairs."

As I rinsed dishes and put them in the dishwasher, I kept thinking about the challenges Jane had faced and had yet to go through. And her direct question. Did I want kids? I had always assumed I would have them. I had dated someone in college who had had a child from a previous relationship, and her son was about a year old while we were together. But I hadn't spent much time with him.

Certainly, Jane would have given whether she wanted kids a lot of thought over the years. But the odds were favorable for her if she had them soon, while she was still young. The risk of having a developmentally disabled child wasn't really all that high. Only 5 percent. Wouldn't you have surgery if the risk of death was only 5 percent?

And even if she really didn't want to have a biological child, there were other ways to be a parent. She would make a great mom. Everyone knew there were tons of children who needed loving homes. She probably didn't want to think about doing that without a relationship. *Add in a serious medical condition, and ...* I sighed to myself as I dried my hands.

When I joined Jane, she was sitting on the bed in a soft, threadbare T-shirt, and nothing else. In the gold light of her table lamp, everything about her was luminous, and I sucked in a breath at the sight of her, the curve of her breasts outlined by the shirt, the lower edge barely hiding her hip.

I sat down next to her and took her hand. "I'm here for whatever you need."

"Thank you," she said, setting her hand on my knee. "I don't think you can know how much that means to me."

I leaned over to kiss her, gently. Fragments of what she had told me over the past week lodged in my brain. Parents gone. Weeks of recovery. Pain and limping. And yet she didn't seem fragile. Breakable maybe, but not like she could be knocked over easily.

I wanted her; could hardly be near her and not want her, sometimes still surprised when I saw this beautiful woman with her tawny eyes looking at me. Tonight I would hold her close.

As I studied her face, I saw a question I couldn't parse out, and I pulled her closer, kissing her cheek.

"Jane," I said as we pulled apart, "I want to. I want to understand. I want to know what's going on, and how I can help. I want to be there in case this surgery is hard. I want to be there for you."

A soft smile crossed her face. "Thanks, Peter. That's ... it means a lot." She leaned into me and kissed me. Without thinking, I pushed the soft T-shirt out of my way and saw the silvery scar from the laparoscopic surgery she'd told me about. I didn't want to look at it, or think about what was ahead, so I covered it with my hand and brushed my thumb under the curve of her breast, using the pressure to push her flat again.

"Mmm ... Peter."

"Wait!" I jerked my hand away, but it was trapped inside her shirt.

Jane froze, eyes open wide in surprise.

"Can we do this? I mean, sex raises your blood pressure. Am I putting you at risk?"

Her face relaxed into a smile, as she rolled toward me again, and laid her hand on my cheek. "Yes, we can totally do this."

In the morning, I drove us into Chicago, to Rush. "Are you scared?"

"No, not really. Just want to get in, get it done, and get home."

Jane led us through the hospital, and it was clear she was at ease here. She didn't pause to look at signs or ask directions. I followed her to check-in, then to the waiting room, into the pre-op area, and watched her barely flinch as someone started an IV.

Then a nurse in a puffy blue cap whisked her away, pushing the hospital bed out of the small room and around the corner. I stood in the hallway, watching as she disappeared through a set of double doors, hands in my pockets.

Around me, the pre-op area buzzed, with nurses walking efficiently from desk to room and back, machines beeping or screeching. I walked back the way Jane and I had come and found the hospital cafeteria.

Jane had warned me to expect a long day, but I wasn't prepared for eleven and a half hours of waiting room time. I had gotten my computer from the car, but there wasn't much I could do without a faster internet connection and some reference materials I didn't have. I went back to the cafeteria, picked up the day's *Tribune*, read the whole thing, and watched the sunset. It was almost dark when a nurse came to get me.

In the ICU, Jane still had an IV, a bunch of wires hooked up to her chest, and a nasal cannula blowing oxygen up her nose.

"What's that for?!" Was she sick, had she not done well? Panic slid into my stomach. What if something had gone wrong? "Why does she need oxygen?"

"We always have surgical patients on some extra oxygen for about twenty-four hours afterward."

A man in a white coat and a full head of dark hair with just a few streaks of grey at his temple, his name embroidered in a classic red, stepped through the sliding glass door into Jane's room and offered his hand. "Peter, right?"

"That's right." I shook the offered hand.

"Dr. Chay, but Jane just calls me Joe." I nodded. "Jane did well in surgery. She's had some concerning arrhythmias in the past, when we've had to work close to her heart. But this time, she sailed right through. She'll have to stay for a couple days while we monitor for clots and make sure her blood pressure is stable, but she usually does quite well."

"That's great; thank you for taking care of her."

"It's my pleasure. We've worked together a long time. Jane is a great patient, dedicated to doing everything she can to keep herself healthy." He smiled, looking at Jane in the ICU bed. "Do you have questions?"

I opened my mouth, but no words came out. "I—I—yes. But I don't know where to start."

Dr. Chay gave me a sympathetic look. "It's my understanding you and Jane haven't been dating all that long. I'm sure this is overwhelming for you."

"Jane said she can't have kids. Is that true?"

He nodded, as if he'd expected my question. "With HHT it really goes patient by patient. Some people have peripheral venous outgrowths, which we can manage easily. Others are like Jane, who can have the smaller venous malformations, but just as often has larger ones. We'll have to see how this surgery resolves, but because this malformation was creeping up into her pelvis, that gives me more concern."

Dr. Chay walked over to Jane's bed and peered at a beeping monitor before silencing it. He turned his attention back to me.

"Certainly, many women who have this condition choose to bear children, and successfully. But for others, the risk is very high. Jane faces a significantly higher risk of pregnancy complications compared to many of my HHT patients."

"If she wanted to, could she have kids?"

He tipped his head back and forth: yes and no. "We'd have to monitor her very carefully, and she'd likely have to be on bed rest for her whole third trimester to prevent a potential malformation rupture."

"I assume you'd screen her more regularly, if she was pregnant." I felt my arms cross involuntarily.

"We could, but a nuclear PET scan is required to see the vessels fully, which would expose her to a fairly high dose of radiation. Doing that more than twice during a pregnancy could be harmful to the fetus. And with someone who has had so many significant malformations, I would worry about not being able to monitor her *at least* once per trimester." He frowned. "There isn't a lot of data on how pregnancy affects the development of these venous malformations."

"And what about having children a different way? Adoption or surrogacy?"

"Obviously that wouldn't be the same risk to her as a pregnancy, but since we don't always know when these will pop up, especially in Jane, I would be cautious there too. Increased stress levels, heavy lifting, these all play a role in how Jane would fare, long term."

"I see. So, it's risky, but not impossible." If Joe was such an expert on HHT, why was he saying pregnancy would be so hard to manage?

"No, not impossible." Dr. Chay crossed his arms as well. "I'm curious why you are asking. Jane has been very clear to me in the past that she doesn't want to have children. Has she been talking about wanting to have a family?"

"We've talked about children, and her condition a few times. I want to make sure I understand everything."

"Jane's a tough cookie, and she stays on top of her health more than most of my patients." He turned to look at her again, with a softness in his eyes I would not have expected. "If she really wants to have kids, we could manage it under very close watch. It's good you are here with her."

"Thanks, Dr. Chay." I stuck my hand out again.

"Peter? Is that you?" I turned to see Jane reaching out from her hospital bed.

"I'll leave you to it. If you need anything, the nurses are just a buzz away." Dr. Chay left quietly.

"Was that Joe?" Jane asked sleepily, scrubbing at the plastic ID bracelet at her wrist.

"Yeah, he came to check on you. He said you did great."

"Okay …" she drifted off again. I guessed I'd spend the night. I hadn't really thought through this part of the day.

An hour later, Jane turned toward me and smiled fuzzily. "You're back."

"I am, I'm right here."

"Peter?" she asked quietly. "Peter, I—"

"What did you say?"

"Peter, I love you," she said, so quietly I wasn't sure she had said anything.

"Jane, you're so quiet, I can't hear you."

"I love youuu …" her voice faded again.

"I'm sorry, babe, I can't hear you." She frowned and her brow furrowed, concentrating. "Get some rest."

I'd heard her, I just didn't know what to say. Was she delirious from the anesthesia meds; or was it real?

The uncomfortable recliner woke me the next morning, and I went to the cafeteria, squinting against the bright lights outside the shadowy room where Jane was still sleeping. A cup of coffee helped, as did a plate of eggs which were surprisingly good.

When I went back to her room, I pushed the door open carefully, not wanting to wake her, but she was sitting up in bed, the shade on the window rolled up.

"Hi!" she said. "I wasn't sure if you'd gone to work."

"Just to the cafeteria. And to get these." I held out a potted plant with pink flowers.

"Oh, cyclamen, how pretty! That's sweet, thank you."

"I'll put them here?" I said as I reached for a shelf.

"Perfect."

Something Resembling Love

I sat on the edge of the bed when she held her hand out for me.

"Best boyfriend ever," she said and stretched forward to kiss me.

Dr. Chay had been right; Jane sailed right through her in-hospital recovery. By the first afternoon, she was walking around the recovery floor, doing calf raises, and making slow laps with her IV.

I drove her home the following evening, and when we walked in, I understood why she'd spent the time she had tidying her house. Whether it was the change from the never-quiet hospital, or something else, the house seemed even more comfortable than usual.

Over the next few days, I traded rounds with Alicia and Lauren so that Jane was never alone. She assured us she didn't need to be watched round the clock, but it made me feel better to know she had someone with her.

I came in one evening and found the three of them laughing. The flowers I'd brought her were sitting on the coffee table.

"What's so funny?" I asked, coming to lean over the back of the couch and kiss Jane hello.

"I just asked Lauren if she'd wipe my ass if I needed help."

"Did something happen? Are you okay?" I grabbed her shoulder, as if to reassure myself she wasn't broken.

"No. Standing is still hard, but I'm fine," she laughed, her hand resting on mine.

"I told her I would if I had to." Lauren's face was set into a look of concentration.

"Grimly, she said it grimly," Alicia added, the three of them laughing again.

When we were alone that evening, Jane and I sat on the couch, her reading and me checking a few datasets on the latest model I had set up. She yawned and set her book aside.

"I want to try to sleep in bed tonight."

"That's great! Do you think you're ready for the stairs?"

"I guess we'll see!" But her face lit up. I couldn't blame her, after two nights in the hospital and another three on the couch. She pushed herself up using the armrest and limped to the bottom of the stairs.

"How can I help?" I asked.

"Put your arm around my waist and just kind of hold me steady. It's not strength that's the issue, just pain."

With each step, Jane blew out a breath, as if she was weightlifting. I tightened my grip around her waist every time she pushed off, trying to take some of the weight.

"How's it going?" I asked, seeing her wince on the seventh step.

"Just dandy." Her voice was strained, and I wished I was strong enough to carry her up the stairs. Mentally, I counted down the last five steps. Jane let go of me and limped to the end of the bed, rubbing her quad.

I looked at her, worried the trip had been too much. "What can I do?"

"Just give me a minute, it'll pass," she said with a tight smile, still slowly rubbing the muscle.

I stood next to the bed, useless, until she held out her hand and balanced against it as she stood and hobbled to the bathroom.

"Thank God for all those squats," I heard her say, laughing. After a moment she called, "Um, Peter? Can you help me?"

"What's up?" I asked, standing outside the open door.

"My good leg won't hold me, now I've done the stairs. I need help standing."

"Oh. Uh, sure." It felt weird to go into the bathroom, Jane sitting on the toilet. I sniffed back my reservations. If she needed help, then she needed help. It wasn't like she'd asked me to—I broke off into a laugh.

"What's so funny?" she asked as I offered my hand.

"I was thinking about you asking Lauren if she'd wipe your butt."

She grinned at me.

I started to pull on her hand, and Jane shouted, "No, stop! You'll pull my shoulder out of the socket that way. Put your hand under my opposite elbow. Now put your other hand by my hip. I'll rock forward, and on three, help me up."

She stumbled a bit as she stood but stayed upright. When she nodded at me, I let go and left her to finish on her own. I sat on the edge of the bed, scrolling aimlessly through the news on my phone. I heard her brush her teeth and shake out some pills before she stood in the doorway.

"Can you help me into bed?"

"Of course!" I jumped up.

Jane sat on the bed, scooting herself backward until her legs dangled over the edge, and swung her good leg onto the bed. "Okay, now lift my leg and help me swing into bed."

She sighed and leaned her head back against the headboard.

"I thought you were just preparing me for the worst," I said, sitting on the edge of the bed. "Is it always like this?"

"No, not always. I wasn't so weak when Joe worked on the one near my heart, but I was much more tired, and resting for weeks. Other times, like when it was in my hand and elbow, I had pain, but I could ignore it because I didn't have to use my hand so much. Hard using only one leg if you're used to having two good ones."

I felt her studying me.

"Are you totally freaked out now?"

"Honestly?"

She nodded.

"A little. How long will this last?" I felt my forehead wrinkle with worry.

"I don't know. Another few days? Maybe a couple of weeks. It'll get steadily better, but I can't say for sure. My knee was worse—that took seven rounds, every six weeks to be resolved, and just as I was getting back to baseline, back to the hospital I'd go."

I set my hand on her thigh, puffy with swelling. "I hope it gets better faster now, the further away from surgery you get."

"Yeah," she half laughed, "me too!"

JANE

So much had rested on the surgery. My mobility yes, although I hadn't been as concerned about that. I knew Joe and I would figure out how to manage the blood vessels, even if he had to take little bites at a time. But I had hoped that by watching me go through the surgery, Peter would understand my position on not having kids.

When he hadn't immediately followed the logic of "complicated vascular disease means kids are not a good idea," right away, I hadn't been completely concerned. He was a scientist, after all; he would want data and facts and all the information. And since HHT was so uncommon, it wasn't like I could expect him to comprehend the same as if I'd had a history of strokes. But his actions and his questions were still at odds. For the first week, he'd followed me around like a nursemaid every time I'd gotten up, jumping to help if I shifted on the couch, offering to get my water and food. I knew he was worried that I was in pain or that I would overextend and hurt myself, even if he also, at least intellectually, knew that movement was good for my recovery.

It had been nice of him and my girlfriends to take shifts the first few days. Chris even came over one evening and mowed my tiny yard.

August arrived, still hot and humid. I woke before Peter, and sat leaning against the headboard, watching the sun lighten my room around us. I had hoped that going through my surgery together would clarify things for him. For us. And I supposed in a way it had.

Quietly, I got out of bed and padded downstairs, still wincing as I put weight on my left leg, gripping the railing so tightly my hand wanted to cramp. Otis dashed ahead, waiting for me to fill his bowl on a side counter.

I started a pot of coffee and stood patting Otis as he ate, looking into my backyard at the riot of cosmos I'd planted because they had been my mom's favorite.

When the pot was done brewing, I went and sat in the living room where Otis curled up in my lap, purring his appreciation for breakfast. Absent-mindedly, my hands stroked through his long fur while I studied the room. The buttery yellow tone of the cream paint I'd chosen, the arched passage from the front hall to the kitchen, my fieldstone fireplace that currently held candles instead of logs. The photo of my parents sitting on the mantle.

All around me was evidence of the life I'd created for myself. I was happy, but recently it had felt like a lot of work.

It wasn't long before Peter joined me, blinking awake, and frowning. "You're downstairs."

"I was tired of being in bed."

"But ... you could have fallen. Why didn't you wake me?"

"Last night, you looked like you were the one who'd been through the wringer! I wanted you to sleep." His face crumpled just enough for me to see I'd hurt his feelings. "There's coffee in the kitchen," I offered.

He returned in a few minutes, bearing a mug of his own, and sat at the end of the couch. He leaned to kiss me on the cheek, and I resisted melting into it, into him.

"How did you sleep?" he asked.

"Okay. Not great."

"Were you in pain? You should have woken me up. I would have gotten you more meds."

"No, nothing like that," I reassured him as I set my hand on top of the quilt over his leg. "Peter, I think ..."

What? That you haven't been honest with me? With yourself?

"I overheard you, in the hospital, asking Joe about me having kids."

"I wanted to hear what he had to say." Through the quilt, I felt his thigh flex. I had learned it was the first spot he tightened when alarmed.

"Did you not believe me?"

"No, I—it's not that I didn't believe you, I just thought maybe ..." He ran a hand down his face.

"That I was exaggerating?"

He sat up straighter and opened his mouth to speak, but didn't have any words.

"You keep saying that you don't know if you want to have kids. But I think you do know."

"I ... I don't know. I mean, I thought I knew, and then there was this, with you, and ... It really threw me."

I nodded. Once upon a time, I'd had my own assumptions.

"This, with us, with you, feels like, I don't know. Good. Wonderful, actually. Even though I still am surprised when I wake up and you're next to me."

I watched him swallow hard.

"I don't think anyone has ever understood, or maybe accepted, me. As me. I know I'm a little ..."

"Bit of an overthinker?" I filled in for him.

"Yeah," he laughed. "That."

"I do like you. I love you, but—"

"You do!"

It was all I could do not to laugh. At the disbelief and hope on Peter's face. Oh, so eager.

"I do. But Peter," I said, sobering, "I need for you to accept me, too."

"I do!"

As I tipped my head, my mouth twisted in disagreement, and I ran a hand through my hair. "I need to know what you want. To know that *you* know what you want. And if kids are important to you ... I didn't want to get six months into this and be in love with you. I don't want to get further, and then have you decide you need to be a dad."

"Okay, but—"

"You should figure that out. On your own." I had to cut him off before he got any further, asking what he could do to prove to me he didn't want kids.

He frowned. "What do you mean 'on your own'? Are—are you—are we breaking up?"

"We need a break. You need space away from me, and surgery and complications. Away from the conflict between presumption and reality. I ... hesitate to call it a breakup because I think there's a chance that this could work; that we could work. But—"

"But it's kind of like a breakup," he finished.

"Yeah." I watched the thoughts pass across his face. Hurt, disbelief, the desire to argue.

Peter's jaw worked up and down, trying to know what to say. It wasn't hard to see the objection in his expression, wanting to decide in the moment one way or the other. Maybe in favor of a kidless life, just so we didn't have to end things.

I sat forward to rest my hand on his leg. "This doesn't have to be forever, if you decide you also don't want kids. But I need to know. For you. And so do you. For me, and for the rest of your life."

He inhaled quickly, and I thought I caught the sheen of tears before he closed his eyes. "It makes sense, what you're saying. It just, I didn't ... yeah."

"Peter, I feel all those things too. I didn't just wake up this morning and make this choice."

"I know you didn't. You'd have looked at all the data. Tried staining it this way and that way."

The lopsided, half-amused, half-sad smile he gave me nearly did me in. And yes, so did the fact he knew how I had approached my decision.

"I'm sure we'll still see each other?"

"Of course we will!" The brightness in my voice was somewhat forced. I wanted to believe we'd work this out.

"Just ..." He gritted his teeth. "Will you promise me you won't hate me?"

"Peter." I squeezed his shin. "I could never hate you. I have too much respect and admiration for you."

He nodded, slight movements, as if he were trying to absorb and make sense of everything. "Can I shower before I leave?"

"I'm not kicking you out, not trying to cut you out. Finish your coffee, take a shower. Hell, I can make breakfast for us."

"That would be nice."

In his simple sentence, I saw the same Peter I'd met at the beginning of the year. Unsure, self-conscious, almost shy. And I hated that by taking care of myself, I'd taken him back to that place.

When he left a couple of hours later, I walked him to the door.

"Can I hug you?" he asked, not looking at me.

"Yes. I want to."

He wrapped his arms around my ribcage, holding me tightly to himself. The sound of his sadness when he sniffed echoed down my spine. Abruptly, he let go and turned out the door.

When he reached the sidewalk, I closed the door and rested my forehead against the solid wood, my own tears slipping down my cheeks, hot on my skin. I turned to lean against the wood and would have slid to the floor if doing so wouldn't have made me scream in pain.

I thought about Margaret, inviting me for Christmas, of William telling me I was resilient. My heart squeezed as I thought about Chris and the way he looked at Lauren. And I wondered, not for the first time, if I'd always be this way: happy in the life I'd created, but never chosen.

PETER

I all but slept at the lab for the next several days. I hadn't been working nearly as hard as I should have been for the last several months. Now Jane and I weren't together—or were we? Had we broken up, or taken a break? Was this a Ross and Rachel *Friends* kind of situation and in three months I was going to be comedically yelling, "We were on a break!"?

Not if I couldn't answer her question, I supposed.

I sighed to myself and rolled back from my monitors to walk to the windows. On the lawn outside the building, people were playing frisbee or lying in the grass. I wanted to be doing that.

"Hey," I heard Chris' voice behind me.

"Hey." A timer dinged, and I walked over to the table where a row of test tubes sat, finishing a new cycle of hypermethylation I would run through a computational model to see where the CpG islands had caused protective cancer genes to be silenced.

"You're here early," he commented. "Or …"

I looked down at my shirt, which I had absolutely been wearing the day before.

"What's, uh, going on here?" Chris was looking at me with confusion.

"I got wrapped up in things last night, lost track of time."

"You lost track of time," he said slowly, as if he was trying to comprehend a difficult concept. "With Jane to go home to?"

I focused on the lab bench in front of me, switching on the microscope. Nothing Fritz and I had batted around over the past few months had worked. Once again, my boss was telling me I needed to finish rendering data, so I could compile it and publish. As if I hadn't been working on that very thing since I joined the postdoc program just over three years ago.

"Peter."

"Making hay while the sun shines," I said glibly and gestured toward the windows.

"Does the sun not shine while Jane's around?" When I didn't answer, he gave the most Chris response possible. "Dude. When was the last time you were outside?"

"I don't know, yesterday sometime, I guess."

"Come on, let's go."

"Go where? Chris, I have to look at this latest sequencing."

"You can do that later," he said, coming to put his hand under my arm and propel me through the door.

It felt good to be in the sun—I had to give him that, and we walked to the coffee cart that was often on a nearby street. I rarely paid any attention to it. Who spent money to buy frivolous coffee, when there was free stuff in the lab's kitchenette?

"Why didn't you go home last night? You haven't spent a night—or a couple of days, judging by the way you smell— in the lab in months."

Since Jane. Surreptitiously, I sniffed at myself.

"We, um, broke up?"

"You don't sound sure."

"She said we needed a break. Or, that I needed one. From her and surgery."

"Was it really that bad?" Chris asked as he took his coffee from the barista and tossed a five-dollar bill in the tip jar.

"No! It was fine. I mean, I was a little freaked out, but you saw her. And she was only off work for like a week." I thought of her rubbing her thigh, resting, and then getting up again. "But she can't have kids."

"Yeah, Lauren mentioned that. Seems prudent if your blood vessels don't behave."

"But she could adopt."

"So you're on a break, or maybe a breakup, because maybe you want kids?" He gave me a sideways glance.

I slurped the coffee and scalded my tongue. "Yeah. Jane said I needed to figure it out for myself. On my own. Like I couldn't do that while we were together."

"She means without sex clouding your brain," he said dryly.

Oh. "I could figure it out even with sex!" I objected.

Chris shot me a look that said I was an idiot. "And do you? Want kids?"

"I don't know. I thought I did. But Jane is just, she's so …"

"Warm, kind, loving, supportive?"

"Yeah," I sighed as we continued meandering along the sidewalk that curved through mid-campus.

"It's why I like Lauren, too. They are both resilient. In different ways, but they get us and our weird personalities."

"You're not weird, Chris."

"You only think that cause you're weird in the same way. We seem normal to each other."

I laughed. Maybe he was right, I thought as we continued in silence.

"Did you want kids?" I asked.

"I did."

"But then, you got Sebastian out of the deal," I said, feeling dejected. He'd at least ended up with a teenager.

"Yeah. But you know what, I would have loved Lauren, asked her to marry me, even if she didn't have Sebastian, if she didn't want kids."

"Did you guys finally set a date?" I asked, as much out of curiosity as to stop talking about me and Jane and kids and my life.

"We did. Next fall. Between the custody battle with Dean and then summer the way it is for Lauren, she hasn't had a minute to think about planning, so we decided to take longer and not make it stressful. I told her I would find us a venue."

I couldn't imagine finding a place to have a wedding. What if my bride hated it? But Chris was grinning.

"Look," he said," I don't know what the answer is for you. Maybe not having kids is a deal-breaker for you. But Jane is right, you need to figure that out."

"How do you do that? Decide the answer to what may be a nebulous concept?"

"Set it up like an experiment." Chris gestured with his cup. "What if Jane could have kids, and wanted to, but then you guys couldn't get pregnant? Or she kept miscarrying. Would you still want to be with her?"

"That's diff—"

"It's really not."

I tossed my paper cup in the next trash can, thinking about what Jane had said, which Chris was now also saying. I looked around us at the nicely manicured lawn, the frisbee players who dashed across, the trees that towered overhead, and nodded.

"There's one other thing you should do," Chris said as we turned around to walk back.

"What's that?" I wasn't sure I wanted to know what other task he was going to assign me.

"Go shower."

I laughed, shaking my head. "Yeah, I'll go home."

"And then come over for dinner. This is my last week in the lab."

"I'm painfully aware of that." Chris had published a short paper on one of his wild hair ideas I'd been scoffing at. A local biotech company had seized on it and given him an insane offer. I felt even more behind. And now who was I going to talk to?!

"In a couple weeks, after the end of summer party, things will have settled down for Lauren. You and I can get a drink, hang out. Be men." He puffed his chest.

"Fine. But I'm only coming because Lauren is prettier than you. And nicer." I resisted the urge to flip him off.

Over the next weeks, Jane's question was never out of my mind. I had to thank Chris for that.

But then I'd had a Zoom meeting with Fritz and expressed my frustration with not making any progress on the methylation sequencing.

"Peter," he had said, sounding not unlike my dad when I was in high school. "The work is the job. The puzzle is the work."

At first, I'd thought it had been a mistranslation from German to English. But the more I thought about it, the more I realized he'd said what he meant. And "puzzle" was an apt word for learning about cancer.

We're both scientists, Jane and I, I thought as I checked on another slide. *Every experiment starts with a hypothesis, a belief that becomes a question to prove or disprove.* Whether or not I wanted kids was no different.

My assumption that I would have kids of my own was probably born out of societal expectations. I liked kids, even if I wasn't always very natural with them. But were they something I wanted, or had I gone along with the "meet someone, get married, buy a house, have kids" model?

Jane had had reason to think about it, to know. It wasn't her fault she was at risk if she got pregnant. Would I break up an otherwise good match just because she didn't want to be a mother? Wouldn't that make me a total asshole?

Lots of people didn't have kids because they couldn't or didn't want to. Even Chris. And he was happy. *But isn't Sebastian more like adopting?*

I sighed as I flopped into the chair behind my computer. It was just a damn circle, and I kept going around and around.

I hadn't always been this way. Geeky yes. Marching band and science Olympiad. But in high school and college I'd dated like a normal human. Did I think that having kids would make me more ... cool?

Jane was everything else I had ever thought I wanted. She got me in a way that no other girlfriend ever had.

She hadn't been at Chris' end of summer party, and neither had Alicia. I'd wondered, but had tried not to dwell, and certainly hadn't asked. Maybe Lauren would mention it when I went to their house for dinner tonight.

But, I had promised Chris I would meet him for a beer first. "To get you out in public," he'd said.

I had to credit Chris; he never picked dive bars or restaurants, or anything else, really, that wasn't hip. This restaurant, with its industrial-looking bar and polished wood tabletops was no exception. When I sat down at the booth with him, I was surprisingly glad to be there. I was starting to see why Chris made an effort to do other things. Besides, standing over the test tubes staring at them didn't make the experiment go any faster.

"Goose Island, please," Chris said to the server.

She returned a moment later to pour beer into our glasses from a pitcher. He flashed her a huge smile and she flushed. Chris tended to have that affect.

I suppressed a shudder, doubting whether the pitcher was sanitary, sitting in the open for so long.

"It's alcohol, you weirdo, it'll kill off anything you might be afraid of."

He knew me too well.

I didn't mind his razzing. We'd been friends too long now for me to be offended by it anymore. "So why are we here on a chilly fall evening, when we could have gone straight to your house?"

"Because I wanted some time alone with you," he winked suggestively.

"Greeeeeat."

"Cheers! To being friends."

I looked at him skeptically, but banged my glass against his.

Chris set his glass down and looked at me. "There's something I want to ask you."

"No, I'm not experimenting in threesomes with you and Lauren."

He fake pouted, then looked at me normally. "That's not what I was going to ask."

"You're already engaged to Lauren. I'm not going to marry you." It was entertaining to give him the same kind of obnoxious answers he normally gave me.

He grabbed his chest, pretending to be hurt. "I'm wounded. You know my true feelings, yet still you spurn me!"

"But you love Lauren!"

Chris grinned, clearly pleased with the banter. "It is related to Lauren, though," he said. "I'd like you to stand up for me at the wedding."

I choked on my beer.

"You're one of my closest friends. It would mean a lot to me to have you there."

"Wow. That's really …" I grabbed a napkin and clapped it to my mouth as I coughed. "I'm flattered."

"So, you will?"

"Of course I will."

"Thanks, Peter." Chris' voice was sincere as he held my gaze.

"You're welcome," I said with equal sincerity.

We each took a drink. Chris was probably thinking about Lauren, and I wondered if she had asked Jane the same thing.

Chris threw a twenty on the table. "Right. Time for dinner."

"Why didn't you ask me at your house?" I stood as he did, giving a last cough.

"What if you'd said no? Then we'd have been forced to have dinner together while I evaluated our friendship and the meaning of life."

I laughed, following him through the door and down the street to his car.

Lauren's blonde hair was pulled up in a messy bun when she moved to hug me as Chris and I walked into the kitchen. "You came! I wasn't sure with …" Her gaze slid to Chris and back. "Work and everything."

"I'm trying to be more like Chris and not always be in the lab. How's real estate season wrapping up?"

"Really well! I have three houses under contract this week, and another couple that should be in the next weeks. By the time we get to Halloween, I should be set for the winter. Like a bear going into hibernation," she laughed at herself.

"You don't look anything like a bear ready to hibernate." Chris poked her in the side, and she giggled.

I felt a pang. Watching them reminded me of being with Jane. It wasn't just the affection; it was the loneliness of lab time. One of the great things about being with Jane was that I could tell her what I was working on, and she would listen with genuine interest.

But if Jane and I weren't going to be together, maybe I could get through this hurdle with the DNA, and then I could go out again, maybe meet someone.

Like it's so easy, a little voice needled. *You might be a good scientist, but no one notices the lab rat.*

Something in my gut clenched. I ignored it.

Lauren's cell phone let out a chirp, and she grabbed it. "Let me just see what this client—oh! It's from Alicia! Aww look, they're in front of the Eiffel Tower." She turned the phone to Chris, then to me.

Staring back at me were Alicia and Jane, in her retro red sunglasses, both grinning like idiots, holding ice cream with the Eiffel Tower in the background.

"Hmp." I nodded, focusing on my dinner.

"She looks so well. I know she was worried about that new medication. Doesn't look like it's slowed her down at all."

I looked up sharply. "New med?"

"Yeah." Lauren clicked the screen dark. "Her doctor started her on a new medication that basically stops the extra vessels from growing. He said she will probably still need surgeries, but she's at much less risk now."

"Wow. Good for her."

If it was good news, why did I feel like I had gotten ripped off?

JANE

I hadn't gotten through my parents' deaths and my many surgeries and leaving my hometown behind by wallowing when things got gloomy.

When I walked back into the lab—okay, limped—my coworkers gave me a round of applause, and a huge banner was hanging in my office that read, "Welcome back, dirty girl!"

I turned around to beam at them. It didn't matter what happened with Peter, I assured myself. I had these people.

Near the end of the week, Kip, in his standard button-down and dress pants, appeared in my office, where I was resting my leg and working on lab reports.

"I know you're just back—"

"I wasn't not here that long."

"Felt like it. You know you're the only one who can control Rodriguez." I rolled my eyes at him, and his smile said he was glad I had played along.

"Anyway, don't forget the brass is in town."

"Why do you think I brought those?" I pointed to the heels that sat on the chair in the corner.

Kip closed his eyes and shook his head. "Just don't kill yourself."

That evening, I made a few last notes to myself on the slide I'd been looking at, turned off the electron microscope, and hung my lab coat on the peg in my office. Twenty minutes later, I was taking a glass of cabernet from the bartender.

"Jane is the one who has been leading our research into chemical-free fertilizer," Kip explained to Aziz, in full-blown Director Thompson mode.

"Very good work you're doing. How did you go down this particular path?" Aziz asked.

I smiled immediately, welcoming the questions about my research. "We've always known that manure is an excellent fertilizer. Sure, it's got nitrogen and phosphorus. But what else? And why? What is it about manure that is so beneficial? I figured if we could decipher that, there would be a way to extrapolate it for home use. Because no one wants to put cow dung on the rhododendron outside their kitchen window!"

Aziz chuckled. "I have a colleague who would be interested in hearing about your exploration of the makeup of soil. He's outside of Florence, Italy. I'll connect the two of you."

"I'd like to talk with anyone doing similar work. Thank you."

And that had been that. My life back on course as August rolled on. Until I saw Joe for a follow-up appointment.

"Jane, I have good news," he said when he came into the exam room for my one-month post-op.

"The next bundle of vessels isn't nearly as large as we thought, and I can put off surgery for another six months?" I joked, tapping my heels against the end of the exam table.

"Sort of. You're right, the bundle isn't as large as we feared. But more importantly, there is a new drug that was just approved by the FDA for your condition. It blocks the vessels from growing." He offered me a printout.

"Really?"

"Yes, and in clinical trials, it was 93 percent effective."

My chin jerked in surprise. "At preventing new growth, or stopping what is already there from spreading?"

"Both, actually. This might not mean you'll be surgery-free for the rest of your life, but it would significantly reduce the number of procedures."

"Wow!" I said as I scanned the paper.

Something Resembling Love

"And more importantly, it would reduce your day-to-day risk from injuries or a random rupture. No more worrying about how fast it's growing, and if you'll hemorrhage internally. Jane, it's possible you could have kids if you wanted!"

"Wow," I repeated, more quietly.

"I know. Science these days. Someday soon, we'll hear some lab rat has figured out how to prevent cancer from replicating."

"No doubt," I said dryly.

"If you want to try it, I'll get you a sample today."

A million questions raced through my mind. "Yes," I said instead of fixating on any one of them. "Yeah, a sample would be great!"

When I walked back to the waiting area, I texted Lauren and Alicia immediately.

> I need to talk to you guys. Tonight.

Lauren:

> Everything OK?

> I think so. My place at 7?

Alicia:

👍

That evening, sitting around my dining room table, wine half drunk, I told my friends about the medication.

"That's incredible, Jane, just amazing. I'm so happy for you!" Lauren said, setting her hand on mine.

"It is. But." I raised my hands, shrugging them open in defeat, "I don't know what to do with it."

"I'm confused." Lauren's head tilted. "Why wouldn't you want to take the medication if it's as good as he says?"

"Not about that." I shook my head. "I'm going to start the med. But the part about kids. I mean, if this is the thing that drove Peter away …"

119

"But I thought you didn't want kids?" Alicia frowned.

"I don't. Or at least I thought I didn't. I don't know anymore!" My emotions were in turmoil. I was excited about not having to worry so much about the stupid extra blood vessels and their consequences. I'd still get my semiannual scans. But this development had the potential to change everything.

"How am I supposed to know which part is true—the not wanting kids, or only believing I didn't?"

"I'm sure there's someone you could talk to about it, some expert," Alicia suggested.

My mouth tightened in a frown. "The drug is so new, though, I'm not sure there is anyone like that."

"If I know you, you will figure out a way to find those answers," Lauren said with a single decisive nod. "You will pester Dr. Joe until he finds the right article or the right person, and you'll go from there."

I gave my girlfriends an awkward smile. I had, in fact, already thought about digging deeper, and had used my government credentials to log in to PubMed and find the abstracts and articles on the clinical trials. So far, I hadn't read anything concrete.

"And in the meantime, how about a little distraction and escape?" Alicia asked, putting a brochure on the table between us. A photo on the front looking like *Under the Tuscan Sun* stared back at me.

"Oh, that looks wonderful. I want to go!" said Lauren.

"We could all go," Alicia said with excitement.

"I can't—it's the last mad rush for home sales coming up. Now until about Halloween. But you should totally go. Find some hot Italians to drive you around on their Vespas!"

"I think that's Paris," I said dryly.

"Whatever. Do it!"

Alicia and I laughed together, and when I looked at her, she was staring me down.

"You don't have to spend time convincing me! Let's do it."

"Next month?"

"Sure, why the hell not." I faced Lauren. "And yes, I will do more research on the medication."

Something Resembling Love

A week before Alicia and I boarded our flight, I visited a new red brick building along a side street between Evanston and Chicago. The curved tops of its front windows gave it a welcoming feeling.

The pregnancy specialist, Dr. Hyatt, ushered me not into an exam room, but a comfortable office. With her tight grey ringlets and sparkling blue eyes, she looked both intelligent and warm. "Dr. Chay told me a lot about you."

"You as well." I took a seat in a comfortable armchair. "Thank you for fitting me in so quickly." I gripped the mug the receptionist had given me, the coffee in it now cold, and felt it slide in my sweaty grasp.

"Dr. Chay sent over a few of your most recent labs and your last three PET scans. I'm not an expert on HHT like he is, but I see his female patients if, like you, they are considering pregnancy. Let's dive right in, shall we?" She flipped open a blue file folder. "I talked with Dr. Chay about his take on this new medication, the extent of the vascularization you've had over the years, and the number and scope of surgeries you've had."

"Sure."

"Your risk depends on a number of factors."

"That is why I came to see a high-risk pregnancy specialist," I said dryly.

She smiled, amused. "From my conversations with your geneticist, and your pulmonologist, it sounds like your condition could be very stable, and then it could run rampant for a few months, necessitating surgery quickly, but it has never been consistently one way or the other. Dr. Chay also said that while the surgical treatments have been effective, they are also risky due to potential for increased blood pressure, as well as just the additional stresses on your body. He told me that the new medication you are on has been helping, not just in clinical trials, but also it appears to be going well for you—although, it's too soon to know how it will work long term."

I nodded.

"We don't know how the medication would affect you during pregnancy, and there are no clinical trials, as of yet, to determine what the risk might be to a fetus. What we do know is that a pregnancy will raise your blood pressure, no matter how healthy and active you are going in. Birth, even more so. It would not be impossible to carry a pregnancy to term, but there are risks."

"I know about some of them from what Joe has said over the years."

She nodded. "There are those we know about. With no capillary connection transition from artery to vein, the increased blood pressure can cause the connection to rupture. This could be minor, or it could cause some kind of organ failure, or a stroke event. What we don't know is, if becoming pregnant might exacerbate the disease and cause it to produce the extra vascularization more rapidly, even with the drug. Like I said before, we don't know how the drug itself would affect you during pregnancy, or the fetus. And of course, there are the risks for the child associated with your HHT—things like increased chances of birth defects, developmental delays or disabilities, or even that the child might inherit the HHT themselves."

"Joe and I have talked about those risks."

"Are you considering becoming pregnant?" She tilted her head, regarding me kindly.

"No, in fact, I'm not even in a relationship. Right now. I mean, we're apart, but I don't know if the relationship is over and it's ..."

"Complicated with this new drug."

"Yeah," I breathed, relieved that Dr. Hyatt got it. "The question of kids, or not, was ... he said he didn't know, and I do. I've never wanted kids. I mean, I guess at some point I assumed I did, but I don't. And then when this came up, I wondered if ..." I stared out the window for a long moment. "I wondered if I was being selfish. I knew a lot of this already and suspected much of the rest of it. But I thought ..."

"You thought maybe you should find out more. That knowing more might help convince you of one course or another."

"Yes," I said, still looking out the window. "Convince me that I was wrong, that I truly do want kids, and I was just afraid." I turned back to look at her. "But I'm not."

"Cheers to us!" Alicia said, clinking her glass to mine. Her hair had an ombre green streak in it now. In honor of Italy, she'd told me.

"Agreed—to us and new adventures!" I said over the rumble of the plane's engines.

Alicia had taken charge of our trip, planning the flights and transportation, the hiking tour we would take, where we would stay in Florence once the hiking part was over, and for our final week, in Paris. I'd been happy to let her analyze all the options and hand over my credit card.

"Did you get any resolution on the medication and possible pregnancy?"

"Yes and no. There are no more medical answers, no surety one way or another."

"But you came to a conclusion of your own?"

"As you guys knew I would."

"Science is kind of your jam," she said with a small lift to the shoulder nearest me.

"Dirt. Dirt is my thing. Not veins and pregnancy and babies and the psychology of … Wow. Anyway." I saw Alicia grinning her amusement and took a gulp of my champagne. After a moment, I continued, "I think I wanted to be convinced. I think I wanted someone to come along and say, 'Silly girl, here are the facts. Of course you want kids. Now, call Peter up and tell him.' But that's just not the case."

"I never thought it was." Alicia tapped her glass to mine.

I leaned my head back against the seat, eyes closed. Alicia had been right; this was a good idea. My life was more than this relationship. If Peter decided being a father was what he wanted, I would be fine, I would find someone else. Maybe someone better. Maybe I could find a rich Baron, or whatever the Italian equivalent was, who already had five adorable, but grown children. I shifted to face the window and settled in to sleep.

When we arrived in Pisa, Alicia and I found a mismatched-looking collection of travelers near baggage claim. One tall man seemed to be in charge, and he herded the small group to two Mercedes travel vans. I dozed as the van rocked up hills and around corners.

"We will rejoin for dinner in the evening. You will find the tables in the lower level," the man said. I was yawning as he handed our key to Alicia.

We found our room off the courtyard and unpacked, trying not to succumb to the comfortable-looking beds. Then, Alicia and I wandered the old stone building. Down the stairs, we found a room with long tables and a wood stove. Several other people had pulled up chairs and were enjoying Moretti's.

"Yes, you must be Alicia and Jane." Our guide came to shake our hands. More alert than when we'd arrived, I noticed first how tall he was, and second, the short-cropped dark hair that made him look like a monk. His eyes were nearly as dark a brown, and they were alight with interest.

"We are. This is Jane." Alicia nudged me forward. "And I'm Alicia."

"It is good to meet you both." His gaze shifted from Alicia to me, lingering. "I am called Matteo Rossi."

When he turned to the next person coming down the steps, Alicia gave me a quirky smile. I grabbed a couple of beers from the counter, and we found a seat.

As we sat in the half circle around the wood stove, I glanced at Matteo from time to time. The long, confident strides. The concentration balanced against a welcoming expression. I felt Alicia nudge me in the thigh.

I raised my shoulder at her. "He's not *not* cute," I mumbled.

PETER

I hadn't been able to stop thinking about what Lauren had casually mentioned about Jane's medication. It didn't help that Chris had announced he was planning to throw a Day of the Dead party. Even though Jane hadn't been at the Chris Labor Day weekend party this year, she would probably come out for this.

Chris claimed it would be something small. But I knew what that meant. Fifteen or more people instead of thirty growing to fifty. People just wanted to be around him. Unlike me, who couldn't keep a girlfriend.

I shook my head at myself. That wasn't fair. To Chris or to me. I'd had a girlfriend, and maybe I still did.

Jane was off living her life, traveling in Europe. On vacation. What did it matter if there was a medication that could help her? She still had the condition. Would it change her mind; would she want to have kids now? Did I?

Hunched in front of my laptop on my couch, I Googled hereditary hemorrhagic telangiectasia again.

I read a statistic on the Cure HHT website that said 90 percent of people who had HHT were undiagnosed. And another, that since its discovery in the 1880s, not much more was understood about how it worked.

The arteriovenous malformations grew spontaneously, almost anywhere in the body from fingertips and noses to around organs and in brains. HHT was genetic, autosomal dominant. Genetics wasn't my specialty, despite my work with DNA, but I knew "dominant" meant it didn't skip generations and, unlike autosomal recessive genes, only one parent had to transfer the gene. And "autosomal" referred to genes that were numbered, not sex related. Just like cancer.

But HHT could still skip a generation if the parent with HHT didn't pass on the gene with the mutation in it. So Jane might or might not pass it on. It was like my blue eyes, I supposed. My mom had brown, but she had a copy of a blue-eyed gene to pair with my dad's recessive gene'd blue eyes. There had been no way of knowing which of my mom's gene copies I'd get until I was born. If my mom had passed on her brown copy, I'd have had brown eyes. Just like it would be for Jane's kids. One copy would be enough to give them HHT, too.

Jane hadn't told me about the genetic connection, but then again, I hadn't asked more.

Further down the Cure HHT webpage, I found links to research being done on the genetics at most major hospitals, and then a short white paper talking about the new use of a drug.

Lauren and Alicia knew about how HHT impacted Jane's life, and so probably Chris did too. But did the people that she worked with? Maybe her boss, in case of an emergency, but anyone else?

And speaking of emergencies, who was her emergency contact? She and Lauren had lost contact for a while. I didn't know how long she had known Alicia. Certainly, it wasn't me, because she would have told me that. Did she even have an emergency contact?

I let out a long breath and slowly closed the lid of my laptop.

Over the next couple of weeks, I all but abandoned my own research in favor of reading about HHT. Some of the ideas used to develop the medication could be useful for stopping or slowing tumor growth, but that wasn't why I kept coming back to them.

On the computer next to me in the lab, code rolled across the screen, but I ignored it, rolling my lower lip between my fingers as I sifted through what I had found, reading about the research that had been conducted to understand the genetics. Much like cancer, there was no good explanation for where the mutation had first come from.

Something Resembling Love

I went back to the white paper and searched the name of the drug. I came up with a dozen papers on the initial research for the drug's development and the results of clinical trials. Roche had done a lot of the testing, and now manufactured the medication. I shook my head at the irony.

The initial publications explained the proteins and growth factors involved in how HHT expressed. My knowledge of tumor growth helped me wade through the jargon. "Huh," I mused out loud, startling myself. "Angiopoietin-1. Interesting." I didn't know much about biological development, but it looked like they'd developed the drug to block the effectiveness of this protein in the body.

It plays a critical role in mediating reciprocal interactions between the endothelium and surrounding matrix and mesenchyme and inhibits endothelial permeability, I read. *The protein also contributes to blood vessel maturation and stability.* Further down: *Activation of* "insert random cell receptor," I mumbled, *which ultimately leads to endothelial cell migration, tube formation, sprouting, and survival.* I remembered from my long-ago biology classes that endothelial cells lined blood vessels.

There were citations to papers on how blood vessel development, or rather inhibiting it, was being used in cancer treatment. I clicked through a few of these as well. Someone had extracted the technology of using vascular endothelial growth factor to slow down the growth of blood vessels to tumors, extracted that technology, and applied it to the angiopoietin.

When I reached the end of the article, I stood up, walked to the window, and watched the remaining leaves shiver on the trees. I had known that Jane's HHT was scary, and on some level, I had heard her say that it was life-threatening. But I hadn't realized how real that threat was. She'd been dealing with this her entire life, mostly on her own. She'd lost her parents, and then had her world turned upside down again when she'd found out about this unpredictable disease.

I'd been waiting for her to say, "You know what, I'd love to have kids with you." I'd listened to all the things she had said about HHT, and to Dr. Chay in the ICU after her surgery, and still tried to get him to say it was fine for Jane to have kids.

When she'd ended things, or put us on a break, or whatever was happening in our relationship right now, Jane had said that she loved me. Her voice had been so matter of fact; not the sweet, soft way I had imagined hearing it. From her or anyone else.

What else could I have expected, though? She'd been waiting for me to hear her when she said kids were not in the cards for her.

I wished I had known all of this, in this much detail, before. *Before what? Before you refused to listen to her? Before you ignored what is arguably the most important factor in Jane's life? Before you refused to see the way her brokenness makes her her?*

Her words echoed in my head: "What if something awful happens, and I end up in the hospital for months? Or worse, die! Can you imagine trying to parent a scared five-year-old who doesn't understand why mommy can't even pick him up?"

Could I really blame her for not wanting to jeopardize her health, or put a child in the same position she had been in, losing her parents young? If she'd been Lauren, instead of my girlfriend, I probably would have thought the decision reasonable.

The voice in my head was right. I had been unkind, selfish even. In not fully understanding; in not trying to understand.

And I loved her. Even though I had never told her so. I sat back down in the chair with a thud. Why had I never told her? Why had I been so hung up on how much my parents liked her? Why couldn't I have been a normal boyfriend and thought it was great she and my family got along so well?

I set my head in my hands. Despite loving her, I had still tried to convince her she should do something she didn't want to do, and which could have killed her.

If I really loved her, wouldn't I accept her as she was?

"Fuck," I whispered to myself.

I could feel Chris' reaction to my realization, smacking me on the back of the head, not just rattling my chair. "Good job, asshole," he'd say. "Took you long enough."

Even though she was still in Europe, I wanted to call her now, this moment. I wanted to tell her I was sorry; I'd been an ass. I wished I could go over to her house right this minute and hug her and tell her that I loved her, too.

For once, I couldn't wait for Chris' party.

Something Resembling Love

 I clicked over to the event page Chris had set up on his website and checked *Yes*. My face hurt from my smile when I saw Jane had RSVP'd that she was going as well.

JANE

Our group of thirteen reached a summit along the Cinque Terre.

"Look at that view!" Alicia turned in a circle with a sweep of her hand. "Blue skies and ocean as far as the eye can see."

I breathed in the heavy air. I'd been trying not to think of Peter every day, but it was hard not to wonder if my nudge for him to make up his own mind had had any impact.

"I'm not sure I want to go back," I said, squinting against the sun. "Surely I can apply my knowledge of dirt to sand, or something, right? I could stay here and test and retest which kind is the best for sunbathing, playing volleyball, reading a book, walking on, docking a boat …"

"Such a great idea. And I can be your research assistant."

"Perfect," I said as we dissolved into laughter.

I bent over to catch my breath. "Are you all right?" Matteo's voice. I looked up to see him holding out a hand, frowning concern at me.

"Yeah, I'm good, just laughing too hard," I said, automatically taking his offered hand to stand up.

"So long as you are not sick."

I put a hand on his arm, "Thank you, Matteo, I'm fine."

He looked me over, head to foot. Satisfied, he nodded and turned back toward our descent down the hill. I watched him walk nimbly around the boulders and rocks that littered our path. He didn't look like the "guido"-styled Italians I had come across in Chicago or Philadelphia, overly friendly in a hyper-masculine way.

A three-or-so-foot drop greeted us at the end of the trail. Matteo waited, offering a hand for everyone to grab as we jumped down, but he didn't release mine right away. I glanced at his weather-worn palm, then smiled up at him. "Thank you."

He gave a quick nod.

When we reached the café in Monterosso, all of us were ready for a beer and a sandwich. I noticed Matteo talking with each person in the group, checking to make sure they had refilled their water, had enough to eat, still felt okay, if they needed more sunscreen. He carried a backpack, which I was sure had a first aid kit, but I wondered what else he carried. More socks? Tubes of sunscreen? I gave a half laugh to myself. Just like when I went into the field.

"Have you everything you need?" He sat down between me and Alicia.

"It's so beautiful here, Matteo," Alicia said, as she scanned the view to the ocean. "I can see why you do this all year round."

"Even for us annoying tourists," I chuckled.

"You are not annoying. What would make you think that?"

"Nothing in particular, just that tourists usually are. Not knowing local customs or history. We infiltrate churches, taking pictures; we are more steps on the fragile landscape, bringing dirt from who knows where and depositing it in vineyards."

Matteo's dark eyes considered me for a moment. "I see what you are meaning. We have those issues, yes, but that is why the government is so dedicated to maintaining *i nostri parchi*, most especially the Cinque Terre, because there are so many visitors."

"I'm glad to hear that. It must be so peaceful in the winter, with fewer of us in the forests. Snow on the branches and in the vineyards."

"We have little snow here. It is too close to the ocean. Where your agritourismo is, they will have some. Only the Alps have the snow like I think you mean. But it is beautiful, you are correct." His gaze stayed on me. "You like the land, I think. The winter would also bring you enjoyment."

"You're right, I do like the land," I said, not looking away.

"Is this a side job, or are you like Jane and nerd out on forests and dirt?" Alicia asked.

"No, this is only what I do. Being outside is freedom. I like sharing that with people, even if it is a few days only."

"I understand that."

"Tell him about your fertilizer work." Alicia nudged me under the table. Hard.

"No," I shook my head with a half laugh, "no one wants to hear about manure."

"It is important to do things naturally, to use the things nature gives us in positive ways," Matteo said quietly.

"I couldn't agree more." I smiled.

"You would enjoy all the seasons."

"I'm sure I would."

Matteo kept his eyes on me for another moment, then got up to gather the group.

Alicia nudged me as we sat together on the train back to Riomaggiore. "He likes you."

"He does not." I waved her comment away. "He's only being polite."

"Your radar has been damaged by that idiot you dumped."

"I didn't dump Peter."

Alicia raised an eyebrow at me. "Matteo likes you. He's just reserved about it because you are his guest. It would be different if you were in a bar."

I rolled my eyes. "Whatever you say."

I wasn't sure how I wanted to feel about Alicia's supposed observations. Matteo was attentive with everybody, but he did linger with me a few moments longer than the others.

A couple of afternoons later, Matteo guided us into a small town off the path we had been hiking in the Garfagnana Valley.

"There is a small perturbation coming into the area with too much rain to continue trekking safely." Matteo looked up, studying the clouds. "When this area was still home to many small farmers and peasants, they cared for these forests. The chestnut trees are big and strong, which helped people build houses. But if there is wind like this perturbation will bring, the trees can fall. We have had many great mudslides in areas where chestnut trees are most prevalent. Instead, we will go back to the house, and I will take you to a special restaurant close by."

Something Resembling Love

We were more than damp already, so the news was met with mixed feelings—wanting to finish what we had started, but also being lured to an early beer.

In the evening, dry and clean, our group piled closely into one small tour van and drove to Castelnuovo Garfagnana, the nearest town of any size. As we rumbled along, ABBA came on, and we belted out the words to "Fernando." With a half chuckle, Matteo turned the music up and sang along. We turned toward each other, grinning, singing. The amusement in Matteo's eyes was palpable. Was this how he was when he wasn't guiding and worrying about people who were more or less fit?

At the restaurant, I was less surprised than I might have been, when Matteo slid into the chair next to mine. He had endless stories: the history of the area from medieval times up to current events; tales of what he had seen in the forests we were hiking.

Near the end of dinner, Matteo stood to address the group. "I tell you of the chestnut trees many times, I know. But they are an important part of our culture in the Apuan Alps. I have told you how the people who lived in these mountains harvested the nuts for food. All over the mountains, the chestnut trees grew large." He spread his arm wide overhead, setting his hand on my shoulder as he finished his gesture. "The people laid branches over hot coals, spread the nuts to dry, and ground the dried nuts to a powder. Chestnut flour. It was used in baking for centuries, long before wheat flour was a staple, readily available."

"That seems like an awful lot of work," commented someone at the end of the table.

"Yes, but the chestnuts were nutritious. To finish our dinner, we will have brownies made with this chestnut flour."

"Did you grind it for us?" someone else joked.

"Haha, no, I did not. It is commercial now, but I think you will like them still."

The plate of brownies made its way around the table, followed closely by more wine. I offered the bottle to Matteo, who wrapped his fingers over mine, but quickly looked away. "You would like more, Jane?" he asked, concentrating on my glass.

"I would." In my head, I was agreeing to more than wine.

"It has been a pleasure to know you, Jane," Matteo said the next night over dinner, as we sat at one of the large tables in the cellar of the *agritourismo*.

"Likewise." Alicia caught my eyes and raised her eyebrows several times. I felt myself grow warm.

"What will you do when you return?"

"We don't go back just yet. I am meeting a colleague in Florence, Alicia and I spend a couple days there, and then we are going to Paris for another week."

"You have colleagues in Italy?" Matteo furrowed his brow.

"He's really more my counterpart. Someone who does what I do for the Italian department of agriculture."

"Who is this person? I may know him."

"Tonelli, I think. I don't recall his first name."

Matteo seemed to consider this. "It is good you go to Florence. It holds many beautiful things."

After a large sip of wine, he stood up. "Tomorrow," he began, silencing the dinner conversations, "we have our last hike together …"

His announcement was met with groans from everyone.

"Can't we hire you for another month?" someone asked, to ensuing laughter and applause.

Our last day was both my most favorite, and my least.

Our hike was along the nearby *via della Contessa*, which Matteo told us had been used by villagers during the tenure of Pope Gregory VII. Local legends said that Pope Gregory VII and Countess Matilda of Tuscany, for whom the path was named, used the roads and passes in the late 1000s to meet for political discussions … and also romantic ones.

At the end of the hike, the drizzle that had accompanied us all day turned into a downpour. I was jealous of those with hiking poles as the small hill leading to the car park became a slip and slide. When I stepped onto the path, I skated on the mud the rest of the way down the hill, arms flailing.

"Oof!"

Something Resembling Love

For the span of three erratic heartbeats, I stood still, evaluating if I was upright, and then realized not only was I not only wasn't lying in mud, but I was held securely in Matteo's muscular arms.

"Are you hurt?" he asked.

"Just embarrassed," I said, pushing wet hair out of my face. "Thank you for catching me." I looked into his eyes.

Matteo's hands held firmly, one on my hip, the other behind my back, for a moment longer, staring into my eyes. Then he set me away from himself.

"*De nulla,*" he murmured.

It's nothing? I wondered if that was true.

When we returned to the *agritourismo*, our hosts Bernardo and Rosalba were ready with beer and *vin Brulé*, the Italian version of mulled wine. We peeled our wet layers off and set them on chairs, crowding around a wood-burning stove, sharing stories and photos from the afternoon.

During my shower I thought about the past week. I was certainly attracted to Matteo. His easy way of being in the world was comforting, and very much the opposite of Peter. I loved being outdoors, and Matteo's similar enthusiasm was refreshing. And I was glad we had more places to visit before we went back to Chicago. While I wasn't going to give Alicia the satisfaction of admitting it, I wasn't quite ready to let go of this fantasy world.

Later, we joined for a hearty meal. By the time dessert was served, the rain had passed, and a lovely evening in the courtyard beckoned. Bernardo, who had been with us each evening, appeared in the courtyard brandishing bottles of homemade grappa, and a portable stereo from which was blasting traditional Italian music. He offered second helpings and poured more wine and, I thought, enjoyed this small group more than most that came through.

Our after-dinner drinks quickly became a party. Each of our thirteen hikers got up and danced, with varying degrees of gracefulness. Alicia laughed, enjoying the revelry, and we bumped hips, clapping along. I had felt any number of emotions throughout the trip, although while we had been hiking, I hadn't really had the opportunity to feel sad. Some of the hikes had been challenging.

Matteo came around and grabbed me into his arms, twirling us in loops to the sound of the tarantellas.

"Told ya he liked you," Alicia chided, when I paused to catch my breath.

"Maybe a little," I admitted, with an amused smile and self-deprecating half shrug.

"Do something about it."

"I am."

"I don't mean dancing. Go, you know …" she wiggled her eyebrows.

I rolled my eyes at her. While Matteo was attractive and kind, I wasn't sure that sleeping with him would solve the rest of my problems.

A few minutes later, Matteo reappeared, offering a glass.

"You may have to carry me to my room tonight, if you keep giving me grappa."

Next to me, Alicia snorted. I ignored her to take Matteo's hand.

As we neared the end of the evening, the volume of the music lowered, and instead of dancing, our group chatted, sipping the last of the grappa, or nibbled the anise cookies Rosalba had brought out. I took mine and wandered around the far side of the building. What would life feel like when I got home? The hot tickle of tears streaked down my cheek. I didn't want to go home—and not in the way that tourists often felt at the end of vacation.

I had come because I needed to be distracted. I wanted to stay because I felt settled. *But*, I reminded myself, *it's not over*. Alicia and I still had another ten days of traveling ahead of us.

"Is everything fine?" I heard Matteo behind me.

"Yes, just admiring the view in the moonlight." I quickly swiped at the tears.

"Have you been crying?" He came to stand in front of me.

"No. Well, a little. I suppose I am sad to leave."

"Hmm." Matteo's eyes stayed on me for a heartbeat, before he turned to face out over the hill that dropped down to the next village. "You are unhurt from this afternoon?"

"Thanks to my knight in shining armor coming to the rescue." I smiled at him, looking at his profile as he studied the stone clock tower that rose from the hill below us.

After a moment, he turned, facing me, maybe looking for evidence that I hadn't been hurt. He leaned toward me, hesitated, and then kissed me gently.

Something Resembling Love

Automatically, I turned toward him, reaching for his shoulder as he slid an arm around my back. I felt like I could let go, step over an edge of the courtyard, and he would keep me from falling. A tiny corner of my brain registered that this was different than Peter. There was no hesitation, no reassurance required. Only a man kissing me like he was sure he wanted to. Like he knew what I needed.

Then there was nothing else, no thought. Just the slide of his tongue over mine. A tiny nip at the corner of my mouth. Him sucking on my lower lip, his focus on one spot, while his hands pressed into my back, keeping me tight against him.

He stopped abruptly, and I blinked my eyes open. The clock on the bell tower showed twenty-two minutes had passed.

He stepped back, his arms dropping away. "That was—I am sorry, I should not have pressed you," Matteo stuttered.

I reached for his hand. "I'm glad you did."

He glanced at our hands and then looked at me with concern. "Your friend will think you have fallen down."

"I doubt that," I said dryly. When he looked at me oddly, I quickly added, "She won't be worried."

When we returned to the courtyard, the rest of the tour had dispersed. Matteo walked up the hill toward the building his room was in, and I leaned against the old stone wall of mine, breathing in the damp chill air, feeling a thousand different things. The thrill of the way Matteo had kissed me, more confident than Peter, and my accompanying desire. Guilt and disappointment. Longing to be kissed again, but also just to be held.

I blew out a long breath. The memory would be a nice souvenir to take home.

I found Alicia in our shared bedroom, folding clothes into her suitcase. "Out enjoying the … scenery?"

It was hard to keep the bubble of giddiness out of my voice. "Sure was."

She paused, folding a sweater. "I'm happy for you. You really had a great week, didn't you? And you didn't pick up a single handful of dirt!"

Saying goodbye the next morning to the friends we had made was bittersweet. We exchanged contact information while Matteo and Bernardo loaded luggage into the small bus that would take us to Florence. Jokes were shared, promises exchanged to send photos, and hugs were given.

As we started to board the bus, Rosalba came over and grasped my hands. She spoke to me in rapid Italian, earnest in whatever she was saying, a single word familiar to me: *tutti*. *Everything*. When she finished, she grabbed me suddenly to hug me.

Startled, I looked at Matteo. When Rosalba released me, he came over to hug me too, an enigmatic look on his face. "She says that everything will be fine."

I glanced at the woman who was nodding, hands clasped under her chin.

"Right." I forced a hesitant smile.

"Here is my email and phone. It would be a shame to lose a lovely friendship." Matteo handed me a scrap of paper, then helped me onto the bus.

I sat across the aisle from Alicia, staring out the window. When we reached the motorway, I finally looked at the paper. The ones drawn in the European style that always looked like sevens made me smile. I folded the paper and tucked it into my wallet.

Although Alicia and I only had three days in Florence, we more than made up for it with diligent sightseeing. Alicia and I dragged each other across the city center, crisscrossing our previous paths. The Duomo, the Uffizi Gallery, shopping over the Ponte Vecchio, indulgent meals, and the Pitti palace, as well as wandering the streets.

On our last afternoon, I made my way to the local office of the Ministry of Agriculture.

"You are Jane!" he said as soon as I walked in.

"Pietro?"

"Yes, yes, is me." He waved me forward with both hands, ushering me toward an office. "So glad to meet you, please come in. I get you espresso."

I sat, taking in the shabby office furniture and new computer.

"Here you are." Pietro returned, bearing two demitasse of scalding and bitter coffee. He reminded me of Thompson. A shorter, greyer, less bureaucratic version, but just as dedicated.

"Tell me how I can help," I said, as I carefully stirred in the two accompanying lumps of sugar.

Something Resembling Love

"It is the farmers, you see, we have a problem with this fungus in the soil. But Secretary Aziz, you know from the American Department of Agriculture?" I nodded, and he continued, "He says you maybe can fix it."

Aziz had a high opinion of me. "Tell me more about it, and I'll see what ideas I have."

We spent the next four hours drinking coffee and trading stories, problems, and suggestions. Pietro was probably thirty years my senior and had thoughts on all aspects of agriculture. Although our respective interests didn't overlap, they complemented each other.

I left feeling renewed in my work. Excited for Paris, but also ready to return to the lab.

PETER

I sat down at my kitchen table desk, working on a paper I hoped I could get published. Fritz had been calling every couple of weeks to ask what progress I'd made. Just as often, he asked about my setbacks, not judging me.

The draft stared at me from the monitor, mocking me as I stared at the blinking cursor. Scrabbling my fingers through the hair at the sides of my head, I reapplied myself to the task at hand.

Our first findings of hypermethylation in DNA ... I wrote, adding an electronic sticky note to remember to add a citation to the previous research.

Since reading about Jane's HHT and finding out that Roche had done most of the drug development, I'd doubled down on my own work. Maybe the mystery of cancer replication would never be solved. Maybe it couldn't be. Perhaps it could be, but not by me. But I had to try.

Maybe it would be solved somewhere like Roche, by someone like Fritz, who was still dropping offers to support my work. But I remained adamant. I would do this outside of industry. I wanted, as I'd told Jane, for the research to be pure. Untainted by Big Pharma.

Hours later, my phone rang, breaking me out of my focus and forcing me to the surface.

Something Resembling Love

"Isn't it lonely there without me to brighten up your days?" Chris said when I answered. I could picture the lopsided grin he always gave when trying to get me to react.

"Hell, no! I get way more work done without your sorry ass trying to distract me."

"I *knowwwwww*." He drew it out, pretending to be a fluttery girl. "I miss you too."

I laughed. Chris was right; I missed having him around. Even if he'd been a pain, trying to tell me how to run my love life or my career.

"I'm glad you're coming tonight," he said. "It'll be good for you to get out. Jane's going."

"Yeah, I saw."

"Ah. That's really why you're coming."

"That's not why." *Yes it is.*

"If you say so. I hope you figure out what to say and apologize for being such a dumbass."

I let his comment soak in before speaking solemnly. "Chris, I messed up with her. And I don't know what to do."

"Tell her that." He was quiet for a moment. "I'm glad you're coming."

That evening, I carefully painted my face: a white curve coming down from my hairline, dropping over the bridge of my nose, and cutting off to the side under my jawline. The remainder was filled with black. Everyone else would have colorful and intricate designs—flowers and spider webs, teeth drawn across their lips. But pretending to be the *Phantom of the Opera* was as good as it was going to get for single me. Was I single? Were we still together in some way? Had Jane moved on in the past two and a half months, met someone in her travels, or at work?

I peered at myself in the mirror and then gave up on the face paint to change.

Crap. Why had I not thought of this before? Carefully, I drew my T-shirt up over my head, keeping it as far away from the artwork as possible. If Jane had been here, she would have reminded me to do this beforehand. Hell, any girlfriend. I didn't really want to wear a button-down shirt, but ruining my handiwork was less likely that way.

When I automatically reached for my black jeans, I heard Jane's voice in the recesses of my memory saying, "Weeeell … it's not the eighties. Black jeans aren't exactly cool anymore. How about the dark blue ones instead."

I grabbed my keys and looked around my apartment. Mail piled up. Cups scattered on surfaces. Soulless.

When I walked into the room Chris had reserved for the party, I twitched. We were in one of the newest swanky bars in the city. Naturally. Lights cast an orange glow from the floor up the wall. Glass chandeliers hung from the ceiling. Behind the bar, the orange light theme continued behind the shelves of liquor; the bar top was a polished, smoked glass. The curtains were some kind of draped heavy cream velvet. One long table sat along a wall with hors d'oeuvres.

This sucked. I felt awkward and invisible. Just like my pre-Jane life. I spotted Alicia talking to a guy I remembered from a couple of gatherings. "Hi Alicia, and it's Zach, right?"

"I'm glad you came," Alicia said as she hugged me hard. Did that mean Jane would be happy to see me, too?

"And miss one of Chris' parties? No way!" The excitement was feigned, but I *was* glad to be there.

"Isn't that the truth," Zach agreed, raising his glass slightly in a toast. A gregarious muscular guy, he looked over most people's heads as he scanned the room. "How did he find this place? I hadn't even heard of it, and I live three blocks away."

"You know Chris. Somehow, he just knows these things." Alicia waved her drink in a circle to encompass the room. "It's like he has this internal radar for the newest and hottest."

"Maybe it's for the priciest!" Zach joked "I think I paid ten dollars for my beer."

"I don't know where you've been drinking, but that's Chicago!" Alicia laughed.

"Maybe I just don't get out much. Old age is catching up with us!"

"We're not old!" Alicia punched Zach lightly in the shoulder.

"Maybe not." He leaned over and wrapped his arm around her shoulders, giving a little squeeze.

Watching them, I felt even more out of place.

Chris appeared, wearing a tux with tails but no bow tie, Lauren in tow in a ruffled dress. Both of them sported perfectly painted sugar masks.

Something red flashed in my peripheral vision. Jane. Laughing with someone on the other side of the room.

"Peter! You came!" Lauren said, leaning to hug me and blocking my view. Why was everyone so surprised I had come?

"Now you're here, we can wrap up and go dancing," Chris said, throwing an arm around my neck.

Several blocks of walking later, I noticed Jane ahead of me in the line to get into the club. She leaned over the counter, and suddenly our entire party was being waved past the guy taking cover. She was waiting too, to make sure that every one of our group got in, before turning for the bar.

I followed her, signaling to the bartender for a beer.

"Too many choices," she commented, leaning on the bar top.

"I've never known you to not know what you want." The words sounded bitter.

"I just spent two weeks in Italy drinking red wine and homemade grappa. Hard to shift back. Negroni, please." She gave a charming smile to the bartender and then turned back to me. Tiny jewels dotted around her eyes, making her even more radiant than usual. "How are you?" she asked sincerely. "How's work?"

Work was the last thing I wanted to talk about. "Fine. I'm working on a paper that I hope to have ready for submission in the spring."

"Peter, that's great! I'm so happy for you!" I felt her hand on my arm, warm and comforting.

Shrugging, I changed the subject. "How's Otis?"

Her smile faltered a little. "He's good. Fluffy as ever."

"How's your dirt?"

"Just peaty!" She made a face at her own joke. Dead air lingered between us. "It really is nice to see you, Peter. I hope your paper goes well. Let me know when you finish it. I'd like to read it."

"Sure," I agreed automatically.

I watched her walk away, full ruffled skirt swaying. I followed her into the crowd. Someone else had noticed her too, someone not from our group. He was tall with dark hair, wearing a suit. As Jane walked past him, he grabbed her hand. She shoved the fox mask he'd been wearing up onto his forehead. He was as good-looking as Chris.

Before I could take another breath, they were swaying to the beat, his hand on her lower back, pressing her up against him. I watched the scene unfold from about two-thirds of the way across the dance floor. Just like the lyrics blasting overhead, I felt it in my chest. But not when she looked at me; when she looked at him.

I don't know how it happened, but before I knew what I was doing, I was walking slowly toward them.

The pain beneath my ribs made no difference. All I could feel was an insistent pounding, like someone had a hold of one of my ribs and was crushing it in time with the music. *Bound to be together, bound to be together.* He spun her again, and her glowing, laughing face registered on my retinas.

She looked just the way she had on that New Year's Eve. Alive and gorgeous. No trace of a life-threatening vascular disease lurking beneath the surface. I felt it in my chest, the punch of her attention, the surprise I'd felt that night that this vivacious, beautiful woman could care so much that I was included.

I could almost feel the rise of her hip beneath my hand, the singer belting out that the girl he was dancing with was his destiny. Then the music stopped abruptly, a scratch of the record as the DJ transitioned to the next song.

The guy bowed to her, and she curtsied in return, laughing. When she turned, she saw me. Stopped. Her eyes locked on mine, a questioning tip to her head. Was it an invitation?

One side of my mouth tipped up, some sort of weak apology.

She turned away, and I didn't follow her.

Even before I opened my eyes in the morning, I was kicking myself. The night before had not been my finest hour, not by a long shot. What had I been thinking? Following Jane, staring at her. I'd wanted to talk to her. For real, not just some barroom banter. Instead of telling her that, I'd nearly stalked her. *Jesus. What an idiot.*

Something Resembling Love

But seeing her had solidified what I'd been thinking about since Chris and I had talked about kids and families; throughout the reading I'd done about HHT. Jane wasn't being unreasonable. And she'd been right, I could see now, to tell me to figure it out for myself. Without sex as an influence, as Chris had translated for me.

I grabbed the phone off the small table next to my bed and texted her, before I lost my courage.

> It was great to see you last night. Can I come over?

I sat up, scrubbed my hand over my face, and stood up. The stack of dishes in the sink caught my eye, taunting me. I wasn't going to be mocked, so I grabbed my heavy winter outwear, collapsible windscreen, and ice fishing pole, using the app to find a nearby street-side car to rent for the day, and drove into Wisconsin. I set myself up on the frozen lake and waited. Anything was better than going to the lab or trying to run computational analysis, hoping that Jane would text me back.

I'd been out there for a few hours, cold enough to not be checking my phone, when she texted me back.

> Hi Peter. Do you want to get dinner tonight?

I wasn't sure if she meant to come over. She probably would have said exactly that if she'd meant it.

> That would be nice. What were you thinking?

> The place we went on our first date?

> Absolutely.

It felt auspicious that she had chosen that restaurant, like maybe she too was thinking about our beginning and starting over and being together. Quickly, I packed up my fishing gear and raced through the traffic along I-94 back to my apartment.

The clutter was still there, so I started laundry, and folded and hung the clothes I knew were clean.

With clothes no longer cluttering the floor and the dishwasher grumbling, I felt inspired by my progress. I grabbed a sponge and attacked the bathroom. It made me recall the morning I had woken up to Jane cleaning in here. I had been horrified. I shuddered at the memory, how embarrassed I'd been seeing her cleaning the toilet.

When I sat down for a break, my place looked like someone who cared might live here. It was nowhere near "Jane" clean and tidy, but it was respectable. My linens were clean, that coffee ring on the counter was scrubbed, and I had plates to put my food on.

If Jane and I ended up back here tonight, no matter how unlikely that might be, I wouldn't cringe when she walked in.

The feeling of accomplishment carried with me when I walked into the wine bar that night and saw Jane sitting at the bar.

JANE

The morning after the Day of the Dead party, my alarm went off early, just like every other day. I did not leap out of bed, though. Instead, I reached down to scratch Otis, his fluffiness comforting. Peter had been awkward, staring at me in that weird way—sadness and longing. Well, he knew what he had to do, and I didn't have time to worry about it this morning, anyway. Under Secretary Aziz was in town for his quarterly visit, and I knew he'd want an update on my manure project.

When I walked in, Aziz and Thompson were seated together in the small conference room we sometimes used when we needed to present information. I waved. Thompson raised his hand back to me.

I checked on my newest batch of test plants, routine garden vegetables, and watered them. After going through my morning checklist, I went to my office. I love my job, I told myself, looking around the painted concrete block walls that held my degrees and certifications and photos from being on location. But since returning from the Tuscan hills, I'd found my mind wandering back there often. I should hang a photo of me and Alicia, I thought, and logged on to my computer. In early December, part of our team would go to New Mexico for a week, and I needed to order sample baggies and sunscreen.

I looked up at the knock on my door. "Aziz," I said, surprised to see him in my office, but also that he wasn't wearing a suit.

"Hello, Jane," he said, sounding just as formal as every other occasion I'd seen him. "I'm just on my way to the airport, but wanted to talk with you first."

"Um. Okay." I started to move the things that were sitting on my desk so there was a clear place in front of my guest chair.

Aziz brushed my actions away. "Don't bother. This will only take a moment."

I stopped shifting papers and looked at his well-groomed bearded countenance. He didn't look upset, but then again, I didn't know Aziz all that well. "How can I help?" I asked brightly.

"Were you planning to attend the industry conference later this month?"

I started to speak, but Aziz kept talking. "If not, you are now." He chuckled at himself. "I'd like you to present your research on the extraction of micronutrients."

"Like on a panel?" I frowned.

"No, as a speaker."

"Oh … it's not really ready. I was planning to publish mid-next year." After the full study was done.

Aziz took a step into the room. "It's a well-designed study and I know you have data already."

"I do, I just—"

"Weren't planning to present it yet. But you should. Get credit and recognition now."

I blinked, hearing the unsaid words. *Before someone else does. So I can show off my region.*

"Thompson has all the details. I look forward to seeing you in a few weeks." He turned and walked out of my office, my attendance at the conference, stellar speech in hand, a foregone conclusion.

A few weeks!

I picked up my phone to text Lauren and Alicia and freak out … Instead, I saw a text from Peter, asking if we could get together. I glanced back at my wall of photos and suddenly, desperately wanted a glossy red pinot.

I texted Peter back, suggesting the wine bar he'd first taken me to.

Something Resembling Love

Peter wasn't at the restaurant when I arrived, so I took a chair at the bar, searching the menu for a Tuscan pinot.

"Jane." I heard his voice next to me a short while later.

Warmth flushed through me at the sight of his familiar physique and the sound of his voice. "Hi," I said, smiling broadly.

"Hi," he said, voice quiet and hesitant. He cleared his throat. "Do you think we could grab a table?"

I picked up my glass and followed him across the room to a booth.

"You look really pretty," he said.

I touched my hair. I didn't feel pretty in jeans, having come from the lab. "Thanks."

We made small talk for a while. Peter's lack of progress and frustration with his boss. My invitation to speak. It felt like we were on a first date again. Well, I *had* picked the same restaurant.

"Jane, I ... the reason I wanted to see you is because I've, um, I've been doing a lot of thinking. About what you said. About not wanting to have kids, not wanting to be a mom at all."

I nodded, holding my breath.

"I'm sorry," he said, reaching across the table for my hand. "I didn't listen to you. Or, I guess I did, but I didn't hear what you were saying."

"Thanks, Peter." Even if he still wanted kids and this was the end of our relationship, that alone made me feel better. This was the first time someone I had dated had acknowledged my perspective.

"I researched HHT. Read a bunch of papers."

I had to smile. "Of course you did."

He nodded. "Especially after Lauren told me about your new medication."

Oh. So that's where this was going.

"It's bad, the way HHT is for you. It's serious. I didn't see that. Or maybe didn't want to." Peter gripped my hand as he spoke. "I wanted you to know that I read everything I could, all the publications on the clinical trials. It's amazing there's a drug that will keep you safer. I'm ... happy. I'm happy for you."

"Thanks," I said with a sad smile.

"I did what you asked. I figured out what I want."

My eyes closed against a slice of disappointment. "That's wonderful, Peter. I'm happy for you, too."

"I want you." His voice was sincere.

My eyes flew open, finding Peter's face. Open and earnest. Eager and excited.

"I love you," he said, hunching forward across the table toward me. "I don't know why I never said it before. Maybe I was afraid you didn't love me too. Or that you—you—I don't know. It doesn't matter." He shifted, leaning closer.

I looked away from him, to the fake candle on the table, unsure what to feel. I picked up my wine glass with my free hand and finished the last swallow.

"Jane?" I heard the worry in Peter's voice, now that I hadn't responded.

When I looked at him again, I was beaming. "That's ... I missed you."

"I missed *you*."

We gazed at each other for a long moment with small smiles until Peter said, "Can I take you home?" I nodded, and Peter put some bills on the table. There was more we should talk about, but right now, all I wanted was to solidify the emotions.

"There's no snow this time," I said as we walked to my car, holding hands.

Peter's eyes dropped to my lips, lingered. I could feel time pounding out.

"I don't want a kiss on the cheek this time."

"No. I don't want to kiss you like that." He took a step forward, pinning me against the car door. "What I want is for you to take me home with you."

He crushed his lips to mine, and I lifted my chin, seeking him out, wanting to feel everything. I heard a small moan escape me. "Get in the car."

The Monday night streets had minimal traffic, and I didn't bother parking in my garage. I could feel Peter close behind me as I unlocked the front door.

When I closed it behind us, he pinned me to it, hands on my hips, holding me in place as he crushed his mouth to mine again. Peter's breath

Something Resembling Love

was harsh in my ear as one hand continued to hold me and the other pushed under my sweater, finding my bra, pulling the cup down until he could tug on my nipple. Under his hand, I arched, seeking both release and more at the same time.

"Up—upstairs," I said through my hitching breath.

Peter ignored me to push my sweater up, over my head, arms pulling out of the sleeves, turning them inside out. His mouth was on my peaked nipple again before the sweater landed on the corner of the couch.

"You're so beautiful," he said, face still pressed between my breasts. And then the hand on my hip grabbed my hand and pulled me away from the door and up the stairs.

The bedroom was completely dark, and I fumbled for the button on his jeans, pushing his grey shirt out of the way as well.

"Peter," I whispered, as I felt his chest against mine.

Then his fingers were undoing my bra, and he was turning me, backing me against the bed. I lost my balance and fell onto the smooth, cool bedspread. While my body warmed the fabric beneath my back, Peter finished undoing my pants and pulled them off. I could barely see him in the dark, but I felt the tickle of the hairs on his legs as he stepped between my thighs. I shivered.

He must have been able to see me because he asked, "Are you cold?"

Yes. No. "I don't know."

"I read about that too. How the changes to your circulation can make you cold."

One finger traced up the inside of a thigh, leaving goose bumps in its wake. When the motion stopped, his finger was resting against the lace of my panties, pressing the scratch ever so slightly against me. I let out a shaky breath until Peter's hand moved, taking the clothing with it.

Then his finger was back, touching, pushing, sliding, probing.

"I missed you," he said again.

The next thing I felt was the weight of his body on mine, his erection nudging against me. He paused. "You still have an IUD, right?"

"Mm-hmm." The sound came out desperate and needy, and then he pushed into me. It felt ... nice?

I had missed his enthusiasm, but the moment felt rushed.

"Shit," he said, the sound harsh through gritted teeth. His hand came back to my breast, squeezing in time with every thrust.

"Pe—peter." The air whooshed from my lungs as he thrust once more and pushed as deeply as he could go.

"Jaaaa—ahhhhh."

For a long moment we lay like that, my head not quite on a pillow, Peter flopped on top of me, panting, until he dropped his hip sideways and shifted to lay next to me.

In the darkness of my room, I breathed quietly, feeling every place on my body where Peter had touched me, every word he had said, and a small space of longing still left.

"Sorry, I was—I missed you." Peter rolled to his side.

I flicked on the bedside lamp we'd neglected to turn on in our rush, and looked at him, his eyes on mine.

"It's fine." He had just been in a hurry, I decided. Next time would be more satisfying.

"Jane." Peter's eyes dropped, searching out my hand to hold between us. "I'm sorry. That I didn't listen. Didn't hear what you were saying. You have every reason to think I'm a total jerk and decide you don't want to be with me. But I … I hope you don't," he finished, eyes still on our joined hands.

"What made you decide you were okay with not having kids?"

"Bits and pieces. I talked to Chris. I read the papers. I thought about why you don't, can't, have them and don't want to adopt. But mostly, I thought about what my life would be like without you. We wouldn't need kids to be a family."

Peter's gaze flicked to mine, and I gave him a small smile as I looked at where he held my hand.

"Okay then."

"Okay, like … okay, we're back together?" The hopefulness in Peter's voice was endearing.

"Yes."

He lurched across the space of bed between us and pulled me to himself as he kissed me again. "I missed you. I'm sorry, and I—" His words ended when our lips met, his arm around my waist. "Can we celebrate?" he asked the second he pulled back.

"Yes!" I reached between us to find him fully ready to party.

In the morning Peter woke me again, earlier than he ever had, no words needed to translate the question he was asking.

I was humming when I walked into work. Rodriguez winked at me across the lab bench. "Seems like you're having a good start to November."

I didn't pretend to not know what he was talking about. "I am," I grinned.

"Are you going to be ready for both a weeklong expedition to the desert and to be a star presenter at the conference?"

"Desert, yes. Speech ..." I tipped my hand back and forth. "I'm devoting every waking moment to it though."

"Not *every* waking moment," he said, and winked again.

"What would your wife say if she knew you were harassing me like this?"

"Ah," he scoffed. "She knows you're way out of my league." His hand went to his chest, where I knew he wore his wedding ring on a chain during lab days.

My laugh came out as a startled breath. "Smart woman."

Rodriguez's smile was huge. "Seriously, though. Are you ready?"

I shook my head as I sat back. "Not really. Aziz said just present what I have so far, but that doesn't seem like enough. I need to review the first results and probably run two more sets of analysis to get enough data."

"However I can help, I am here. Even if it means staying late."

"Don't flirt with me like that, Rodriguez. I might take it to heart." It was my turn to wink at him. His cheeks took on a gratifying flush.

I took a moment to adjust the microphone and look out at the audience. There were far more people than I'd expected. My mind was calm in one area and whirring in another. I'd been back from Italy for barely two months. It had been less than three weeks since Aziz had walked into my office, in essence demanding I make this speech.

I could have said no, I supposed. Refused to talk about what I had felt was scant data. But I'd had a bare-bones outline, and I'd always wanted to speak at the annual USDA industry conference.

Now here I was, under the glare of the spotlights in the convention center.

"I cannot claim all the credit for what Director Thompson has just said about me. I could not have collected all this data without the help of my distinguished colleagues," I said, naming them, "or without a few million cows." The audience laughed.

"For centuries, humans have used the droppings of the animals they encounter to assist in the growing of crops. But for the last hundred years, cows have played a particularly important role ..."

At happy hour that evening, crowded into a ballroom, I received hundreds of thanks and congratulations. Thompson sought me out as well. "Jane, I don't have to tell you how pleased I am with your research. And your speech was excellent. Not our usual scientific lecture," he chuckled. "I'd like you to meet Mr. Hamer, the Secretary of Agriculture. James, please meet our bright new star."

"Jane, it's nice to meet you in person."

The Secretary of Agriculture had seen my talk? "Secretary." I pulled my professional self together and nodded at him, like we ran into each other routinely.

He continued, gesturing to a shorter, stocky man standing next to him. "And may I also introduce my counterpart at the Italian Ministry of Agriculture, Food, and Forestry, Vincenzo Gonzaga?"

I shifted my gaze to the man who was wearing a suit cut differently than everyone else's.

Gonzaga offered his plump hand to shake. "Your director told me you did a good deed for our colleagues in Florence."

"Minister, it's a pleasure to meet you. Yes, I met Pietro Tonelli earlier this fall. I was already in Florence after having spent a week hiking in the Apuan Alps. It was an enlightening experience, and I learned more than I ever thought I'd need to know about chestnut trees."

The Italian minister chuckled.

"The forests are so diverse, so untouched. Still, I managed to refrain from bringing back any of the soil to look at in our labs here! I don't know that my thoughts were all that helpful, but I enjoyed the opportunity to share what I could."

"Pietro said you were generous with your time. He would like to have you back, perhaps even go out into the forests together," Gonzaga said.

Something Resembling Love

"I would have enjoyed doing so. I'm sure Pietro and I could share many stories and scientific thoughts!"

When I got home three days later, I was still glowing. At the end of the week, Alicia and I met Lauren and followed her from store to store, examining every piece of footwear she could find, for nearly two hours.

"I don't understand how you can already be shopping for shoes. You don't have a dress!" Alicia said later, as we sat down under the same twining vines of the tapas bar Lauren had taken me to the year before.

"It took so much longer than I anticipated!" Lauren said.

"It took about as long as I expected." Alicia's voice was dry.

"That's awful!" I scolded.

"What, she always takes forever shopping." Alicia waved an arm at the bags next to us. "And these are her wedding shoes. I didn't say it was bad, just that I wasn't surprised."

"She has a point, Lor," I said with a wry smile. "Maybe we should ask for compensation." I gave the shopping bags side eye.

"Like what?" Alicia asked, leaning forward.

"Like we should be bridesmaids, or something."

"We don't even know when the wedding is. Maybe you'll be in the midst of another lab cleaning bleach-fest, like you were while Peter was in Germany, and won't be able to walk down the aisle straight."

"Oh! Peter and I got back together!"

"See. I told you you were the science babe!"

"Hello, details!" Lauren chided.

I took a breath and filled them in on the conversation Peter and I had had. Excitement coursed through me as I shared the exchange of *I love you*s and I couldn't help the smile that was so big it hurt my face.

"That's almost as exciting as Lauren finding the shoes for her wedding." Alicia looked at her pointedly. "For which there still isn't a date."

"We have a date!" Lauren interrupted.

"And thank God for a place for these shoes," Alicia deadpanned.

I snorted, still smiling. "You sound like you might be jealous."

"I don't blame her," Lauren said. "My momma always said, 'shoes are the foundation of every outfit'."

"And there's the Oklahomey drawl," Alicia laughed.

Lauren laughed too, shaking her head. "You're two of the best ladies I could imagine being friends with. You are so dear to me." She started to tear up, and waved a hand in front of her eyes, as if that would stem the tears. "Will you be bridesmaids for me? October sixth."

"Hm ..." Alicia said, tapping a finger to the table. "I don't have my calendar with me, but I think I might already have something on that day."

"Alicia!" I scolded and turned to Lauren. "Of course, we will."

"I don't know," she said. "We only got a glass of wine after traipsing all over for those damn shoes." She tossed back the rest of her Prosecco, Rebel Wilson style.

"Of course we will," I repeated, glaring at Alicia. She shrugged, throwing up her hands in acquiescence.

Lauren beamed at us, eyes shining. She sniffed back her emotion. "Okay, so the reception will be at the new hotel, The Langham. It's lots of white and grey, so the colors don't have to compete." Lauren gazed past us, her eyes seeing something we didn't. "The ballroom has a honeyed parquet dance floor with a full view of the river from floor-to-ceiling windows on three sides."

"She's in realtor mode again," Alicia stage-whispered to me.

"I thought it would be too expensive," Lauren said as if she hadn't heard me. "But you know Chris." She refocused on us and beamed.

PETER

From the Day of the Dead party to Thanksgiving, November flew past. On the mornings I woke up in Jane's bed, I lay there for a minute, even if she was already up, smiling to myself. I had almost lost all of this. Warmth and comfort and sex. I thought the same thing when she was at my place, but with less emphasis on the comfort part.

When Chris asked if we were coming to Friendsgiving, I said yes, with no hesitation, and felt less like a grad student fighting my way through life. As Jane and I sat across from each other at dinner and played footsie under the table, it seemed like I had finally reached adult status. A serious girlfriend, who had set up a makeshift office for me in her spare room; friends who had careers of their own. Even if my findings were still slow, I was doing it.

I watched her lean to the side to talk with Sebastian, the kid's face lighting up as he described a school project. Jane followed him out of the room after he asked to show her something. They came back a few minutes later, Sebastian holding a large page with an intricate pencil drawing.

"You guys have got to see what Sebastian did this semester!"

He wrapped an arm around her and beamed.

"Hey, how's it going up there?" she asked the next morning, when I wandered downstairs.

I'd been checking a few calculations. "I made some adjustments, so we'll see how those go. It'll probably take most of the day to run."

"Wanna hang out on the couch in the meantime? I lit the fire."

I shivered involuntarily as another gust slammed pellets of ice against the kitchen window. "That sounds great!"

We settled comfortably into opposite ends of the couch, facing each other, Jane with her legs crossed under her, me with one foot on the floor.

"I think Sebastian has a crush on you." I nudged her with my foot.

"Nah. He's just a teenager who's happy to be noticed."

"By the girl he has a crush on."

"You sound jealous," she said, a teasing note in her voice. "Do you have a crush on me too?"

"I do," I said, voice serious. "Did you know, it's been a year since we first met?"

I could see by her smile that she was pleased I had remembered. "I did," she grinned. "It makes me happy."

"It does?"

"I love being with you, Peter. You make me happy."

My eyebrows raised involuntarily. "I'm still always surprised to wake up next to you. It makes me happy, too."

"There's no one else I'd rather share my fire with."

"It's really nice in here, with it lit," I commented. "I didn't even know the fireplace worked."

"It's one of my favorite things about this house."

"It's nice. Cozy. Makes me think about what it would be like to …" I hesitated, not sure how far I wanted to go. "Be together all the time."

There was a moment before Jane said, "And?" with a slight lift to her eyebrows.

I sighed, sinking back against the arm of the couch. I thought of my best friend, and his extremely well-received paper, having finished his postdoc and gone straight into a position in industry to lead a lab at a biotech firm. "With Chris gone ... I still have a lot to do on this research, plus my boss isn't helping matters by telling me to do it differently."

"Have you thought about doing it the way he's suggesting?"

"But it doesn't make any sense!" I swept my hand through the air. "Doing it his way means abandoning everything I've done up to this point and essentially starting from scratch. I've already been at this for three and a half years! I don't want to still be working on the same thing in another year and a half." My hand fell back to the couch, defeated by the possibility.

"I totally get that. But Peter, he's been doing this for decades now, what if he's right?" She sat forward, clutching her coffee to her chest. "What if you need a fresh perspective on the problem? Or, what if by trying it his way, you make some other discovery that gives you the answer? Sometimes breakthroughs come when you step outside the box. When I've had a big problem, if I've stepped away from it and come back at it from a different angle, I could see the pieces differently."

"That doesn't make any sense." I shook my head.

"It doesn't have to," she said earnestly. "It just needs to work. I'm not saying it would solve all the blocks. But it can't hurt."

"You don't understand, though, how this kind of research works," I insisted.

Jane jerked back against the arm of the couch. "You're right, I don't," she said after a minute.

"Sorry." That had been a stupid thing to say. "I'm just frustrated."

"I know. And not to make it worse, but don't you think that all upgrades in understanding come because we changed the way we did things? You can't get to a new place by doing the same things you did to get to the old place."

I turned to look at the fire, a cheerful soundtrack to the good coffee in my hand. There wasn't a table turned desk across the room, littered with journals and notebooks, making me feel guilty for relaxing. "I don't want to go back to the lab on Monday."

"Can I suggest that part of the problem might be that you're working too hard? If it feels so good to not work, maybe it's because you're burnt out."

"Now you sound like Chris," I grumbled. I sat watching the fire leap and sway for a moment, thinking that I was doing something very Chris-like, enjoying this time. Maybe he was on to something. "You know, in high school, I read all the time. Like, real books, not journals or textbooks. And I played the saxophone in the marching band. I guess I could do that again. I still have my saxophone."

"I'll bet you made an especially handsome band geek." Jane set her mug down and scooted across the couch to kiss me.

"You're wonderful," I told her.

"You're pretty all right too." Her breath brushed over my ear, reassuring me that she was close.

I pulled back and ran my eyes over her face. "I love being with you. You make me feel like a whole person," I said.

"You are a whole person," she said quietly.

I wanted to lean into her hand as she brushed her fingertips across my temple. "It doesn't always feel like that."

"You are invested in your work," she kissed one cheek, "driven," the other cheek, "smart," forehead, "fabulous," one temple, "fun in bed," she whispered, kissing a cheekbone, and "handsome." She kissed my mouth, warm and tender.

"Darling Jane."

"Hello, Peter!" Mom practically sang when she answered my call the next afternoon.

"Hey, Mom."

"Peter, you sound tired. Are you getting enough sleep? Of course not, never mind." I could see her brushing away the statement, as if she knew and was already disappointed in my answer.

Internally, I sighed. Even if she was right, I didn't want to be nagged by another person, and certainly not my mom, who always thought she knew what was best.

"How was the church bazaar?" I redirected her.

"Oh, it was very successful. We raised over ten thousand dollars for the food bank."

"That's great, Mom!"

"How's Jane?"

"Fine." She was up to something. Usually, she'd rattle on and on before asking anything personal. I hadn't told my parents about our break.

"Your father and I liked her very much when we met her over the summer."

"I could tell." By how my mom had put her arm around Jane, the way my dad had looked after Jane had spent an hour talking seriously with him about his birdwatching.

"It's so sad she doesn't have any family." After a slight pause, she rushed on with enthusiasm. "Why don't you both come home for Christmas!"

I hadn't come home for holidays since I'd started my postdoc. "Mom," I stated flatly.

"You haven't been here in years for the big family get-together. I'm hosting this year. You don't have any plans, right?"

She was right, I didn't. Jane and I hadn't talked about it at all, and I didn't know what she usually did for Christmas anyway, since she didn't, as mom had pointed out, have any family. I wondered if she spent Christmas with Lauren.

I didn't want to spend more than two days with my parents. But I also knew my mom was right—it had been years. I liked it like that. I already knew Jane would say yes if I asked her. "I'll think about it."

"All right, but don't take too long to decide. Here's your dad …"

I tried to call home when I thought my dad might not be there, but that wasn't possible during Thanksgiving weekend.

"Peter."

"Dad."

There was an awkward silence as we both scrambled for something to say.

"Your mom is eager for a visit."

"I told her I'd think about it. Did she mention that she'd like me to bring Jane home?"

"Yes, and I think it's a wonderful idea. She's singing while fixing dinner. I haven't heard that in a long time!"

"Mom sings?" I asked, incredulous. I'd heard her sing Christmas carols and the wrong words to songs on the radio, but that wasn't actual singing.

"Songs from the sixties mostly. She loves Carole King."

"Huh." I tried to picture my mom standing at the stove, belting out "I Feel The Earth Move." The image didn't fit with the apron-wearing woman I'd known all my life. Then again, Dad had a photo on his dresser of the two of them in college, bell bottoms overwhelming my mom's slight frame, both of them with long hair, and Dad with the mustache he hadn't had since I was little. "I'll ask Jane if she's interested."

"It would be nice to have her here. She's not like your other girlfriends," Dad observed.

Yeah, all those other girlfriends I'd had. I made a non-committal noise.

"I'm just saying that we like her. That's not a bad thing, is it?"

"No, I suppose not," I admitted grudgingly.

"All right. We'll talk to you again soon."

"Mom and Dad would like you to come home with me for Christmas," I said without preamble when I came downstairs.

"Whaaa?" Jane paused in the process of draping a glittering pine garland artfully across the mantle and looked over her shoulder. "Like for the weekend?"

"The whole thing of it, sister included."

"I don't know what to say."

"Just say yes. I don't want to go without you, and if I don't come home again this year, they'll be hurt." When she kept gaping, I continued. "We'd have to leave the weekend before though, because my mom will want us there to go pick out the tree. It's only about a six-hour drive to Owensboro. Stay the weekend. We could drive back the following Saturday. I don't see any way for us to leave the day after Christmas."

"You make it sound like a prison sentence." She was still holding the garland in place.

Something Resembling Love

I shrugged and came to help her with the fake evergreen. "Dad is always trying to tell me how to do things. Mom meddling with my life."

"Do you want me to go?"

"I just said I don't want to go without you. Please come with me."

Jane finished arranging the fake pine boughs and then turned to me. "I'd love to. It would be nice to be around family for a change. Maybe I'm ready."

We packed Jane's car while there was snow on the ground and clinging to the trees, making it look like Christmas. As we drove south, the snow faded, but the grey skies followed us to my parents'.

My mom rushed out of the house as we arrived. "Jane!" she drawled, coming to embrace us. "It's so good to see you!"

Jane hugged her back as if they had known each other for years. "Thank you for inviting me, Margaret. I haven't had a real family Christmas in a long time."

"Jane, thank you for being the excuse we could use to get Peter down here." My dad hugged her too and then took her suitcase.

"Where am I going to sleep?" Jane whispered, as we followed my parents through the house.

"In my room."

"Where are *you* going to sleep?" she asked, wide-eyed.

"Probably on the pull-out couch in the basement." I watched my mom walk up the stairs and pause at the linen closet to get an extra set of towels. "Sorry, I know they can be a bit much."

Jane had a small smile on her face as she tipped her head toward me and quietly said, "They are wonderful; they remind me of my parents."

My sister came in later, stomping snow from her boots, her hair, dyed a festive blue, spilling out of a beanie. She dropped her bags and bounded over to hug Jane. "Peter has told me so much about you!"

"He has!?" Jane asked, pulling back in surprise.

"No, not really. But he's talked about you some and I pull what details I can out of him. You know, threatening to spill his deepest darkest secrets."

Jane glanced at me, then leaned toward Catherine to ask in a stage whisper, "Will you share anyway?"

I was doomed. We'd see what Christmas looked like when there was a house full of aunts, uncles, and cousins and second cousins—most of whom were under seven.

After dinner, Mom claimed tiredness and an early start to the following day. Jane headed for bed not long after, and I was left at the table with Dad, with only my sister for protection.

"She's a nice girl," he commented.

"Jane is many things, Dad," Catherine said as she poured herself more bourbon, "but a girl she is not." Her eyes cut to me as she set the bottle back on the table. "How do you keep your hands off her?"

"With my well-cultivated self-restraint." I glared at my sister.

"Ah yes, Peter, the poster child of self-deprivation."

"Catherine ..." my dad warned. "How's work going?"

I would rather have detailed my sexual exploits with Jane than talked about my research with my dad, so I didn't say anything. My dad took the opportunity to give me more advice. "Have you tried to write the code the way I suggested? Now I know you don't want to listen to your old man," he continued as I took a breath to object. "But I have some experience with this."

"Dad, you learned to code in the sixties. With COBOL. Now there are a dozen languages to choose from, and none of them can be used to program until I know what to program *for*."

"There's a simplicity in COBOL that the newer languages don't have. You'd be surprised how effective it still is."

"How 'bout them Bengals!" Catherine said. "They're playing tomorrow, right? I've got five bucks that says they lose in the first quarter." She slapped a bill on the table.

An hour later, when I could extricate myself without looking like I was avoiding the problem known as my dad, I stuck my head in the door of my room. Jane had fallen asleep sitting up, the book she was reading face down in her lap.

I took it from her hands to put it on the nightstand, but she woke. "What time'sit?"

"About eleven. Go back to sleep, babe." I kissed her on the forehead.

The next morning, all five of us picked out a Christmas tree at a live farm we hadn't been to since I'd left for college. Mom insisted on baking, and she and Jane spent the middle of the day making peanut brittle and rolling out and decorating sugar cookies.

In the evening, we put the final decorations on the glowing tree. Catherine and I had been tasked with making the popcorn garland. On the other side of the area rug, Jane was helping my parents string cranberries.

"All they do is fawn over her," I said to Catherine as we sat in the corner, eating more popcorn than we were stringing.

She stopped stringing popcorn and looked at me. "Is that bad?"

"No. Yes. I don't know."

"They just want you to be happy, Peter. I know you've been chafing, but look at Jane. She looks so relaxed. Maybe you've forgotten that she hasn't had family to be with in years."

"Of course I haven't forgotten!" Then I lowered my voice. "But I don't know how I feel about it."

"You love her; why wouldn't you want her to be part of our family?" She looked at me expectantly.

"I can see Mom and Dad inviting us to visit all the time. And Jane wanting to come. For that very reason." I shoved several pieces of popcorn in my mouth and mumbled around them. "She's just so ..."

"So what, Peter?"

"So perfect."

"So perfect that she appears to love you even though you're entrenched in your way of doing things and won't listen to suggestions. So perfect that she challenges your view of how things are supposed to look. So perfect she lost her parents and has had to live life alone. So perfect she's got a serious health condition. So perfect that our parents like her a lot. So perfect that she's exactly what you've always said you wanted," Catherine scoffed. "Sounds like you've got a real coyote there."

"I haven't said anything about what I want."

"You don't have to say anything out loud for me to know. I'm your sister."

"Younger."

"Smarter."

"You have blue hair."

"So?" She stared me down. "Look, you love her, she loves you."

"Maybe I don't want to share."

Catherine rolled her eyes. "I think there's something you're not telling yourself. Or maybe it's something you're not telling Jane ..." She waited for me to reply. When I didn't, she let out a disappointed breath. "Whatever it is, you need to figure it out and start acting like an adult."

She got up to join the other three, leaving me stewing by myself.

JANE

I woke to the smell of fresh coffee, and stretched. Peter's childhood bed was surprisingly comfortable, and the blue checked bedspread made me wonder what he had been like in high school.

There was no snow in Owensboro, but the chilly grey skies made it feel seasonal. Margaret set a cup on the counter for me as I walked into the kitchen, and waved me to follow her into the living room, where the tree had sprouted a mountain of presents overnight.

I'd carefully selected a few small things that I thought might appeal to Peter's parents and taken my best stab at what Catherine might like based on Peter's minimal guidance.

As we sat around the tree, I watched Peter and his family together. The double helix key chain Catherine gave her brother and William's broad smile when he opened the mosaic coaster I'd chosen.

I unwrapped a gorgeous, chunky, hand-knit sweater in a bright red.

"For when you get cold," Margaret said.

I pulled it on immediately, the cable pattern soft against my skin.

After we finished unwrapping presents, I followed Margaret to the kitchen, while William and Peter stayed behind to clean up the mess of wrapping paper.

"What can I do to help?" I asked, as she set a ten-pound bag of potatoes on the counter.

"Nothing; you're our guest." Her brown eyes sparkled, bird-like, as she watched me.

"I can't not do anything. I'll be bored."

"You will be many things today, Jane," Margaret said, raising her eyebrows at me over the pile of potatoes. "But bored is not one of them. Still, I won't pass up help." I saw her shoot a look at Catherine and Peter as he sat down at the kitchen table next to her.

"I can do just about anything, but I'd really like to make the pies, if you'd let me. My mom and I always did that together." I glanced down at the counter in front of where I stood, somehow missing my own parents even more now.

"Isn't that lovely. Of course, if that's what you'd like to do." Margaret's always present but slight southern accent grew stronger for a moment, and she shoved a can of Crisco toward me.

Margaret had been right when she said I would not be bored. I made eight pies, two each of pumpkin, apple, pecan, and sweet potato. I peeled potatoes and made gravy. Peter and I set the table.

While the turkey roasted, Peter and I chased young boys around in the yard, waving sticks as swords. Little girls tugged on my pants, wanting to show off their princess tiaras or dolls. I saw Peter eye the babies needing to be held, a mixture of expressions on his face, hesitant and excited. For a while, he held his youngest relative, a month-old little girl, who slept peacefully in his arms. I talked with aunts, fourth cousins, and uncles—a houseful of people whose names I would never remember.

"I think Mom invited the entire family when you agreed to come for Christmas," Peter commented, following me to the bedroom that evening.

"Oof! I am so full. And so tired!" I fell back into bed. Peter sat down next to me, both of us leaning against the headboard. "There were so many kids! And they never slowed down! You seemed to enjoy yourself, though."

"They're my cousins. And I like kids."

I felt the weight of his eyes on me, and then it lightened. Maybe I was making more out of it than he had meant. "They seemed to like you more than me."

"Kids think I'm one of them."

"You'd make a great mom."

I rolled my eyes at him. "Not in a million years. Now go away, you're interfering with my beauty sleep."

"Nothing could diminish your beauty." Peter kissed me, and I felt his longing.

I kissed him back. "Now go away before your parents see and have heart attacks that their son isn't as pure as they believe!"

"Maybe I'm willing to risk it."

"I'm not! I like your parents way too much."

"Ugh." Peter banged his head against the headboard. "Mom keeps dropping not-too-subtle hints about you and me, and all my dad wants to talk about is my time in the lab. He has so many *suggestions*. It's like he thinks he's been coding for thirty years."

"Well, hasn't he?"

He rolled his head to the side, looking at me out of the corner of his eye, still propped against the head of the bed. "Peter," I said, propping myself up on my elbow to look at him, "Your parents only want what's best for you. Maybe they don't know how to show that. But they really are just trying to help. Do you think you could listen to them not as people trying to tell you what to do, but as people who are trying to help you out from their experiences?"

Peter heaved a sigh. "Catherine's the one with the blue hair."

"Catherine," I said carefully, "doesn't walk away from the conversation."

"I don't, either. I've listened to both of them all week!"

"Can I just make an observation?" I reached for his hand. "I know you think because you're not physically walking away, that you're listening. But watch Catherine. She says thank you if they offer her some advice. I'll bet she doesn't take most of it, but she acts like she's going to take it into serious consideration. And she hugs both your parents often."

"She's a girl."

I rolled my eyes. "So am I, and I haven't hugged them since we got here. It's a measure of how much she appreciates and respects them."

Peter looked at me like he had no idea what I was saying. "I respect them, too."

"As far as it goes. But Catherine respects their opinions, she doesn't scorn them."

Peter looked at me, eyes wide in disbelief. "You think I'm being a jerk?"

"I just think you could be a little more open. I get it's hard to take advice from parents. No one really likes to hear it, because it always makes us feel like we're doing something wrong."

He looked away and up at the ceiling, and I could tell he was stewing. "I'll bet you were great at it."

"Peter, I was a teenager when they died. I was horrible."

"It seems like my dad thinks I'm an idiot. And my mom thinks I don't have a social life."

I raised an eyebrow in disbelief.

"Maybe not an idiot." He kept looking at the ceiling. "It just feels like he wants to tell me what to do. It feels so much like they are meddling."

I thought about the fights I'd had with my parents as I'd grown up, sure I knew everything. "Maybe it's because you resist it so hard. If you answered his questions instead of trying to evade them, it might feel better because he wouldn't have to work so hard to get your attention."

He heaved a sigh. "I suppose that makes sense."

"Your parents are wonderful people, and they love you."

"They love you, too."

I closed my eyes against the sharp slice of grief. It would probably never go away.

"I'm sorry your parents are gone, Jane."

"I am too." A single hot tear ran down my cheek. "It was really nice of your parents to include me."

Peter put his arm around my shoulder and pulled me close against his chest.

"I saw the way those kids climbed all over you the other day." Margaret gave me a knowing look over the cranberry sauce during dinner on our last night. "And you so patient with them. That's a skill you have. I hope you're planning to use it," she commented as she passed the bowl to Catherine.

"My friends' kids seem to like me all right."

"That's not what I meant, and you know it." Margaret smiled.

"Mom, what are you doing?" Peter nearly growled.

Something Resembling Love

"Merely pointing out the obvious, that Jane would make a wonderful mother." There was a quick glance between the two of us before she said, "I mean it, honey." The glance returned to Peter and turned meaningful.

"I'm afraid I won't be having children, Margaret." It was sweet, even if she had caught me off guard. "My vascular condition would make pregnancy very dangerous."

"There are plenty of ways to be a mother." She sounded just like Peter.

"I made a choice a number of years ago, when I was first diagnosed, that I wasn't going to have children. Of any kind. I never know when I'm going to need another surgery or what it will be like—I'm sure Peter told you how difficult the one I had in July was. Besides, I'm not very maternal." I was desperate to remain polite, but I was on a knife's edge between tears and anger. I did not want to be having this conversation.

"It's not so hard when you have a kind and caring husband." Margaret smiled at William while I groped for Peter's hand under the table. After a moment, I found his knee and his hand rested on mine.

"I'm only making an observation."

My fork made a sharp metal clang against the wood of the dining room table, and both of Peter's parents looked up. Catherine's head turned, looking back and forth between her parents and me. "I don't mean to be rude, but I am firm in my decision not to have children. It's a perfectly valid choice for me to make, my health condition aside. I do not want to adopt, and I don't want to run the risk of leaving a child without a mother just because I felt I should have a traditional family with two point five kids."

"It's just that—"

"Please let me finish. I know you think I'd be a great mom because of whatever cute interactions you saw me have over Christmas dinner. But that was six hours out of an entire life. I can like kids and still not want to be a mom. I can want to spend time with them and not need any of my own. And while I get that you and William would really like grandkids, it is not my responsibility to fulfill that wish for you."

When I finished, William was blinking at me, and Margaret's mouth was open. Under the table, Peter squeezed my hand.

"I ..." Margaret trailed.

They were never going to invite me back. Which was a shame, because I really *had* had fun with all the kids, and the week had been my nicest Christmas in a long time.

But across the table, Catherine was grinning at me. "Mom, is there any pie left?" she asked. Her hand popped to the front of her chest, giving me a supportive thumbs-up.

After a moment we all picked up our silverware.

"So, how about them Bengals?" Peter asked.

I buried my smile, looking at my plate, as Catherine snorted her laughter.

In the morning, William came to Peter's room for my suitcase as I pulled my new sweater on. I took a breath, but he beat me to it.

"She can get a little carried away when she gets excited. It's what made her good at keeping her students engaged. But sometimes she forgets that not everyone needs to be parented. Least of all you, on your own for so long."

I looked at him for a long moment, seeing so much of Peter in his face.

"Of course, now she likes you even more," William said blandly as he bent to pick up my suitcase, making me laugh. I followed him down the stairs.

As William and Peter packed the car, Margaret cornered me, taking my hands in hers.

"Jane, I'm so sorry about what I said last night. I shouldn't have pushed at you like that. It's just that you're so ... well, everything we had hoped for, for Peter. And then watching you with all the kids ... But of course, your reasons and decision are your own. And are totally valid." She hugged me tightly.

"Thank you." Tears pricked behind my eyes. More than anything, I'd missed this feeling of family.

William hugged me too. "Have a safe drive back. Bring him home more often."

We each waved out the windows as Peter drove down the driveway.

"I'm sorry about my mom, she was out of bounds pushing you last night," Peter said as he merged onto the interstate. "They're both, but her in particular, ready for grandkids. And neither Catherine nor I are close to giving them to her."

"She apologized to me before we left this morning. It's fine, she just got carried away. But I think she thinks you should marry me." I was only half-teasing.

"She's right, though," Peter continued, ignoring my comment about marriage. "You would make a great mom. And she's also right that you don't have to give birth to be a mom. Look at how you take care of your friends. And Otis!"

"Did you really just compare having a human child to taking care of a cat?" I laughed.

"I think Otis might think he's human." He glanced at me, grinning, and looked back at the road.

"Thanks for being there."

"I would have said something, but you didn't really need me."

I rolled my eyes at myself. "It's a talk I'm used to giving. But I do need you. Even if it's just holding my hand."

He reached over and squeezed my knee before focusing on the road again. I looked out the window and smiled to myself. It had been a long time since I was sorry that Christmas was over.

PETER

The Monday morning after Christmas, I went around the lab, checking the cooler temperatures, booting my computer, and pulling up the logs of algorithms. I had never been away from the lab this long for something that wasn't a conference. But all seemed to be in order.

I checked my email and saw I had a message from Fritz, saying Merry Christmas and Happy New Year. In it, he reiterated his offer for me to come work for Roche.

"Come to Switzerland," Fritz had been saying nearly every time we'd talked since last spring.

The offer was tempting. A large salary, virtually unlimited funds. There was so little time left on my funding. And when it ran out?

I shook my head. My life was here. Jane was here. I picked up the ball Chris used to toss at the wall while he'd been thinking and turned it around in my hand. I wished he was still in the lab with me. He'd probably tell me to take the offer, and he'd have some solution about Jane and her career.

I lobbed the ball myself and found the repeated action oddly soothing, letting my brain wander to ponder the past week, even the time since Thanksgiving.

On our last night, after that terrible conversation with my mother, I had kissed Jane good night and walked through the living room to see my parents

Something Resembling Love

snuggled next to each other on the loveseat. In the glow from the colored lights on the tree, they had been drinking bourbon and talking quietly. I'd stopped at the edge of the room, feeling like I was intruding, but caught. Seeing them alone made Jane's comments replay in my head. Usually, all I could see was my *parents*, but for this tiny moment, they were just another couple.

Catherine had attached herself to Jane over the course of the week until any stranger might think Catherine was Jane's sister, rather than mine. I'd watched Jane teach my mom how to make the pie crust the way she had. Or looked out the window to see my dad showing Jane how to chop wood.

I kept coming back to that image of my parents in the colorful glow of the Christmas tree, struck by how together they looked. Flashes of Jane waving a stick, chasing two of my young cousins across the crunchy leaves, and then running back toward me as they chased her, played in my mind.

On the lab tabletop next to me, my phone dinged. It was Chris.

> Don't forget about NYE!!! 😘
> 😘 😘 😘 😘 😘 😘
> 😘 😘 😘 😘 😘 😘

I chuckled and texted Jane.

> Chris would like us to not forget we are going out for New Year's.

> I know! And you can kiss me whenever you like instead of being surprised when I kiss you! 🍃

I emailed Fritz back and wished him a happy new year as well, ignoring his offer, and returned to the sequencing at hand.

This year, I did not arrive to dinner by myself. Jane came with me, rather than Chris and Lauren, but I still offered her my hand when we got out of the car. I didn't feel as out of place in my rented tux or standing next to her. Under her coat she wore a strapless red dress that curved over her breasts and dipped between them, offering me a tantalizing view of what I would get to see later.

She grinned when, in the lobby, I pushed her coat off her shoulders, my hand brushing over her breast as I did so, and I smiled back, enjoying the moment—that she was mine this year, and I didn't have to watch her from afar.

Chris' same friend was hosting the same party in The Signature Lounge, and as we rode the elevator, I rested against the back wall, pulling Jane against my chest. I didn't feel awkward when I put my arms around her waist, feeling the slip of the red fabric and the roundness of her hip under my hand. She leaned into me and dropped her head back on my shoulder. I kissed her on the cheek.

"Hey. No making out in the elevator," Chris said.

I pretended to glare at him while Jane looked back and forth between us and laughed. "Are you jealous, Chris? Is Lauren not giving you enough love?" Jane turned in my arms to face me and kissed me like we were alone.

"Ow-owww! Peter!" Alicia called.

I wanted to be embarrassed, but around my friends, I couldn't be. Instead, I grabbed Jane's ass and pulled her closer.

Then the doors opened, and the sound of the bass filled the space as we filed out and headed for the bar.

As soon as we entered the room, Chris grabbed someone and pulled him over into a back-slapping hug. "Stewart! These are my friends," he said, naming us all. "And, of course, you know Lauren."

"Glad everyone could make it. A friend of Chris' is a friend of mine. Enjoy the evening!" he said with a quick bow of his head.

At every turn, I thought about this same room a year ago. I could still feel the stone I'd had in my stomach as I'd watched Jane talk to Fritz, the way she'd casually set her hand on his arm. As my friends and I danced away the last few hours of the year, I remembered the way Chris had had to drag me away from the wall to come dance the last ten minutes.

Something Resembling Love

"What are you smiling about?" Jane asked, her mouth close to my ear in the loud room.

"Last year. Chris forcing me to join you guys. You. Being excited you kissed me."

"I'm still excited to kiss you." She stepped closer, no longer dancing, her arms around my neck as we swayed.

"Me too," I said and moved to brush a kiss over her cheek.

Just like the last time, in this same place, she turned her head and kissed me fully. This time, I laughed against her mouth and tightened my arms around her.

When the DJ quieted the music and announced we were getting close to midnight, we stepped apart to stand side-by-side, but I didn't let go of Jane's hand.

I took a flute off a tray that passed by and handed one to Jane, then took one for myself. We tapped our glasses together. As the one-minute countdown began, I looked at her. This beautiful woman who had given me a second chance.

Moments from our time together over the last year popped into my head. Her clapping when I'd showed up in the circle of our friends here, last year. The way she had called me out on the not-kiss after our first date. Sitting on her couch talking about work—hers and mine—and the way being on the couch had often become more than holding hands and talking.

I thought about how much my parents liked her. It was kind of nice. And I saw her as she had been, sitting on the floor in front of the Christmas tree, playing patty-cake with my youngest cousin.

As the crowd around me shouted, "Ten!" I focused on Jane's face again. She'd been bumping hips with Alicia at the beginning of the countdown, but now she stepped close to me.

I skimmed my hand up into her hair, still a short bob, feeling the silkiness run through my fingers.

"Three ... two ... ONE! Happy New Year!"

Behind me, I heard the boom of the fireworks, but I didn't turn to look. In her heels, Jane was a fraction taller than me, but it made no difference as her hand dipped under my arm and around my shoulder, pulling me to her as much as I was holding her against myself.

I didn't hear "Auld Lang Syne" finish, and only recognized we were standing still when someone smacked me on the ass.

"Has Jane really corrupted my reserved friend so much that he's ready to have sex in public?"

"Oh please." Jane rolled her eyes. "As if you and Lauren weren't doing the exact same thing. Just because you finished prematurely doesn't mean Peter needs to follow your lead."

Chris staggered back a half-step, clutching his hand to his chest. "Jane! I didn't know you had it in you."

I pulled Jane close to my side. "Mine. You have your own."

"Lauren," he said, turning his head but still looking at us.

"Yes, dear."

"Our friends are being mean to me."

Lauren smoothed her hand down the side of his face twice. "Well, it's your own fault. You made Peter come with us."

Chris fake pouted for a few seconds. "Well done, man," he said, grinning, and clapped me on the shoulder.

I shook my head at him, then watched him and Lauren fade away from us. "I guess we should drink these?"

Jane lifted her champagne glass to mine. "Happy New Year, Peter."

"Happy New Year, darling Jane."

After we drank, and I set the glasses on a passing tray as I tugged her back onto the dance floor.

All through the ride home, the bass from the music still pulsed through me, and I could feel Jane's hand run up my thigh while she sang along quietly to lyrics I didn't know. Just like they said, my hands had started to tremble, and I stared at her, the chatter of our friends fading. Her knowing, answering smile only made me want her more.

When she pushed open the door to her house, turning to glance at me, I rushed in. "I need you out of this dress. It's been driving me crazy all night," I said, fusing my lips to hers. She breathed a laugh as I slid my hands around her hips to her round ass, pulling her to me.

"I debated between wearing this dress tonight, and the white one I wore last year. Did I make a good choice?" she asked between deep kisses.

I groaned when she stopped kissing me. But she took my hand, our fingertips curling around each other's. I eagerly followed her up the stairs, my eyes glued to her butt as it moved with each step.

She glanced over her shoulder, lips parted to say something, but she smiled instead. "Oh, so that's what you like. I can accommodate that." With each remaining step, she put a little more swing into her hips.

At the top of the stairs, I stopped her, holding her in place, pulling her back against my chest. I smoothed my hands over the red satin to the front of her hips and up her torso. My fingers traced along the curved top edge of the dress, following the dip until my hands were resting lightly under her breasts.

"Peter," Jane breathed, leaning back against me. She made a plaintive sound as I stepped back.

"I need you now," I told her as I jerked the zipper down, exposing her back, "I've needed you forever."

"I need you, too."

One hand and then the other slid inside the back of the dress, skating around her rib cage until I could cup my hands under her breasts, feeling the weight of them. Gently, I squeezed her nipples. She hissed, arching into my hands.

"More," she whispered, sounding desperate.

My hands glided down her torso to her waist, turning her to face me. All evening, this was what I had been thinking about, this moment, when I could have her alone, to myself. Reveling that I could.

One hand stayed inside the edge of the dress where I had unzipped it, pinning it between us. The other I wrapped around the back of her neck, holding her against me as I kissed her, touching my tongue to hers. She squeezed my ass with one hand and everything inside of me tightened.

I tugged the dress down, helped her carefully step out of it, and came back to run my hands down her sides.

"My turn." Jane gave the bow tie a sharp tug, kissing me thoroughly while she easily unbuttoned each one of the tiny buttons I had fumbled with. It was rather erotic to be standing there, her hands inside my open shirt and tux jacket, and her in only skimpy, smooth panties. Like some scene in a movie.

"Are you ready?" she breathed in my ear. "Because I've been waiting for this all night."

The tip of her tongue ran up the edge of my ear, and my pants fell to the floor. I tripped over them in my eagerness to get Jane onto the bed.

As she fell, she pulled me with her. We paused, both panting, looking into each other's eyes, and pulling each other close. I rolled and took Jane with me, landing her straddling me.

She was the sexiest thing I'd ever seen. On the dance floor that evening it had been the same, the curve of her hips and the swell of her breasts over the top of the dress begging to be held. I indulged now, running my hands up her arms, down the front of her body, and guiding her hips as she sank lower on me.

"Mmmm ... Peter." She settled, and I felt the sensation everywhere she touched me.

"Jane, that feels so good." I raised my hips, feeling her warmth around me.

"No, wait, I just want to feel you. This is what I wanted, to be here in this moment, just before I can't wait anymore."

"I can't wait, Jane," I said, rocking under her just the slightest bit.

"Just another minute," she said, making a matching tiny movement. Again and again, until my vision blurred.

My hands rested on her thighs. With each movement she gave, I moved them up her body. Feeling her ass in my hands, holding her hips, the ripple of her ribs under my fingers as my hands drifted up her torso, until they were holding her breasts again.

I tugged on one nipple, and she gasped. "Again."

I did the same on the other side, and she fell forward, her hands braced above my shoulders. Her hair fell forward; the strands soft on my cheeks. I felt myself stiffen more, remembering how her hair felt against my stomach and trailing over my erection.

I pressed one hand on her back, coaxing her further forward until I could close my mouth around her nipple. She stopped moving, eyes closed as she leaned into my mouth. My hips raised underneath her as I sucked harder.

"Ahh. Ahh. Ahh." Her voice came in time with every thrust.

"Jane," I said, pulling my head away from her chest. "You feel so good."

Her eyes opened, and for a moment she stared at me. I squeezed her breast in my hand. She shifted back hard, grinding against the front of my hips. I could feel her everywhere.

I panted. "Don't stop, babe, I need you."

Jane reverted to the little rocking motion. "What do you want from me, Peter?"

Right now, right here, I wanted everything from her for the rest of my life. To have her in bed like this, to be able to roll over and fall asleep tucked next to her, to reach for her in the middle of the night, to wake up and have coffee. Over and over again.

"Everything. I want everything," I said hoarsely.

As if she had been waiting for the right answer, Jane moved again, wildly, small whimpering sounds escaping as she climbed higher. The pause had pushed me closer to the edge, and I roared with pleasure at my release.

JANE

I stretched in the cloudy morning light. The first workday of the year. Next to me, Peter shifted in his sleep. Otis stood from where he was curled by my feet and stretched, before coming to sit on my chest and yawn in my face.

"Yes, I will feed you," I said softly, scratching his neck.

I got out of bed and pulled on a robe and slippers against the chill of the terracotta tiles. After I'd returned from Italy, I'd bought myself a small espresso machine, and while Peter preferred drip, I still experienced a small thrill with every first sip, remembering all the tiny cups I'd had in Italy.

My phone let out a soft chime where it sat on the counter next to the machine. When I glanced at it, there was a new message from an unknown international number.

Frowning, I picked it up. Perhaps Pietro wanted to ask me a few more questions. But he had my work email, not my personal one. Or my phone number.

I skimmed it quickly, then reread more slowly.

Buon Anno, Jane,

I hope to find you well, and you have found happiness even though you were sad to leave Tuscany. Did you solve the problem you were going to help with in Florence? I have thought of you many times

Something Resembling Love

since you returned to America. Perhaps you will need to come back and give more assistance. If so, I would be pleased to see you.

Matteo

That was unexpected.

But was it? I had thought of Matteo as well. Especially now, as I sat savoring my espresso and hearing his voice in his words. I thought of the way he had held me, looked after me, kept me from falling. For a brief moment, I closed my eyes and let myself remember the kiss we had shared.

Then I shook myself. Peter and I were together again. That moment had been part of vacation. I looked up as Peter came into the kitchen. Quickly, I closed the app on my phone, feeling guilty.

"Happy New Year," I said, handing him a mug.

"That was yesterday," he said, running his hand across the top of his hair.

"Let's pretend it's today."

"Does that mean we can go back to bed?" He yawned broadly, and affection swelled in my chest.

"Maaaaybe. Except I'm not all that sleepy anymore."

Peter choked as he was drinking. He set the mug down, sloshing liquid onto the countertop. "You must have superpowered the coffee this morning, because suddenly I'm wide awake."

"You're just excited for the new year." I picked up his mug to wipe the spilled liquid, making a show of being casual.

When I turned to take the sopping cloth back to the sink, Peter's hand caught my waist. He took the dishrag out of my hand and tossed it across the room.

"I want to pretend it's still New Year's morning," he said hoarsely.

In an instant, his mouth was on mine, his arm behind my back, snugging me up against him. My robe had come undone, and I could feel just how badly he wanted this morning to not be January second.

For a fleeting second, I imagined he was Matteo, cautious but in charge. Then I flexed my hand into the soft flesh of Peter's back, reminding myself who I was really kissing.

His hand came to my face, holding me in the sweet way that he did, and all thoughts of Italy and other kisses dissolved.

"Darling Jane," he murmured in my ear. "Come back to bed. It's much too early on New Year's Day to be up."

I giggled and took his hand to follow him up the stairs.

A couple of hours later, I pushed him out the door with a kiss. As I packed my work bag, I closed my eyes, smiling at the past couple of weeks. The easy way we'd fallen back into our relationship, and how there was less friction now Peter knew he could be content without kids.

I looked at our cups, sitting on the counter to dry where Peter had washed them. What would it be like for us to live together? He'd already used my spare room over the holidays to get a bit of work done and had marveled at the space, at not having to sit hunched over his coffee table.

New year, new moves, right?

Rodriguez was already at work when I arrived, late, and raised an eyebrow and grinned at me. I rolled my eyes but grinned back, and started to hum as I walked past, making him laugh.

Over the short week at work, I focused on preparing for the spring ahead. I ordered more supplies—the rate at which we went through slides really was alarming. I cleaned out my desk and went through my email.

As I did so, I thought about the message from Matteo, sitting in my WhatsApp, the only un-replied-to message there.

I pulled out my phone and read it again. His message sounded slightly formal. But then again, he'd said he would want to see me again. I doubted I would go back to Florence, at least for work. But, I reasoned, no harm in keeping the friendship alive.

> *Buon anno, Matteo! What a pleasant surprise to hear from you. I think I was helpful to my colleague in Florence. He reported that the solutions we had come up with were successfully implemented in a few places. I doubt very much that he will need my help again, now that his issue has been resolved. I've often thought—fondly—of the week we spent hiking and exploring the small villages you showed us. If the opportunity arose to go back, I would do it in an instant!*

I read it again after I hit send.

"Happy New Year, Jane."

I looked up to see Kip standing in front of my desk. I gave him a radiant smile.

Something Resembling Love

"This came for you. Someone in the mailroom thought it was mine. It looks like it's from Italy."

Frowning, I took the plain envelope from him. The stamp was decidedly Italian. Printed on the back, an unfamiliar logo. A simple but beautiful card with an olive tree adorned in Christmas lights slid out easily.

My eyes widened as I read it. "It's from the Italian minister." I kept reading. "Wishing me a merry Christmas and a prosperous new year. He says he enjoyed meeting me at the conference and hopes we'll have an opportunity to run into each other again."

"I guess you *can* get recognized for bull shit."

I laughed at the joke with him. After he left, I finished the note.

Pietro sends his best and wishes to thank you once again for your thoughtful approach to the fungal infestation. I am additionally personally grateful as one of the vineyards affected belongs to a cousin, and was first planted by our great-grandparents.

"Huh," I said out loud to myself as I set the card on my desk. The minister's words were slightly formal as well. Maybe I'd get to go back to Florence after all.

I sat back in my squeaky office chair and thought about that week. More accurately, I thought about the kiss Matteo and I had shared, hidden from the rest of the group, as the village clock had moved too quickly. Matteo had been embarrassed by his actions, but as much as I would not have admitted it to Alicia, a small part of me had stayed in that spot for the last few months.

What I'd said to Lauren, not long after we'd come back, had been true: in Evanston, my life had a set path. Coming back had been like sliding a well-oiled drawer into its place. Easy. Undemanding. Natural.

But there had been moments when I had missed the peacefulness that had come from being away from the city. Chicago was a solid place for the career I had strived for. I had wanted my parents to be proud of me, and I knew they were.

Why was I even thinking about this, though? I looked around the painted concrete walls of my office. They were covered with photos from trips, smiling colleagues with arms around each other, sweaty or muddy, high on the adrenaline of exhaustion.

I tapped the screen of my phone, and lit up a picture of me and Peter, sitting on Lauren's couch at Friendsgiving, holding hands, my head on Peter's shoulder.

I rolled my eyes at myself. Sometimes the beginning of the year was like this. I got melancholy, missing my parents, and thought about uprooting my life. Usually after watching my friends or coworkers come back from warm holidays with their families. Maybe my brain was just doing its routine. Automatic pilot, despite my own wonderful holiday season.

Whatever. I stood and walked to my lab bench. Some good old-fashioned poop would help.

By the middle of January, I was back on track. Despite my presentation, I still had more work to do before the extraction of micronutrients was commercially viable. Like plants, I needed a balance of bacteria: enough to spur my growth, but not so much that the unsettled feeling would return and run rampant. Much like Peter, I was treading a fine line between too much and too little. But I seemed to be making small progress, while Peter was still talking about being stuck. Well, cancer was cannier than minerals.

I smiled as I cleaned up my lab bench.

When I got home, Peter was already there, the oven heating.

"Um …"

"Don't worry, I'm not cooking. It's to bake the bread to go with dinner."

"Dinner!?" I dropped my bag and coat by the back door and came to hug him from behind.

It was just a regular night. Wine and dinner and talking about our days. But it felt homey. As we put dishes and leftovers away, I wondered again if Peter might consider moving in.

"Come to bed," he said, as he wiped down the counter.

"You want to go to bed? Now?"

He shrugged. "It's January. It's cold and dark. Aren't we supposed to, like, hibernate or something?"

"All right," I laughed. "Let's go to bed." He followed me up the stairs, the air chilly away from the warm kitchen.

I shivered, and Peter put his arms around me, looking into my eyes. "Darling Jane."

I shivered again and dropped my head to his shoulder. He held me tighter.

"How will I get your clothes off if you're so cold?"

I laughed. "Quickly?"

Peter took the word as a challenge, starting with my jeans and fuzzy socks. He helped me under the covers before he took his own jeans off and then slipped in with me.

"That was an excellent idea," I said between kisses.

"Are you warmer now?"

"Much."

Peter stripped his shirt off and then helped me to sit up to take off my own. He gazed traveled my face, to my lips, trailing down my torso to my breasts.

"You are so beautiful. I am so lucky."

"So am I," I agreed, reaching between our bodies to run my fingers over him.

Peter grunted and closed his eyes. I ran my fingers over him again.

"Stop," he gritted out. "I'm going to …"

"I thought we were hibernating?"

He laughed. "Then let's hibernate."

He was no longer looking at me, but dropped his head, his tongue touching each of my nipples, a quick swipe of warmth that left me shivering in anticipation. I went back to touching him, stroking lightly along his shaft until he was shaking.

"What are you doing to me? God, I love when you do that."

With a sure hand, I guided him to where he felt best. Together we moaned and moved in rhythm. Under me, Peter tightened and gave a quick double thrust that felt amazing. He relaxed before I came, leaving me suspended above my orgasm.

When our heat became too much, Peter flung the covers off his body. The cool air hit my back, making me shiver, but I didn't care.

I buried my face in the pillow, smiling to myself. I was definitely going to ask him if he wanted to move in.

When I woke in the morning, Peter was not in bed. I lay still, listening, until I heard him running water in the kitchen. Ooh, was he up making coffee?

I put my robe on and went to find out.

"Sorry, I don't know how to use that." Peter pointed at my espresso machine.

"Any coffee I don't have to make for myself tastes good." I took the mug he offered me with a smile and followed him into the living room. "This is a nice way to start the weekend."

We sat in silence for a few minutes as Otis jumped up on the back of the couch and settled himself.

"I wish I wasn't so allergic. He really is a nice cat."

"He is. Peter, there's something I want to ask you."

"Okay, but can it wait? I need to tell you something first."

"Sure," I said, frowning. He sounded serious.

"You're so pretty." He reached for my hand. "And patient with me. Understanding. Smart. You care for me in a way I never have been. I love spending time with you."

I felt tears well in my eyes and gave him a watery smile. "You mean a lot to me, Peter. I love being with you, too."

He watched me for a moment, then took a deep breath. "I've been thinking about work a lot recently. Everything was going well with the DNA and ..."

"I think you're doing a great job. Cancer is so adaptable, and you're so dedicated." I swept my thumb back and forth over his knuckles.

"Fritz keeps offering me a job in Switzerland," he blurted. "I keep thinking about my life in ... in general." In Peter's face I could see worry, sorrow, heartache, and self-loathing.

"And then, Christmas ..."

"I'm fine, Peter. Your mom just got carried away."

"No," he shook his head, "it's not that. I want to be with you ..."

I felt my heart swell, warmth and love overtaking me.

"But I—" He looked down at our joined hands. "I thought I knew what I wanted. And then Christmas showed me I was wrong."

My brow furrowed, not following.

"Jane, I ..." Peter looked at me, held my gaze. "I do want to be a dad. I want to have kids."

The words took ten times longer than they should have, to register. The human brain was so fast, but not like this. When the sounds made sense, I felt as if I'd landed on my back from three stories up, the wind knocked out of me completely.

"I ... you ... what did you say?"

"I want to have kids."

"I ... see." The tears that had been building, hearing how much he cared about me, what had sounded like Peter's way of parsing through a future together, spilled over, hot and angry.

"Seeing you playing with my cousin's kids, holding their babies. You walked my infant second cousin up and down the hall while her parents sat and drank a beer. You let her suck on your finger and you two held a conversation ... you babbled with her all evening. Even the way you are with Sebastian, playing video games."

"So I played with a baby."

"You're just so *good* with them. So comfortable and natural."

"That's because I don't have to be responsible for them!"

"I know why you don't want to have kids. I get it. But Jane, we could do this. We could figure out a way to have kids."

I pulled my hand out of Peter's, cringing at how excited he was by the idea of us being parents.

"You know *I* don't want to." I hated how cold my voice was, how angry, but this was ... how dare he. "I was clear on that from the very beginning. I gave you every opportunity to tell me this early on. Hell, I pushed you away so you could figure it out on your own and you ... you lied to me!"

"I didn't lie!" He grabbed my hand again. "I spent a lot of time thinking about it, and I thought I knew."

This was it; this was the moment in my life from which I knew I was going to be alone forever. I'd been more upfront with Peter than I'd ever been before.

"Last night was a lie. You knew you were leaving."

I'd given him every opportunity, and still I was alone. I yanked my hand away again and stalked to stand in front of my fireplace. "*This* is why I asked. Pushed. I didn't want to get here, be in love with you, and have you decide you wanted to have kids."

"I know," he said with a sorrowful nod. "I'm so sorry." Tears rolled down his cheeks as well, one after the other.

I nodded again, swiping ineffectually at my own tears, a mix of anger and heartbreak.

It seemed like hours, and also only minutes, before I walked into the kitchen.

Peter followed me as I grabbed a glass, turning to hand it to him with my other hand still on the knob. The memory of this same motion the first time we kissed came crashing over me, making me dizzy. I grabbed at the air, trying to steady myself, and the glass slipped from my hand.

Together we watched it fall and shatter. How fitting.

"I should probably go," he said after a moment.

"Right. I guess so."

I trailed after him, watching him pick up his bag, and walked out the door behind him.

He turned around. "This is hard. I didn't want to hurt you."

"I know." My last look was Peter walking down the sidewalk.

When I finally closed the door, the tears fell in earnest, and I slid down the inside of the door sobbing.

Otis sat down and stared at me, his yellow eyes blinking.

"I know you liked him. I liked him too, but I don't think he's coming back."

Otis climbed into my lap and settled, not caring that my tears soaked his fur.

PETER

The day I broke up with Jane quickly turned to Martin Luther King Day which became late January.

I reverted to who I had been pre-union with Jane, and worse. The pile of mail sprouted wings that occasionally spit pieces onto the floor. I used and rewashed a single mug, the rest lingering on the counter for a week at a time. And I ignored Chris' texts and phone calls until one night, he showed up on my doorstep.

I swore as I looked through the peephole, then glanced behind me at my apartment. Nothing I could do about it now.

"So you're not dead," he said when I swung the door open. "Just hol—… eeeeee shit." Chris' eyes swept across the apartment behind me. "Peter, what the fuck?"

"I've been working."

"On what? World record for most ingrained butt print on a couch? Most stubborn coffee ring?" He glanced at me. "Jesus, man. Put on some pants, we're getting out of here."

I heaved a sigh and turned to my room. I could hear Chris moving things around and when I came back out, he was starting the dishwasher.

"You're such a domestic goddess."

"It's the real reason Lauren loves me."

We walked a few blocks to a neighborhood pub. Someplace Chris had frequented pre-Lauren.

"What the hell was going on back there?" he asked as soon as he'd ordered beers and burgers for us. "Shouldn't you be with Jane? Or at least not making your apartment some place she would never set foot in?"

"I broke up with Jane," I stated flatly.

"You what!?"

"I broke up with Jane." I didn't look at my friend. Couldn't.

He leaned forward, trying to see my face. "Why!"

"It was the right thing to do." I still didn't look at him.

"Because …?" He was still trying to get me to look at him.

Because my life was a mess. Because I wanted to be a dad. Because I felt like I was falling behind. Because nothing made sense except for her. "You wouldn't understand."

"Try me," Chris said, somewhat angrily.

I sighed, shoulders slumping. "Because I want kids."

"What the fuck, dude? You told her you didn't, that you could be content without them. After she broke up with you so you could figure out this exact thing!"

My head came up in response to his accusations. "I thought I could. But then at my parents', all my cousins and second cousins. Hell, even Sebastian. Seeing her actually with kids." I hung my head. "And besides, I need to finish my postdoc."

"Not having kids would make that easier, you know."

"She was everything I thought I wanted," I said as if I hadn't heard him.

"You're being a coward. Being a parent is not all it's cracked up to be."

"Says the guy who got a built-in family."

"Sebastian was in high school already when I met Lauren. He's more like hanging out with a young adult than having a kid to raise."

Chris paused, waiting for me. I picked at the edge of my coaster, still not looking at him.

Something Resembling Love

"Aside from not wanting to, not being able, to be a parent, you have no qualms, right? I mean, she loves you; she gives you a home, and you guys have great sex." Chris ticked off the list on his fingers. "She makes you feel good about yourself, takes care of you when you're sick, likes all the other same things you do. Doesn't care that you spend every free moment in the lab, and doesn't judge you for all the excuses you make."

"I'm pretty sure Jane would not want to ice fish."

Chris snorted in what was, I hoped, amusement. "And what is happening at your apartment?"

"I've been working." My voice was defensive. "Now that I'm not with Jane, I have more time to focus on the research, the process."

"I guarantee you're not making any more progress."

"Yes, I am," I lied.

"I've seen you make some interesting choices along the way, but this is by far the stupidest. You don't want to be stuck here? Fine. Quit." He swept his hand around, as if waving the pub and the city away. "Go join industry. Work fifty hours a week instead of a hundred, go home to Jane every night, get laid, and have a life."

"You know the research we do here is important."

"Oh right!" Chris slapped his forehead. "I forgot. The only pure research is academic research. Of course, how could I have forgotten the golden rule?"

"You know how I feel about that."

"And the advances that Fritz and his team have made are irrelevant because they were made by a corporation? That's some logic you've got there," Chris said with a disbelieving shake of his head. When I said nothing, he continued. "Do you think any of this is anything other than fear?"

"Oh, so now you're a psychologist in addition to a genetics PhD? Screw you." I sat back in the booth and turned away.

"Do you have any idea what you are throwing away?"

"As a matter of fact, I do." I crossed my arms over my chest and glared across the table.

We finished our beers, and Chris left some cash on the table. As we put our coats back on, Chris set his hand on my shoulder. "Don't throw your whole life away because of one thing. Don't think you can fill the void with another rung on your career ladder. You will regret this."

"Go away, Chris. Go back to your perfect life and leave me to my choice."

At home, alone in the dark, I sat on the couch, staring into the grey light of my unlit apartment. I *was* upset. Mad at myself for throwing out a relationship with the woman I loved.

And I was frustrated. Even with all the extra time in the lab, which, if I was honest, had only been about ten hours more since we'd split, I wasn't any further.

I replayed the last night Jane and I had spent together in my mind. The meal I had brought, her surprise and delight when she'd seen me using the oven. I could still feel the way her house felt, calm and inviting. Warm colors on the walls, red kitchen appliances. Watching her make cupcakes for Rodriguez, and not feeling jealous.

On its own, my hand flexed, as if Jane were underneath it. She'd been so cold that night, and I had loved warming her up. Even now, by myself, knowing I'd never see her again, my body was responding to the memory of her.

I'd barely been able to sleep, knowing what was coming in the morning. I'd been worried I would chicken out.

When I'd woken up, the sky had been starting to lighten, the stars burning out. Carefully, trying not to wake Jane, I'd rolled, pulling a small pair of scissors from the nightstand. With them in my fingers, I'd lain there watching Jane, stroking her hair. Miles and weeks away from her, I could feel her hair on my fingers as I'd brushed it back, exposing a lower layer. Carefully, I'd picked up a small section of her hair and cut it off, a few inches from her scalp.

After, I smoothed her hair back in place, running my fingers through it as I watched Jane wake.

The strands were in a tissue now, curled on themselves, tucked away.

JANE

I couldn't tell anyone immediately. What was I going to say? My boyfriend, whom everyone loved for me, who I had loved for me, and who I had been on a break with to solve this exact issue, had broken up with me because I couldn't have kids.

If I'd been conducting a study, this would have been damning evidence that I was irretrievably broken.

From where I was curled up on my couch, the fire in my fireplace doing its best work to cheer me up, I could see the ice coating the hydrangeas that ran along my side yard.

I picked up my phone and sent a text to my friends.

> Dinner at my place tonight? I'm making stew.

Lauren responded first.

> Yes. Good. I haven't seen you since NYE.

Elizabeth Standish

Alicia:

> What kind of stew? I'm only coming out in this weather if it's Tuscan.

I laughed out loud in my quiet home.

> You'll just have to chance it. 5 pm.

The imminent arrival of friends got me off the couch. There wasn't much to do except thaw the beef and chop the veggies, which gave my mind time to wander.

Sometimes I loved that; my brain's meanderings were how I had come up with the initial idea for my current research, how I'd gotten over snags in the past.

Eventually I tired of listening to the same "Yes, but" go around, and I laced up my running shoes. Screw the cold; that was why I had a water heater and a fireplace.

As I ran, tears froze on my face. Up Sheridan, over to the lakefront, down the sidewalk through the park. Until I was cold enough and tired enough that I no longer cared, could focus my thoughts on seeing my friends.

I pulled the stew out of the oven where it had been keeping warm. Alicia poured us all chianti as we sat at my dining room table.

"I just have to say, you looked so hot in that red dress on New Year's!" Lauren said, aiming a huge smile at me.

"Too bad that Stewart guy is such a jackass. He totally checked me out and then sneered," Alicia said.

"He was probably just jealous of Zach. We all looked great," Lauren said as she pulled photos up on her phone. We swiped through them together, reminiscing. "We're a good-looking crew."

I gave them as much of a smile as I could muster.

"I guess I have to admit this was worth coming out for," Alicia said as she tore off a last piece of bread and swiped her bowl clean.

"Even if it wasn't Tuscan?"

"Even then."

"Where is Peter tonight?" Lauren asked as she stood and collected our dishes.

"He probably had to go home and get some work done. I'm sure you guys have been staying in, in this cold weather." Alicia gave the words 'staying in' special emphasis.

I spun the stem of my wineglass between my fingers, feeling it bounce back and forth between them, quiet for a moment. "Peter broke up with me."

I heard Lauren throw something in the metal sink. "What the fuck?" she said, coming back in the room, her face stony.

"When?" Alicia asked.

"About a week ago. I should have told you guys sooner. I just … couldn't deal. I've been working a lot." My laugh came out as an ironic huff. I looked at Lauren. "I would have thought he would have told Chris."

Alicia frowned. "Why? I mean, did he say why?"

"Turns out he *does* want kids?"

"That asshole," Lauren said, the angry look on her face hardening as she sat back down next to me and covered my hand with her own.

"I just—" I sniffed. "I thought it was going to be different this time. I gave him every opportunity to make this decision early on, and—" My voice caught, choking me. "And he couldn't."

"I think you need this more than the rest of us," Alicia said, and poured the last of the wine into my glass.

I gave a watery laugh and took a drink as tears spilled down my cheeks.

"Apparently it was seeing me with his family's babies that did it. And I guess because I play video games with Sebastian," I said, looking at Lauren.

"Playing video games made you mom material?" Alicia asked.

"I don't know; maybe he thought I could keep our kids entertained while he worked?" I shrugged and let out a shaky breath. "Here's the worst of it, and I feel so stupid, but I—" I swallowed hard. "I thought he was proposing. I mean, we weren't even living together, or talking about it, but he was so sweet, and things had been *so* good since we reunited in November."

I stopped, realizing that November had only been two months ago.

"And now I feel even more stupid. How could Peter, of all people, have decided in such a short time frame that he wanted to get married?"

Alicia leaned forward onto her elbows. "We all get pulled into the fantasy at some point."

"Do you—God, I hate to say this," Lauren said, cringing, "but do you think he thought you might change your mind?"

"Fuck, I hope not! I was so clear."

"I'm sure you were. But you know how he can be. I mean, his work bears that out," Alicia reminded me.

Next to me, Lauren nodded emphatically. "Chris says the same thing, about Peter's lack of flexible thinking."

I nodded as well, in resigned agreement. I knew Peter was like that, had heard him talk about his work that way. Even his relationship with his parents. But I had seen them be warm and interested. Not meddlesome.

I sighed. "Anyway. Happy New Year to me." I raised my glass again, in mock toast.

"Give me that," Lauren reached for my glass. "I'm gonna stick it up Peter's backside."

Work was one thing I could count on. It, and my coworkers, had been there for me for years. When I'd been dating, when I hadn't been. When I'd been brand new and more recently, as my work was being nationally recognized. Briefly, I wondered if Peter was jealous.

Not that it mattered now.

I was somewhat surprised to receive another WhatsApp from Matteo before the end of the month, congratulating me on my success with Pietro. I had assumed his New Year's message was a quick hello, maybe thinking back on favorite groups he'd guided over the previous year.

Over the next few days, I thought about the week of hiking, the days in Florence, meeting with Pietro. The time in Italy had been healing. Matteo had been a part of that. The space away from my normal routine had been a good break. If I'd come back from Italy and Peter and I had never gotten back together, that would have been a peaceful ending.

But this being jerked around, even if it hadn't been intentional, was devastating.

Something Resembling Love

Matteo had been attentive to me. And he was attractive in a rugged way that was nearly a hundred and eighty degrees from the softness Peter carried from being indoors so often.

Which made me stop to think—how well-matched had Peter and I truly been? Yes, we both worked in a lab ... but I got out. Maybe that was because he was focused on his career, which I could appreciate. But he wasn't terribly physically active, either. And then there was the stupid kids issue, which we were polar opposites on.

As I drove back and forth to work, I let myself imagine seeing Matteo again. Remembering our kiss in the Italian moonlight was an easy distraction. Still, I couldn't help myself wondering how he would react to my limitations.

In the first week of February, Kip walked into my office, bearing two cups of coffee and another envelope.

"Don't tell me. I got an early Valentine's Day card from the Italian minister?" I gave him a cheeky grin.

"Ah, not quite."

At his hesitant tone, I gave him a wary look.

"May I sit down?"

I gestured to the chair opposite mine.

He took a moment to sit, handing me one of the paper cups, and settling in the chair, ramping up my curiosity but also my concern. "It seems Secretary Aziz and the Italian Minister of Agriculture have been talking about you."

"Is that a good thing, or a bad thing?" I blew on the hot liquid.

"I suppose that depends on how much you liked your time in Italy. The Minister would like you to come and consult."

Was that all? "Sure," I said, setting the paper cup down with a satisfied smile. "I'd be happy to go to Italy and help Pietro out some more." Italy would be a welcome change, and I could get away from any lingering ghosts of Peter. "How long are they thinking they'd want me to be there?"

"Six months. To start." I couldn't quite decipher the look Kip was giving me.

"Oh! Well, six months is doable."

"No," he said, shaking his head, "Six months to *start*. The Minister wants to give you a permanent job, but he only has funding for the first six months. Ideally, he wants you to move and stay."

I choked on my coffee. "He—" cough, "he wants me to—" cough, cough, cough, "to move there?" Cough, cough. "Permanently."

Kip raised his eyebrows above his brown eyes. The same ones that had looked at me with concern and care when I had first told him about my medical problems were now laced with amusement. "Apparently Pietro was quite taken with you, and your suggestions solved their fungus problem."

I immediately thought of the minister's great-grandparents' vineyard.

"And here I thought you might be coming to fire me," I joked.

"No," he laughed, "Unless you considering kicking you out for a promotion firing."

"How soon do I need to decide?"

"Maybe two weeks at most."

"Okay, I will give it serious thought."

"Good." Kip sat a moment longer before standing. "Let me know if I can play intermediary," he said as he rose. "And Jane," he said, turning back at the door, "don't take too long. This is an incredible opportunity for you. I know you've had a rough few months, personally. Consider this a gift for getting through that, as well as everything you've contributed to the industry."

He was wearing a half smile. It made me do the same. "I will. I do. Thanks, Thompson. Would you mind closing the door on your way out?"

I sat back in my chair and glanced around the room at the same diplomas, certificates, and photos that I looked at every day: graduating from college with honors, getting my masters, my first job, my first promotion. The day I had been given this office, the publication of my first paper, and my second and third, too. I had wished my parents were still alive to share and celebrate all the milestones with. I didn't have any friends left from the life I'd had with them.

Right now was one of those "I made it" moments I wished I could share with them.

Something Resembling Love

Instead, I sent a text to Lauren and Alicia and named a favorite place of ours..

> Meet me for happy hour.

I was already ordering a round for us when Lauren and Alicia walked in together.

"You didn't even wait to order? Must be serious!" Alicia grabbed her martini off the bar.

"I had a meeting with my boss today," I explained as we wound our way to a low table.

"A good meeting, I hope. I can't tell by your face," Lauren said.

"I've been offered a consulting gig in Italy."

"As in move to Italy and buy a house kind of consulting?" Alicia wanted to know.

"Maybe. Six months, and then, if there's funding, permanently."

"Holy shit! That's amazing! When do you leave? You're going, right, don't tell me you're thinking about turning it down!"

"I only found out this morning! I mean, I'm pretty sure I'm going to do it. But it's a big change, and I have a settled life here. A house, to be exact. Full of furniture."

"So what, it's just furniture," Lauren said. "People leave all kinds of crap behind when they move. I have seen it all!"

Alicia looked at Lauren and nodded once, sharply. "Exactly. So you have a house, and a car, and some furniture. Your health is great. It's not like you have a husband or kids …" she winced. "Sorry, I didn't mean it like that."

"Yeah, I don't have any of those things," I said a little sadly. "But I do have great friends, and a life, and a job I already know that I love. Plus my house, which is 'just a house' as Lauren would say."

She shook her head. "I help people buy and sell houses all the time. But your house is your home. You bought it when you first moved here, you used money from the house you grew up in to buy it. It's not just a house. It's a connection to your parents and how you got from there to here."

I swallowed hard, trying not to cry. "Yeah," I sniffed. "I don't want to sell it. Maybe Italy doesn't work out, and I want to come back; maybe it does, and I still want a house in the States."

"This is an incredible opportunity," Alicia interjected forcefully. "And I know someone who would happily rent your house and take care of it just like you'd want."

"Who, you? I thought you loved your place?"

"I do, but it's a condo. I've been thinking about moving anyway—maybe I want a realer place to live. Lauren can get me top dollar for the condo. And then, if it doesn't work out and you want to come back, Lauren can help me buy a new house. Oh, and, I can hang out with my favorite guy Otis! Seems like a win-win!" Alicia was grinning at the idea.

"You guys aren't making it easy for me to come up with excuses to turn it down."

"Because you *shouldn't!*" Lauren said, with a slap of her hand on the table.

"I have one built-in friend, so that would be nice."

"That Pietro guy you met with while I went shopping? Isn't he, like, twice your age?"

I laughed, "I didn't mean him."

"Are you talking with Matteo?" Alicia gasped.

I gave a coy smile and nodded.

"Why didn't you tell me my matchmaking efforts worked?" She reached out and smacked me on the arm.

"Ow," I laughed, rubbing the spot. "I wouldn't say your match made us. We've been exchanging WhatsApp messages since the first of the year, that's all. Nothing as sexy as you're envisioning."

"Wait, Matteo's the guide you guys had, right?" Lauren clarified.

"The super-hot guide we had who totally had a thing for Jane."

"And you made out with him."

"Mmm ..." But I couldn't totally keep my smile hidden.

"It's fate," Alicia declared. "You have to go!"

"All right, all right," I held my hands up in surrender, "I'll go!" I laughed.

Something Resembling Love

Although I had initially agreed with my girlfriends, I hesitated. Six months was one thing; the possibility of permanency another altogether. In my quick chat with Joe he said he'd want another PET scan before I left, but didn't have any real concerns now that I had the new medication.

In the end I decided if I hated it, I could put in my six months and turn down a permanent position. If I loved it, then Alicia would already be taking care of my house.

A week later, it was me who was bearing two cups of coffee to Kip's office. He gave an amused shake of his head when he saw me standing in his doorway. "You're either trying to butter me up because you're going to break the Minister's heart, or you've brought coffee because champagne is frowned upon during the workday."

I laughed. "The latter. Which you knew."

"Indeed," he chuckled as I handed him his beverage and sat across from him. "Unfortunately, knowing how much you like facts and being able to organize them, I don't have a lot to share. The Minister would like you to be in Italy as soon as you can."

I nodded. The lack of forethought made some sense: I'd heard it said that in hell, the Swiss were the lovers and Italians ran the trains.

"You're used to going to a lot of different places, I know, but you seem even more calm about this than I would have expected," Kip observed.

"You know me," I said with a shrug. "I like the next adventure, the next new place to explore. And Italy was … good to me. I'm excited to have a reason to go back."

"Yes, I know that. And it seems like more."

I sighed, slumping in the chair. Kip and I had known each other for almost a decade. "I don't know if I can explain how the end of my relationship impacted me."

He gave a solemn nod. "I saw. You're practiced at hiding things, but not from those of us who care about you."

It wasn't pity I saw on his face, but the understanding of someone who had known me a long time; someone who had become a surrogate family. I gave several small nods as I inhaled. "Evanston was a life I made for myself. To a degree that's been tarnished. When I was in Italy last fall, I had a chance to step back and get some perspective, but then I was back and into the routine. I loved being in the forests every day. I guess I'm just looking forward to having more time in that mental place. The friend was our tour guide, and he'll be a good resource. And I really liked Pietro. I think it's going to be exactly what I need right now. Although I'm going to miss everyone here, and these conversations," I finished with a slightly sad smile.

"You'd better believe I'm coming to check on your research and contributions over there! I need to make sure our governmental asset is making us look good."

"So you can drink wine to celebrate the success of your mentoring?" I joked, lifting my paper cup in lieu of the glasses we didn't have.

Kip laughed. "Something like that."

There was no reason for me to hold back on continuing a conversation with Matteo, and my excitement spilled over, a release of the heartbreak I'd been trying to tamp down.

> *If you had known Pietro Tonelli, who I visited in Florence, I would almost suspect you had a role in what just happened. But, since you didn't, it seems that I am just very fortunate. I hope that when I come back to Florence in a few weeks, you and I can connect. Chatting is nice, but it would be more fun to talk in person.*

Now that I had a reason to go back to Italy, I was suddenly nervous that Matteo would have forgotten all about me, despite the messages we had been exchanging. I didn't want to admit to Alicia that she was right, but I did really like Matteo, and I really wouldn't mind kissing him again, and exploring where else that might lead. And if I was honest, Alicia had been right about that too—he had been more attentive to me. I'd told Lauren I was independent and capable, but I'd liked how Matteo had looked out for me.

> *This is an excellent thing to hear! I am happy you will have a reason to come back to Tuscany so soon. How long will you be here for? Where will you live? There are many questions, but I would like to help you be settled. It will be nice to see you as soon as you are here.*

Before responding, I waited a couple more days. In the meantime, I did some of the planning Director Thompson had, not unfairly, accused me of needing to do. I booked a flight and happily paid for it with my government credit card. I explored weather charts and bought a new pair of hiking boots. Matteo didn't know that I was delaying, of course, but I didn't want to seem overly eager to see him. I felt incredibly excited about my new work, the opportunity, and the change. Would he be different with me not as a guest? Was that kiss our last night merely a stolen opportunity and nothing more?

> *I fly in March first, to Florence. I don't know where I'll be living yet. It would be nice to see you, as well. I am excited but also nervous, as my Italian is rudimentary at best! Will you show me the best hikes near wherever I get settled?*

When I woke up the next morning, I checked my phone before I even got out of bed. Matteo's response was waiting for me.

> *I will lead a tour when you are arriving. But let us plan to meet soon after. When you know where you will stay please tell me, and I will visit you. It will be good to have this friendship in person again.*
> *Matteo*

I was pretty sure he was flirting with me, referring to our kiss. I grinned to myself, and then flung back the covers, irritating Otis. "Sorry, buddy, I'm just excited. We have a lot to do."

On the last day of February, I stood in the terminal with Alicia and Lauren, having just checked my luggage. All that was left now was to get on the plane. My first-class seat awaited—an upgrade I'd gifted myself. I didn't want to make such a lengthy flight uncomfortable and ruminating on what-ifs.

"Okay, one last hug for the road. Oh, I love you both, I'm going to miss you so much!" I said as I pulled my friends into a last hug.

"We love you too," Lauren said, at the same time Alicia said, "Don't forget about us."

"My contract is only six months."

"Right," she scoffed, "like that'll be the end of it." We laughed together as Alicia handed me my backpack.

"Send me lots of pictures of Otis," I said to her.

"He's not even going to remember who you are, I'm going to spoil him so much."

I paused just before I walked through the scanner to wave and blow a kiss to the two of them, standing with their arms around each other, waving back.

Finding my seat took no time at all, and the flight attendant offered me a beverage. "Prosecco, please." If I was moving to Italy, I was going to celebrate properly.

The jetliner rumbled slowly down the tarmac. I was excited to be going and at the same time, sad to be leaving my friends behind. But if I stayed, what would I be staying for?

Thompson was all but pushing me out the door. I'd be ignoring the pull and the happiness I'd felt when Alicia and I had taken our trip. Settling for a life I knew, when I could be branching out.

I thought about the hills and the fog, the towns and the churches, the cappuccinos, and the tall chestnut trees, and smiled to myself as I finished my bubbly wine.

***

"*Salve,*" the customs agent intoned as he inspected my passport and visa.

"*Buon pomeriggio, come sta?*" I replied. He looked up sharply, and I smiled. He smiled back. "*Ottimo.*"

"*Bene! Grazie.*" I doubted he was "very well," but maybe all customs agents had to pass a gruffness test before being hired.

Squeezed into my tiny rental car, I drove northwest for an hour, stopping briefly for a few necessities and several bottles of wine.

The short-term apartment was small but functional and as I unpacked, I video called the girls, showing them around the space.

"I wanted you guys to know I arrived safely. Now I'm exhausted!"

"Go to bed."

"It's too early," Lauren objected.

"I don't care that it's only five p.m. I'll have a glass of wine and some store-bought pasta and sleep."

"Remember, she likes to get up early." If they'd been together, Alicia would have been nudging Lauren in the shoulder.

Something Resembling Love

When we hung up, I poured myself a second glass and heated my dinner. I whispered a silent apology to all of Italy for having a pre-made meal. And then I collapsed into bed, a heap of excitement, sadness, heartbreak, wonder, and anticipation.

In the morning, my alarm went off an hour after my usual time. Unable to commit myself to details immediately, I set off to find the closest bar for at least two, and maybe more, cappuccinos.

At the first hit, I smiled, deeply gratified. Nothing in the US compared to this, and I was prepared to turn over several euros each day for the pleasure.

I had a week in which to set up a bank account before I was to report to the Florence regional office of the Italian Ministry of Agriculture, Food, and Forestry Policies. Supposedly most everyone in the office spoke reasonably good English; my Italian, though improving, was nowhere near ready to communicate about dirt.

"*Questo è un bellissimo sporco,*" I practiced in the mirror. That is beautiful dirt.

The memory of Peter shaking his head at my enthusiasm for dirt surfaced in my mind's eye and tightened my throat. *No*, I whispered to myself, and him. *It doesn't matter that I don't understand why. Why you lied to me for months. Why you lied to yourself. None of that matters; I'm in Italy now, and you don't get to come.*

I pulled up the various web pages I had bookmarked to look for a more permanent place to live. All I knew about my job at this point was that I would work out of the Florence office, but I would spend time in the field to the north and west, and Pietro had suggested I find a rental around Lucca. So here I was. At least I had been here for one day with Alicia, so I could imagine the lay of the land more accurately.

By the end of the week, I had accomplished all but my biggest goal. I had a car of my own, I had a bank account, and I had met with a few of my new colleagues, who did all speak English, thank God!

I still didn't have a permanent place to live, but hoped Matteo would have some ideas. Maybe a friend had a place to rent.

PETER

Weeks after Chris' surprise visit, I was in much the same spot, doing almost exactly the same thing. I'd been sufficiently embarrassed, though, to deal with the mess I had let accumulate. I mean my best friend, a guy who said "dude," no less, had loaded my dishwasher.

His last day in the lab had been months ago, last year! And still I sat here working on the exact same hang-up I'd been toying with on his departure. I was smart, dedicated, checking and double-checking my data. Consulting with my colleagues. I'd even brought my boss in for brainstorming, rather than listening to him tell me what I was doing wrong. But I was barely any further. I'd been sporadically able to replicate the methylation with the enzyme I'd used just before I'd broken up with Jane; that was it.

I pushed back roughly from the computer, wandered over to the window, and stared at the bare trees.

Why couldn't I get this one thing to work?

My body landed heavily in the chair again, wishing I could feel the jolt of Chris shaking it. It wasn't hard to imagine his life now that he was done, had a job, and was making a real contribution. I was sure he did it all while looking as perfect as ever, no doubt after having had morning sex with Lauren and collecting accolades from his colleagues. He'd leave about four-thirty, go to the gym, be home by six for that downtime he swore was so important.

Yes, I was jealous.

Turning away from the lowering sun outside the window, I reassured myself I was on the right track. I hadn't gotten this far by going home early.

During my next attempts over the following weeks, I adjusted the concentration, hoping a solution with nano amounts less would break the bonds, but keep the strands intact. If it worked, I would have slightly better than a 50 percent success rate.

One more try, I thought to myself as I carefully added the enzyme I'd been working with for months to the strands of DNA in the petri dish. *Just one more. If it doesn't work this time, I'll give up.*

When the micropipette was empty for the last time, I stood up and stretched. Turning to the computer, I watched the progress bar moving slowly at the bottom of the screen, as it analyzed the data I'd entered last night. Or had that been early this morning?

Outside the window, the trees were no longer completely bare; tight buds were starting to form on the branches. An endless cycle that never failed. Unlike me, who failed as often as I saw any progress.

I sighed to myself as I watched people walking across the quad without coats. The last few warm days had been teasing hints of spring. Was I destined to stay forever a postdoc, to always be crouched over a lab bench while outside, the seasons changed, the people around me succeeding and moving forward?

"Come to Switzerland," Fritz kept saying. "Let us help you finish your research." The last call had been two days ago, the same as ever. *We're doing great work here. I have a dozen research assistants I could put at your disposal. I know this is your goal, to determine how to stop this replication. We have a bigger budget.* And the last one, the one that tugged at me now: "Come join us, I can have you here anytime you wish."

Maybe I should take Fritz up on his offer. Screw being "unbiased." Wasn't the more important thing finding a cure? I knew Chris would take the opportunity. Hell, Chris had taken the opportunity. Abandoned his postdoc before our research was complete and jumped at pursuing his own theory.

"I don't know," I said out loud to the empty room.

Wouldn't taking a job with a well-respected pharmaceutical company be the biggest end to this mess? I could show Jane I'd done it. Made progress, made a decision, asked for help. Any of the things that would mean I had accomplished ... anything.

I could tell myself I'd made it. Most importantly, I could get out of here. I thought of the bareness of my cabinets at home, the spoiled milk I'd thrown away yesterday, the bags of chips lingering in the trashcan fifteen feet away.

Taking a job from Fritz would mean ... getting away from this dumpster fire that my life had become. Leaving behind all the things that triggered memories of Jane. No more walking into the grocery store and feeling sad when I remembered picking out tomatoes with her one random winter's day.

You could have had everything you wanted if you'd been willing to compromise.

"That ship has sailed," I muttered to myself. I wasn't sure I wanted kids as much as I had insisted. But there was no going back. Besides, she was probably already wrapped up with someone else. A woman like her, as beautiful and caring and funny and smart, would never stay single for very long.

I shook myself. My plan was in place. Suddenly it occurred to me that meant I could be staring out a window, baffled and frustrated, for the rest of my life. And then ... I looked across the lab space—empty now, but often buzzing with colleagues hard at work on similar projects. Even if I figured this out, someone would still have to develop a drug that would work in a human the way an enzyme worked in solution; the very work that Roche did.

The golden cast of the sun on the grass beyond my window told me it was late afternoon. Probably why my stomach was growling. I grabbed my wallet and headed for the cafeteria. I decided to take the scenic route and walk outside.

Students were playing frisbee in the quad as I passed through. I took a deep breath, and the scent of coffee wafted down the path, where I noticed a new cart. Coffee sounded like a good idea.

Il Carrello del Caffè read the sign on the side of the red truck. Behind the counter, a shiny espresso machine, a larger version of Jane's, hissed.

"Just a cup of regular coffee," I said.

"For here or to go?"

"To go, please. You offer 'here' cups?"

Something Resembling Love

"Sure, man. Gotta do our part," he responded, as a coworker handed out an espresso to a woman standing off to the side. I glanced at the small cup, distracted.

"Here's your coffee, man."

I reached up automatically, still watching the woman stir sugar into the cup.

That's probably exactly what Jane had done last fall when she had been in Italy. Being fawned over by tall, elegant waiters who served espresso in tiny cups. Giving them that same doting smile she'd given to me.

I threw some cash on the counter and turned hastily, food forgotten.

I packed up my computer and rushed home. The same mountain of mail greeted me, and for the first time in a while, I sneered at it.

I dumped my bag in a chair and sat at the counter, tossing junk mail onto the floor, embarrassed at myself all over again. For hours I sorted and pitched, hauling a bag down to the trash, for once abandoning my rule of shredding.

I picked up the phone. It was midnight, but with the seven-hour difference, my call would be at a reasonable time.

"Fritz?" I said when he answered, "It's Peter. I've given more thought to your offer. I want to come."

"Peter, hallo! This is *fantastisch* news! Yes, yes, we will love to have you join us."

I listened to him describing the process to me and what I would need to do. In the back of my mind, I was already discarding my things.

When the phone call was over, I wandered around the living area several times and then sat down hard on the couch. Had I made the right choice?

Yes. I have. It wasn't like I hadn't been thinking about this for months already, not like I'd made a rash choice in the heat of the moment. I might never get back to Evanston again. I might never see Chris. Inwardly, I shook my head—of course I would see Chris. Our fields were similar enough that we'd be at the same conferences. I would come to visit my parents, and I'd probably come back to Chicago. This was a rational decision.

I gave up sitting on the couch and any pretense of watching the algorithm run, and went to bed. It would be there in the morning—complete or not. Staring at it wouldn't help.

In the morning, gray skies and flurries had replaced yesterday's sun. The clock read seven-thirty. I got out of bed, grabbed a T-shirt, and started a pot of coffee. I would need it. It would take all day to back up my data. And then I had to tell my boss I was leaving the program.

God, it would be so good to get away from that critical jerk.

But first things first. I hit Chris' number and put him on speaker.

"You're up early," he greeted me.

"Ha ha."

I could envision him leaning back in his chair, the way I'd seen him do thousands of times in our years together. "Have you made any more dumb decisions since I last saw you?"

"I called to tell you something you might actually be pleased to hear."

"You've pulled your head out of your ass and realized that Jane was the best thing that ever happened to you, and screw it if she doesn't want kids, because you don't actually care as much as you say, and never did?"

God, I wished that were true. Any of it.

In my silence, Chris continued, "Peter, you're so entrenched in your work you can't see anything other than the choice you have made, can't tell if there's another way to fit the pieces you want together."

"I'm doing something new. Hopefully, this decision will turn out better than the last one."

"What did you do?" I could hear both wariness and excitement in Chris' voice.

"I took the job with Roche."

"You did!? Wow, that's great! Good work."

"You don't think it was the wrong decision?" I wanted the Chris stamp of approval. He made smart decisions, always.

"I think it's an excellent decision," he said sincerely. "If this is really the work you want to do, it's best to do it somewhere you have full support."

"I do, you're right."

"This is great news, Peter. Congratulations!" I could hear his smile in the words. "When do you leave?"

"Two weeks. I'm going to close down the lab this week, pack up the stuff I can ship to Switzerland, sell the rest, and spend a weekend with my folks."

"What do they think about this?"

"You're the first person I've told."

"Aww, I feel so honored," he said, and I could picture him setting his hand on his chest.

"You're such a jerk," I laughed.

"But I'm a jerk who's happy for you. Let me know if you need any help getting rid of stuff."

It was raining steadily when I landed in a dark Zürich on April 3. I collected my two large suitcases and headed for where Fritz said he would meet me.

"Hallo, Peter!" In a trench coat and fedora-looking hat, rain beating down, he waved me over. "Do not worry, your luggage will fit," he chuckled, at the look I gave his car.

A few minutes of jostling and they did.

"Brrr," Fritz said, as he slid in behind the wheel, shaking his head like a dog. "Terrible weather for you to come in to. But it is winter still, so it rains. I will take you to the hotel now, and tomorrow I will pick you up."

In short order, we were unloading my luggage at a large building. We hefted my bags onto a cart and wheeled them to the room I would have for a week. I sniffed at the musty air, wondering what kind of mold might be growing in the cracks.

"It is the old grain smell. This building was a mill. Ahhhh," Fritz took a deep breath. "Smells pleasant, yes?"

"Mmm," I agreed noncommittally.

Alone not long later, I laid down on the bed, staring at the ceiling. I woke a few hours later, shivering, brushed my teeth, and got back into bed. At the first hint of sunrise, the neighbor's rooster woke me, *cock-a-doodle-dooing* his heart out. I would have loved to have covered my head with a pillow and gone back to sleep.

Instead, I hauled myself out of bed and took a hot shower. At least the coffee was strong. And the breakfast enjoyable, I thought as I ate my *rosti*, the

Swiss version of a potato pancake. Fritz appeared as I was finishing my meal and ordered a coffee for himself.

"Today, I will show you the lab you will work in, and you will meet your apprentices."

"Apprentices? I don't know that I'm qualified to be teaching anybody."

"Maybe this is not the right word. Assistants? Anyway, you will meet the people you will work with." He waved the nuance away. "Tonight, you and I will have dinner with my director. He is excited about your research, as am I."

I merely nodded, not seeing what anyone could be excited about. But that was why I was here. To work with people with more experience and deeper pockets. I could see, looking at Fritz's dress pants and button-down shirt, that I would have to upgrade my wardrobe. Maybe not for the lab. But certainly to socialize. I was glad I had one suit that fit.

The day went at a breakneck pace. I met no fewer than twenty-two lab techs. Some were students doing an internship, others were like me, partway into their career. Most were European, and all, thankfully, spoke English. My German was passable, but not scientific.

In the evening, Fritz picked me up at the hotel again and drove me to dinner. "Tomorrow I will take you to a few places you might live."

"Sure," I nodded. I expected some of this—a hotel upon my arrival, meeting Fritz's boss. But a hotel for a week, a ride from the airport, and help with housing were beyond what I had imagined.

"We are glad you are here, Peter. This is an area we are very much interested in having a breakthrough. I know your research has not been as successful as you would like."

"Or at all," I said, mostly under my breath.

"Yes, or at all," Fritz chuckled. "But you see, you are only one man. It is too big a problem for one person. We can crack this puzzle, I think. We have many good minds, and more money. Then we can say we cured cancer! And we will be famous and wealthy."

I cringed a little at the excitement Fritz had for the wealth. But, it was a pharmaceutical company, and profit was important. It was also why they had the deep pockets to fund this research. I nodded. "It would be good to do something so momentous."

Something Resembling Love

In the morning, Fritz did as promised and took me to look at several possible housing arrangements. The apartments were as small as my place in Evanston had been and would have suited me just fine. But Fritz had other plans.

"I showed you these so you would know your options. But I think you do not want an apartment. I think you will want a house. This one is just for sale; it could be good."

He was right. A twenty-minute train ride to the Roche office, it had a traditional high-peaked roof on its small footprint, and a creamy stucco exterior. The small yard had a tiny brick patio, and was planted with shrubs and rose bushes. Jane would have made them bloom; I'd probably kill them within the year. The kitchen held functional Nordic-looking cabinets, and the walls were white everywhere. But the parquet floors made the house inviting.

It reminded me a bit of Jane's house, and I wondered if she knew I had left.

"I'll take it," I said, before I could overthink the decision. I wasn't going back to the US any time soon, and I could afford a house now. If this was my new life, I might as well jump right in.

"You have not even seen the whole thing," Fritz laughed at my outburst.

"You said you thought I would like it." I gazed around the empty rooms. "I am sure you have already vetted it as livable or you would not be suggesting it. It's close to the office, and it seems like a nice place."

"I will have the agent come to the hotel tomorrow if you like."

I turned back to Fritz. "Thanks for arranging all of this," I said, sincerely.

Only eight days after I landed in Zürich, I walked through the front door of the cute house again, and set my keys on the counter. My bags were once again in Fritz's car and he had promised to bring them by that evening.

I walked from room to room. In a few hours my furniture would be delivered. I'd spent my weekend charging to my credit card the things I would need. A bed, pots and pans, a table, a couch, a TV. A set of sheets, a set of silverware and dishes.

I could be happy here, I decided. I *would* be happy here. Fritz would help me be successful. He could mentor me, and I already knew from our previous conversations about my research that he wouldn't make me feel like a failure. Working with Fritz would be far better than with my boss at Northwestern. *Screw that guy*, I thought, as I looked out the kitchen window to the backyard and the wall that faced the street.

I picked up my phone and called Chris.

"If I didn't know you were seven time zones away, I'd wonder who had snatched your body and gotten you up so early," he answered.

His greeting made me smile. "Good to hear your voice."

"Have you unlocked prostate cancer's biggest mysteries yet?"

"No, but I did just buy a house."

"You're moving fast." I could picture his face, open with shock.

"It's great here, Chris. I wish I had done this six months ago, or right when Fritz first presented the idea. You were right."

"Say that again."

I laughed. "You were right, Chris. How's Evanston?"

"You've only been gone two weeks. Nothing has changed."

"Did you guys go out for St. Patrick's Day?"

"You would have hated it. Alicia karaoke'd Dropkick Murphys." I heard him grinning. "I'm happy for you, and glad to hear you are moving forward." His voice was sincere.

"Thanks, Chris. See you at that genetics conference over the summer?"

"Wouldn't miss it."

I was moving on. That's why I was here. It was good for my career. I ran the tip of my finger along the edge of the house's key. It was good to be away from all the reminders, the not-so-chance encounters.

After my first month at Roche, I was sure I had made the right choice. Even though I hadn't yet had any further success with the hypermethylation. But as Fritz had pointed out, if it had been so easy, someone would have accomplished it already. I didn't miss my old lab at all, but I found myself wishing

Something Resembling Love

Chris were around to toss insults and ideas my way. In his place, there were a few other lab rats, and five of us had quit the lab early yesterday and gone for a beer. The local Kölsch had me anticipating Oktoberfest, still months away.

Chris would be proud of me, I thought as I closed my laptop. I was working, only briefly—checking a few stats on a Saturday morning. But now I was heading out. I double-checked that I had filled my small pack with water and added a nutrition bar.

I'd overheard one of my coworkers talking about a hike he had done with his family, going up Uetliberg, Zürich's home mountain. He had started in the city, which I discovered would be a long hike. I'd decided I could probably do the least steep climb, and be home to catch the Swiss soccer—no, football—team play the Italians.

The trail was even steeper than I expected, and I climbed slowly. My last couple of weeks in Chicago had been a whirlwind: getting rid of furniture, packing, ending my lease early, and trying to reassure my parents, or at least my mom, that this move was a good choice. My dad had been strangely complimentary.

Just a few weeks in, and things were already looking far better. Except for no one at home, no one to eat dinner with, or hold hands with, or all those other fun things Jane and I had done together. Closing my eyes while I paused to catch my breath, I tried to banish the memory of that first New Year's we'd spent together, her grabbing my hand to pull me into the center of our group of friends and dance.

That was where this had started—all of this. Where I'd first talked to Jane, first let myself imagine being with her. But it was also the night I'd met Fritz. How could one night have changed my whole life so completely?

If Jane and I had stayed together, one of us would have had to sacrifice. Her job, her life, was in Chicago. She couldn't move wherever just because her boyfriend had been offered a position. If I had stayed, I would have continued on as I had been, never making progress, falling further and further behind.

At the summit, I examined the panoramic guide to each of the mountains in view. Snow topped them all, but below, the city was green. I took a few photos and sent them to Chris, needing to show him how different my life now was.

In a couple more hours, I was walking back through my front door. I flipped on the television, letting the sound of the German-speaking announcers fill the downstairs. I ran hot water and jumped in the shower. Closing my eyes against the spray, I remembered coming home from ice fishing last December. Jane had been in the desert for a week, and I'd gone directly to her house the afternoon we'd both come home.

I shivered now, remembering how cold my whole body had been, and how quickly it had warmed when Jane had snuck into the shower behind me, her breasts pressed to my back.

"How's the fierce hunter?" she'd asked, wrapping her arms around my waist, reaching up to wash my chest.

"Grrr, me man, me eat meat," I'd grunted.

"Catch anything?" Her hands had run down my body to capture my now defrosted and quickly responding parts.

"No, but I'd like to."

"I'll make it easy for you …"

I shut the water off now, blocking the rest of the memory, of her pulling me, both of us dripping wet, into bed.

Nope, not thinking of that. I pulled on sweats and headed for the fridge to reheat the barley soup I'd found at the grocery store. While it slowly bubbled on the stove, I texted Fritz.

> I will take you up on your offer for dinner.

Almost immediately, he responded.

> Come Thursday.

"Peter! How wonderful you came!" Fritz's wife opened the door mid-knock, ushered me into the house, and took my jacket all in one motion.

Inside, the yellowed cream walls showcased family photos and a breakfront held papers and knickknacks. Candles wavered on the mantle above a small fireplace.

Something Resembling Love

"Here, Peter," Fritz handed me a beer. "Let me introduce you—you have met my wife before," he said, kissing her as she brought a plate with a variety of cheeses. "These are my children," he named all three, ranging in age from ten to twenty-two. "And this is my niece, Anja. She is living with us since she has started a new job in the city. The commute was too far from where my older brother lives."

"Hallo, Peter, it is nice to meet you. My uncle says you moved here from the US," Anja said.

I blinked. "I-I did, several weeks—a bit ago. In April." Blonde, blue-eyed, buxom. She looked ... comfortable. But her gaze was direct. I felt pinned, but in a good way.

I automatically followed her into the family room, Fritz and the youngest of his kids ahead of us.

"Are you settling in?" Fritz asked.

"The lab is great, and I'm finding a routine. I had hoped to have more results to show by now, but having other scientists to share ideas with has been invaluable."

He laughed. "You and I struggled for a year with ideas, and you wanted it to be solved once you got here."

I cringed as he laughed at me. "No, I—"

"I think this is *fantastisch*, Peter, really *fantastisch*. This is the kind of attitude that will help you solve the problem eventually, this desire to see results."

So, he wasn't laughing at me. "You've put a lot of resources into this project. I don't want to let you down."

"From what *Onkel* Fritz has said, you seem very driven," Anja said. "He talked about you even before you moved here, your ideas about stopping the prostate cancer. My dear friend's father has it, and it would be good if he didn't."

"Are you a scientist too?"

"No," she shook her head. "I am at the Rietberg Museum. But *Onkel* Fritz talks about what he is working on. We all must listen." She gave Fritz a smile that said she was teasing him.

"I cannot help that I enjoy what I do!" he laughed, throwing his hands up in excitement.

Over the course of dinner I relaxed, feeling less like Fritz and his family were taking pity on the new guy who couldn't make any friends, and more like I was sincerely welcome. Fritz was older than me, but not as much as I had assumed, given his role at Roche. Maybe late forties. His brother must have been much older for Anja to be thirty, as I found out over the evening.

When I got home that night, the bare essentials of furniture reminded me of how alone I was.

It's only been a month, I reminded myself. And I worked a lot. I thought about having Anja over. Would she be dismayed, compared to the home she lived in with Fritz and his family—the large house, the homey atmosphere?

I resolved to find some artwork over the weekend.

JANE

At the beginning of my first official week, I drove to the train station and rode to Florence. The train was more convenient, and parking in Florence was both a hassle and expensive. The city had restricted traffic even further since Alicia and I had visited.

In the office, Pietro introduced me to the secretary, the other field officers, and a couple of younger, college-aged guys who were interning. Pietro assured me that despite the successes they had had with my earlier advice, no one expected miracles. They were simply glad to have another, more modern perspective.

By the end of that week and through the next, I was tagging along to farms and commercial vineyards.

The first few weeks were a blur of new faces, names, places. Rolling hill after rolling hill covered in grapevines and olive trees that were starting to leaf out with the warming days of spring.

"This is Jane," Pietro would say in rapid Italian. "She is new to our office."

The response would go one of three ways. Either I would be scrutinized and watched carefully, or I would be given a dismissive glance and completely ignored. On those occasions I felt like the big shot lawyers in the movie *Erin Brockovich*, going to cattle farms in heels and waving for attention from outside the pens. But sometimes I would be welcomed warmly, taken in for a tasting of olive oil on fresh bread, my delight at the experience making up for my wholly inadequate Italian.

By the time Matteo was back from his tour, I'd been tasting home-produced oil and wine for almost a month.

Fussing over which dress to wear, I twirled in front of the computer screen, hoping Lauren and Alicia could decide for me.

"The pink one!" Lauren exclaimed, "You look darling in it."

"No, the orangey one," Alicia disagreed. "It's a stronger color, goes better with your hair. Besides, it will make you feel confident."

"I need that right now."

"Confidence? Nah, you got this," Lauren cheered.

"I just keep thinking about Peter," I said as I came to a stop in front of the camera. "There's so much *why* in my head."

"Don't let him ruin Italy for you," Alicia said.

"I'm trying really hard not to. But … *why*? You know? I'm so mad. At him for not being truthful from the start. At myself for trusting when he said he knew what he wanted."

"I believed him," Lauren said. "I think he really thought he had it figured out. He just didn't have all the data he needed. Like seeing you with kids."

"But he dated someone with an infant! How does that not make you think about whether you want kids!"

"He didn't see *you* with kids. Dating someone is different than spending all your free time with a child and thinking seriously about what's next. Besides, boys are dumb. Sometimes they have to be hit over the head with something."

Alicia snorted.

"I doubt Chris does anything that dumb."

"Maybe not quite that bad. But he's done some interesting things, for sure."

"And I've seen him in action," Alicia added. "So, the consensus is, boys are dumb sometimes, and some are dumber than most. But I have a feeling Matteo isn't one of the dumb ones."

"Then the question is do I want to feel like a girl, or do I want to look like I'm more sure of myself than I really am?"

Something Resembling Love

"Save the pink one," Lauren grudged. "Use it when you really need to play the soft and feminine card."

Laughing, we signed off. I picked up my brush to sweep one side of my hair back, to do something with it for a change, and *What the he—* ... I held up a top section of my hair, and strands only a few inches long filtered through. With the upper hairs pulled away, I could clearly see a straight line where a two-inch-wide section of my hair had been sheared off.

I dropped the hair and picked it up again. I thought of Peter's inability to meet my eyes the morning he broke up with me. *Had he...* surely, he wouldn't have cut my hair off. Would he?

I watched the shorter hairs float down as I picked up the same chunk again. I was horrified. And then I started to laugh. A snort at first, because how ridiculous it was to save the hair of the woman whose heart you were about to break. The snort turned into a giggle, and the giggle into hysterical laughter that had me grabbing the counter edge and sinking along the wall in tears, laughing and sobbing at the same time.

As I took some deep breaths, the hysterics subsided, and I stood to look at myself in the mirror. I decided to forgo sweeping any part of my hair back.

As I looked at myself, brushing my hair straight, I spoke out loud. "You really know how to make a girl feel special, Peter."

I put on a bright lipstick and walked out the door.

※

As I walked to the town square, I pushed the thought of my sheared-off hair from my mind. Dwelling on it wasn't going to help me settle into the evening. Considering, I realized, I'd never seen Matteo in anything other than nylon pants and hiking boots. I doubted he'd wear that, but I couldn't imagine him dressed any other way. What I was sure of was that I was excited that spring was peeking out, it was warm enough for a dress, and I was going to have authentic Italian food.

Waiting outside the restaurant, I was drawn to the window of the shop next door, and I didn't hear Matteo behind me. I jumped out of my skin when he set his hand on my shoulder.

"Sorry, I made you startled," he said as I turned.

"You did!" I returned the kisses he brushed on my cheeks, letting him take my hands briefly. He was wearing a loose-fitting, short-sleeve button-down over dark brown pants.

"This is fine for dinner?" he asked, gesturing toward the narrow entry to the bistro. I studied his sturdy and sinewy hands.

"I haven't had pizza since I left Italy last fall. I was afraid I would be disappointed." My mouth was already watering, thinking of rings of calamari.

We took a small table outside, and he ordered chianti and pizza. "Your journey was satisfactory?"

"Yeah, not quick, but easy. My first few weeks have been nice. I've done a little sightseeing, met the people I'll be working with. One of them helped me buy a used car."

"What is your job?"

"It used to be fertilizer. Chemical and organic, and why some work better than others. Now I get to do whatever the Italian Ministry of Agriculture wants, since I helped solve a fungus problem." I shrugged. "The outstanding question seems to be not only how much damage is done to the land mass in vineyards from erosion, but also how the nutrient levels are impacted by the erosion. It's a project only budgeted for six months right now, so we'll see how good I really am, if they decide to renew it."

"You are very smart; they will want you to stay." He wasn't looking at me when he said it. The words were more a statement of fact, the way he would say *this is the best pizza in the town.*

"That's sweet. But I don't think how smart I am has anything to do with it. I think it's more about the money and whether they see any results. Six months isn't a lot of time to try something new."

"You are the best, they say."

"Who says?" I tilted my head, unsure what he meant.

"The government. Your bosses?" At my furrowed brow, he admitted, "I Googled you."

I burst out laughing. "You Googled me!? Why?"

"It was after your tour was over." He ducked his head. "You had been interested so much in the trees in the forests and plants. Then you were gone, and I thought maybe I had missed you a little. I wanted to see about you."

Something Resembling Love

I chuckled, then took a large drink of my wine, which Matteo promptly refilled. But I had done the same. He was harder to find than I knew I was. Government work and papers and conference presentations made it impossible to avoid having an internet presence.

I regarded the last piece of pizza, trying to decide if I had to share or not. Matteo subtly pushed the tray closer to me.

"Where will you live while you are here?"

Describing my odd work arrangement, I said, "I don't know yet. I need to be able to go out from Lucca, but also go into Florence every week."

"So you will work in Lucca, but not live in Lucca?"

"It's kind of like you. You have a house near here somewhere, I presume. But sometimes you will go elsewhere, like when you were guiding us all through the forests, and you stay wherever the group you are leading stays. Some days I'll go visit vintners or farmers, other days I'll stay at home and work on plans for them, sometimes I'll go to Florence to meet with my teammates."

"Ah, yes, now I understand more. And you like where you are living?" Matteo asked.

"It's fine for the moment, but not ideal. I've been able to extend where I'm living a few weeks, but the landlord says I have to be out by the end of April. At home, our government would have paid for me to live in a hotel the whole time. But that's not how it works here."

"That would be very lonely, would it not?"

I considered; I'd lived in hotels for a couple of months at a time before. Probably it had been a touch lonely. But I'd always known I was going home at the end of those few weeks. I shrugged.

"You will stay with me, then."

I laughed again, but he didn't join me. "We hardly know each other; I can't just move into your house. What if we don't get along?"

"Is no problem. I am very busy in this time of year; I am often not there for several days."

"And where would I sleep when you are there?" I envisioned a studio sized apartment or tiny house with just enough room for a bedroom, bath, and small kitchen. I might not know Matteo well, but I was fairly certain that he would be perfectly content to live the way he had for the week he had been guiding us: sparse bedroom, small bathroom, hot pad stove—just the necessities.

"In your room, of course," he said, brow furrowed. "Ohhh. Hahaha." Now it was his turn to laugh at me. "No, Jane, I have a home. It was my parents' house until they moved to the south. Now I live there. It is a very nice house; you will like it. Would you like to see it?"

I felt a flush creeping into my cheeks and covered it with an enthusiastic, "Yes!"

"Tomorrow I will take you there," he said with a decisive nod.

An hour or so later, Matteo walked me back to the short-term apartment, pointing out shops and restaurants I might want to check out in the coming days. When he was satisfied that I was at the doorstep to the actual apartment, we said good night. I wanted to run my hands through his close-cropped hair. Instead, he bent to brush kisses over my cheeks again.

I particularly liked this Italian custom.

Not three days later, I was settled in Matteo's home, having shoveled my luggages, as he'd called transferring my things. As was the local style, the house had stone walls, plastered and painted with rich colors of terracotta, gold, and French blue.

There had been a minor disagreement about rent.

"Are you sure? That you want to share your home with me, that is. What will your girlfriend say?" I was certain he was not married, but wasn't sure he wasn't otherwise attached.

"Girlfriend?"

"*La findanzata.* I don't want to be tripping over someone unexpectedly in the middle of the night." At his blank expression, I gave up. Clearly, there was no girlfriend either. "Never mind. How much do you want in rent?"

"No, nothing, there is no rent."

"Don't be ridiculous, of course, I'll pay rent."

"I do not want it; I do not need the money." Straightforward, matter of fact. Night and day from wishy-washy Peter.

"It doesn't matter if you need it, I'm not paying nothing. Besides, your expenses will go up. Water, electricity."

"Is *irrilevante*."

Something Resembling Love

"It's not irrelevant!" I nearly stamped my foot. "You have no reason to provide me with a place to live for free, and if you won't take money, then I'll find someplace else to live."

"We are friends, no? I have this place, why would I not share?"

"I'll pay 500 euros each month." That seemed fair, a good chunk off any mortgage, although I suspected the house was already paid for. I glared at him.

"Yes, yes, fine," he chuckled. "I can see you will not give up."

In so many ways, rural Tuscany was like a land out of time. Small farms were everywhere, producing just enough for the village nearby, sometimes only enough for the family. In many of these, the tasks were done by hand by one or two people, vines carefully selected and trimmed, and scrutinized individually. This was still true in the large operations that sold to regional stores or even exported, to a certain degree, although many of them had large machines for harvesting.

But the chemistry of the land had been changing over the past decade, and while the soil still appeared fertile, pests presented more of a problem, and harvests weren't as fruitful as they once had been. My job was to figure out what had changed, how much modern farming had sped up that process, and if it could be corrected. No small task in an area where agriculture was slowly losing its foothold, subtly altering everything from the traditional way of life to tourism.

Word spread quickly of my arrival, and the farmers became less reluctant to talk with me. A few were already expecting when Pietro made his introductions. My Italian was improving, but not always in useful ways. I could say, "The cultivator is damaging the soil structure," with confidence, but still stuttered when asking for help finding the correct size pants.

I'd seen Matteo hide a laugh when I tried to say, "These pants are too big in the butt." What I'd actually said was, "My butt is very large." When he'd be able to look at me with a straight face, he'd gently corrected my Italian.

Sometimes, he'd weigh in on what I was considering—those hiking boots aren't sturdy enough, try this jacket.

"Oh, look at this beautiful store," I'd said one afternoon, slowing past another artful front window.

"In there, it is frippery."

"Let's go in." I tugged on his hand.

"You go," he said, releasing my hand and stepping away. "I will be at the bar."

I snickered to myself as I went in, glancing once more to watch Matteo hightail it down the street.

But hours later, he was singing a different tune.

"That red looks very nice on you," he said of my pashmina, as he held a chair for me at dinner at a small restaurant near his house.

"Thank you. I bought it today. In the shop you refused to go in," I teased.

"Hm," he considered, leaning to the side, and inspecting my entire outfit.

I shifted the scarf, wrapping it fully around my shoulders and back, and threw a flirty smile at him over my shoulder.

We ordered the *chinghiale bolognese*, a standard meal, but prepared in the Tuscan style, with wild boar. Afterwards, we strolled over the bridge toward the car.

I waited while Matteo unlocked it and opened the door.

"*Grazie mille.*"

In less than a second, he had trapped me between the car door, the front panel, and his arms, and he was kissing me thoroughly. I leapt into it, my body saying *hello*, and *yes please*.

He took advantage, his tongue stroking mine, hands on either side of me, caging me against the car as he shifted forward, pressing his lean body against mine.

"Were you waiting all night to do that?" I laughed between kisses.

"Yes." He was breathing heavily, as if it took great effort to restrain himself.

Then he suddenly stopped, stepped back, offered his hand, and helped me into the car.

My heart pounded the whole drive home. When we parked in the crushed stone drive, Matteo was at my door before I'd managed to undo my seatbelt, offering his hand to help me out. His arm slid around my waist as we walked in, feeling very comfortable.

Something Resembling Love

In the kitchen, he turned me toward himself and resumed the kissing he had broken off so quickly.

I leaned toward him, remembering the kiss we had shared at our *agritourismo*. Sadness washed through me. I had been there while Peter had supposedly been making up his mind about kids. But this, I thought as Matteo's hands skimmed up my sides, this was far better than the early days of having to convince Peter I wanted him.

When I felt Matteo pull back, I opened my eyes. He was looking right at me, his hands wrapped around the pashmina still resting around my neck. "Perhaps I like this frippery," he said, smoothing his hands down the front of the soft material, and over my body. "I said I was sorry I kissed you so much the last night of the trekking." His voice was hoarse. "But I wasn't."

"I wasn't either," I whispered. It had been almost two weeks since I'd moved in, itchy nights knowing he was at the end of the hall, hoping Matteo might do more than kiss me, unsure how he truly felt.

"Good." He wrapped an arm around my waist again, guiding me up the stairs to his bedroom.

His hands still on my waist, he reverted to who he had been on that terrace, kissing me with quiet concentration. "This is all right for you?"

Rather than reply, I stood on my toes and crushed my mouth to his, stumbling him back a step. His hands tightened on my waist, stepping me backward until my knees hit the bed and I fell, pulling him with me.

"I am glad you are back," he said, unzipping my dress at the side to run his thumb along the ribs exposed by the opening.

"I am, too," I agreed, unbuttoning down his shirt and pants.

"I am glad you are living with me here." His hand pressed into my knee, opening it to the side. The cool air of the room hit my skin, and I felt exposed in the most delicious way.

"I am, too," I repeated, unfastening his pants, hearing his shoes hit the floor.

"Come with me," Matteo said, voice low in the twilight of his room.

I let my body follow his as he stood, his hand holding mine and helping me up.

"*Bellissima.*"

Under the scrutiny of his gaze, I felt myself blush, though I kept my eyes on him. One of his fingers rested at the base of my throat, and then he twisted his hand, his fingers cupping the back of my neck and his thumb sweeping over where his finger had just been.

After another long moment, he used his hand to pull me against him, kissing me the way he had by the car. Not patient and tender, but devouring. His free hand played with the edge of my skirt, gathering it into his hand until it was out of the way, and he could place his hand on my skin, using the leverage to drag me even closer to him.

"Matteo, please," I whimpered, my own hands resting on the smooth fabric of his pants.

The hand that was at the back of my neck dropped and found its way under the other side of my skirt, until he was pushing the entire thing up. I shivered when the fabric left me, as much from excitement as anything else.

"You are cold?"

"Some."

"This way," he said, picking up my hand to turn me back toward the bed. I noticed for the first time that it was covered by a patchwork quilt. In the brief moment before Matteo sat next to me, guided me to lie down, I wondered if someone in his family had made it.

Then he was lying next to me, his shirt off. In the shadows he looked sculpted, like Perseus after slaying Medusa, and I ran my fingertips over his chest.

He did the same, and I could feel the callouses on his hand rough against my skin as he ran his hand underneath and then along the side of my breast. He didn't stop, and I felt the same sensation across the top of my chest. When he reached my nipple, I exhaled, leaning into the feeling.

"This pleases you?" He was studying my face.

Instead of words, I put my hand on the back of his and shifted so I could work my other hand under the open waistband of his pants. My God, he had a nice ass. I gave a slow but firm squeeze, and Matteo sucked in a breath.

"Does this please you?" I mimicked.

He watched me for a few seconds and then moved, covering my body with his.

"I think you should take your pants off," I said as I looked into his dark chocolate-brown eyes.

Something Resembling Love

"Hmph," he grunted and sat on the edge of the bed. He was back quickly, moving his hips until he lay between my legs. There was no question about what he wanted to do.

He didn't go for the easy answer, though. Instead, he kissed me again, thoroughly, deeply, passionately, leaving no corner of my lips unexplored. A thumb worked its way under the edge of my panties, and he lifted himself away as he edged the finger closer to my center.

When he finally set his thumb against me—not pushing, no parting, just a warm spot against my skin—I jumped.

"I am glad you are back. I thought of you many times since you left."

"How did you think of me?" I asked as I took advantage of the space between us and set my hand against him. "Like this?" His short boxer briefs were snug over him. I moved a single finger up and down.

He grunted and pushed my hand away. I felt his fingers in my low back as he hooked his thumbs at the sides of my panties, pulling them down my thighs. Kisses trailed in their wake.

He tossed my panties to the edge of the bed and sat back to take his briefs off. He was gorgeous. Muscles defined, subtly, from days spent hiking rocky trails and wooded paths. Toned abs but not in a scary, hours-in-the-gym kind of way.

I reached to set my hand on his upper thigh, the muscle hard under my hand. He settled himself between my legs again, but he didn't rush. I watched him slowly and carefully roll a condom onto himself. And then he came back to kissing me, across my cheeks, and down my neck, to my collarbone. As he reached the hollow at the base of my throat, he moved his hips, edging up against me. I pulled my knees up around him. Matteo accepted the invitation, still moving slowly until his pelvis pressed against mine.

My breath came out in a rush.

"You are fine?"

Instead of words, I canted myself toward him.

As slowly as he had entered, Matteo drew away from me. His return was less subtle, and I cried out at the impact.

He stopped. "Are you hurt?"

"Hm-mm, no," I rolled my head side to side. "Do it again."

I saw a flash of white teeth, and Matteo repeated the motion. Over and over until I wrapped my arms around his back. He grunted in my ear and then groaned with his last few thrusts, taking me with him.

For a few minutes, the only sound was our ragged breathing. Matteo turned on to his back, carrying me with him.

As I lay on his chest, he said, "It is very good you are back."

I laughed softly and snuggled close, his arms coming to hold me. My breath came out in a long, shaky exhale, releasing something I hadn't been aware I'd been holding on to.

PETER

I sat at a table a high-school-aged kid showed me to, fingers folded as my thumb moved rhythmically. When Anja walked in the door, I leaped up, as if a loaded spring was under me.

Fritz had taken it upon himself to have me over every Sunday evening since his first offer for dinner. I didn't really have any friends yet, and Fritz's family had been welcoming, so I'd gone.

Iia and I hugged hello; she didn't let go immediately. "It is nice to see you so soon." Today her hair was rainfall straight.

"Thank you for agreeing to meet me," I said awkwardly. *What is this, a business meeting?* "I mean with such short notice." *Jesus, Peter, shut up.* "Anyway, hello, how are you?"

Iia chuckled. "I am well. The museum is preparing a new collection. My *Onkel* says you spend a lot of time in the lab at Roche. Is it going well?"

"I think as well as can be expected, given that we are trying to stop cancer from growing." I didn't really want to talk about work. "How is your job—you've only been there a few months, right?" Although we'd had several family meals together, I didn't feel like I knew many details about Anja.

"Since the beginning of the year. I like the museum, there is so much there, even just a brief walk through. The first few months were a lot of learning about the collections. It is interesting to see what we have and what we might buy or take on loan."

I liked that we were both still getting settled in jobs we'd only had for a couple of months. "You never said what you did there."

"I work in conservation. It is a well-respected museum, but all the art is non-European. There are challenges with acquiring and displaying art which may not have been cared for properly."

"Your English is as good as Fritz's," I commented.

"We all learn English in school. And I went to school in England. For communication, but I have always loved art, so I have a minor in fine arts, and now I am here." She spread her hands to encompass the restaurant, but also Zürich.

I relaxed as the conversation went on. It bounced around from why did she love art so much, what was school like in the US, how did I choose epigenetics, to what was her family life like at home?

When Anja stifled a yawn, I glanced at my phone—two hours had passed already! "I'm sorry, you probably have earlier mornings than I do. Let me walk you home."

Overhead, trees were leafing out, light green and delicate in the glow from the streetlights, which were more artistic than the glaring lighting all over Chicago. I took Anja's hand, and out of the corner of my eye, I thought I saw a small smile.

"How do you like living with Fritz and his family?"

"His wife is like a second mom to me. I have known them since I was young because Fritz and my father are very close. It's been nice to have a family to come home to, especially when I first moved into Zürich and didn't know anybody. I loved my cousins, too, even when they were young. When my family came to visit, our parents would go for dinner and leave me to take care of everyone. I had so much fun designing games for us to play."

"Sounds like you like kids." I didn't hold my breath intentionally, but since Anja had brought it up …

"Yes, I always have. You know no one here except Fritz, yes?"

"Yeah, Fritz and his wife are my only friends."

"That can't be true."

Something Resembling Love

"I have gone out with a few of the people I work with, but we haven't hung out on a weekend or anything. But now you are my friend, too." I gave her a hopeful look.

"That is true." As she laughed at us, her hand squeezed mine.

"Can I see you again?" I asked as we stopped in front of the house. I wondered what had made me so bold. Normally I would have had to go home and screw up my courage for days.

"I hope so," she said, pulling my hand just a little.

Did she want me to kiss her? I leaned down a bit, waiting to see if I had interpreted her correctly. Her eyes closed, and I took that as my cue.

Anja's hand tightened on mine, encouraging me to step closer until our lips explored each other's..

"I don't want Fritz to see us out here," I said, reluctantly pulling away, "I need for him to not be mad at me."

She laughed, "He would not be mad at you!"

I kissed her again briefly. "I hope I get to see you again soon."

"I hope that too."

I practically skipped back to my house. Yet when I got there, I felt deflated. Despite the painting I had hung on the wall in the living room, it still felt bare. I missed going to Jane's house, the way it had felt like a home, how she had fully invited me to be there with her. I could paint the walls, or hang curtains, but when would I ever have the time?

It was all right, I reassured myself. I'd only been here a few weeks. There was time for me to do those things.

A week later, I stared, unseeing, at the computer screen, trying to focus and failing miserably. The back of my chair shook, and for a moment, past and present collided, and I thought I was in the lab with Chris, being jostled out of my ruminations.

"Peter!"

But no, Fritz hadn't shaken the chair nearly hard enough. "*Guten morgen*," I greeted him.

"Peter," he grinned, "it is noon, not morning! Let us get some coffee."

Dutifully, I followed Fritz out of the lab and across the Roche campus. He had a favorite *Café* I knew we would go to. It was a chilly spring day, alternately spitting rain and sun shining brightly.

Fritz insisted being outside was good for thinking, so we took advantage of a clear moment. Even in a sunny spot, the breeze made it cool, and I thought of Jane. Once we were seated, he asked, "How is your work going now that you are more settled?"

"As you know, both hyper- and hypomethylation can cause prostate cancer. The issue we keep running into is determining which is happening in any given scenario. It seems every week, another epigenetically regulated gene is identified, in addition to the known DNA mutations. This feels like a task that can't be accomplished," I admitted.

"But the amount of information you have generated so far is incredible!" Fritz sat forward, face animated. "It is helpful for us, Roche, but it is also useful for doctors and will be the basis for more discoveries and developments in the future. Why did you pick this course of study?"

"It was interesting, I thought I could make a difference. The opportunity was available when I was looking for the next step in my education." I shrugged. As I'd told Jane, I'd hadn't gone in with a plan.

"Do you miss your home, Chicago?"

"No," I frowned, "not at all."

"Not even your friends?"

"Sure, I miss a few of my friends," I admitted, unsure where Fritz was going with this line of questioning.

"I think you focus too much on work, and not enough on life. I have heard you sometimes sleep here."

"Yeah?" I didn't need another Chris in my life, telling me I was living my life wrong.

"You have been spending time with Anja."

It wasn't a question.

"She is a very bright girl, who likes beautiful things," he said as he sat back. "We could not drag her out of art museums when she was young. She has always been happy, but when she first moved to Zürich, she was sad, missing friends she had in London, and not having anything in common with her old grammar school friends anymore. She looks happier the last couple of months," he finished, looking directly at me.

I took the hint. "How could I provide a life for her, for anyone, if I can't get my career off the ground?" I'd left Northwestern to finally have a career, and even with all the resources, I was still struggling.

Fritz shook his head at me, as if I wasn't quite grasping a simple principle. "Your profession is the research. It is not fixing the problem. It is finding the pieces of the puzzle and working to make sense of them. You cannot see the forest for the trees."

I dropped my eyes.

He tapped his finger on the table twice. "Wisdom comes from failure."

I considered Fritz's words as I walked home that evening, at a reasonable time. My house still didn't feel any more like a home than it had after my first date with Anja. I had a couple more pieces of art up, but it looked forced. Maybe Anja could help me paint or pick out curtains.

In my mind I saw Jane, bouncing on the couch she had helped me pick after the old one had literally collapsed underneath us.

"This one seems sturdy," she'd said.

"Maybe we should look at another store."

"Peter, we have sat on literally every couch in this building. Do you really think you're going to find another couch you like better than this one, at a better price?"

"No, probably not," I'd had to admit.

"Okay good. Let's take it home and break it in," she'd said, raising her eyebrows at me.

That couch had gone the way of all my other furniture, gracing someone else's living room. *Wasted opportunity.*

I punched Anja's number on my phone, and almost instantly she was brightly saying, "Hallo!"

"Do you want to come over for dinner?"

"Peter, is that you?"

"Who else would it be?" I asked suspiciously.

"I did not know you could cook."

"Of course I can." Surely, I could cook something. At the very least, I could order carry out, right?

"It would be nice to have dinner. I have not seen your house yet," Anja reminded me.

"Oh right. Well … it's not like your house. I mean, it's not very homey. But you could come anyway."

"I'll see you soon. *Tschüss.*"

Maybe this isn't *a great idea*, I thought, looking around at the kitchen. At least there weren't dishes stacked in the sink. But still I wanted to impress Anja.

I took a deep breath and pulled up the next number. "Hi, Mom. I need your help …" Desperate times called for desperate measures, right?

"Of course, Peter, what do you need?" Her voice was raised, with a hint of concern.

"I need to make dinner. For, uh, my boss. He's invited me over to his house, and I'm returning the favor."

"Peter, that's wonderful! I'm so glad you are making friends. I think you could roast a pork loin. All you need to do is throw some herbs on it." I scribbled a note as she told me what to mix, and how to cook it. "See if you can find some carrots, too. You can roast those alongside."

"Thanks, Mom," I said, blowing out the breath I had still been holding.

I ran down the street to the butcher, not caring how much the loin cost. I grabbed a bottle of mixed dried herbs similar to what my mom had listed out and raced home to throw everything in the oven.

While it cooked, I threw clothes in the hamper and straightened the piles of journals and books on the coffee table. The one benefit of having had to buy almost everything new was that I didn't have much to clutter tabletops. I checked I had an extra toothbrush, just in case.

When the bell rang forty-five minutes later, I was just pulling on a fresh shirt after a quick shower. I glanced around before I opened the door. It wasn't fancy, but at least it was tidy.

Iia stood on the doorstep, holding a couple of beers.

"You look …" *Hot.* She looked hot in a short black leather skirt and a fuzzy, cropped white sweater. "Fantastic."

I suddenly felt under dressed, even in my place.

"I came from work." She stepped in and put her arms around me. For a split second, I felt how I had when Jane had held me, as if to tell me she was right there with me. Anja's hair tickled my cheek, and I held tighter.

"I can only cook a few things," I admitted as I forced myself to step back from her warmth and lead her to the dining area.

Dinner passed more easily than I had feared, and in what felt like minutes, we were washing the dishes, drying them, and moving to sit on the couch.

"Do you like it here?" Anja asked, looking around the room.

"I like the house, yes. I don't spend much time here, although I'll spend more if your uncle has anything to say about it. He thinks I'm working too much."

"Yes," she chuckled. "Fritz is a fan of working well, but also having time with your family."

"I'm alone."

"Your family might live far away, but you have Fritz—he is quite fond of you—and you have me! It is not so long we have known each other, but it is pleasant spending time with you. If you were here often, we could spend time together more."

She did look at home on my couch.

"I thought I might paint," I said as I glanced around. "But when would I find the time?"

She shifted to face me. "This weekend we could. We could pick a color and do it together. This room," she swept her arm around it, "and go from there. If you like."

"You'd give up your weekend to help me paint my house?" I looked at her in surprise.

"It wouldn't feel like giving it up, because we'd be spending time together." Anja set her hand at the base of my neck.

"Yeah, I guess that's true," I smiled, enjoying the feel of her hand. "Can I give you a tour of the rest of the house?"

"I'd like that."

"You've seen the downstairs already." I gestured with my glass. "Follow me for more excitement."

I showed her the empty room first, then the hall bath, which was completely bare of any decoration, followed by the room I used as my office. It wasn't large, either, but I had a small IKEA desk and a bookcase that someone at work had been getting rid of. The window faced out onto the yard.

"And last is my bedroom."

"Are you sure I should see this?"

"No tour would be complete without it."

"Hm," she said from the doorway. "Maybe this room should be painted first. You have white walls and a white comforter."

"My sheets are blue," I protested.

"I'm not sure I believe you," she said, running her hand along the narrow windowsill.

I walked over and took her glass away, "Maybe I should show you. I don't want you to think I am completely anti-color, or you'll take back your offer to help me paint."

"That would be beneficial. Are these light blue, royal blue, pinstriped ..."

"Navy," I said as I kissed her.

"Mmm, I can work with navy," she said, returning my kiss.

She pulled my shirt over my head immediately. Her fuzzy sweater tickled my chest, bringing my body to life. I ran my hands up her body, and into her loose curls, where my fingers tangled. They had always slid right through Jane's sleek dark hair.

My hands trailed down her back and under the sweater, pushing it up and over her head. *Buxom* was the only way to describe her. Fascinated, I moved my hands underneath the sheer black bra, around the sides, up along the straps, and back down to hold her.

"Do you like the way I look?" she asked.

My eyes found hers. "Very much."

She held my gaze as she unhooked her bra, letting the full weight of her breasts rest in my hands.

"I want us to be together," she said, her hands resting at the button on my jeans. I felt something scratch against my skin and looked down to see the corner of a condom wrapper sticking out of her hand.

Something Resembling Love

Where had that come from? I pulled her against me and crushed her mouth to mine as she undid my pants and then unzipped her skirt.

I wasn't nervous about measuring up. Anja had already made it perfectly clear that I was what and who she wanted. Had I felt that way with Jane? I pushed the thought aside as I rolled on top of Anja. In the next instant it didn't matter, and I groaned as I pushed inside her. She gave an excited cry and raised her hips to mine.

It wasn't like the first time I had slept with Jane. There were no lingering kisses, no slowness and savoring. Just urgency. Panting, I reassured myself that I was lost in the moment.

"Peter, I want more," Anja begged.

If she wanted more, I would give it to her, driving harder into that place of forgetting until she was gasping and I felt her tighten around me.

I rolled to the side to catch my breath, staring, dazed, at the ceiling. Next to me, Anja worked her hand under my back.

After a while she said, "I like your house."

"Mm."

"You are right, this room is the place to paint first, though. We can do it this weekend."

"If you're here to help me." My eyes were closed, but a smile bloomed involuntarily.

"Painting is no fun. But it would be together."

"Then, I'm up for it."

"Are you up for anything else?" Her fingertips danced on my sternum.

"I most definitely am," I agreed, rolling on top of her again.

Although Anja went home after the tour of the house, I felt the effects of her presence long after she was gone. Even in the morning when I went to work.

The stark white space had been a place to sleep and eat. Now I wanted it to feel like a home. I did as Fritz had suggested, and spent less time in the lab over the next week, instead browsing home websites, considering colors, and wondering how they would look in my house.

By the weekend, I had a few gallons waiting when Anja rang the doorbell.

I glanced around the room again just before I opened the door. This was it, the moment I would have a home. I smiled, thinking of Chris.

"*Süßer*," Anja said, giving me a warm hug. Her hair was straight today, a waterfall of blonde that made her look less cute and more modern.

Yes, this would do.

"Hello, *Mausi*, I need a kiss."

"Just a small one, and then more later, after we paint."

"Mmm, fine," I said, pressing my lips to hers, putting my hands on her rear end, and pulling her close.

"No, Peter, we must paint first! Or it will never get done." She swatted at my shoulder.

"Right." I let go, but I couldn't help grinning.

"Follow me," she commanded, starting up the stairs.

The vision of Anja's snug jeans swaying blurred into a memory of Jane's hips wrapped in red. I rubbed my eyes and raced up after Anja.

Painting the bedroom didn't take as long as I had expected, and when I realized I'd forgotten lunch, we sat down for an early dinner.

"I would have come earlier and brought you something," Anja scolded lightly.

"Since I just forgot, I guess I wasn't all that hungry. I'm glad for this soup, though!" It was something Fritz's wife had sent over with Anja, simmering while we painted.

"But you know I'd be happy to bring you something."

"I do." Jane had said similar things, sending me into fits of frustration. I was a grown man; I could fend for myself. But the offer felt different coming from Anja.

"You have paint on your cheek," I said, running a finger along the streak.

"I have paint in a lot of places," she said, examining a smudge on her arm.

"Do you need help getting clean?"

"I think I can manage."

I leaned across the table to kiss her, hoping she would pick up on my innuendo "I still need those kisses you promised …"

Something Resembling Love

When she said nothing, I left the dishes on the tabletop and pulled Anja behind me, up the stairs, into the bathroom, never letting go of her hand until I lifted her shirt.

Iia's fingertips trailed up my back as she pushed my shirt up, digging into my shoulders briefly before removing it entirely. *"Mein schöner Peter,"* she said, grabbing my jeans to yank me against herself.

"Pretty Anja," I said, cupping her butt to return the favor, before breaking the contact and fumbling to undo her jeans.

"Are you nervous?" she asked coyly, stepping into the shower spray.

I shed my own jeans quickly. "No," I said, following her. "I just want to have you."

"You can always have me," she replied, with a flirtatious tilt to her head.

I squirted soap into my hands, rubbing them over her body, in places where there was paint, and where there wasn't. Soon, we were both covered in suds.

With my arms wrapped around her waist and her breasts pressed to my chest, I felt invincible.

Soon, Anja's hands were on my cheeks, holding me as she kissed me deeply. Her hands skidded down my arms in the water until I felt her fingers wrap around me. I closed my eyes and let out a shuddering breath.

Something hit the shower floor, and I opened my eyes. But it wasn't a bottle of shampoo; it had been Anja's knee hitting the metal.

"I—what are you doing?"

"Making sure there is no more paint," she replied, looking up at me from under water-darkened lashes. And then she wasn't looking up at my face. Because hers was pressed against my skin, her tongue supporting the length of me.

I groaned and smacked my hand against the wall as she moved. *Fuck* that felt good!

"Iia," I groaned again.

She pressed her thumb into the skin above where I was hard, and I came immediately.

"Fuck," I whispered to myself. What had just happened? Anja still had her mouth around me. I was panting. "Stand up. That has to hurt."

"Enh." She shrugged.

"That—you ..." I grabbed her face in my hands and kissed her hard. Her nails bit into my back, enough to know that she had enjoyed it, too.

When Anja left the next afternoon, after we'd painted the living room something with a soft grey undertone she had picked out, I flopped on the couch and looked around. It already felt more inviting. Inspired, I sat up and dialed the landline my parents had insisted on keeping, even after they'd gotten cell phones.

"Peter, this is a surprise!" Mom answered.

"I have something I want to tell you guys. Can you get Dad on the phone?"

"Is everything all right?" If we'd been in the same room, she would have been reaching forward to touch my arm. "Here's your dad."

"Peter."

I got up from the couch to walk to the other side of the living room. "I just, um, wanted to give you guys a, ah, to tell you guys—Mom, you remember when I asked you for something to make for dinner?"

"Of course. I thought it was nice you were having your boss over for dinner."

"It wasn't my boss. It was his niece. We're dating," I blurted.

"Oh honey, that's fantastic! I know you were very upset over you and Jane."

I ran my hand back and forth through my hair, pacing the living room. "Right. Anyway, you guys will love her. She works at a museum, and she went to school in London, and—"

"She sounds great, Peter," my dad said.

"I, um, I know I've only been in Switzerland for a few months. And I'm coming back later this year for Chris' wedding, but ... well, maybe you guys would like to come visit? You could meet Anja, and Fritz."

"Honey, that sounds wonderful. We'd love to come!" I could picture my mom looking at my dad, smiling and nodding.

"Great, that sounds great. Maybe in August?"

"We'll be there, Peter," my dad said.

Something Resembling Love

When I hung up, I felt the buzz of anticipation. Fritz thought I was doing good work. I had a girlfriend. My parents were coming—because of an invitation *I* had issued.

JANE

"Here you are," Pietro said, handing me a demitasse of espresso. I didn't know if someone, Pietro maybe, had bought the machine in the kitchenette or if it was standard government issue for Italy. Either way, it beat every single coffee I'd ever had at a USDA office or meeting.

"This is the farm you go to tomorrow," he instructed as we bent over a map in the main room of the office in Florence. "It is near to where you live."

I'd settled into a routine over the summer. One day each week in the Florence office, writing up reports and talking with my colleagues. The historical and agricultural knowledge they had was invaluable, as were the details of when a vineyard had changed hands, been left alone for years, or continuously harvested.

Other days I was on my own, visiting vineyards and olive groves. Every week and a half or so, I'd head to a lab in town where I rented time, looking at the dirt under a microscope. Pietro's contemporaries in the office had shaken their heads, wondering why. So had one of the interns. The other sometimes went with me.

My research on fertilizers, and my knowledge of phosphorus, calcium, nitrogen, and potassium, was just as applicable here as at the USDA. But there were other particles at play in the Tuscan soil that affected grapes differently from wheat or corn.

Something Resembling Love

I'd been fascinated the first time I'd looked under a microscope and seen the tiny flecks of mica, so numerous it had looked like glitter mixed in with the clay. As I toured vineyards and explored the soils, I learned about wine as well. How a few hundred feet of elevation change, or a negligible difference in the ratio of rain to sun over the course of a growing season, could completely change what grape variety would thrive. Too much change, and a crop could be destroyed.

I expected a difference from Midwestern soil, but seeing it with my own eyes, feeling the difference in the texture of a handful, made me giddy.

"You will take via Ludovica, past the *Ponte della Maddalena*," Pietro instructed, tracing his finger along the winding line.

"I don't know where that is."

"Ah yes, that is the proper name. Mostly it is called *Ponte del Diavolo*."

"Oh, right." I'd seen the bridge as our hiking group had driven between towns, its mismatched arches reflected in the Serchio river.

"They hide her in plain sight," he muttered to himself. I knew from experience he was talking about Mary Magdalene, of whom he had a small statue in his office. He resumed his directions in a normal tone. "Then you take the next three right turns."

That was how all the directions went. Most days I was on my own, navigating the roads with verbal instructions like Pietro had given me, and an address that always seemed inadequate. Where I went it was mostly rural roads without house numbers or street signs, and amongst the hills, GPS often got turned around.

My phone rang after lunch. *"Pronto,"* I answered, hearing static on the line. I sighed quietly. Another perk of driving the beautiful hills.

"Jane, can you hear me?"

"Hi, Matteo."

"Are you all right? Are you lost?"

"Not today!" I sang, as if I had successfully done something particularly tricky.

"That is good," he chuckled.

"I'm getting better!" I insisted.

"You are, yes."

Matteo frequently called on days I was driving in areas new to me, making sure I hadn't gotten lost. That had been helpful a few times that I actually had been lost.

"I will see you tonight," he said, hanging up.

I smiled to myself as I drove under broken clouds. As one of our fellow hikers, an older British man, had said, using it as a gauge for how to dress, today there was enough blue in the skies to make a sailor's trousers.

It was nice to feel like someone was concerned for me. Different from the anxious worry Peter had had after my surgery, which had always felt more as if he needed reassurance than like he was taking care of me. Being with Matteo felt like having a particularly watchful protector. A large sentinel who would only spring into action if I, the heroic damsel, signaled I was in distress.

When I pulled in the drive that night, my car was making a whirring sound. I frowned at it as I turned the engine off.

"How was Cutigliano?" Matteo asked from where he stood at the counter, chopping vegetables.

"It was good. Muddy. Some of the best olive oil I've ever had."

"You say that everywhere you go." He laughed out the words.

"It's always true," I said, picking up an olive off the tray on the counter. "But I think I need to take my car in. It's making some odd whirring noise."

"Describe this sound."

"I don't know. Not like the fan. A different kind of whir."

"You have been driving often. Let me check."

"What are you doing?" I asked as he marched outside.

I watched from the front porch while Matteo opened the hood of my car, pulled a long metal stick out, ducked into the garage, and climbed under the car. Twenty minutes later, he reemerged, with black streaked down one side of his face.

"It is fixed. You were low on oil. It needed to be changed, too."

"So you just …" I gestured toward my car.

"Yes, of course. I love you; I want you to be safe," he said, kissing me on the cheek as he passed me, heading into the house.

"Did you just—you can't just—say that!" I turned to follow as he walked past.

"But you know this, do you not?"

"Saying it is different!"

"How?" I watched him frown in confusion.

"You can care for someone and do things like that," I said on an exasperated exhale. "You don't have to love them."

"Don't you have a kind of love for all your friends?" He was wiping his hands on a towel, as if nothing extraordinary had happened.

"Well, yes." I paused, considering, before returning to my original exclamations. "But that's not what you said!"

"No, it is not. I do have love for you as my friend. But also, as much more than that." He brushed another kiss to my cheek as he headed toward the kitchen.

"I am very grateful. For both of them. And I love you, too."

"Good, now let us have dinner."

I smiled at how matter of fact he was about the knowledge that we loved each other. "The ground must have been chilly, wet from all the rain," I said to his back.

"Yes."

"Are you cold?"

"Some. But I will warm."

"How about if we speed that up?"

I wrapped my arms around his waist from behind.

Matteo made a *hmmm*ing noise, the sound vibrating into my chest. He turned toward the stairs, and I followed him.

I walked backward along the hall, kissing him as he kissed me, pushing his shirt up. He'd had on a light jacket to lie in the mud under my car, and as I skimmed my hands down his shirtless back, it was still chilled.

"Mmm. That feels nice," Matteo said against my mouth. "Again."

I repeated the motion, seeing goose bumps spring out along his arms and shoulders. "I'm making you colder."

"It is only my body, which likes when you do that."

"Is that right?"

"Do it again. Lower."

I gave a half smile. "Like this?" I asked, running my hands down his torso and lightly sculpted abs.

"Lower," he whispered.

I brushed my hand across the front of his hiking pants as I backed into the bedroom. He made a sound of appreciation. "Yes, that is better. I am feeling warmer."

"Okay, great," I said, and stepped around him. "Do you need help with dinner?"

"Get back here, Jane," he growled, grabbing my wrist to pull me up against himself.

I laughed, enjoying him. "I thought you said you were all warmed up."

"Warmer. Not warm." He yanked at my cotton pants, and it was my turn to shiver. "Come here, *cara*," he said quietly, guiding me onto the bed and pulling the quilt over my back as I lay on his chest. Underneath the cover, his hands ran over all of me.

I fumbled for his fly, shaking from the attention and the chill. Matteo's hands were warm again, and as soon as he pulled my shirt over my head, he had them on the sides of my breasts. I relaxed into the warmth he was radiating.

"I didn't do a very good job of warming you up."

"It seems I must do all the work." He lifted his hips slightly, pressing himself into my softness.

"You don't seem to mind." I breathed out the words, leaning into the friction.

"You still have the goose bumps; I must ensure you are fully warm," he said, rolling me over so the warmth of his body lay over mine.

"If you must," I agreed. I gasped as he slid himself out and back in, each stroke warming me from the inside, until wave after wave of heat rolled through me.

"Jane," he said, voice harsh as he pushed hard against me once more and stayed.

I clutched at him until the tension drained from us, and we slipped to the side, lying face-to-face. The streak of oil had smudged along his cheek.

In the quiet of the old house, we lay together. A chill raced through me, and Matteo pulled me back up against his chest, the hairs a reassuring rasp against my still sensitive skin. "What did you do in America to warm up when you were cold?" he asked as he placed his warm hands on my back.

"I have a cat," I said into his chest. "Otis."

"Why did you not bring him?"

Something Resembling Love

"I wasn't sure how long I would be here. Alicia is renting my house, and he is living with her. Or maybe I should say, she is living with him."

I felt the laughter in Matteo's chest. "If you stay here, will you bring him?"

"I want to. There are rules, but he's healthy and has all his shots." I lifted my head suddenly. "Please tell me you aren't allergic."

"I am not."

"Do you even like cats? Or animals at all?"

"I love all the animals," he answered, smiling down at me.

In the morning, I dashed out the door—into the rain, hoping it wasn't a deluge. "Shit!" I yelled; my hair plastered to my face already. I ran back to the house. Matteo stood under the roof of the front porch, holding my open umbrella out to me. "Thank you." I kissed him.

"I both kinds of love you," he said with an amused smile.

"I both kinds of love you, too," I called as I ran for my car again.

It felt good to yell it out loud, to not hold it in, to know the person on the other side wanted to hear me say it.

※

"Do your friends worry about you?" Matteo asked over cappuccinos one afternoon, as we sat on the small porch and watched it rain.

"No," I said, somewhat puzzled. "Why would they?"

"This is far away from home for you. I heard part of your chat."

"Ah." Lauren had been lamenting how long it had been since we'd had happy hour, and how much she missed having me around for Chris' events. "I think they worry more about themselves. They miss me."

"You miss them, yes."

"I do. When I left, we all said they would come visit."

"Why do they not?"

"They have jobs. It took me awhile to get settled," I said with a smile, acknowledging his role in that.

"Must you be, for them to see you?" he asked, genuinely confused.

"I thought it would be good for me to be able to drive us without getting lost, find a place for them to stay."

He turned to me with a questioning look on his face. "They would stay here, would they not?"

"This is your home." I gave a dismissive wave of my hand. "I can't just randomly invite my friends to crash it."

"It is your home too. There is plenty of room."

"This is not my home, it's yours. We're roommates."

"Jane," he said, his face and voice serious. "We are more than roommates, you know this."

He was right. I'd slept in "my" room for about two weeks, until the night of my frippery, when I'd willingly given in to Matteo's affection. Now we went to bed together every night.

"You should ask them to come," Matteo said, gently squeezing my hand.

"I have to go back in October, and that's not far away."

"Back?" Matteo looked stricken.

"No, not back like my job is up. I mean, it might be, by then. I haven't heard anything. But my friends Lauren and Chris are getting married."

"Ah yes," he nodded, looking relaxed again.

We sat watching the rain together for a few more minutes before I asked, "Would you ever want to go visit the US?"

"I have been. I would go again, with you, yes."

I was quiet, pondering the wedding. Peter would be there, and while I was happy in Italy, I wasn't sure how long the job would last. I could receive notice there was no more funding and be going back for the wedding with all of my belongings, the six months a nice tidbit to add to my resume, and nothing more. And if there was no more money, where would that leave me and Matteo?

"What is wrong, *cara*?"

"I was just thinking."

"Something serious. You have the frown."

What the hell, no time like the present. "Do you think you will lead hikes forever?" *What a dumb way to start this conversation.*

"As long as I am able, yes."

"Would you ever want to slow down, have a family?"

"No."

"No, just … no?"

He shrugged. "I have no calling to have more children."

"More!" My head whipped to look at him. *More??*

Next to me, Matteo let out a long sigh. "When I was at university, we were irresponsible, and the woman I was with …"

"Got pregnant."

He nodded, slowly. "Yes. Her parents were very strict. I convinced her not to terminate the pregnancy, even in secret, but they would not let her marry me. They took her out of university, and she was wed to someone else." Matteo's voice was steady, but I heard a thread of sentimentality.

I stared, eyes wide, not sure what to say.

"After I graduated, I started my trekking business. She sent me photos. I wrote to her, thanking her for the photos, asking how I could help. But she said I could not. We traded a few letters. Bruno is fifteen now.." He closed his eyes, and I waited. "It took a long time for me to forgive myself for my part in our irresponsibility." He gave my hand a light press.

"And you never, all those years …"

"Some time after Bruno was born, she wrote once more. After that, her husband forbade her from contacting me."

"But surely you could find her, or Bruno, now. With the internet and social media …"

"It is too long now," he said, shaking his head. "I have always hoped she has had a comfortable life, and it does not seem fair to disrupt their lives."

I set my hand on this thigh. "Did you ever think about having kids again, after you had your business up and running?"

He turned to look at me. He seemed sad, but also not upset. "I wish sometimes I had kept in better contact with Bruno's mother. Insisted. Her father and husband were influential men, powerful and rich. But also, maybe it is better this way. I think I would not make a very good father. My life is the hills."

My breath clogged in my chest, and I felt the sting of tears behind my eyes.

"And you? Is it your wish to have a family?"

I shook my head while I swallowed, trying to get the stone out of the way of my voice. "No. I don't. And I can't."

"Can't?" Matteo frowned.

"I have ... you were right to worry about me when we were hiking. I have a vascular condition that means, among other things, I shouldn't have kids."

"Jane!"

"It's fine," I waved my hand, brushing his concern away. "My doctor at home was diligent about screening me, and now there is a new medication I have been on for almost a year, which has reduced my daily risk and the screenings. But I still can't have kids. And that was ... an issue. In my last relationship."

"This is why you were sad, that night in the courtyard."

I shouldn't have been surprised. It was Matteo's job to be on alert for threats to the people he guided. Washed out trails, sunburns, overexertion. And apparently emotional distress as well.

"I had paused our relationship, told him—Peter—he needed to decide what he wanted. After Alicia and I got back to Chicago, he told me he was okay not having children." I sniffed, willing myself not to cry over something that didn't matter anymore. "Then, he changed his mind, decided he actually did."

Matteo picked up my hand, holding it between his own. "This is unfair. I can understand how hurtful that must have been. You loved him, but he did not love you."

"No, he did—"

"Perhaps. But not all of you. To love you, he would have accepted your position."

I closed my eyes against the tears that spilled over. Yes, that was it exactly. And I hadn't been able to put it into words, damn it. Not even for myself.

"Would you come with me? To the wedding?"

"Will this Peter be there as well?"

I thought of how close he and Chris were. "Yeah," I choked out a laugh, wiping away my tears with the cuff of my sweatshirt.

"Hm." Matteo nodded, looking out across the drive. "Yes, it seems only right."

"Are you going to protect me?" I asked, half-joking.

"If I must."

PETER

I drummed my fingers on my knee as I waited for my parents to arrive at baggage claim. It was probably normal to feel this jittery. I wasn't only introducing my parents to my girlfriend; they were flying over from the US to meet her. And while it hadn't been that long since I had seen them, in fact, less time than between our usual visits, it felt like a bigger deal. Real job. Owning my home. A girlfriend who was almost living with me. They weren't staying with me this time.

My mom appeared in the crowd, waving her hands wildly. My dad was right behind her, carrying both of their bags.

"Peter!" she practically shouted as she threw her arms around me.

"Hey, guys."

"It's good to see you," my dad said, hugging me once my mom had relinquished control.

"I'm glad you're here," I said, and found that it was true; I *was* happy to see them. Maybe my time with Fritz and his family had made me appreciate my own parents more.

"Your hotel is just up the street from my house," I told them as we headed for Fritz's car, which I had borrowed. "Breakfast is included. I took the week off for your visit."

"When will we meet Anja?" Mom asked.

"Tonight. Fritz invited us all over for dinner at his house. He's excited to meet you guys, too. Dinner is later here, though, so we won't be going over until seven."

I pointed out churches and museums as we drove, places I thought my parents might be interested in seeing up close. "This is it." I parked the car.

"How far is your house?" my dad asked.

"About a mile. I need to run to the store. That should give you guys enough time to get unpacked."

I left them in the lobby, commenting to each other on how they were getting an actual key instead of a plastic card. When I returned a couple of hours later, Mom and Dad were sitting at the hotel bar having a local beer together. My mom was wearing a skirt and heels, my dad a sport coat.

"You guys didn't need to get dressed up."

"We're meeting your boss, Peter; of course, we did," my mom chastised.

"Okay," I shrugged as they got off their chairs and followed me to the car.

"*Grüezi!*" Fritz's wife said when she opened the door for us. "We are so happy you are here with us."

"These are my parents, Margaret and William. Mom and Dad, this is Fritz, and his family. And this is Anja," I said, as I put my arm around her shoulders. Her hair was parted on a diagonal, and she wore wide-leg faded jeans that stopped in a fray just above her ankles, and black Doc Martens. Maybe my parents would think that was the standard here, since the shoes had originated in Germany.

"Hello Mr. and Mrs. Livingston, it's very nice to meet you."

By the time the *Apfelstrudel* was on the table, Fritz and my dad were in serious conversation, and my mom had jumped right into talking with the kids.

"Yes, you should have your father to the lab," Fritz said over the conversation the rest of us were having.

"Oh?" I asked.

"I will lead him on a tour. You can show him your lab as well."

"Oh," I repeated. "Sure, that sounds like a good idea." If Fritz was leading, maybe it wouldn't be awkward.

It didn't take long for my parents to start yawning. Between their quiet lives at home and the time change, they'd had a long evening.

"We are being rude." Fritz moved to stand. "Keeping you up after your long day of travel. Peter can take you back to your hotel. I hope you will join us for dinner at least once more before you return home."

"It would be our pleasure," my dad said rather formally, shaking Fritz's hand. My mom nodded her agreement behind the hand she was using to cover her yawn.

The ride back to their hotel was quiet as they both struggled to stay awake. Anja rode in the back seat with my dad. "It was a pleasure to meet you both," she said as we all got out.

"Very nice to meet you, too," my mom said. "Peter, we're so glad to see you," she said as she hugged me good night.

"I'm happy you guys are here. Dad." I hugged him as well.

"Good night, Peter."

The next few days were full of tourist adventures. We wandered museum after museum, Anja took us on a tour of the Rietberg, we sat in more churches than I knew Zürich had, and drank afternoon coffee every day. Both my parents seemed to be thoroughly enjoying themselves. Anja sometimes went with us, sharing her knowledge of places we passed, statues we saw, and the history of the artwork.

As we wandered the streets, Anja and I held hands, but I shied away from anything stronger. My parents knew she and I were serious, that she often stayed with me, but I still couldn't bring myself to do any more than hug her in front of them.

"Are you upset with me?" she asked one evening, as we got ready for bed.

"No. Why?"

"You avoided me today. I am used to kissing you when we like, even in public."

"I know. It's my parents. I'm self-conscious around them. They're old-fashioned; I want them to like you as much as I do."

"If you kiss me in front of them, they won't like me?"

"That's not really what I mean. I don't want to offend them."

Iia frowned.

"I'm not explaining it very well. They're not as accepting as Fritz. I think they need to get used to it."

Her frown lessened. "If you think that's best."

"It is. But I will kiss you now," I said, cuddling her close.

The next day, Fritz followed through on his promise to take my dad on a tour of Roche.

"The top floor is where our executive offices are," Fritz explained. "We have four floors dedicated to pharmaceutical research. We are working on a new medication for Alzheimer's, and we have started testing for one for Parkinson's," he said as we walked along the hallways.

"In here, our people are looking at the cellular makeup of brain tissue before and after direct application of the solutions we are experimenting with," Fritz continued as we watched people in blue gowns, booties, puffy surgical caps, and eye shield glasses through the windows that lined the hallway.

We walked down the stairs. "This floor houses our newest research starts. We have a CRISPR machine which we are still experimenting with to determine how best to use."

"This is incredible," my dad said, in genuine awe. "It's a far cry from science experiments and technological advances in the 1970s."

"We have come a long way," Fritz grinned. He seemed to be enjoying my dad's enthusiasm as much as my dad was appreciating the tour.

"What's your favorite part?"

"I think it might actually be Peter's work that I am most excited about," Fritz answered. "If we can crack epigenetics, it opens a new field of opportunity for Roche to help treat, perhaps prevent, many terrible diseases. Peter's work has been invaluable for filling in blanks."

"That's terrific!"

I wasn't as excited as Fritz to show my dad this part. It was one thing to accept what Fritz said, that the research was the work. It was another thing to not have anything tangible to show my dad.

"Wow! This isn't at all what I was expecting," my dad said.

Something Resembling Love

I looked at it through his eyes. Coolers lined two walls, and lab benches stood in the middle, with sinks between them. A few of my colleagues in lab coats looked up when we walked in; one waved.

"Each cooler houses a different strain of prostate cancer that we have as part of our medical research agreements with hospitals around the world. Some are only a few strands; others are whole prostates that were removed."

"Peter, why didn't you tell me about all of this? This is amazing work!"

"Well, I—"

"Peter is hard on himself and doesn't think his successes are enough. I've told him, though: every piece of information is a win."

My dad nodded enthusiastically. "I've told him that, too. But he didn't want to hear it from the old man."

I was still thinking about my dad's enthusiasm when I walked in the door after dinner that evening.

"How are your parents?" Anja asked, drying her hands on the kitchen towel.

"Dad loved the tour Fritz did, he can't stop talking about it." I scratched my head. "He asked me a few questions over dinner, but it didn't feel like an inquiry."

"Does it usually?" Her brow furrowed.

"Yes. Or it has in the past," I explained as I got a glass of water.

Iia tipped her head. "Is that not what parents normally do?"

That was exactly what Jane had said. "I guess. Maybe? I don't know. But I was away at school, and he wanted to talk every week; ask me about my engineering classes, make suggestions. Even after I got to grad school. It got annoying. Like he thought I didn't know what I was studying."

Iia continued to look at me. "I learned to love art because of my *mutti*. She loves to paint. When we were little, my brother and I, she says she couldn't because there was so much to do with young kids. But when we grew up, she painted again. We had many long conversations about the Dutch masters."

"It sounds like you liked it?"

"I did. Do. She still asks about my work. It is something we share."

"It never felt like that with my dad."

"Perhaps with this visit, you will have more in common."

"Maybe," I agreed, following her upstairs. We brushed our teeth, my mind still turning over the time I'd spent with my dad. For the first time in as long as I could remember, talking with him about my work hadn't felt like a fight. I startled when Anja touched my hand and pulled me toward herself.

"I don't really know what to do with today," I said as she kissed me.

"Do you know what to do with tonight?"

"Yeah, of course," I replied, putting my arms around her back to hug her close. "It felt like for the first time he saw me as competent on my own."

Her lips touched mine again, her hands trailing down my back, finding their way under my shirt.

I gave her a quick kiss in return. "I just wonder why he was so different."

"Peter, can we leave your dad at their hotel? We haven't slept together since before they arrived."

"Right. Yes, I've missed you, too," I said, distracted, kissing her and reaching for the zipper at the back of her skinny black pants. Under my hands, I felt the edges of the detailing that gave the pants a moto vibe.

In the dark afterward, Anja's breathing slowed as she fell asleep. Lying there with my thoughts, I imagined what Jane would have said, how it was wonderful that Dad and I had had a good day, an easy conversation. She probably would have said, "I told you so," but nicely. I was starting to see what she had wanted me to appreciate—my parents loved me, admired me. They wanted to be part of my life.

I could have told Jane that. I had told Anja, but unlike Jane, she hadn't seemed to understand the impact on me, all the ways my thoughts were swirling.

They're different people. I flipped to my side. If my relationship with my parents was different, did it matter if Anja knew all the background?

The rest of my parents' visit was completely different, and I found myself feeling sad at the thought of their departure. Snippets of our conversations from when I was in high school had come back to me as we talked. I reflected on my dad helping me on science projects, the time we'd spent building my first computer at his office. Somewhere along the way, I'd started to feel smothered by that time together. But now I wondered if it hadn't been him, only me rebelling as a teenager against what I'd seen as parental oversight.

Something Resembling Love

When I dropped them at the airport, Dad hugged me tightly. "Good to see you, Peter. Don't make it too long before you come home."

I hugged him back, saying, "I promise to visit," and meaning it.

They video called me the day after. "We're home!" Mom sang.

"How was your trip?"

"Easy. No lines in customs!" Mom said. She glanced at my dad. "Peter, we know you feel like you've found your place at Roche, but we were surprised—it seems you and Anja were already living together ..."

"She's a nice girl," my dad rushed in.

"She lives with Fritz, but yes, we spend a lot of time together," I hedged, not wanting to admit that Anja was with me most nights.

"Maybe you're rushing it. Just a little?" Mom suggested.

"We want the same things."

"Such as?" Dad asked.

"Well, kids, for one." I watched my parents exchange another look.

"Well," my mom said quickly. "If Anja makes you happy, then that's what's important."

"Thanks guys, that means a lot. I'm really glad you came to visit, and I kind of miss you."

"We miss you too," Dad agreed.

"Come home for Christmas, Peter."

"I don't know if I'll be able to. Chris' wedding is in October, though. Maybe Anja and I could come down after that." I wondered if Mom would make us stay in separate rooms, even though she saw us as already "living" together. I wasn't sure that Anja would be as chill about that as Jane had been.

"We'd love to have you, whenever."

After the video ended, I stared out the window, past where I had propped my phone for the call. If only I had followed Jane's advice and invited my dad into my research years ago. I couldn't believe how different things were between us, and with my mom, as a result.

I knew that my job at Roche had changed me. Maybe things would have been different for Jane and me if my boss for my postdoc had been as supportive as Fritz. I couldn't always maintain confidence that what I was contributing had value, but at least I wasn't beating myself up every day.

I shook off the conversation when I heard Anja coming up the stairs.

As she washed her face and brushed her teeth, I sat on the bed, watching her reflection through the doorway. Today her hair was back to soft curls.

I got up to join her and brush my own teeth. She walked into the bedroom, leaving me to watch her reflection in reverse. The T-shirt she pulled on barely covered her ass, and I grinned around my toothbrush.

She was on her side, setting her alarm when I got into bed behind her.

"Pretty Anja," I said, running my hand across her butt to the top of her hip and down her leg.

She turned to smile at me over her shoulder. "*Mein schöner* Peter."

My hand trailed back up her leg to where the shirt hit, bunched higher against the sheets.

"Mm." Anja closed her eyes, smiling. "Again."

This time I was more firm, hand skidding along her skin until I could cup her ass. I squeezed and let go, pulling on Anja's shoulder until she was flat on her back.

"I missed you, while my parents were here."

"I was here."

"That was different," I said, as I moved until I was straddling her hips. I pushed the shirt up, over her breasts, framing them.

"Aren't you going to touch me?"

"I wanted to look at you first," I said as I set my hands on the outside of her breasts, pressing gently but firmly. Just touching her turned me on, and I shifted to make myself more comfortable.

"I am not sure why you bothered with your boxers." Anja's hand running down my chest sent waves of sensation through me.

"You're right," I said, and stood to the side of the bed to pull them and my shirt off. As my shirt came over my head, I saw Anja was naked too, round and soft.

Something Resembling Love

I wanted to go fast, to fill myself with her. But I also wanted to be slow. I lay on top of her and pushed in. She let out a soft groan in my ear, making me pull back and slide in again.

My body screamed at me to go faster, but I refused, staying slow and pushing hard. Each time, Anja met me with her own movement. Over and over until I started slipping.

"Oh Anja, oh, oh God," I panted.

"Yeess-ss-ss-sss," she breathed in my ear.

The release ripped through me. "Iia, yes, you feel ... oh, God. I love you," I ground out as my eyes scrunched. I collapsed on top of her, feeling badly until she put her knees up and hugged her legs around me, her nails a light scratch on my back.

"And I love you, Peter."

I lifted my head.

She nodded, the light blonde framing her face, making her look angelic. "I do. I am glad you love me."

My head dropped down, and I buried my face in her hair.

It felt like I was on cloud nine. Anja had said she loved me, and now there was this.

I pushed back from my computer in the lab, smiling. The results of the last round of attempts at demethylation were in. And they looked good! We'd had a few early successes where the DNA strands hadn't completely disintegrated, but we'd been unable to replicate them with consistency. Until this month. It was all about timing the dosing of the enzyme. Success. Replicable success!

I called my team together. Sometimes it was still hard to believe I had a team of scientists and lab techs who worked under my direction. Would I have ever gotten this far if I had stayed where I was, not taken the chance and quit my postdoc?

"Some of you have already seen the latest findings. Our work with 5-azacytidine has paid off. The last month of experiments proved we can demethylate without destroying the DNA. This is a huge win for us!"

Applause and cheers filled the room.

The group broke up, heading back to workstations or clean rooms. I went to my computer to send the report to the company officers. Emails composed, I leaned back in my office chair, looking out the window at the leaves whose edges were just tinged with color. I thought again of Fritz's advice early on, that my job was not to flip a switch and cure prostate cancer; that it was in the research. We wouldn't take today's new information, or tomorrow's, and hand it to oncologists. There would be years of more work before there would be treatment.

I glanced at the chart on my whiteboard. Checks, *X*s, and scribbles filled the boxes. The checks were far fewer in number. But I knew now that the *X*s and scribbles were just as important.

I thought about what Fritz had said, as I walked home: wisdom came from failure. Enjoying the fall air, I reflected back over the past twelve months. Chris and his cockiness had driven me crazy, but I felt like I could conquer the world. If this was how Chris usually felt, it was no wonder he assumed everything would work out in his favor!

"We had a great day!" I told Anja when I walked in the door. I shared the success we'd had. Anja knew what I was working on, but she didn't understand the details the same way Jane had. That didn't matter, though; she didn't need to know the names of the enzymes we used in order to appreciate the success.

"I am happy for you." She hugged me.

"Kiss me," I said, pulling back enough to do so. "Such a good day."

She was smiling at me, excited for me. I buried my face in her hair, the curls a soft cloud where I could smell her perfume. It felt like I could ask for anything.

"Move in," I said, between kisses.

"Move in?"

"Here, move in with me. I know it hasn't been very long, but I want you here. Move in. I love you."

Iia kissed me, once, twice, "When you came to dinner the first time, I knew I wanted to be with you. I love you." She kissed me again. "Yes, I will come live with you."

"You will?!"

"Yes, of course. If we love each other, why not?"

"I can't wait to tell—"

She cut me off, pressing herself against me.

I didn't need any encouragement, and I felt myself harden. "I need you, Anja. Painting, making dinner, sleeping. In the shower, with your family. In bed." I shuddered a breath as I held her face, looking into her blue eyes. I felt as if I had passed some test.

At the end of the following week, with Anja at an art opening, I poured myself a beer, logged on to my computer, and settled back on the couch.

"*Wie geht's?*" Catherine said, in an overdone German accent.

I lifted my glass in response.

"Ah, here too," she said.

"It's the middle of the afternoon."

"But it's the weekend," she said in a sing-song voice. "In summer," she added.

"It's the end of September."

"Spoilsport." She pouted.

"Why are we doing this on a Saturday? Don't you have friends?"

"Sure I do. But I am here to help my older, if not wiser, brother."

"Help me with what?" Thousands of miles away, I narrowed my eyes at her.

"Make good choices."

"What the hell does that mean?"

"Mom and Dad said Anja is practically living with you."

"Who are you, my mother?"

"No. But in her absence, it's my duty." She held up her fingers in the Girl Scout's pledge. I rolled my eyes. "Mom and Dad know you think they interfere, so they won't say anything, but *I* have no such qualms."

"So you're here to tell me that my girlfriend shouldn't move in because the rest of you think I can't make my own decisions?"

Catherine shrugged like *if the shoe fits*. "I met Jane before you guys moved in together."

"We never lived together."

"Exactly," she said, as if I had proved some law of physics. "It's too soon, Peter."

"This from the girl who changes boyfriends almost as often as she changes the color of her hair." I cringed as soon as the words were out of my mouth, but my sister was unfazed.

"I'm a free agent, dating whomever I like. Plus, I like change. You," she pointed at me through the video, "do not." She paused, waiting for the dust to settle. "You're still recovering from Jane."

"That's ridiculous. I have a girlfriend, why would I be hung up on Jane?"

"Because you love Jane, and you fucked *that* up royally. Just because you have a girlfriend doesn't mean you've moved on."

"Your logic is flawed. I have a great job and finally have respect. I have a nice girlfriend. I have a good life here! Why are you trying to ruin it?"

"All I'm saying is that you never described Jane as 'nice.' What do Mom and Dad think?"

"About me having a girlfriend? I don't know, I think Mom is pleased. You know how much she wants grandkids."

On the other end of the line, Catherine gave an unladylike snort. "If you both want kids, Anja might throw out all the condoms."

"We're only moving in together."

"First comes love, then comes marriage, then comes the baby—" she taunted.

"All right, all right." I cut Catherine off. "They don't know that Anja is moving in."

"I'm pretty sure they're aware their thirty-four-year-old son has had sex," she said dryly, sounding much like Jane had.

"Why would they? I've never lived with anyone before."

"For being a doctor, you can be remarkably dumb and naïve." She paused, clearly waiting for me to respond. "You brought Jane home for Christmas, for crying out loud! And you can't even tell your parents you asked your girlfriend to move in?"

"I only brought Jane home at Mom's request."

Something Resembling Love

"That's the biggest load of shit you've ever tried to feed me."

"I've moved on," I assured my sister.

"You don't love A*nj*a. More importantly, you did love Jane. And you still do."

"Even if that were true—which I can assure you, it isn't—"

Catherine spoke over the end of my thought, giving a shake of her head. "You really are a wuss. One I love, but a wuss, nonetheless. This is a bad idea, Petey."

"I love Anja," I said through gritted teeth, feeling the conviction I'd had for weeks dissolve under Catherine's steady gaze.

"If that's the case, act like it. Call Mom and Dad and tell them. Aren't you going to see them after the wedding? They should know you're living together. Mom might even let you sleep in the same room."

"This was so fun, I'm glad we had this chat." I sneered at my sister.

"Look," she said with none of the ribbing that had carried through our conversation, "I love you, despite the fact you can be so dense. We all want you to be happy. I'm sure Anja is great, but you're not ready."

After we signed off, I stared into my pint of Hefeweizen. I wasn't hung up on Jane. And I would prove it to everyone when I saw her in a few more weeks.

JANE

In the last days before Matteo and I departed for Chicago, I carefully packed my suitcase with my bridesmaid dress at the bottom. I wondered how Matteo would feel about meeting all my friends and what was sure to be a week of parties and socializing.

He had assured me that he was excited to know everyone, but I couldn't help but wonder what seeing Peter would be like. For me, but also for Matteo.

It will be fine, I told myself, repeating the words that Matteo had said to me countless times over the past week.

Then we were on the plane, going home, and the skyline of Chicago along Lake Michigan was a colorful sight. Matteo squeezed my hand when he caught me staring anxiously out the plane's window.

I hadn't even rung the doorbell, and Lauren was dragging me through the front door. I was barely through the entryway when she and Alicia surrounded me. "You're here!" she said loudly.

"I am. We are," I laughed, stepping out of the circle of their arms.

Chris was leaning his shoulder against the wall with an amused look on his face. He stepped forward to hug me. "Glad you're back, Jane."

"This is Matteo." I took a couple of steps back to grab his hand. "Matteo, this is Lauren, the crazy loud one, Lauren's soon-to-be-husband,

Chris. Alicia you know, and this is Zach. I didn't know you'd be here this afternoon, it's good to see you again."

"Someone had to take your place," Chris joked.

"I'm sure," I said dryly, noticing how Alicia had floated to Zach's side and wrapped her hand around his muscular bicep. He towered over her.

"It is nice to meet Jane's friends. Thank you for having me," Matteo said formally.

"We're so glad you're here!" Lauren was practically bouncing as she came forward to hug him. I laughed at the surprised look on Matteo's face.

"Hey man, great to meet you," Chris shook Matteo's hand.

"Is Peter coming? I expected he would be here."

"He said he would be. You know how he is, always late."

We followed Lauren into the living room and then onto the deck, where she'd set out snacks and chilled wine and beer. "How many people are you expecting!" I asked, looking at the spread.

"Just a few."

"Is that Chris' idea of a few people, or yours?"

"Chris'," Alicia answered.

"Oh boy." I turned to Matteo. "Prepare to be overwhelmed."

"It will be nice to meet these friends." He gave Chris a genuine smile that carried to the rest of the group, and I relaxed. Even in his casual slacks, he fit right in.

"Just so you know," I said to Lauren, still looking at Matteo, "we are not staying late. We just got in, and I'm already ready for bed."

"Jane!"

"It's like ten p.m. our time! You want me to be able to go out for your bachelorette, right?"

She gave an overblown pout. "Fine."

I grabbed a beer and handed one to Matteo. No way was I pouring wine for us; it would never measure up to home. Drinks were distributed, and the six of us sat around the deck table. Lauren filled us in on her busy summer of real estate sales. She'd closed a three-million-dollar home a few days ago.

I filled the group in on my Italian language woes.

"She is too modest," Matteo interjected, picking up my hand. "Jane's Italian is quite good, but she doesn't believe."

"I can navigate the grocery store by myself now. It has only been five-and-a-half months."

"Are you still guiding?" Alicia asked Matteo.

"I am. It is quite rewarding. Next year I think I must hire another person for my small company, to run the business for me."

"Maybe we'll come hike with you ne—There he is." Chris stood up. "About time you got here!"

I didn't have to turn to know who Chris was talking to.

"Sorry. We got stuck in a customs line a mile long."

I turned in my seat as a woman said, "He's lying, it was not so long."

When I saw her, I froze. Anja was the spitting image of who I had imagined, and feared, Peter would meet on the trip he'd taken just after we'd started dating. Wispy blonde hair. Big blue eyes, lined with black eyeliner and heavy mascara. And as busty as me. Well, that wasn't a surprise; Peter had always liked my boobs.

I hadn't expected the chunky boots, though, and blinked. Obviously, she was Swiss. But she carried a nineties grunge vibe, in a sophisticated way. "You must be Anja," Chris said.

"Yes. It is nice to meet you."

I finally stood. "Jane!" Peter rushed forward to hug me, and I stuttered a step.

"H—hi." He looked exactly the same. T-shirt, albeit tucked in, and jeans. He still carried the same extra pounds, but he wasn't hesitating the way I would have expected after our split.

"How are you? How's your dirt? And Otis?"

Whatever I'd been expecting, it wasn't this enthusiastic reunion. "Um. Fine," I answered, feeling thrown.

"You'll have to ask *me* about Otis," Alicia chimed in, coming to stand next to me. "I'm his roommate these days."

In Peter's abrupt entrance, I'd forgotten he didn't know about my move to Italy.

"His roommate, what?"

"I moved to Italy this spring. Alicia is renting my house. This is my boyfriend, Matteo," I said, wrapping my arm around his waist.

Something Resembling Love

"Um. Hi. Pleasure to meet you." Peter glanced at me and then up at Matteo.

"And you." Matteo's voice said it was not, in fact, nice to meet him.

Peter looked at where Matteo's arm held me close against himself, and it seemed like the two of them were glaring at each other. Then Peter gestured behind himself and said, "This is my girlfriend, Anja."

"I gathered that. It's nice to meet you." I held out my hand, and she stepped forward to shake it with a smile on her face.

By seven p.m., the backyard was full of friends and acquaintances. "If you would like to stay, I am pleased to stay with you. If you are ready to leave, I can be your excuse," Matteo said quietly.

I turned, taking his hand, and stretching up to kiss him. "I think I've done my duty. Let's go home."

Matteo nodded his assent, kissing me on the forehead. Still holding his hand, we wound through the guests. I hugged Alicia, interrupted Chris to do the same, and then found Lauren.

"Thanks for being such a good sport tonight," I said as we drove to my house.

"It was enjoyable meeting your friends." After a short pause he added, "Most of them."

I gave him a sharp glance.

Matteo gave me a nonchalant shrug. "It is hard to like someone who has caused a loved one pain."

As I drove the familiar route, I was glad our reunion was out of the way. Even though it had been weird, seeing Peter with a girlfriend, at least the wedding wouldn't be tense. "Well, here we are, home sweet home. I wonder how much Otis is going to hate me for abandoning him."

"He will not hate you," Matteo said with surety as I unlocked the door.

I waited while he examined the main floor, glancing up the stairs and gazing around. "It looks like you. Even without your things, I can tell this is your home," he turned to smile at me, making my lips curve in return.

I led the way to my bedroom, feeling pensive. It was good to be here, but I also felt out of place. I wasn't sure if Alicia had left the curtains, or put them back up for me, but the room looked just as it had when I'd left. Curled up in the middle of the bed was Otis. "How's my big guy?" I scratched his head.

Otis leaned into my hand and began purring noisily.

"It seems he forgives you," Matteo chuckled.

We unpacked our bags. I took a shower to wash off the day's traveling and was almost asleep when I felt Matteo's cool and toothpaste-minted kiss.

"I'm so glad to have you in my house," I whispered in the dark, pulling his face back to mine. "Thank you for making this trip possible."

"Of course; it makes you content, so we must do it."

"You know what else would make me happy?" I asked, setting my hand on his hip.

"Hm," he half-grunted as I trailed my hand forward to the front of his square-cut briefs. "I think that would please me, too," he said, pushing the edge of my T-shirt out of the way to trail his hand across my stomach. "But you are very tired, so perhaps we should sleep." He rolled onto his back.

"Don't you dare!" I laughed, coming to hover over him. In the dark, I could just make out his teasing grin. "I love you," I said quietly.

"I also love you," he said as he pushed his hands gently up my ribcage.

In the morning, I made espresso. Matteo smiled, watching me work. I hadn't realized, until he was standing in the kitchen with me, that every time I had used the machine, I'd been reminded not just of Italy, but of him.

During the day I took him to my old office, showing him around the lab and introducing him to my colleagues.

"We miss you at happy-hour trivia," Kip said. "And Rodriguez pined over you every day for the first three months," he finished, raising his voice.

Rodriguez took off his goggles, looked at Matteo, and glanced at where he held my hand. "How's the humming going?"

I snorted, then said, "Really well," around my laughter.

I took Matteo to my favorite Chinese place for lunch, and then we went back home so I could get ready for Lauren's big night.

"Are you sure you'll be all right on your own tonight? It'll be early morning before I'm back."

"It will be fine. Otis and I will share a Peroni."

I glanced at him in the mirror, where he sat on the bed, Otis purring under the deft scratches Matteo was giving him. It made me smile, and briefly, I thought of Peter avoiding Otis. It wasn't Peter's fault he had a bad allergy, but I'd harbored some small resentment I hadn't known until I'd seen this scene.

"Just don't keep him up past his bedtime."

Matteo chuckled, smiling back at me in the mirror.

Outside, a horn honked, and Matteo followed me onto the driveway.

Lauren waved from inside the open limo door, a fuchsia satin sash glowing across her torso. "You will have fun, I see," Matteo said as I turned back to him, grinning at my friends' antics. He kissed me. "Go, have your fun," he said with a shooing motion.

I laughed and stretched up to kiss him again. Longer, deeper, grazing my hand through his short hair.

From behind me, I heard Alicia. "This is not *your* wedding we need practice for!"

I came out of the kiss, laughing.

I wasn't surprised by how fun the night was, or how much time we spent on the dance floor. Lauren had refused to wear a fake wedding veil, but the sash we'd forced her into said, "Future Missus."

I'd missed her, especially after having reconnected, and Alicia's over-the-top personality. I'd missed going out with them and being in a mix of people. Maybe not always missing the sweaty crush of a dance floor, but the energy of so many people.

"Jane," Lauren said, as she and I sat in a booth at the VIP level.

"Lor."

"I missed you," she said over the beat of the house techno mix as she threw her arms around me. "And I love Matteo for you."

"He's pretty great, isn't he?"

She flopped back on the bench next to me, recalling previous times we'd gone out and had one too many. "Quieter than I would have imagined for you. But exactly who you need."

"I think so, too."

Lauren grabbed my hand. "Just don't hate me," she said.

"For what?"

"At the wedding. We had to put you and Peter together."

I must have looked stricken, because Lauren squeezed my hand. "Just for the ceremony. And then the wedding party is at tables near the front, but nobody has to sit near anybody else."

Under the thumping of the bass on the dance floor below us, I felt my heart pound. *Excitement? Nerves?* "I'll be fine." I squeezed back.

After a week filled with last-minute preparations, the scene was finally set. Alicia, Lauren, and both of her sisters—one the brunette version and the other a younger, nearly carbon copy—and I had a relaxing morning in a hotel suite, getting shoulder massages and pedicures. We spent the rest of the day primping.

"I hope we don't get any rain!" Lauren fretted, looking out at the cloudless blue sky.

"Stop worrying, Lor, it's going to be beautiful. And if it rains? Rainbow!" Vanessa admonished as her phone dinged. "All right, the limo is waiting for us."

"Am I going to like it?"

Lauren still didn't know where she was getting married—Chris had sworn all the bridesmaids to secrecy.

"You're going to love it!" Alicia promised from behind her, as she and I finished tying her dress up.

Her eyes went wide as she stepped out of the limo onto Northerly Island, a small peninsula that jutted out into Lake Michigan behind the Field Museum. "He never ceases to amaze, does he?"

Even though I had known it was coming, I was still floored by the sparkling of the water that surrounded the strip of land, blooming bushes and flowers perfectly landscaped surrounding the permanent white structure where the wedding would be held. I felt sparks in my belly.

"It's all going to be fine." Alicia's voice was low in my ear as we walked into the building. "An hour, and then you can go back to Matteo and dance all night. Maybe spark your own happy ending."

"I think it's a little soon for that," I said dryly.

"Maybe just the in-bed kind, then." She winked.

"Alicia," I laughed as Lauren stepped up onto the small platform in the bridal room.

"What? It's totally obvious you guys are having hot sex. I can tell by how he looks at you! I can also tell just how much he loves you."

Something Resembling Love

Vanessa untied her sister's dress and spread out the train. I handed her a champagne glass, and the bridesmaids toasted her happiness.

"Off we go," Vanessa said.

The wedding coordinator stood in the doorway. "The gentlemen are lined up. Lauren, you look stunning! I'll be back for you in just a moment."

We set our glasses down, retouched lipstick, and filed into the hallway. I had to hand it to Lauren; her eye for design extended even to the dresses we were wearing. The jewel tones suited us individually: bright red for me, royal blue on Alicia—who had a matching chunk in her hair, and emerald and purple on her sisters.

When I stepped next to Peter, he turned to look at me, and I felt his lingering gaze. "Hi," he said softly, almost apologetically.

I cleared my throat. "Hi." While I'd been twisting one side of my hair into a complicated braid, I'd decided I wasn't going to say anything to Peter about his midnight chopping of my hair. It was still a couple of inches shorter than the rest.

He offered me his arm, and I threaded mine through.

"Sorry we didn't get to catch up at Chris' the other day."

"It's okay; I think we were both off time zone."

"Yeah." He paused, still looking at me, and then faced forward. "This is going to be some wedding, huh? I can't wait to see what Chris has planned."

"Undoubtedly something over the top!"

The processional music began, and we inched forward, waiting for the coordinator's signal. I closed my eyes as we waited our turn.

Once, I'd imagined this could be us. But, I reminded myself as I took a deep breath, waiting for the cue, out there was a man who loved me as much for everything I wasn't as for what I was.

We walked slowly down the aisle to the sound of a quartet. Peter escorted me to my place at the end of the bridesmaid line and then took his spot on the opposite side of the raised platform.

The quartet started the wedding march, the curtain at the entrance to the aisle parted slowly, Lauren and her dad standing together.

Then it happened. A bass beat dropped behind the main melody—a turntable appeared, tucked behind flowers that were rolled out of the way. Lauren had gotten as far as her first step before she burst into laughter. The quartet kept playing, and then a trumpet player I hadn't seen before stood to add in the song's fanfare.

The crowd burst into cheers as Lauren wiped her tears of laughter away and continued down the aisle.

"You ass," I heard her say to Chris when her father stepped back, but she wore a huge smile.

"You deserved something special," Chris said, and kissed her on the cheek.

The minister, a former client of Lauren's, waited as the crowd settled down and began the much more traditional ceremony.

Just beyond the kissing couple, I saw Peter clapping along with everyone else, his eyes glued to me. I felt my smile falter for a moment and looked for Matteo amongst the other guests. Like everyone else, he was smiling and clapping loudly.

After Lauren and Chris were beyond the rows of guests, we filed out of the room in the same order we had come in, and I had to wait, Peter watching me the whole time, until he took my arm again.

Guests filed across the lawn to their cars while the wedding party stayed for the obligatory photos. When the photographer finally declared she had enough, I helped Vanessa situate Lauren in her limo, and then found a seat in one of the town cars.

In the ballroom, modern chandeliers hung over tables, and gold light washed up the walls. For all that she could behave like a giggly girl when she was with her friends, Lauren was as sophisticated as they came. The pieces she had put together fit her and Chris perfectly.

Bridesmaid duties discharged, I headed for the champagne, but Matteo beat me to it. "For the beautiful lady." He handed me the glass with a small bow, looking formal and edible in a slim-cut black suit.

I gave him a tiny curtsy in return.

"You look most beautiful in this dress." He slid his arm around my waist and held me close, voice brushing against my ear. "It is just the right color for you. Like a perfect pinot."

Friends I hadn't seen in the months since I had gone to Italy, or before, found their way over, and even through dinner, I had to pause from time to time to stand and hug someone, saying, "This is Matteo, my boyfriend." And, "Yes, all the way from Italy."

Something Resembling Love

When dinner finished, we turned to watch the newlyweds cut the multilayer cake. The crowd laughed as Lauren and Chris smashed pieces on each other's mouths and shared a kiss. Even if they hadn't been in wedding attire, anyone could have seen how smitten they were with each other.

Against my will, I glanced at Peter, partway around the table of ten. He was clapping along, smiling but not laughing, and behind where Anja was watching the happy couple, he was looking at me. I looked away quickly, turning so I could bat my eyelashes at Matteo in the chair next to mine.

He smiled broadly at me and leaned to give me a kiss.

Everyone remained standing as Chris led Lauren to the floor for the first dance, a spotlight on them as he wrapped her in his arms. Elvis crooned from the speakers, telling us how much he couldn't keep himself from falling in love. Matteo stepped behind me and looped his arms around my waist as we swayed to the melody.

I remembered an NPR article I'd heard about the inspiration for the song, a French classic more than two hundred years old named *Plasir d'amour*—literally, "Pleasing Love." The original song focused on the brevity of love contrasted with the longevity of pain it could cause. After a failed year with Peter, I had certainly felt the pain. I knew better what Elvis was talking about. Sometimes love was inevitable. And now I knew what that felt like, too.

As I turned my head to kiss Matteo, my gaze swept over Peter. His girlfriend, with her clouds of blonde curls, rested her head on his shoulder, and his arm was around her back. But he was looking at me again.

I let out a breath and on my exhale, Matteo spoke softly. "I should have made you sit not at this table, but another." Apparently, Peter's looks hadn't escaped Matteo's notice. "Are you all right, *cara*?"

I rested the bridge of my nose against his jawline and breathed in. "I am."

The song ended, and the guests clapped, catcalling when Chris dipped Lauren low and kissed her deeply. Not missing a step, the DJ set up the next dance.

"And now, let's have the wedding party on the floor, too!"

Matteo squeezed my hand and kissed me on the forehead. When he let go, Peter had stepped around the table and was holding his hand out for me.

I started to smooth my dress, my hands hovering above the snug bodice, but stopped when I recognized the look in Peter's eyes. I took his hand instead.

It wasn't surprising the DJ played another love song. It was a wedding, after all. Even if I had everything I needed now, seeing Peter brought his lies and the hurt to the surface.

He twirled me and pulled, landing me hard against his chest. It felt awkward to come into contact with him. Mentally, I readjusted myself. "You look beautiful," he said as we stepped side to side, turning slowly in a circle on the spot, making me wish we weren't face-to-face.

"Thanks. You look more comfortable in a tux than you have in the past." I gave a smile and a small laugh, hoping to lighten the feeling that surrounded us.

"Yeah," he agreed with a chuckle. "I guess I have Chris to blame for that. Or thank, depending."

"How is Zürich?"

"It's good. We had an important breakthrough just a few weeks ago."

"Peter, that's great! I'm thrilled for you."

He didn't seem excited though, which made no sense. Until he said, "I wish I could have shared it with you."

"Oh," I gave an uncomfortable half laugh. "Well, you are now."

"I meant like before."

Under the weight of his gaze, I felt pinned, and I shifted, trying to create some space between our bodies. "You can't say things like that."

"Why not? It's true."

"We're not together. I'm with Matteo. You're dating Anja—who seems very nice."

He hesitated, looking closely at me for a moment until abruptly he relaxed. His focus on my face softened; his grip on my body too. "She is," he said simply.

I waited for him to say more, but he went back to me instead. "Matteo is not what I pictured for you."

"Oh?" *Oh?* He'd been picturing me? Even after he had been the one to end things?

Something Resembling Love

"Yeah," he shrugged, our hands rising with the movement. "I guess I thought you'd end up with a professional. Someone more scientific, or something."

"Someone like you?" I raised my eyebrows.

"Yes." The weight of his recent declaration resurfaced. "You like your lab so much."

Even with his major career move and recent success, Peter was still comparing himself. I lifted one shoulder. "I do. But there are other things I appreciate, too."

"Right. Of course." The change back to relaxed Peter was jarring. "It seems to suit you, your new life."

"Yours does, too. A boss who you respect goes a long way."

"It does," he agreed, finally giving me a genuine smile.

The song ended, faded, and another was layered on top.

"Excuse me."

We turned to see Matteo, jaw set.

"May I have my *ragazza* back?" He was practically glowering at Peter.

Peter narrowed his eyes at Matteo, and I saw him take in the ease with which Matteo occupied space, his comfort in his own sophisticated suit. "S-sure. It's good to see you, Jane." He let go immediately, but lingered a moment until Matteo glared at him and he turned away abruptly.

"Are you claiming me?" I joked as Matteo pulled me to him.

"No. I am not jealous of *him*. But you have no duty to spend the evening with him, and it is mine to protect you."

I looked up into his handsome face, so different from his more rugged everyday look.

"You are mine, *cara*," he said fiercely.

I didn't know what to say. I'd never seen this possessive side of Matteo. I was kind of enjoying it. "Thank you."

"You are welcome." He inclined his head until his forehead touched mine. "Now may we dance?"

"Yes, please!" I grabbed at his suit jacket and let him guide me onto the dance floor and tuck me, secure against his shoulder, under his chin.

PETER

I could see that Anja, in her bold, one-shoulder orange dress, was where I had left her when the wedding party had been called to dance, sitting at the now half-empty table, talking with Alicia's date, Zach.

I made a sharp turn and a direct line for the bathroom. I needed to get my head together. Ever since I'd come back to Chicago, I'd been feeling scattered, driving streets that held my former life and seeing places Jane and I had gone.

When Chris had mentioned he'd refused to tell Lauren where the wedding ceremony would be, I thought he'd been setting himself up for an immediate divorce, judging by the stories other friends had told about their wives and the obsession that could go into every wedding detail. But then he'd played that ridiculous rendition of the wedding march, and Lauren had laughed.

I was jealous of the easy way they were together. The way Jane and Matteo were. *The Italian stallion*. I shook myself, trying to rid my head of the image of her leaning into him, watching the first dance.

I had my arm around Anja, too. I splashed my face.

"Get it together, Peter," I whispered fiercely to my reflection in the mirror. "You love Anja, and she loves you. That's all that matters." I dried my face with a paper towel and went to find my girlfriend.

Something Resembling Love

When I got back to the table, she was alone. A quick glance around showed me that Alicia and Zach were on the floor. The DJ had turned the music up and the Black Eyed Peas were exhorting us to have a good, good night.

"Hi, I'm back, sorry." I bent to kiss Anja, and she smiled just before our lips touched.

"It's okay … I talked with the other people. Your friends are all very nice, and welcoming."

"They're good people," I agreed. I straightened and offered my hand.

We joined the crowd on the dance floor as the DJ played one upbeat song after another. I even saw Lauren's parents dancing together, her dad doing an awkward side-to-side step.

Chris' family was around, too. His mom had so far been sitting at the family table, upright in her ornate shalwar kameez, but clapping and laughing with other guests.

Through the evening, larger or smaller groups of friends gathered in circles, dancing like we were back in high school, formed a conga line, and blew bubbles. Chris, bow tie undone, tux jacket off, spun Lauren in fantastic circles, catching and kissing her. I tried not to look for Jane but couldn't help myself. As people left and rejoined the dance floor, I saw her heading for the ceiling-height doors that led outside.

Iia patted me on the arm. "I need some water," she said in my ear.

Latching onto the excuse, I dashed after Jane. "Warm in there, isn't it," I said, forcing myself to step calmly over the threshold. She was resting her elbows on the sturdy balcony edge and turned to look at me. Below us, Chicago traffic honked and whirred.

She smiled in agreement. "Are you and Anja having a good time?"

"Yeah. I had forgotten how Chris' parties can be. You miss one season and …" I shrugged.

"Right," Jane laughed. "And just being back in Chicago is a contrast to where Matteo and I live."

"You guys live together?" *Already?* What was I thinking "already" for? Anja was about to move in with me, and we'd only been dating a few months.

She tipped her head, maybe conceding how quick it had been. "I couldn't find an apartment, so Matteo offered me a place with him."

So, they weren't living together like *that*.

"Then, there was already this spark between us. Once we were sharing a house, it took off." She gave a small laugh to herself.

"That was convenient."

"I don't know how long I'll be there, though. The Italian government only hired me as a consultant." She shrugged, as if the unknown didn't bother her. "What about you and Anja?"

"She's Fritz's niece."

"Ah, the inimitable Fritz."

"Yeah." I felt one corner of my mouth pull up. "I owe him a lot."

"I'm happy for you, Peter." She straightened from where she had been leaning on the balcony wall.

"What about you? Are you happy?" *What a stupid question.* Just look at her. The rosy cheeks, the sparkle I'd seen in her eyes when Matteo had bent to whisper something to her. "Are you healthy?" I added, to cover my tracks.

"It's—yeah. Joe found a brand new medication that has reduced my risk drastically—probably developed by someone like you!" She gave me a bright smile that was infectious. "And then, I didn't think my career could get better, but being in Italy has been a tremendous experience. And having Matteo as my friend before I even arrived just made everything so easy."

It took me a minute to put it together, to realize she'd met him while I was off flailing about whether I wanted children. What a mistake I'd made. Maybe all I'd really needed was a better boss and to not be working alone. Well, and a better relationship with my parents.

"My parents came to visit, a couple months ago. Fritz gave my dad a tour."

Jane's eyebrows went up. "How did that go?"

"Surprisingly well. He and I … you were right, you know. He, my dad, they both just want me to be happy." I paused, watching her look at me, face open and interested. "I wish I had listened to you before. It's a good feeling to not dread talking to them." I gave an ironic laugh at myself.

"It's good to have parents," she said simply.

Something Resembling Love

"It is." I looked down where her arm lay along the top of the stone wall. "Jane, I'm sorry."

As if sensing my desire, she withdrew her hand from where it rested. "It's over now." The words were spoken with kindness.

"No, I owe you a real apology." I picked up her free hand with mine. "I really fucked up with you."

She pulled her hand out of mine. "You just didn't know. You didn't have all the data," she said with a wry smile.

"We could have had an amazing life. Two scientists saving the world."

"And their kids," she said with heat.

"Maybe. I know that's what I said I wanted, but I wonder if—if it was like my career. I needed to get to a better place to see what was real. If I hadn't had Fritz always offering me a way out, if I hadn't taken it, I think I would have felt inadequate always. I'm not like Chris," I said with a rueful laugh.

"No," she laughed with me. "You're not."

"But once I got to Roche, and saw how many people were doing similar work, and also not making fast progress, or sometimes any, it was different. I saw my struggles differently."

"Didn't you see that at the conferences you went to? Research only half completed."

"People only present the good stuff at conferences."

She tipped her head side to side in acquiescence.

"Anyway. I wanted to tell you how sorry I was, am, that I didn't listen to you. About my parents, mostly. But also, my boss. And I wanted to say thank you, for always listening. For taking care of me and loving me. Even when I was trash at reciprocating."

"You weren't trash, you were just trying to prove you could do it. Any of it. All of it. On your own."

"I guess I was." I looked at her, her smile, and the way her hair fell; the sparkling clip in it that made her look even more like a fashionable woman from the Roaring Twenties. "Thank you." I stepped forward and put my arms around her.

I noticed the hesitation in her body before hers came around my neck. For a flash, I felt the way I had when we'd been together. "I'm really proud of

283

you, Peter. You're an amazing scientist. Chris called you a true friend, and you are. And you were a good boyfriend."

I squeezed my eyes and arms tight. I felt her tense.

"Peter?" Anja's voice was behind me, sounding distant.

I immediately let go of Jane and stepped back, brushing a hand over my eye to catch the few tears I'd felt well up. "*Mausi.*"

Ila frowned. "They are playing more music. We should dance."

"Definitely. Let's!" I held my hand out as I crossed the balcony. Just before we stepped through the door, I glanced back at Jane. She was already turned back to the view.

The reception lasted until the early hours of the morning with Chris and Lauren on the dance floor the entire time. Upbeat songs that made the room feel like a club, and slow ones that made me nostalgic for New Year's Eves with Jane.

We watched Chris take off Lauren's garter, making a show of only using his teeth. I would have expected nothing less. And then Lauren turned around, tossing her bouquet high overhead. Jane wasn't even trying, yet it landed upright in her hands, as if she'd been carrying it all along.

I forced myself to smile and clap with everyone else.

When we sent the newlyweds off, they came through an aisle of friends and family that wound from the cake table, all the way around the room, and finally to the door.

"We love you all," Lauren called, as they finished their great escape.

A week later, after a few days in Chicago and a quick visit to my parents, Anja and I were home. Anja had the opening of a new installation at the museum, and I was continuing the work from the lab team's success.

I woke early, unable to sleep through the excitement. By this evening, only a few short hours away, Anja would never have to leave. I was looking at her, watching her, as she opened her eyes. She smiled.

"Hi," I said quietly, but with a huge smile of my own. I stretched forward along the pillow to kiss her.

Her hand rested on my face for a moment, and then we got up. She followed me downstairs, and I watched as she measured coffee grounds.

Something Resembling Love

Sturdy mugs in hand, we sat at the kitchen table, watery sunlight filtering through the windows.

"Did you like Chicago? Have a good time?"

The slightly worried expression on Anja's face softened. "I did. I liked meeting all your friends. Especially Alicia."

"Good, that's good."

She didn't say anything more, just looked at me.

"What's wrong? If this is about moving in, if it's too soon, we can wait."

"No, Peter, it is not too soon. It's just—" Anja's gaze left mine, looking past my shoulder to the living room, where the lighter shade of grey she'd picked for the walls looked just right with the couch I'd chosen haphazardly. "I don't think we can be together anymore."

"What? *Why?*"

She set her hand on my wrist and let out a long breath. "Because, Peter, you are still in love with Jane."

"What!"

"And I cannot be with someone who loves someone else."

"But I'm not! I don't."

Ila's face said she disagreed. "I saw you with her, at the wedding. The way you danced with her. And then, outside."

"She's my friend. I care about her!"

"The way you held her—" She gave a slow shake of her head. "You have never done that with me."

"That's because you and I are different. Our relationship is different. We do … other things." I looked down at my coffee.

"I saw you with your friends. You are more relaxed with them."

"Because I have known them a long time." I reached to grip her hand.

"But you should be that way with me, too, if we are together. If you want me to live with you."

"Don't you think that comes with time? If we lived together, that would be another level." I was frantic, completely off course. Yes, I loved Jane. But not how Anja meant. Jane was my friend, a part of my friend circle. We had cared for and about each other. I couldn't just dump that to the side because I was dating someone new.

"Peter, I have very much enjoyed the time we are spending together. But if I were to move in, that would mean it is serious."

"It is! I am! Serious about us."

"I believe you believe that. But what I saw, you could not keep your eyes off Jane the whole time." I opened my mouth to object, but Anja continued. "You have not seen any of your friends in half a year. And you did not look at Lauren that way."

"Lauren was marrying my best friend!"

"Or Alicia," she continued, ignoring my rational objection.

"Ew."

"She is also kind and pretty."

"But Alicia was my coworker. Sort of. And she's not my type."

"Physically we look the same; she's just a little heavier. And she has blue dyed into her hair." Anja brushed her comment away, as if the hair color was an insignificant difference.

"So does my sister. That doesn't mean I'm attracted to her."

She took a quick breath. "My point is, she and I are similar, and yet you did not look at her all night."

I couldn't argue with that. "That doesn't mean I love Jane … or that I don't love you. Because I do." I turned my hand over under hers and grabbed it.

The hand I was grasping slid out of mine. "You are not ready," she said, her face serious. "And I am. So, I cannot move in with you."

lia rose from the chair and walked upstairs. I slumped back in my seat, dumbfounded. How could this be happening?

She returned a few minutes later, carrying her work satchel and an additional bag.

"*Auf Wiedersehen*, Peter. *Ich wünsche dir alles erdenklich Gute.*"

I didn't move from the couch. Couldn't. What was I going to say? *You're wrong?* I'd already said that, and Anja hadn't believed me. I focused on the empty cup Anja had left across from me.

Something Resembling Love

I thought about Jane, in the red dress she'd worn for New Year's, not even a full year ago. Of the lip print note she'd left in my suitcase, just after we'd started dating. How she had fit so well with my family.

And then I thought of Anja. Not minding my nerves on our first date. Offering to help me paint and making the house feel like a home. Almost everything in here, she'd had a hand in. How I had never felt inadequate around her, never thought about the extra pounds I carried around. Her playfulness with Fritz's younger kids.

I dropped my head into my hands.

The fourth Thursday in November felt no different than any other. The alarm clock beeped. I showered while coffee brewed. At home, Mom and Dad would wake up and start the turkey. Catherine would have spent the night. Midmorning, aunts, uncles, and cousins would arrive. The rest of the weekend would be spent putting up Christmas lights, drinking hot chocolate, and playing bridge.

When the sun sank low, the late November sky darkening earlier every day, I turned off the overhead lights of my office before returning to my chair. The darkened city flooded my vision. Cold night air. The warm yellow from the lights out front marched in a half-circle around the stories of the Roche buildings, climbing into the sky that I was floating in. In one direction, I could see the snowflakes filtering through the pools of light and over the dark patch where the lake sat. I swiveled to look more squarely out the bank of windows, and the illuminated opera house gleamed with its classical sophistication through the evening darkness.

As I entered the opera later that evening, I felt myself stand up straighter, and I was reminded of going to the opera house during the conference just after Jane and I had started dating; after Chris had introduced me to Fritz. That night, I'd bought a standing-room ticket so I could enjoy the music and the costumes of whatever opera had been playing. Even though I had enjoyed the show, all through that evening, I'd thought of Jane, wishing that I could have shared it with her.

The arching marble columns and marquetry along the walls added to the sense of magic. I flashed back suddenly, to running down the aisle to stand over the orchestra pit of the concert hall in Columbus, watching the small orchestra for a musical tune-up, seeing the clarinetist and saxophonist, the small block for the conductor to stand on, and the faint glow from the lights clamped onto each music stand. Just as suddenly, to my mom, humming along with the classical station, tucked away in a memory I hadn't remembered I had.

I missed those days, I realized. Missed being young and carefree, not having expectations and failures and loneliness on me.

More memories flooded my mind. A glimpse of my mom, her dark hair swaying as she pretended to conduct the orchestra on the radio. A flash of my dad, twirling her through the kitchen. Jane, moving her wrist back and forth in the air in time with the music.

Someone jostled me from behind, and I realized I'd been standing still in the middle of the aisle. "*Entschuldigung*," I mumbled, and found my seat.

The view from so high up was, I thought, one of the better ones. Sure, I couldn't see the individuals in the orchestra as well, but I had a better view of the columns, arches, swirls, and flowers that decorated the walls.

The house lights dimmed, the conductor appeared, and the audience applauded. The Romance-era melodies, heart-wrenchingly beautiful, pulled at me, and at the emotional conclusion the audience was on its feet with applause. I felt wetness on my cheeks.

Back at home, I tossed my jacket on the couch and called my parents. They were probably just finishing Thanksgiving dinner.

"Hi, Peter." My dad answered on the laptop in the kitchen. "Let me get your mom."

"You should be here, loser," Catherine said, leaning against the counter behind the small built-in desk in my parent's kitchen, a glass of bourbon in her hand.

"Today, I am grateful I don't have to put up with my dear sister."

"Children," my mom half-scolded as she sat in front of the camera. "We're glad to hear from you. What a nice surprise. Are you and Anja doing anything?"

"Uh. Well, no. She, she broke up with me."

I saw my mom's gaze travel up and I imagined her looking at my dad over the top of the laptop.

"Just after we got back from Chris' wedding," I said, answering the unasked question.

"Sweetie. Are you all right?"

I could see my sister and my dad, listening with surprise. "Yeah. Yeah, I'm fine," I lied. "I went to the symphony tonight, instead of Thanksgiving."

"That's wonderful. I remember when we used to take you kids when you were little."

"I remember that, too."

"You do?"

I nodded. "I remembered it tonight. Looking over the edge of the orchestra pit."

My mom clasped her hands against her chest. "We were always afraid you were going to tumble headfirst over the railing." My dad stepped forward to lean over her shoulder. "For a while, I wondered if you might take up music as your career."

"Really?"

"But then you gravitated towards math."

"There's a lot of math in music," Catherine added, still leaning on the counter.

"Peter," my dad said, turning the camera toward himself, "We're really proud of you. I think your mom would agree that we're grateful to have our son making such important contributions to science advancement."

"Thanks, Dad."

"He's right. We wish we could celebrate your success together, in person."

"I wish we could be, too," I said, and meant it. "I promise to be there for Christmas."

When we hung up, I noticed an hour had flown by. That was what I was truly grateful for this year: my improved relationship with my parents. Maybe I'd needed to be further away. Perhaps I'd needed success to be able to believe in myself.

I called Chris next.

"Happy Turkey Day. How's it feel, to be working while the rest of us are gorging ourselves?"

"You'll never make it if you keep taking all these days off," I ribbed him back.

He laughed. "It's good to see you. Thank you for making the trek for the wedding."

I paused, considering what I wanted to say next. "I really messed up with Jane."

"We all do. Sometimes it leads us someplace better. You have a great job now, you're happy in Zürich, and you're dating someone you like. How's it feel, having your woman in your home?"

I flinched, then let out a long breath. "She broke up with me." God that sucked, saying it twice in an evening. "Said I wasn't over Jane."

His look pierced right through me, even through the screen. "Are you?"

"I don't know," I said with a sigh. Chris waited for me. "Maybe I'll come for New Year's. I'm going to see my parents for Christmas."

"I'll start putting it together."

I chuckled to myself. "Happy Thanksgiving, Chris. Give Lauren and Alicia hugs for me."

"Will do. Happy Thanksgiving," he hung up.

I shut the lid to my laptop and sat there for a moment. Would it be fun to ring in the new year with my best friend and all my old friends? Sure. But I'd never not remember Jane in her white backless dress, pulling me into the circle to dance.

I went upstairs to shower. I had left Jane behind along with my pots and pans, the patio furniture I had bought the first summer we had been together, that I had hardly used, and the couch she had helped me pick out. Chris was right, you couldn't what-if.

I had been unfair to Anja. I'd thought changing directions meant I was ready. Part of me had been. But as Anja had pointed out, not all of me.

A towel wrapped around my waist, I reached into the dresser. My fingertips grazed the embossed lid of a small box. Everything inside of me stilled, as the chill I'd chased away in the shower prickled across my skin again. Slowly,

Something Resembling Love

I reached for the box. Holding it in the palm of my hand, I sat heavily on the bed.

I knew what was in it; I knew how it would make me feel.

What ridiculous choice had I made by committing the details of her body to my mind as a last memory? What idiocy had possessed me to stash scissors in the nightstand?

I carefully took out a piece of tissue and unwrapped it from its precious cargo. Inside, a small chunk of Jane's silky hair was coiled on itself. I had been careful to cut the hair from a few layers down. Sitting on the side of the bed, holding a clipping of hair from my former lover and friend, I could see her perfectly in my mind: an open smile above eighties retro red sunglasses.

JANE

It was a gorgeous fall day as Pietro and I and several others from the Florentine office toured one of the large vineyards. The owner led us between the rows as we tasted the grapes for their four varietals. On the weekend, the nearby town would host a festival for *la vendemmia*, the harvest of the grapes for the year's vinting.

After several hours, the five of us got into Pietro's car. Matteo met me at the train station. "Are you fulfilled?" he asked.

"Yes, and very full," I said, placing a hand over my stomach.

I watched the leaves blur past in the near-dark as we drove the half-hour home. "It was such a beautiful day today."

"You are happy?"

"I am," I said, turning to look at Matteo. "I'm glad you're going to come with me tomorrow."

In the morning, we set off early, the promise of fresh espresso beckoning me. As we passed the same golden leaves, going in the other direction, I thought how different this was. Before I met Peter, I had gone to the farmer's market on Saturday mornings, or out for an early run. That mostly stopped when we got together, in deference to his preference for sleeping later.

Matteo parked the car, and we walked hand in hand several blocks to the town square, where faux grapevines adorned tents. The scents of freshly brewed or steamed coffee nearly drowned out the fresh baked goods—*cantucci* and loaves of bread for soaking up olive oil.

"Can we wander?" I asked.

"As you like." Matteo squeezed my hand.

We tasted every olive oil, sampled every cheese, sipped innumerable tiny cups of wine. I bought more flowers than I could carry and filled our bags with freshly harvested truffles. Loaded down, Matteo made a trip to the car while I went to find Pietro and the rest of the office.

"Do we go to all of these?" I asked, dipping a small piece of *cantucci* into yet another cappuccino.

"No," Pietro laughed.

"That's a shame," I sighed, and he laughed again.

"I wish to offer a toast for each of us," he began, raising a small cup of wine. "We have worked well this season." He gave a tiny tip of his head toward me. "Jane was very helpful last year, and I was glad to have her 'new' ideas in our office. We are all guilty of thinking the old ways are the best way, the only way. But Jane and her microscope opened our eyes, I think."

"I thought my career would be farm visits," said the intern who had scorned my lab visits. "But Jane showed me we need both the traditional ways of farming and the new technology if we are going to save our beloved Tuscany."

"I'm happy to have been able to help," I said as I looked around at the familiar faces with fondness. "It's been a pleasure and an honor to spend the last six months with you. I'll be sad to leave."

I had tried not to think too much about whether I would be leaving. Matteo and I hadn't talked about the fact I was just past my six-month contract, and Thompson hadn't said anything. I knew I was avoiding the topic, but I loved my life in Italy, and everything that went with it.

"We hope you will help us more, teach us all to use your fancy microscope and what you see." Pietro brandished an envelope of heavy paper with an ornate crest.

Frowning, I took it from him. It wasn't sealed, and with a questioning look, I opened it at the table.

Elizabeth Standish

Jane,

I am pleased to be able to ask you to remain with the Italian Ministry of Agriculture, Food, and Forestry on a permanent basis. Tuscany appreciates the dedication you have to her, and it would be our pleasure to offer you a position as Director of Land Management with the Italian government, and, should you choose, Italian citizenship.

Best Regards,
Vincenzo Gonzaga
Minister, Italian Ministry of Agriculture, Food, and Forestry

I read the letter twice. "Really?" I looked at Pietro, eyes wide.

"Yes-s-s," he laughed.

"I accept!" I said, throwing my arms around Pietro's neck.

"*Cin cin*," said one of the men, raising his glass. He'd been less than welcoming when I'd first arrived.

By the time Matteo found us, the conversation had become social, just a group of colleagues enjoying a harvest festival on a perfect fall afternoon, with lots of wine. By the time we were saying our goodbyes, more than a few cheeks were pink.

"You had a good day with your colleagues," Matteo observed, his arm around my waist, guiding me back to the car.

"Even better than I thought it would be."

"What made it so good?" he asked as we got in the car.

"This." I handed him the envelope with a flourish.

He took it from me, reading it slowly. I saw the corners of his eyes crinkle before he looked up from the page with a wide smile. "I am not surprised."

"You're not?"

"No," he shook his head as we pulled out onto the road home. "This is what they say. Your bosses, the governments, all your fancy papers. You are the best."

His words made me smile, too, a grin of my own at his surety in me. I knew I was good at what I did, and that I brought knowledge and protocols to the table that weren't standard here. It was fulfilling to have those things recognized.

"I knew it was so."

I shook my head, amused, but feeling the certainty of staying in Italy surrounded me. The hesitancy I'd been carrying since coming back from the wedding lifted and floated into the golden air. We drove the rest of the way home in silence.

In the driveway, Matteo turned off the engine. I turned to smile at him, and he gave me another broad grin in return. As we walked toward the house, he swept me up, spinning us in a circle. "The best one!"

"Only you think that," I said, laughing at his enthusiasm. "But I don't mind."

"Come, let us celebrate," he said. He set me down, but grabbed my hand as he ran toward the front door, yanking it open, and dragging me up the stairs.

It wasn't every day that we got such lovely weather after the grape harvest. Mostly late November was colder, and rainy. Occasionally, I had been told, we would get some light snow. Nothing, I'd been assured, like what I was used to in Chicago.

This week, the hills were empty. American visitors would be at home spending time with family and friends for Thanksgiving, while European visitors were more likely to come after the Advent season had started. Therefore, I was out hiking a little corner of the *Alpi Apuane*. Hiking back in the US had been different—flatter. These were mountains—not tall like the Rockies, but rugged all the same. I chuckled at myself, and my naiveté when Alicia and I had visited. I'd considered myself in good shape, and I had been, just not for climbing steep, hilly, barely recognizable trails. Now I knew better, even if I never would be able to keep up with Matteo's long strides and his mountain-goat-like agility.

Back home, I would have been putting canned foods in a box at the gym, donating to the food banks. Instead, I was strapped into hiking boots, already well worn, and a bright red down jacket. It might be sunny now, but on the way back down it would be much cooler, and I still didn't like being cold.

Elizabeth Standish

Below my feet, the larger towns and cities were preparing for Christmas markets. Most would open next week. After my parents had died, I'd shied away from Thanksgiving, the emptiness of that first holiday, a mere week after they'd been killed, always lingering. But Matteo had thought the idea of setting aside a day to give thanks was a nice one, and I was different now, too, so we were having a few friends over. The only traditional dish would be pumpkin pie, made from actual roasted pumpkin. I wasn't surprised pumpkin wasn't found in cans in Italy, but I was amused, nonetheless.

At the summit, I dropped to the ground and gulped water gratefully. I could feel the flush in my cheeks from the climb and felt alive! The sea was too far away for even a glimpse, but I oriented myself facing west, anyway. It wasn't that I was looking toward home, really. This was my home now, and I loved it. But was I missing my friends? Absolutely.

Very little had changed for me since I'd accepted my official job offer. I'd received a phone call from Kip about a week after I'd received the letter from the Italian Minister of Agriculture.

"Jane," he'd said, "congratulations! I hate losing my protege and star, but I'm happy you took the consulting job."

"I am, too. It was the right choice for me on many levels."

"I'm glad to hear that. I was also glad to meet Matteo this summer." There was no mistaking the question in his voice: had my heartbreak been fixed?

I'd laughed softly at that. "Yes. We knew each other before I moved here, but yes. It's like you said: this opportunity was a gift. But I miss the old office and working for you."

"This is the direction you were meant to go. I get it; I had some out-of-the-blue opportunities in my career as well. Sometimes I wish I had taken more of them."

"Thanks, Boss."

He chuckled. "Stay in touch, Jane. And Happy Thanksgiving."

A small twinge came over me, remembering the phone call. Tuscany was where I had moved forward—great relationship, amazing career moves. But it was also where I had reconnected with my love of dirt, the place where I had first seen a tiny glimpse of something beyond Peter.

It wasn't lost on me that we had both ended up moving to Europe. I wondered now if he was as happy with the choice he'd made as I was with mine. I hoped so.

Something Resembling Love

It had only been a few weeks since I'd received my formal offer, left the life I had known behind, all my friends and a lifetime of memories thousands of miles away. Permanently. But Italy and Matteo were my home now.

I had gone back one more time, packed up my things, gotten a last scan—which had shown that my vessels had barely changed in the nearly year I'd been on my new medication. Joe had found a new vascular specialist for me in Florence but had promised he'd stay involved in my records and care as long as I wanted him to. We'd hugged each other hard, a little tearful, on my last visit to his office.

Otis had had a last vet visit to get his health papers, and I'd bought him a horribly expensive travel carrier. He was adjusting, too, pouncing on bugs and the occasional mouse, critters he had never seen in Evanston.

The hills and valleys spread out before me. Blue skies sat above the treetops, filling the valleys below. The view was incredible, a whole panorama of bright possibilities.

I sat on the foothill for a long time, looking out over the valley below. Mist filled in along the river that snaked through the small towns, but the skies stayed blue as the sun started its descent. I would have to go soon; the wild boars didn't present much problem unless you threatened them, but tripping on a tree root in the dark could be downright dangerous. Still, I stayed seated, watching the gold light of late autumn fall on the various trees: dark greens, red-orange, and golden yellow, glowing in the last of the light. I felt my heart squeeze. How lucky I had been to have become friends with Matteo, to do something drastic and move so far away, to have found such a beautiful place in the world.

After a few more minutes, I pushed to my feet and set off down the sparse trail. In half the time it had taken me to hike up the tall hill, I was back in my car, following the river until I crossed over.

When I reached home, I noticed the lights on in the kitchen, which meant Matteo was cooking. A small smile came over me, before I dashed from the car into the warm space. As I suspected, he was standing at the stove, and I walked up behind him to wrap my arms around his waist and rest my cheek against his strong back.

"Hello, *mia tesora*," Matteo greeted me, a rumble vibrating into me despite his quiet voice.

"Hello, *caro*."

"How was your hike today? It is quite dark now; you were safe coming down?"

"Yes, I was safe." I smiled to myself.

He turned around, studying my face. "Yes, I think you had a good day," he agreed, bending to kiss me lightly on the lips. "I am finishing the sauce for tomorrow's meal, then we will eat."

I nodded.

"Go to shower, and come back." He smiled, then kissed me again.

I floated out of the kitchen, and then returned in charcoal straight-legged sweatpants and a fuzzy sweater.

Over dinner, Matteo told me about the young couple backpacking along the *Apennine* Mountains, which he had guided today. Just out of college and headstrong, it sounded. I wondered what made them choose this time of year, but mountain man that he was, that question never crossed Matteo's mind. As he described the couple, I watched him intently: the way he moved his hands, how far under the table his long legs stretched, the intensity on his face, and how still the rest of him was.

"What is wrong?" he interrupted himself. "You are very quiet tonight."

"Nothing is wrong. I enjoy listening to you."

"Yes, but now you are not all the way present with me."

I sat back. "Just that today, I was doing a lot of thinking about how much my life has changed." I stood to take our plates to the sink.

"Are you regretting your settlement to come here? To live with me? You were not so happy when you came."

I had turned around to deny I had any regrets. "Oh, Matteo, do you really think that?"

"I do not know. You American women confuse me!" he admitted with a laughing shrug.

"This is me, though, not some random American tourist. Well, not anymore."

"You are still sometimes American," he said, rising, "even if you look Italian."

Stepping forward, I met him before he could decide if he was going to clean up dinner dishes or go to the living room, and stretched up on my toes to kiss him, barely touching his lips.

Something Resembling Love

He sighed and shook his head, so I tried again, this time more forcefully. One step closer, and he stepped back, bumping up against the table behind him. I raised myself up again, skimming my hand through his short hair to pull his head down and into a thorough kiss.

Releasing the back of his neck, I grabbed his hand. "I love you, Matteo."

This time it was he who reached to kiss me. He wanted to be gentle, tender, but I wasn't having any of it. This wasn't about wooing each other. I wanted him to know how much I wanted to be with him. "Come here and kiss me like you mean it," I demanded, voice low.

He hesitated, so I pushed again, taking what I wanted. I heard him inhale sharply, could feel every ounce of tension, every line of muscle, all the restraint he had placed on himself. Good. I turned around and walked away, still holding his hand.

When we reached the bedroom doorway, he stopped, refusing to go any further. "You looked so far away."

"I was contemplative at dinner, not sad."

He moved from the doorframe, and we sat next to each other on the bed.

"You're right, I was thinking about my old life earlier today. It would be a lie if I said I never thought about my friends, or the people who used to be in my life. Exes included. But I am not unhappy about it. I was thinking how lucky I am to have this new, amazing life, with kind, friendly people in it."

"Rosalba and Bernardo are very nice, it is true."

"Not them, you idiot!" I slugged him on the shoulder. "You!"

He grinned. "You are not sad?"

"No, I am not sad."

"You may still have to convince me of this." His expression was dead serious, and I wondered if he was joking even a little.

I kissed him again, firmly, but not how I had in the kitchen. Slowly I deepened the kiss, making it darker, demanding more until he relaxed and gave back. Moving to stand in front of him, I reached for his belt. He gave another sharp inhale, and I paused to run my hand lightly over the front of his pants, the nylon's shush loud in the dark and hushed room. He was holding his breath, waiting.

Two seconds, three seconds, five. When I grabbed at his shirt to untuck it, he reached for the tie on my sweats. In uncountable seconds, we were both naked atop the comforter.

I hovered over him. "Now, do you believe me?"

He nodded, and when he was settled inside of me, I whispered again, "I love you."

His eyes never left mine, holding us in place as we moved, breathing together in the stillness of the room until I began to tremble. Matteo wrapped his arms around my back, pulling me down to him as he rocked into me, a thud vibrating up my spine that left me gasping in release.

When we were quiet and resting, I asked an important question. "Do you understand that I can miss my friends, can wonder about something I had assumed would happen, even to where it makes me nostalgic, but also *not* want to go back?"

Matteo said nothing as he lay by my side.

I rolled to my side and propped my head on my hand. "Do you know that when I am quiet, thinking about things and people I have left behind, I can be, am, still grateful to be here, and fulfilled with the life I have? Here, with you."

He nodded, eyes on mine, absorbing my words. "Yes, or maybe it is better for me to say that I do now."

"It confused you before?"

"Perhaps yes. My whole life I have lived here, I have never left, nor has my family. I do not think I could leave my home; it would make me very lonely. This is what I think it is like for you. Especially with this holiday you celebrate tomorrow. It is a tradition we do not have here, unlike Christmas, which is celebrated all over the world. Tomorrow, I think you will feel like a stranger, even if only for a little while. So maybe you were thinking today that you would like to go back."

I dropped my head into the curve of his shoulder and smiled against his chest. From his perspective it made perfect sense that I would be sad and lonely, that I might want to leave.

"It's not uncommon in the US for families to live thousands of miles apart. It doesn't mean that I don't miss them, or never will. They can come visit. But this is my home now; you are my family." As I snuggled closer, Matteo's arm wrapped snugly around my back.

"I do understand," he kissed my hair. "*Ti amo, cara.*"

Something Resembling Love

In the morning, the usual clouds and rain were back. I didn't mind, though. The weather made it feel more like the holidays to me; I was always hoping for at least rain, and maybe snow to start off the season.

Matteo was up making cappuccino when I joined him in the same comfy clothes from the night before. A holiday morning meant lazy cups of coffee and homemade *cantucci*. Besides, with no turkey to cook for hours, there was no rush.

The first thing I would make was cranberry chutney, which I had added to the menu when I had seen the fresh blood oranges in the town market. Combined with Tuscan chestnuts, it would be a decidedly Italian cranberry chutney. In the meantime, the pumpkin I had roasted would bake as pie. There was fresh cream in the refrigerator to whip at the last minute. The rest of the menu was up to Matteo and our guests. Probably some kind of pork, maybe even wild boar, given our rural location and the season. I was sure that Rosalba would bring fresh bread, and Bernardo would probably bring a bottle, or three, of his homemade grappa. If so, we'd be dancing the night away.

"What are you smiling about?" Matteo interrupted my thoughts.

My smile got larger. "I was thinking about Bernardo's grappa. Do you remember the night at the end of our tour? He brought some out, and we were all dancing in the courtyard to ABBA and Spanish guitars."

He smiled a twinkly eyed smile. "Yes, I remember that night!" He leaned over to kiss me soundly. "And I found you by the wall."

My breath caught at the way he was looking at me. "Yeah, that too." The words came out wispy, and I swallowed. "Anyway, maybe we'll all be dancing outside with grappa tonight!"

"Just for you." He kissed me again.

In the early evening, before the sun had set all the way, our guests arrived. Matteo's mother, father, and siblings, Rosalba and Bernardo of course, and a few local friends. Charcuterie and cheeses were arranged and spread with olives and bread. Small pots filled with olive oil were scattered across the table. I had guessed correctly about the wild boar. Red wine flowed accordingly. The pumpkin pie was a new experience for all but Matteo's younger sister, who had gone to college in California.

Elizabeth Standish

Dinner took hours, each course lingered over, so different from an American Thanksgiving, where all but dessert arrived on the table at once. We hugged and chatted and caught up over the antipasti. European football was discussed over soup, politics with the mushroom risotto. Finally, we were more serious over the main course, and I led the tradition my close friends and I had always practiced.

"This has been a year of transition for me, big changes," I said, speaking in careful Italian. "When I first came, for a holiday, I was just taking a little time for myself. I came to hike, but afterwards, what I needed was *goditi il sole*," I nodded to Rosalba, who'd found me watching the sunrise in the courtyard. She nodded back enthusiastically. "When I came back, I wasn't sure if I was running away or running toward. Your welcome to me, your acceptance of me as part of Matteo's life, helped me realize, early on, that I was running toward something. What many of you don't know is that I lost my parents when I was still a teenager. I have always created my own home. But here, with Matteo, and each of you, I didn't have to; you had one already waiting for me. *E per questo sono veramente grata*," I finished, close to tears.

Matteo's father raised his glass, "*Cin cin!*"

Matteo leaned over and pulled me into his shoulder, hugging me close, kissing my temple.

One after the other, each guest shared their gratitudes. We laughed at some; were moved by others. When the pie had been finished, we sipped grappa, and cracked nuts, leaving their shells spread along the table.

I couldn't remember a warmer Thanksgiving.

Rosalba insisted they stay to help us clean up afterward, even though it was about two in the morning. But she and Bernardo didn't live far, and it was a help. I had always hated coming out to a sink full of dirty dishes after a big holiday meal.

At last, we hugged them goodbye in the stone driveway.

"*Lo sapevo che sarebbe andato tutto bene*," Rosalba said as she hugged me. She had been right; everything was alright.

"This was nice," Matteo commented as we watched until they were out of sight.

"It was," I agreed. "I'm glad you talked me into it. I enjoyed sharing it with you and our friends."

Something Resembling Love

"Good, we will do it again next year." He gave my shoulders a squeeze and looked down at me, face full of affection. "I like this tradition; it is good to be grateful. Come, it is late, we must go to bed."

I giggled, a little intoxicated from the wine and spirits, and took his hand.

In our bedroom, before I could even unclasp my necklace, he reached for it himself. "I must tell you what else I am thankful for. I am so happy you came back." He started unbuttoning my shirt. "I was very sad—no, disappointed, when I had to put you on the van to Florence, and back to America. I kicked myself all the time I drove home for not staying with you that night, for leaving you with the tears in your eyes after you had responded so fervently to my kisses. And me to yours. I am grateful that you came back, and you have stayed. I would have understood if you had not accepted your job here. You had a life in America. I am glad you came to have a life here."

By now, he had slowly stripped away my shirt, unfastened my pants, and was working on my undergarments. He was still completely clothed. I had made no move to undress him, entranced by his words.

"You make me joyful, Jane, *mia tesora*. You are surprised?" he asked, watching me draw a quick breath.

"A—a little," I admitted.

He bent to kiss me, tenderly but thoroughly. "But what I mean is that I am also grateful for the depth that you have brought to my life. And I would like to be grateful for you in all the ways before the night is over."

Accepting his words and the touch that went with them wasn't difficult. Truth be told, we had always been kind and tender with each other. But who was I to object to or refuse the physical expression of his feelings?

"I tell you often that I love you, and that is true. You show me you love me in this fashion as well." Another quick but true kiss. "I would like it to always be this way."

"I do, too," I whispered.

"You are a true Italian now," he said, playing with my hands. "Be my wife, too."

I glanced down at the sensation on my finger, where a band hovered at the first knuckle, waiting. I leaped for Matteo's mouth, kissing him fiercely. "Yes!"

Even as his lips crashed to mine, I felt the band slide the rest of the way on.

"I love you, *mia tesora*."

"*Mio caro, amore mio.* And I, you."

Wondering what happened to Jane after she accepted Matteo's proposal? Or if Peter did anything different in his life after Anja broke up with him? Get the bonus epilogue to find out!

www.elizabethstandish.com

Acknowledgments

I got the idea for this book when some doctor misdiagnosed me with HHT in my mid-thirties. The pronouncement was life altering, from a mindset perspective. After rounds of genetic testing, the diagnosis was revoked, and I went back to "you live in a high desert" as at least a partial reason for my bloody noses and tiny blood vessel clusters that would randomly burst. Even though I had long since decided I only wanted fur babies, the implications I faced in those six months were very real. They showed up in my personal life, in my mental health, and the hours-long bloody noses I dealt with impacted my ability to do my real-life job. Nothing says "sexy" like making out with a cute guy and having a small blood vessel on your lip break open during said make out, and having to rush to the ladies' room. (Needless to say, we did not have a second date.)

Not long after I was initially diagnosed, my friend Stacey offered me an opportunity to go hiking in Italy. I thought, living a mile high, I was in good shape and would be fine on those hills Stacey and I would be hiking. Boy, was I wrong! As I dragged myself up hill after hill, getting passed by others in our small group who were twenty years my senior, I felt ridiculous. But those Chestnut Gangers, as we dubbed ourselves after the thirty-seventh story our guide told us about the chestnut trees in the hills, never made me feel bad, and cheered me on. I'm grateful to our guide, who I named Matteo after, Sir Gerard and Ann, Andy, and Tony (whose husband incidentally owns the cutest bookshop, Dial Lane, in Ipswich, England, where

I sold my first international copies), Martin, and Tom for making me feel like I belonged with them. I'm thrilled to, a decade out, still call you all my friends.

There are so many other people to whom there are shout-outs for. Kathleen McGowan for her passion and incredible research on Mary Magdalene and the ways in which she is hidden in plain sight, and also for the historical tales of Matilda of Tuscany and Pope Gregory VII across Tuscany and in Lucca. My childhood friend Julie, whose adorable duplex in Evanston inspired Jane's. My Italian friend Fausto for the unique phrases and Italian to English translations like "shoveling the luggages". And to my dear friend Mark, thank you, for teaching me something—anything!—about wine. Not just drinking, but also tasting and terroir.

Huge thanks once again to my incredible editorial and design team: Alexandra O'Connell for making me a better writer and caring about Peter even when he was pissing me off. While my biology background means I can wade through medical journal articles, I am not a cancer researcher like Peter. But he works in such an obscure field, I had a hard time locating someone with time to double-check my genetics. Any errors are mine alone. Thanks to Jennifer Bisbing for yet another meticulous proof. Katherine Patterson for all the graphics she has helped me with since we designed Magnificent Mess together: the quick tweaks, jumping on the "but can we just do this one thing" requests. And Elizabeth Mackey for the *Under the Tuscan Sun* feeling cover. To my Italian checkers, Stephanie Nguyen and Maria Stancato, thank you for your graciousness in reviewing the Italian throughout the book, so I didn't sound absolutely ridiculous with my tourist-level phraseology.

As a brand-new author with almost no social media following, I really want to say a heartfelt thank you to those of you who picked up *Magnificent Mess*, loved it, and shared that in your reviews.

I finished the first draft of this book after coming back from a second trip to Italy, not long after my mom died. Although the storyline of Jane's parents dying was already in place, thinking about her being alone made my own grief that much more potent. For months, the only thing I could do to keep my head above water was write and rewrite this novel. Maybe it was the fact that life doesn't always work out the way we think that kept me from giving Peter the perfect happy ending, but I hope he will get one someday.

About the Author

Elizabeth Standish is an attorney based in Denver, Colorado, who has had a solo practice, presented criminal appeals to the Colorado Court of Appeals, and worked in-house in biotechnology. When she finally tired of telling other people's stories in her legal briefs, and telling happy endings only to herself, she wrote her first novel. Just like her first heroine in *Magnificent Mess*, Emmalyn, she too grew up showing horses. Currently, she shares her home with an ever-changing menagerie of dogs, cats, and her local deer. She recently returned to riding after a twenty-five-year hiatus. This is her second novel.

www.elizabethstandish.com

Made in United States
Troutdale, OR
08/23/2025